MIDNIGHT AT TRAFALGAR

Rebecca Randolph Buckley

This is a work of fiction.

ISBN: 978-0-9819654-6-8
Library of Congress Control Number: 2010911663

Published 2010 as ***Midnight at Trafalgar***
R. J. Buckley Publishing
San Tan Valley, AZ

First Published 2005 as ***Midnight at Trafalgar Square***

www.rjbuckleypublishing.com

Traveling to England is something I have to do quite regularly. I love the countryside, the villages, the towns, and the cities. I've found that not many countries have as much to offer as Britain to my peace of mind and craving for tranquility. I'm drawn to the history, people, and culture as well as to the geography.

Rebecca Randolph Buckley

ACKNOWLEDGEMENT

Sharing my September Seven Virgo birthday with Queen Elizabeth the First was the initial enticement to my delving into the history and writing about England. As a result of researching my own Scottish and Irish ancestors, and while living and traveling throughout England, I fell in love with the British people and culture—past and present.

Therefore, to those I've met personally in the glorious, romantic isle to the northeast, and to those who are of another lifetime in Great Britain, I thank you all for the inspiration of this novel.

And to my blessed cache of people who so kindly consented to read and critique this novel in its early stages, I'll be forever grateful—Dennis Dillow, Anita Schwaber, Hilda Cardoza, Martin and Ali Weller, Kellie Isom, Mary Matejcek, Dennis Smith, Sharon Klykken, and Jim Buckley.

Tons of thanks go to Jeanne Fielding, a terrific free-lance editor. You are the greatest, Jeanne!

This is the first novel of the 'Rachel O'Neill' series, although I've written a screenplay that is a prequel of sorts - "Peace in the Valley" that occurs before Rachel discovers the world across the seas, but is the beginning of her quest to find herself and her legacy.

Rebecca Randolph Buckley

DEDICATION

To my mother, Selma Lee Dearmore McMullen and to my father, James Neal McMullen—

I dedicate this special first novel, written by your firstborn who loved you very much when you were here ... and I still love and miss you, even though you are gone from this earth for now, but not from heart and mind.

PART ONE

London

With long slender fingers, tipped with nails the same color as her ginger hair, Rachel O'Neill traced the fine lines around her eyes and mouth as she leaned closer to the gigantic, gold-leaf framed mirror above the marble vanity. She'd never before been concerned or even mindful of age and the evolution of the aging body because she'd always been one of those very lucky women who appeared to be fifteen years younger at any age. Even now one would think she was in her mid-thirties. She had good genes, but she didn't like what she was seeing in the mirror tonight, regardless.

I wish I were taller!

She stepped back and rose to her toes, striking a pose as if she were a ballet dancer in a robe, hands stretching high above her head towards the illuminated ceiling in the elegant dressing room of the hotel boudoir.

Why couldn't I be as tall as my father?

Her father, Neal O'Neill, had been tall and stately and Rachel thought he resembled the screen star, David Niven. Like Neil O'Neill's father and Niven, they were all British and spoke

1

in a light clipped manner that was tinged with a dry sense of humor. Neal's mother was British as well, an O'Connor from Scotland. She was tall, too, a slender woman with red hair and freckles. But Rachel hadn't inherited the physical attributes of the O'Neill or the O'Connor clans.

Dammit! Why couldn't I have been like them?

She thought about her mother as she took the mascara cylinder out of her new leopard-print cosmetic bag and began applying another coat to her already thickened lashes. Rachel's natural dark hair, almost black, which was sometimes visible at the roots, her olive-toned skin, and her 5'4" height, came from her mother's American Indian branch of the family. Because of that, Rachel felt she was constantly fighting the battle of the bulge and she feared that someday she'd end up with one of those short, stout, matronly bodies that her Indian blood-line possessed. She was puzzled how her own Indian mother, Lily, could be so tall and slim when most other Indians she saw were just the opposite.

Rachel's thoughts drifted back to the day she had made the startling discovery on the Blackfoot reservation in Montana when she found her mother still alive. She spent 35 years thinking her mother was dead up to that point.

She quickly grabbed a Q-tip to dab the mascara that smeared on her eyelid. Her eyes had begun to tear up with the childhood memory. She rested her hands on the countertop for a moment, pausing as she recalled when she was just three years old and her father had lied to her about her mother.

The truth was . . . frantically fearing for her life, Rachel's mother, Lily, had fled after one of Neal's nightly drunken and abusive tirades. The one-sided fights seemed to be seamless in Rachel's early memories of life. She was far too young to know that her father had despised Lily's quest to improve herself by attending college to become a teacher. He made Lily's life unbearable and it came to an abrupt end the night he literally threw her out the door, threatening that if she dared come back to take Rachel, she'd not live to see another day. He warned Lily that he'd chop her up into little pieces and bury her in the backyard.

2

Lily believed him capable of such a horrible thing, for when he was drinking he was an ogre. Although she wanted to take Rachel with her, in fact it felt as if her heart was being ripped out of her body, she left without her daughter and never returned.

"Your mother's dead," Neal told Rachel the next morning when she toddled into the kitchen, all sleepy-eyed looking for her mother.

"My mommy is not dead! She is not!" Rachel cried in defiance. "Where is my mommy? I want my mommy!" She began sobbing, running through the house, calling out and searching every room for her mother.

Neal had remained seated at the breakfast table and poured more Irish whiskey into his coffee, not a flinch or any show of remorse for what he'd just told his little girl.

Rachel stopped crying a few weeks later and after another few weeks, she stopped asking unanswered questions about her mother. Throughout her childhood too much had been left unsaid, but she submerged her questions and feelings deeper and deeper until she didn't have them anymore.

It wasn't long before Neal married Lee Dearmore, his housekeeper, a kind woman who had been taking care of Rachel.

Lee was a godsend!

Rachel removed the white monogrammed hotel robe and reached for her evening dress hanging on an ornate brass hook behind her. She was wearing a black satin one-piece bra and panty undergarment to make the fit a smooth one. As she removed the plastic covering from her new Vivienne Westwood gown, she thought of her stepmother Lee.

Yes, she certainly tried to fill the void, bless her heart.

But, her father's second marriage ended as Rachel approached her teens. Neal became quite successful in the bar business but was caught up in all that went along with it - the long hours and the flirtations that led to ego indulgences. It was inevitable that Lee would become aware of and lose patience with his indiscretions and when at last she faced the truth, she packed her bags, bid a sad farewell to Rachel, and left town.

Rachel pulled the gown over her head, adjusted its fit, and began vigorously brushing her hair.

3

Her father seemed to feel lost when Lee left him. He probably loved her more than he realized. He'd stopped drinking during their marriage, which could only be attributed to Lee's gentle patience and fortitude. But then Neal wasted no time at all in marrying again, this time to a local real estate agent, who turned out to be Rachel's nemesis. All remaining gentleness and kindness disappeared from the household during that marriage. So did Rachel.

She teased her hair gently to create a slight poof. In the past, she had insisted on having hair perfectly shaped; now she liked it better just a bit off kilter. She thought again of how things had worked out over the years.

It's strange how it all was leading me to my mother.

Rachel had lived for so long with unanswered questions surrounding her mother's "death", with her workaholic father's inept attempts at love and guidance, and then with two distressing marriages of her own, it was no wonder that Rachel's emotional state had reached catastrophic proportions that day. She sat, spaced-out, at her desk in a commercial high-rise bank building in downtown Los Angeles. The repercussions of committing a financial error that week that cost her employer thousands of dollars reverberated through her.

On looking back, she realized she'd been a foolish perfectionist, and she couldn't believe she hadn't asked for assistance when she needed it. It could have been so easily avoided, but at the time she truly thought she could handle it herself. She didn't want anyone to know the difficulty she was having. Didn't want them to know that she was in over her head.

Of course, she knew that when stock options were exercised, the certificates had to be dated and processed the same day as the exercise. But she hadn't quite mastered the IBM Selectric and the new program she was using to create the documents. She lost data as fast as she created it and then had to start all over again. And it all crashed down on her during an unexpected stock split, a three-day period of up to thirty stock option exercises a day.

Her boss had to announce the whole mess at a board meeting on that September morning, because the board had to approve payment to the stockholders for the losses caused by her gross negligence. She was terribly embarrassed and disappointed in herself and terribly hurt that she had been guilty of such a tremendous blunder.

So on her lunch hour that hot autumn day after the fatal *faux pas*, she had thrown the rest of her responsibilities to the wind, left her office and hurried to the Greyhound bus station in downtown L.A. She purchased a one-way ticket to the Northwest and boarded the bus without another thought.

But before she left her office, she had placed some notes in an envelope and sent it through inner-office mail to her boss, spelling out instructions as to what to give to whom, meaning her keys and car, and what to do with what, meaning her apartment and belongings. The notes said that she needed to find herself and a life of peace, without stress.

Stress comes from within, remember.

She sprayed her hair with a shine mist and reflected on what she had gleaned from her mother's spiritual influence over the past 8 years. She'd learned from her mother that awareness is the beginning of healing and if a person is continually aware of a fault within, or a bad habit, the fixing will follow.

Awareness is healing, and stress comes from within.

Some days she repeated the words to herself over and over, very aware of her own inclinations and shortcomings.

Awareness is healing, and stress comes from within.

However, she hadn't felt any spiritual awareness that September day, eight years ago—one day after her thirty-eighth birthday—when she left her employer and the professional ladder she'd taken such pains to climb; when she abandoned her son, Devin, his wife, and two children who'd been living with her.

No, that wasn't very spiritual of me at all.

As she laid the brush on a towel, she sighed heavily in remembrance and guilt and then pulled a strand of pearls from her jewelry bag. She loved pearls and diamonds. The necklace reminded her of all the jewelry and clothing she'd left behind that day and how she'd never seen any of it since. Devin's wife had taken it when she'd divorced him after Rachel's

5

abandonment.

I wonder if she enjoyed my things as much as I did.

During most of her son's young adult life, he had struggled with addictions until it had interfered with his ability to support himself. At Rachel's invitation, Devin and his family moved in with her, which turned out to be chaotic for all of them - too many people in too little space with too little money.

No wonder I left, somebody had to.

She picked up a cosmetic moisture container and sprayed a fine mist over her face.

But her job and her son weren't the only reasons she flipped out that morning. She had accumulated an insurmountable amount of debt on her credit cards–purchases of clothing and essentials for Devin's family, along with frustration purchases and rewards for herself. Creditors were calling every day asking for payment. She owed the second half of a down payment on a new Jaguar sedan – her dream car – and was two payments in arrears.

All she had to do was ask someone for help, but she couldn't; it didn't matter whether it was personal, business, or financial. She never asked for help. She wasn't going to ask her father. She didn't have close friends. She couldn't ask her boss.

My ex-husbands were pricks, couldn't ask them. I wouldn't have, anyway. Not their problem.

She ran cold water from the gold faucet as she wondered where her ex-husbands might be. Then she rinsed her hands and rubbed scented lotion speckled with gold dust on her arms, neck and chest.

No, she couldn't have asked anyone for help in those days. No one knew about her dilemma or would have cared. She kept her troubles buried deep within; and knew she had to deal with them herself. It was her responsibility, nobody else's. But it had been too much for her. The strain suffocated her. She had to run to breathe–something she'd done most of her life, although in somewhat lesser proportions. It was her modus operandi to remove herself from unpleasantness even if it meant that she moved from one job to another or from one neighborhood to another or from one man to another. She was never in one spot long enough to become attached or grow roots.

At the time, she'd been dreaming of the Northwest, of beautiful forests, soothing lakes, and the peace one must feel in such blissful surroundings. More than once she had dreamed of an elusive Indian woman beckoning her to a fairytale–like land, way off somewhere in the mountains and forests.

She always paid attention to her dreams and sometimes lived in them. There were times she'd force herself to sleep more than was necessary because she could dream at will. It was her means of escape. So when the time came, when her life became so unbearable that she couldn't continue as she was any longer, she knew exactly what to do. In that very instant, that one September morning eight years ago, she made the decision. She left everyone and everything behind. Off she went, literally following her nighttime dreams and only God knew what else.

It felt as if a huge burden had been lifted off my shoulders, actually.

She remembered how light and giddy she had felt as she rode the Greyhound buses from state to state, day after day, searching for some meaning to life, while she was being drawn mysteriously to the northern states. And then the most incredible thing had happened. She stumbled upon her mother, Lily, very alive and very well, on the Blackfoot reservation in Montana, teaching children.

Yes, Rachel could easily chalk up her smooth complexion to her mother's Indian side of the family. She thought she should be grateful that darker races were generally blessed with smooth beautiful skin.

So why the hell am I wrinkling at forty-six?

"Damn!" she exclaimed, as she pushed the skin upwards from her eyebrows. The thought crossed her mind that maybe the propensity to wrinkle sprang from the other branch of the family tree.

She brushed on a finishing coat of lip gloss. Maybe her wrinkles were from her maternal grandmother's ancestors. She gently pulled her facial skin back towards her ears to see how she would look if she had a slight facelift.

I do look like Grandma Emma.

Not much had been known about Lily's mother. She'd been the granddaughter of one of the first Indian agents in Arkansas, had lived in Indian Territory, and had run off and married a Blackfoot Indian when she was just 13. According to the stories, Grandma had been at the mercy of the worst of evil stepmothers. She'd been at the receiving end of exorbitant cruelty and trauma that could prematurely wrinkle the skin of a grape, not to mention that of an impressionable young girl, and certainly could alter her gene pool. Come to think of it, Grandma Emma's skin had been wrinkled since puberty. Rachel remembered seeing sepia photos of her teenaged Grandma. She knew that a person's cells could drastically change and evolve as a result of an afflicted emotional state.

But then again, it's one's perception of self that makes the changes.

She remembered Lily's words and smiled as she said aloud, "Thanks, Lily. I'm definitely on the path, I am. Well, sort of."

As she looked in the mirror again, reality stared back at her.

Dammit anyway!

The lines in her face were more pronounced than ever on this exciting New Year's night in London and it bugged the hell out of her.

She grasped the skin at the back of her neck, holding it tight at the base of her skull and pulled the front of her neck smooth, free of wrinkles.

"Gawd! I need a plastic surgeon, Ethan!" she blurted out loud.

Ethan Philips suddenly appeared in the dressing room doorway, adjusting his bow tie. He looked very dapper in his tuxedo, especially for an overweight man in his sixties.

"And I need to lose seventy pounds," he said as he tripped over the threshold which pitched him closer to Rachel than he'd planned. "Goodness me!" Embarrassed, he looked at himself in the mirror rather than at her and accidentally bumped her again. He'd misjudged the space his portliness filled between them. "Sorry!" he said, as he sucked in his stomach to button his jacket.

Rachel frowned, "No, no, no. Leave the jacket open, Ethan. It looks too small when you button it." Then she gently pushed him out the door and said, "Now, go on. I need to finish. I didn't mean for you to come in here, I was just saying I need a facelift. Go on."

"Well, I say, you needn't push me! You can be a horror, you know. A bloody horror!" He unbuttoned his jacket, swiftly turned on his heels, and headed for the spacious bedroom of the hotel accommodations he had so carefully selected for this New Year's Millennium Celebration.

"The bloody wench!" he mumbled aloud to himself as he deliberately and dramatically re-buttoned his jacket in protest. He moved quickly into the large oval-ended salon, grabbed a Godiva chocolate from a crystal tray on the buffet as he passed and stuffed it into his mouth. He sat down on the delicately carved, brocade sofa in the alcove and fidgeted.

He loved the London Ritz. The architect had loathed square rooms and designed the suites to appear to be oval by rounding off the salon, or living room as Rachel called it. The peach-colored sofa and two pale yellow, satin chairs imparted elegance to the space. The carpet throughout was of a pale peach plush. The magnificently swaged draperies were of the same fabric as the sofa with natural lace sheers covering the windows. The walls were covered with matching moiré fabric.

Ethan sighed. Here they were at the grand Ritz in London and Rachel still didn't seem happy.

What is her problem?

She was snippy, irritable, and bossy, had been for weeks, it seemed. He only wanted to please her, to do something nice for her, but she wasn't letting him. And he'd planned this trip to make up for being totally consumed with business meetings and operational fiascoes ever since she'd arrived from America. He'd been working fifteen-hour days, including weekends, and they'd had no social or personal life at all. Although most of the time she'd been working with him, he still felt guilty for leaving Rachel to fend for herself, a fish out of water in her new British environment, even though she said she could handle it. But he wondered.

Maybe it's been too much for her.

He felt she was still coping with her father's death.

He had offered her the opportunity to come to England and do some work for him, feeling she might need a change of pace and she jumped at the chance. She arrived in England from the States in June and signed a six-month employment contract with him, after which she'd planned to holiday in Paris and do research for her next writing project.

Rachel's father left her financially independent, but she told Ethan she didn't mind working periodically. She told him that she loved accounting and doing budgets and financial reporting. That had been the way she made her living before her father died.

She offered to work for Ethan on a part time basis for half a year. However, things had taken an entirely different course during those six months. Three months into it, Ethan announced their engagement, strictly a business arrangement, however, nothing more. At least, that was the deal. His board of directors had offered Rachel a five-percent shareholding in appreciation for the work she had done for the company, with the condition she would remain on tap as a consultant, gratis. Ethan had joked about how his forty-seven percent plus hers would give him voting control of the company, if they were married. So, what began as an amusement became a reality, or almost a reality. They weren't married yet, just betrothed.

They'd met six years earlier in California when Ethan was visiting the U.S. on business. Then they'd reconnected several times in the years that followed, sometimes two or three weeks at a time, but nothing of an intimate nature ever developed between them. In fact, he didn't think Rachel was attracted to him as he was to her. She was polite to him, but she insisted on keeping her distance, sleeping in separate rooms, even though they lived in the same house, and she reminded him every chance she got that the impending marriage was to be in name only. But still, he hadn't lost hope.

He thought about her lame excuses for sleeping in separate rooms in his home, one of which was his snoring, which she said she could hear from her room on the second floor. Another was her inability to share a bed with anyone. The list lengthened with whatever reasons of the day would come to mind. But he felt there was more to it than the trivial complaints.

Maybe she just doesn't like sex.

He didn't want to think about that, but from the beginning she made it clear that it wasn't to be a sexual relationship.

Still, Ethan had suggested on occasion, here and there, even after a night of wining and dining, that it wouldn't be harmful if

11

they experimented sexually. Taking into account the fact that they'd both been married before and with the worldly view of premarital sex being what it was, it would have been more or less acceptable to live in what the religiously pious called "sin".

She said, "No."

So Ethan went along with the separate room arrangements in his spacious British manor house. He didn't see any point in being pushy or demanding. Of course he could insist on sexual favors in exchange for her room and board, although he knew that would be disastrous and wouldn't work at all with Rachel. So, he just bided his time and figured she'd come 'round sooner or later.

He had fallen in love with Rachel the very first moment he saw her inviting smile the day they met in California, although she'd been the most difficult person to get close to he'd ever known. She wasn't the kind to divulge her inner feelings. She seemed to have a barrier shielding her feelings from the outer world and it was impossible to penetrate that shield. She was amicable enough, but that's where it stopped. So he hadn't told her that he loved her and he hadn't told her why he kept in constant contact with her through the years or why he dreamed up a reason for her to come to England this time. All he wanted was to have her near. He couldn't tell her because he feared her reaction and he didn't want to lose her forever.

So here we are, spending our first holiday together since the bloody phony engagement. In the Ritz. In London. In separate beds.

He stood, paced restlessly, and then finally opened the French doors to the balcony that overlooked the city and Green Park, the sought-after lush view from the deluxe suites. Glancing at his watch, he bellowed, "It's seven o'clock, Rachel! Rachel? Do you hear me? The cocktail hour began at half past six!"

"I hear you, I hear you. And please don't yell. Why do you do that? As soon as you get in the front door at the house, you start yelling 'I'm home! I'm home!' I can always hear the car coming into the driveway, Ethan. I know you're home. And I know what time it is. I have a watch."

She is a bloody wench! This type of treatment wasn't new to

Ethan; he'd been at the receiving end of it all before. His ex-wife Nora was an expert at making him feel worthless and she continued to chide and criticize him even though they were divorced. She'd even laughed at his lack of sexual prowess. He wondered why he continued to put up with Nora's attitude towards him and why he continued to take her telephone calls every day. *I'm a masochist.*

Nora telephoned Ethan at least once a day at the office, complaining about her life, complaining about what he hadn't done for her, complaining about their daughters, Adele and Vera. Even his daughters were constantly ragging on him, too.

I should tell them all to go to bloody hell.

But he wouldn't. He was too forgiving, sometimes to his own disadvantage. He couldn't bring himself to be unkind to his family, no matter how cruel they were to him at times. Other than his sister, they were his only family. He loved them in spite of themselves. Of course, when his daughters wanted something from him, their attitudes changed considerably. No matter. He accepted them as they were, along with the good and the bad, which included their incessant scorn and rejection.

He knew he could never face total rejection from Rachel. It would be too much for him to bear. He was aware he wasn't an over-the-top handsome man, and not as sensual as Robert Redford, but then how many men actually were? Oh well, it didn't matter; he wasn't going to dwell on it.

What he needed to do was focus on the running of his company. His financial situation was worse than he'd let on to Rachel. He was very near to closing the doors, if he couldn't obtain more financing immediately. He was indeed desperate. He'd scraped from every account, including his pension, to be able to give her a New Year's celebration in London.

So, there wasn't time to figure out how else to woo Rachel; no time at all. He must concentrate wholly on the business when they returned to Stamford. She either wanted him or she didn't. He'd find out soon enough.

3

Rachel was perturbed that Ethan had broken into her thoughts, although she realized it was her own fault, he was only responding to her. She didn't know how she felt about him always being around. They worked together; they lived in the same house. He was always apologizing to her for not being able to spend more time with her when, actually, she didn't want him to spend more time with her. Ethan's attentiveness was something new and foreign to her and she had difficulty accepting it. All her life she'd been a loner, even when she was a child and right on up through her marriages to workaholics and after. Rachel's own father had been a workaholic. She had been grateful that her stepmother Lee was around as long as she was.

She thought about her son. No wonder he had such a rough go of it, no one was ever there.

That was one thing she admired about Ethan, he was always there for his daughters, no matter what.

Every New Year's Eve, Rachel's thoughts dwelt on her family. It was a museful time for her, introspective as well as

14

meditative. She liked to think back over the years to get a perspective of how she was then, compared to now. She was curious how she'd progressed spiritually as well as emotionally from year to year. And over the past year she'd been having inexplicable revealing dreams and visions which led her to believe she'd lived before. She'd discussed it with her mother, who was her spiritual guru and who had given Rachel a multitude of reading material about past life discovery. Rachel hadn't made up her mind whether she believed it or not, but, nevertheless, she was intrigued with the possibility of a person traveling through each life, each time encountering similar experiences of a previous life, each time learning to handle them differently, hopefully better. For several months before coming to England this time, she had vivid dreams of 18th century Cornwall, the southwestern part of England. She had felt as drawn to Britain as she'd been to Montana where she found her mother. So when Ethan asked her to come help him with his company, she eagerly accepted, not only to make some much needed life changes and help him out, but to research the visions in her dreams.

Rachel was interested in the interpretation of dreams, past life regression and Karma. Her mother, Lily, explained to her that Karma was the effect of one's experiences in past and present lives created by thoughts, feelings, and actions. Rachel found the concept difficult to grasp, but ever since she'd found her dear mother, she made it a point to take stock of herself every New Year's Eve in order to understand where she'd been and focus on where she was going.

Subsequently New Year's Eve had become a special time for her. Before her father died, she found out it was a particularly special time for him as well.

After divorcing his third wife, Neal had sold his property and a string of British pubs in the San Joaquin Valley and had become a very successful real estate broker in Los Angeles. He lived until he was ninety years old, and was active right up to the moment he had a debilitating stroke.

Rachel dropped everything to care for her father in his Brentwood home, along with 'round the clock nurses, and spent

15

many hours reading and talking to him. Although they had a tumultuous relationship during her childhood, the last few years of his life proved to be as close and loving as any father and daughter could ever hope for. The doctors had led her to believe he would eventually recover from the stroke, although maybe not fully, so she had been prepared to arrange her life to suit his.

One early afternoon, two weeks into Neal's recuperation, he had been reminiscing about his youth and told Rachel about his dreams since he was a boy.

"My dream was to travel the world, my dear. But most of the time I was ridiculously inebriated in the early days. Your mother wasn't interested in travel, she was off studying at university . . . Lee was terrified of people. And then when Mary came along . . . I was too busy."

"When you get well, we'll go together, Daddy. We'll go wherever you want." She had turned to reach for her cup of coffee, stealing a moment to wipe away the tears that filled her eyes. It was so difficult seeing her father this way.

He hadn't noticed the tears. "When I was a child, I vowed to see every country before I died. I wanted to celebrate New Year's Eve in every capitol city. Remember, my dear, how I watched it on television every year? I pretended to be one of those lucky boys waving at the TV cameras as they panned at the stroke of midnight. Silliness, I know, but nevertheless, a passionate desire of mine."

That explained why he always stayed home on New Year's Eve and watched telecasts rather than go to parties like all the other parents.

At that point he closed his eyes for a lengthy moment and then reached for Rachel's hand. With piercing blue eyes, he looked deep into hers and said, "Promise me you'll live my dream. Promise me you'll go to every country and write about it. Go see the world, my dear. Celebrate New Year's Eve in every capitol."

She squeezed his hand. "We'll celebrate them together, Daddy."

"Never let anyone prevent you from doing anything you want to do. Look at what your mother accomplished. She became a teacher to help her people. You've got that ability in you. Never say in your old age, 'I wish I would have!'"

She blotted her tears and continued to listen to her father struggling to talk, his face contorting with paralysis. Rachel had promised herself to live his dream as well as her own. When he died of a massive heart attack that night, she was devastated. A part of her died with him.

Lily and Lee had come to the memorial service to support Rachel. Although their memories of Neal weren't fond ones, they had respected Rachel's feelings and had been happy she'd been able to learn to love her father during his last years. Lily had stayed for two weeks to help Rachel tidy Neal's home in Brentwood and tie up the loose ends of his business. He'd willed everything to Rachel and she had decided to leave it all in the capable hands of Neal's business manager, who sent her a hefty quarterly check.

After Lily returned to Montana, Rachel flew to Denver to visit her son and his new wife, Kellie. They hadn't been able to come to the service, and needed to be with family more than ever before. The loss had been overwhelming.

After a few days in Denver, Rachel returned to L.A., moved her own belongings into her father's house, and settled into her new environment. At times it had been too much for her, surrounded by Neal's memorabilia and furnishings, so she'd drive up the coast to visit Lee on weekends. As usual Lee partially filled the void. At first Rachel stayed in daily contact with both her mother Lily and stepmother Lee through email and Instant Messenger. Her mother would send her daily words of wisdom and love. Lee was just a drive away and there for her as well.

Lee had turned 76 the day Neal died. She owned an art gallery in Cambria - a Central Coast California artist community, halfway between Los Angeles and San Francisco. She was a talented artist and small-town living was perfect for her. She didn't like the hubbub of the city because people frightened her. She was a quiet, loving, gentle woman, and expressed her feelings in her paintings - large elaborate paintings of women, children, birds and flowers.

17

Rachel gave her hair a good spray of Addict, her favorite perfume.

I should go see Lee again soon. And Lily. And Devin.

She thought of how Lee had begun to show her age sooner than her father, in spite of being 14 years younger than him. And whether it was that, or whether it was Lee's fear and inability to communicate with people, or whatever it was, Neal eventually found younger women to keep him company. Rachel wondered if she could have somehow caught her stepmother Lee's wrinkles, as one might catch a cold or the flu - maybe wrinkles were contagious.

As Daddy would say . . . this is silliness! She smiled at the thought of one of his favorite phrases.

Turning sideways, she checked the mirrored view of her new, very daring, low cut, black crepe de chine gown. Normally, she wore so many layers of clothing that none of her body parts were visible, much less right out there like this. Her breasts looked like they might pop out over the top of her dress any minute. She felt uncomfortable, but she'd fallen in love with the gown when she was in London a few weeks earlier to shop. She couldn't resist it and felt it would be perfect for New Year's Eve.

She dabbed more of her favorite scent on her earlobes, on her inner wrists, and between her double-D bosoms. Tightly pulling in her abdomen, standing straight, shoulders back, she smiled quickly into the mirror. Then just as quickly, she frowned, grabbed her black velvet handbag and mumbled to herself, "Why the hell should I care how I look? What difference does it make?"

She switched off the light and left the room.

Paul Newland picked up the phone and dialed a number. As he waited for an answer, he clicked *January* on the screen of his notebook scheduler and entered a female name on *January One* - Phyllis. Clicked *January Two*, typed Sheri. Linda on the *Third*. On the *Fourth,* he typed a question mark. Someone answered on the other end of the wireless. He responded.

"Yes, may I speak to Carol, please? Paul Newland here. Oh really? Paris? I didn't know. No, no, never mind. Thank you. Happy New Year to you, too."

He replaced the receiver, leaned back in his desk chair, swiveled around, and faced a most breathtaking unobstructed panoramic view of the city of London across the Thames River. Most of the new contemporary office buildings, condominiums, and hotels on his side of the river were refurbished warehouses and had become premium property investments over the past decade. The holiday lights, so carefully strung in trees and across the fronts of buildings on the London banks of the Thames, had begun to twinkle, and from his view he noticed how the traffic traveling over the bridges into the heart of London had increased in the last few minutes. *New Year's Eve celebrants no doubt, out in full force.*

His expansive, richly paneled office and matching oversized mahogany desk was flanked by leather sofas and chairs, grouped in tactical vignettes which were placed to facilitate casual meetings of all sizes and shapes. He liked casual-intimate, as opposed to board rooms with long formal tables. That day there were four such meetings; the last was with the Kawasaki group visiting from Japan. At the last minute, the New York office had arranged the meeting in an effort to woo and entertain the major client they'd just learned was visiting London over the holidays. New contract bids were out and awarding time was near. So, since Paul was the only remaining senior VP in London through the Season, he was chosen to guarantee the renewal.

"Grrrrreat! Just great! What a way to spend New Year's Eve, doing the town with a bunch of Japanese clients!" he said aloud to himself. Thank God he'd be seeing Phyllis tomorrow. Maybe he would call her after midnight tonight and get an early start. Who knows, she might be home early. Yes, that's what he'd do. He'd dump the clients as soon as he could after midnight. A full night and day of sex was in order. Phyllis was his first choice, because he knew she'd go along with whatever he wanted and she could go for 24 hours without stopping. Then he'd have Sheri the next day and Linda the next, three whole days of sex, maybe a fourth. He was getting an erection just thinking about it.

"Excuse me, Paul," a familiar voice sounded from behind.

Startled, he swung around in his chair, "Carol! What are you doing here? Your office said you were in Paris." With his hands resting in his lap covering his sexual mood, his eyes glazed as he focused on her braless breasts pressing against a tight designer tee-shirt. Those breasts had given him many hours of viewing pleasure and he missed them more than he missed her.

"Paul, you bloody fool, quit staring at my tits! I just came by to tell you, I want you to move the rest of your things out of my flat while I'm in Paris, and don't take anything we haven't agreed on or I'll have you in court so fast your head will spin like a top. Do you understand? Paul, do you hear me?"

He watched the expression on her pretty face go from bad to worse as he deliberately remained silent, glancing back and forth from her mouth to the heaving mounds attached to her chest.

"Ohhh! You have no idea how that look always infuriated me," she said. "You need help, Paul. You're really sick!"

Finally, he answered, "Would you please try speaking to me in a quiet, civil tone instead of that shrill, shrieking, irritating noise that spews from your pretty little mouth, sweetheart? It just doesn't fit the picture."

"I didn't come here to pose for you or to have a civil conversation with you, Paul. Nor do I have time for any of your clever, jaded sarcasm." She opened her purse and threw a house key on his desk, carefully keeping her distance. "You can leave the key with the manager when you're finished." She turned quickly, went out the door, slamming it behind her.

"And a rip-roaring Happy New Year to you too, sweetheart," he muttered to himself as only Humphrey Bogart would.

The phone rang. Paul hesitated to answer. Finally, he picked up the receiver, "Hello? Yes, I'm picking them up at half past eight. What? You've got to be kidding! You took my New Year's Eve, and now you want my friggin' New Year's Day? Dammit, Loretta! Okay, okay, okay! But, you're going to owe me big time for this one. I promise you!"

He slammed down the receiver and ran his hands through his hair. How did he end up in this man-eating profession? All he'd ever wanted was to be a painter, in his own studio with wall to wall nude models, and own his own gallery, but no. Here he was, thirty-seven years old, and a freakin' creative director for a cannibalistic ad agency. How the hell did this happen? This was not what he wanted.

Ethan was up ahead and pushed the down button of the hotel lift at the Ritz. Rachel paused in front of another oil painting hanging on the wall.

"Come on, come on," he impatiently called to her as he held back the doors from inside the elevator.

She picked up the pace and quickly entered after him, noting as she stepped inside the elevator that he'd never been one to step aside and let her enter first. He didn't open car doors for her either and didn't walk on the traffic side of the street when walking with her. Ethan bore no sign of the so-called charm and manners usually associated with the British. But then again, maybe it was all a great big myth or propaganda generated by British film makers and her all-time favorite, Cary Grant—the most charming Brit ever. Or maybe it was only unique to the upper echelon and royalty levels of society. Maybe it was the individual, no matter what culture. The elevator moved slowly.

"Lee would love to see those paintings, Ethan. And you

know what? I was thinking I'd like to bring some of her work over here. I bet I could place them in a gallery." She turned and smiled up at Ethan. "Do you know where we're going?"

Not looking at her, he replied, "I'll ask at the desk."

"Are you all right, Ethan? We are going to have a good time, aren't we? Our first New Year's Eve together?"

In response to her rather surprising kind question, he swiftly removed his glasses and abruptly bent down to kiss her. But, the suddenness of his action threw her off balance. With his poor eyesight, he miscalculated the distance between their faces and overshot. It was more of a smash than a kiss. So, between the smashing kiss and Rachel grabbing for the wall railing to steady herself, the possibilities of the moment were somehow lost in the effect. The elevator doors opened. They exited.

"You wait here," he mumbled in embarrassment over his clumsiness.

Rachel watched him charge like a bull down the Long Gallery, bumping into people along the way, without apology. The thought of Broderick Crawford's portrayal of Harry Brock in the movie "Born Yesterday" crossed her mind. Somehow Ethan didn't fit the surroundings or resemble the glorious genteel men standing around with their ladies. His movements were those of a man with a mission. The Ritz Hotels were never a disappointment though, always festive, always beautiful. *It's not that Ethan disappoints me. No, disappointment isn't the word. It's just that he is so different, so unpredictable.*

Her feelings about him were probably more of enormous curiosity than anything else. And in the midst of those feelings, she felt they'd known each other forever and she couldn't understand why.

As she gazed down the corridor, she wondered if the Ritz Hotels in the States were connected to this one. Southern California boasted a couple - Marina del Rey, Laguna Nigel. She'd been to those and also spent time in the New York and Paris Ritz. They were all unique unto themselves, unlike a hotel chain.

Cesar Ritz had opened the first one in London in 1906 and from the beginning the Ritz was frequented by the nobility and aristocratic peoples of Europe. The Royal Family had been part of its patronage since it began, including the Prince of Wales (later Edward VII) and continuing to the present day Prince of Wales - Charles.

She could visualize the scandalous Prince of Wales hanging out here - the first one, Edward. She couldn't begin to imagine the present Prince Charles having a cocktail in public at the Ritz. He just didn't seem the type to mix with the masses. He seemed to be more private.

Rachel walked across the Long Gallery, which was a grand hallway leading from the entrance of the hotel along the full length of the property all the way through to the Terrace Garden. She peeked into Palm Court, which had been a meeting place for young socialites since the 1920s and still seemed to attract the "in" crowd, including film industry giants from around the world. Her literary agent, Anita Schwaber, in Los Angeles had encouraged her to frequent Palm Court that boasted of a high glass ceiling, towering marble columns and a statue fountain. Anita told her that she needed to network in London, which was a major melting pot of writers and producers.

So, in addition to stopping in when she came to London to shop, she had afternoon teas at the Ritz with Ethan's older sister, Elaine. Afternoon tea consisted of assorted finger sandwiches, scones, various cakes and desserts - not to be confused with high tea after 6 p.m. that consisted of heavier foods such as sausages, meats, etc. High tea was originally a meal prepared for the man of the house when he returned home from work each day, whereas afternoon tea was a mid-afternoon snack between lunch and the evening meal.

As a matter of fact, Elaine had taken Rachel to several of the "in spot" afternoon teas. She most certainly knew all the finest and expensive places to go. Elaine, like her brother, knew how to spend money - one of the things they both did well. However there was another side to her, unlike Ethan, she was a bargain hunter. But in every other way, they not only behaved alike, they looked alike. Elaine was a female version of Ethan, a large-boned woman with the same facial structure and the same big blue-gray eyes. One would think they were twins. However, she didn't have his portliness, but was a tall, attractive woman, very imposing, unlike her gentle nature.

When Ethan and Elaine spoke, it sounded as if their mouths were always full of marbles. They spoke through lips formed in a tight pursed oval, a Donald Trump pucker one might say, which made their accent seem much more contrived than normal. They both considered their particular pronunciation as proper English, however. Rachel felt they had developed a dialect all their very own. It wasn't at all similar to anyone else's accent, unlike anyone on BBC's news and talk shows, which was a good measuring stick. Theirs was unlike the Royal Family's sound, which one would think would be nearest to purest. Their sound was unlike the educators whom Rachel had spoken with on her research trips to Cambridge. But Ethan insisted that both he and Elaine had been taught proper English. Rachel decided maybe they were taught it, but they unquestionably added their own slant to it.

She knew that Elaine didn't care much for her and she knew that Elaine told Ethan that Rachel was after his money. Unknown to Elaine, Rachel had never been motivated by money. Besides she had plenty of her own.

In spite of Ethan's request for Rachel to stay put by the elevator, she began walking towards the Rotunda Lobby - a beautifully arched, round lobby. How could she stand there and wait and not move around? She wanted to take it all in, to see it all. As she strolled, she eavesdropped on happy couples partying and chatting to one another; some standing, some sitting on the exquisite sofas, some on the beautifully upholstered Louis XIV chairs. She noticed that most of the women were wrapped in furs; a very pricey representation of every fur-bearing animal on the planet, all on exhibition under this one courtly roof. She was amazed at the number of fur coats, and mentally counted them. *Seven . . . eight . . . nine . . .*

In the States, fur coats were taboo. The animal rights activists had seen to that and very rarely did a real fur coat appear, even on special occasions in such refined surroundings as this, for fear of being spray painted by radicals. Rachel didn't wear fur anyway, because she was too short and she felt it made

25

her look like a giant fur ball.

Suddenly, the hustling-bustling body of Ethan came bouncing back towards her, impairing her view across the Lobby.

"It's on the Seventh Floor," he said as he pulled on her arm and quickened the pace.

"Ethan! You're dragging me."

He loosened his grip on her arm and slowed to a reasonable pace as they walked through the bar area.

She added, "Did you notice all the fur coats?"

"I suppose that means you want me to buy you one," he chuckled.

"No. Have you ever seen me wear one?" She tried to keep up with him. "The one and only time I had a fur coat was in my early twenties. I paid $55 for a three-quarter length mink - 1920s vintage - at a church bazaar. And after wearing it a couple years with my jeans, it fell apart, never to be seen or heard of again. You know, you really don't know me, Ethan. And if I wanted one, I could certainly buy it myself!"

She tightened her lips and looked towards the sounds of music, dancing, laughter, and joy coming from the enormous, crystal chandeliered restaurant at the end of the Long Gallery.

"Now that looks like an exciting party!" she exclaimed. "Why aren't we going in there?"

"It's a benefit gala, four thousand a plate, Rachel. I chose the two thousand pound package, because it includes our room, complimentary cocktails, dinner, and the party."

Rachel moved nearer the entrance to the ballroom where it appeared that everyone in the *Who's Who* of London was in attendance – she recognized some politicians and literary people and she thought she saw Rod Stewart and Sting. *No, it can't be them.*

She did see Jamie Lee Curtis sitting at a table with her British husband, however. Everyone was as festive as the décor. Noise and laughter abounded. But the thrilling part for her was the actual room. It was the most elegant hotel ballroom she'd ever seen. It reminded her of the white columned, gold leafed rooms of Versailles - magnificent chandeliers, huge gilded mirrors, lovely paintings, and candelabras. She loved atmosphere and opulence, was always drawn to it.

"This is really something, Ethan!"

Ethan pulled her back and then a few steps further towards the elevators, "Here we are." He stepped into the lift, holding the door back for her.

"I was just looking; you didn't have to rush me."

On the Seventh Floor, they found their destination - an all black and white, chrome and glass, twinkling mini-lighted, very contemporary setting. It was like stepping into another world. A far cry from the preferable Old World elegance they had just left downstairs. But, it did have one redeeming quality, Rachel noted. The two banquet rooms opened onto expansive balconies, overlooking the beautifully lit Terrace Garden below. That pleased her, she loved night lights and especially gardens.

Inside, the dining tables were set up in one of the two adjoining banquet rooms. The ceiling was concealed generously with black and white helium balloons attached to hanging streamers. More balloons and gaudy plumed hats decorated every dining table. Every patron in the reception room was coincidentally dressed in black except for one woman who was in red and one who was wearing a very short, green-sequined spandex dress. The men resembled penguins and the women resembled the haunting, hollow-eyed, back-up group in Robert Palmer's '80s music videos. The room was very, very quiet and very, very somber. Whispers and the occasional phony laugh were barely audible.

The reception and cocktail area had a black and white tiled marble floor and black leather sofas with glass and brass cocktail tables placed in front of them. On the cocktail tables were geometric crystal and chrome sculptures; artistic, but cold. Canapés and cocktails were served while everyone darted glances, giving each other scrutinizing once-overs.

"I don't like this, Ethan." she quietly expressed. "It's uncomfortable in here. There's no laughter, nothing. Look, no one is smiling! I'm sorry, but what kind of party is this?"

6

Paul opened his eyes, swiveled back around to his desk, and leaned forward in his chair to pull a few tissues from the desk drawer - tissues that always came in handy for mopping up after impromptu sexual fantasies.

"My dearest Carol-in-absentia, I thank you, I thank you, and I thank you. The tee-shirt does it every time, sweetheart," he said as he tossed the tissues in the wastebasket.

He stood up, zipped his pants and went into the executive washroom. His was one of two offices in the London headquarters that was equipped with washroom facilities and a bar. He'd made it clear to the New York office that he would only consent to stay in London if they gave him what he wanted. The bar and washroom were at the top of his list, along with an office with a view across the Thames, and the highest six-figure salary for creative directors in the company. Actually, Paul was given his choice of Los Angeles, New York, or London and had considered returning to the West L. A. office because that was home to him. But, in the end he chose London. He'd just met

28

Carol who tipped the scales in London's favor and he preferred the proximity to Europe where the best ski slopes in the world were just a short flight away. Unbeknownst to headquarters, he would've taken the assignment whether or not they had complied with all of his wishes. His poker face while negotiating talent was one of the reasons he dealt with the most valuable clients of Triple R - Randolph, Ross, & Remington, Inc. His creative genius, of course, was also a contributing factor.

Paul came out of the washroom in his skimpy, burgundy Calvin Klein's and opened a built-in wardrobe. He selected a black stylish tuxedo, a black, mandarin-collared, silk shirt, and an azure blue silk cummerbund with matching fringed neck scarf - exactly the color of his eyes. He kept an assortment of clothing in his office for quick changes rather than having to make the trip up the river to his condo. After quickly changing into his New Year's Eve attire, he draped a long, black, rain-repellent coat over his shoulders, then grabbed his umbrella and rushed out the door.

While he was waiting at the elevator, one of his staff members rushed towards him from her office, donning her raincoat.

Oh no, not now! Although Paul had worked with the woman on several projects, he knew nothing about her and couldn't care less. He made it a point to distance himself from fellow employees. The less he knew about them personally, the better, especially the women. It made his job easier to orchestrate and bear.

"You look like you're off to a party, Paul," she said as she buttoned up and tucked her scarf inside her collar. "Nice tux. Is it Armani?"

He frowned as he replied, "I don't know without looking at the label, Belinda. I buy what fits and appeals to me, and if it happens to be a designer label, so be it. It doesn't matter to me. I think we've had this conversation before."

This was not the first time he harshly reacted to Belinda's obvious obsession with designer labels. And it seemed to go over her head each time, he noted. She refused to get the message that he was not label-oriented and didn't care to discuss the maker of his clothing or any other personal facts with her.

He couldn't put his finger on it, but for some reason she just rubbed him the wrong way, and at times he found it difficult to work with her. Whenever he would give her an art assignment, she would always produce something totally different from what he'd asked, but she was talented. He had to admit that. He had to admit that she had a pretty face too, as pretty faces go. Maybe it irked him because her ideas were usually better than his, although hell could freeze over before he'd ever admit it to anyone. His own bag of creative tricks was depleted of late and he'd found it rather difficult to produce any new innovative ideas. His concentration had been off. At any rate, he didn't need this female upstart nipping at his heels up the corporate ladder.

As he discreetly glanced at what she was wearing, he figured she probably was one of those people who wouldn't purchase anything from an unknown designer or off a rack in an ordinary shop. How she managed to survive on her salary was a mystery to him. She must spend all her money on clothing with her credit cards most likely maxed out. She was a stylish woman. *She is a threat to any man's financial security.*

She was one of London's most promising graphic artists, but Paul thought she was strange. She didn't mix with employees, a loner. She also showed signs of lacking good common sense. Above all else, she was flat chested and a bit too bottom-heavy for Paul, which was another reason he disregarded her. Women should have ample breasts and slim hips. It didn't help that he'd covered that fat ass of hers several times because she'd made a few heavy-duty, bad judgment calls. Not artistically, but business-wise, which only contributed to his viewpoint that women were not business minded. They were made for sex and giving birth, or modeling. That's all. Not even cooking. Men were better. Most chefs were men.

"You got a hot date, tonight?" Belinda asked.

"With the Kawasaki consortium? I think not," he replied as he looked at his watch.

"Sounds like your night is going to be as exciting as mine. I'll be spending it with my mother and her card-playing friends. Are you going to Trafalgar?"

"Wouldn't miss it for the world."

"Well, I hear they're closing the streets all around the area because of what happened last year. So, it might be a bit difficult to get there, although it isn't far from my house." She readied herself to step on the elevator.

The bell sounded its arrival.

He waited for her to enter the elevator, and then joined her. They rode in an uncomfortable silence to the ground floor.

"Here we are. Have a good evening," he said mechanically without a smile, as he held back the door for her exit.

"Thanks, Paul. You too. Good night."

Belinda hurried towards the massive glass doors that led out to the street, glanced back, smiled and waved at Paul before she exited. She had a crush on him for an entire year, but of course had hidden her feelings, knowing it was impossible to capture his attention and affection. She and all the other women at Triple R knew of Paul's promiscuity and preferences and had witnessed the continual parade of sensuous women traipsing in and out of his office. *I wonder what it would be like to make love to him. Oh well, he'd never be interested in me.*

In fact, she knew he would never be interested in just one woman, which was probably the reason he had never married. He was the most ineligible eligible bachelor around. She was continually beleaguered with what to talk about when she found herself face to face with him. She became tongue-tied and unable to think of anything smart or clever to say. She always said something stupid like asking about designer labels that she really didn't care about or asking boring questions about clients or work. Paul was the most handsome man she knew and tonight he looked like he stepped right off the cover of a gothic romance novel. *I'm so glad I bought some romance novels at the newsstand earlier this afternoon to read over the holidays.* And she vowed to increase her visits to the gym as a New Year's resolution, in her serious attempt to reshape her body – smaller butt, bigger boobs. *The boobs might need implants*, she thought as she hailed a cab.

Paul went to the security desk and picked up the phone. He hesitated as he glanced towards the door and watched Belinda disappear into the night. There was something about that woman that left him feeling quite uneasy. Ever since he settled into the London office a year ago, he'd felt intimidated by her. He wasn't sure if it was her extraordinary talent that surpassed his, or her aloofness, or her mysterious, penetrating green eyes. Whatever it was, he felt very inept around her.

He shook the thoughts of her from his mind, dialed an extension, and told the company driver to pick him up at the entrance. One of the benefits of being a Senior VP was having a chauffeured limo on call. Most of the time he preferred using a company van to transport client groups, however tonight warranted a limo, in spite of the pretentiousness that grated against his bohemian grain. He took solace in the fact that it was company policy, not his personal preference to use the limo. It was one more reason he would rather be in a studio loft, painting and minding his own frigging business.

Rachel and Ethan sat at their table.

Thank God the band isn't dressed in black and white too, like everybody else, Rachel thought as she raised her hands while the waiter placed a napkin across her lap. The jazz combo was very good she noticed. The singer had perfect pitch, as perfect as her gold lame´ dress and gold sparkly flower in her golden hair. She was gorgeous and sang mellow and sultry. The combo wore colorful ruffled silk shirts with silk pants in darker hues, giving the room the only colorful holiday spirit it possessed.

"Oh, I love this song - *The More I See You,*" Rachel said as she reached across the table and patted Ethan's arm. "You know, I really do miss singing. You've heard me do this one, haven't you?"

"Yes, yes, I think so." He gave a quick automatic smile, and then picked up a menu card from the plate in front of him. "The courses are listed on the card. It should be quite delicious, you know. Considering the cost."

Rachel straightened in her chair, "Please, Ethan. Just this once, can we go through the evening without costing out everything?"

"Yes, yes. You're quite right. What wine do you fancy?" He picked up the wine list.

"Champagne, what else? It's New Year's Eve."

"Wouldn't you rather have a nice wine with dinner, a Beaujolais? You like Merlot. Cabernet Sauvignon? Champagne will give you a headache." He continued looking over the menu.

She sighed, "Not any worse than a red wine would. But order whatever you want. I don't care. I'll drink anything tonight. I just thought I should stay with champagne, since that's what I've already had today. Usually a headache comes from the mixing, doesn't it? Oh, she is so good! Listen to this. 'Someone to Watch over Me', my all-time favorite."

Ethan glanced at the singer for a moment, and then returned to the wine list. "They're all your favorites." He motioned for the waiter. "We'll have a bottle of Merlot, this one, number 21."

Rachel smiled widely at the waiter as she tilted his name badge towards her in order to read it, "And please bring me a bottle of champagne, Anthony. Surprise me, will you? Not too expensive, a Brut." The waiter flashed a handsome smile back at her and asked if they preferred to have the champagne and wine now or with the first course.

"Now, please," they both said in unison.

Anthony nodded and went after the bottles.

Rachel glanced across the table at a frowning Ethan. "Sorry. I changed my mind. I should stick with the champagne. So, what's the first course?" Rachel picked up the menu card and read aloud. "Fois Gras. No way. I'm not eating duck liver. I've seen how they force-feed the poor things, literally funneling food down their throats, sometimes exploding their stomachs. Ohh! Terrible!"

"Rachel, please. Not tonight." Ethan pleaded.

Ignoring him, she continued, "And smoked salmon with anchovy paste swirls. Oh well, I'll just save room for the main entree."

"Go on. You're going to try these, aren't you? After all the money I've spent?"

She rolled her eyes and looked away as she recalled the

conversation they'd had during the three-hour drive to London earlier that day. He'd kept bringing up how much the trip was costing him, and she'd said that he needn't have gone to all the trouble if it was going to bug him so. They didn't need to stay at the Ritz. If all he wanted was to please her, well, all she wanted was to be in Trafalgar Square at the stroke of midnight and wave at the TV cameras. If he'd only asked her before he made the arrangements, she would've saved him a lot of money, she'd said. What was his problem? His company was doing well enough. Although he wasn't a multi-millionaire, it didn't matter to Rachel. She'd never been impressed with blatant display of power, status, and money anyway. And here she was on New Year's Eve, sitting among these stuffy pretenders at the Ritz, when all she'd wanted was to walk around Soho and Piccadilly Square, on the street amongst the celebrating masses.

May as well make the best of it. If nothing else, the music is good. And although the courses listed on the menu card weren't for her palate, she wasn't going to complain anymore. She felt she'd been pushing it too hard already. After all, Ethan was trying his best to make her happy. She knew that. He probably felt he'd made the right decision in coming here. It was an exquisite hotel, a gorgeous room. So, to make the evening work for both of them, it was up to her. But still, she couldn't control the frown that furrowed her brow as she looked across the table at Ethan right at that moment. He was noisily slurping up the first course that had just been set in front of him, scraping his plate with his utensils. Making clanking noises. He wasn't even waiting for the wine steward to pour from the bottle he'd just uncorked and wasn't waiting for Rachel to begin. By the time the steward poured the wine and champagne, Ethan's first course had vanished. Rachel's food sat on the plate, untouched. She handed it to Ethan.

She'd asked herself many times over the past few months what had possessed her to accept this man's proposal? Aside from business. Maybe her acceptance of the proposal was because she needed a male authoritative figure in her life, now that her father was gone. *No, I don't need a male authoritative figure. God forbid!*

What was it about her that got her into situations that were so awkward? Was it the commitment that spurred uncomfortable feelings and caused her to withdraw? She recalled how it was with both her husbands. Once married, she had become ill at ease, had shrunk into herself, and had wanted out of the trap. She craved freedom. She rebelled against being controlled, same as she had with her father while growing up. She remembered feeling subservient and submissive early on when she was married. She certainly didn't like that. She wanted to be able to make her own choices about everything. If she didn't want to cook, so be it. If she didn't want to talk, so be it. If she didn't want to go where he wanted to go, so be it. If she didn't like his friends, so be it. If she wanted to travel alone, so be it. If she didn't want sex, so be it. She didn't like making plans and concessions to suit the other person. Call it what one wished. That's how she felt.

But here I am, making more damn concessions. Like right now, spreading out the food on this second plate the waiter just gave me, to make it look like I've eaten some of it. She didn't like duck or goose liver. She didn't like pork or pork pie. She didn't like anchovy paste swirls. She didn't like smoked salmon. She never would have ordered this if she were by herself. She didn't like raw fish or pickled herring, and the list went on and on - all of Ethan's favorite foods. She felt he must've cultivated a taste for this cuisine only because it was considered to be the food of the affluent. How could anyone really like this stuff? Even if she were richer than the Pope, she would continue to eat plain foods - fruit, salads, cheese, steak, salsa, pizza, chocolate chip ice cream, and, of course her favorite, marshmallow crème. *Whatever happened to the food one could recognize without having to read a description of its contents?* This wasn't her idea of a romantic New Year's Eve, sitting at a table of strange, exotic food that turned her stomach, in an unfriendly cold room, across from an insensitive man, while she was missing all the fun at Trafalgar Square.

Anthony poured another glass of champagne and wine, wished them bon appetite, and walked away.

"Excellent wine! Would you like to try it?" Ethan asked.

She sipped from his glass and nodded in pleasure. "Yes, it's a smooth Merlot. Would you like to try the champagne?"

"No, thank you. It would spoil the taste of the Merlot."

She took a deep breath and counted to ten, trying not to respond to his abruptness. When she reached twenty, Rachel smiled and said, "This is great, Ethan. Perfect timing for both of us. I'm so relieved I finished the film script on schedule. Fedexed it this morning to Anita. Thanks again for being my sounding board, for reading it with me. Now I can begin my novel. It feels good to be able to get away, doesn't it?"

He nodded as he swallowed a big gulp of wine and poured more into his glass. Ethan didn't sip wine, Rachel noticed, he gulped it like water. Usually, he ordered a large bottle of sparkling water immediately upon being seated in a restaurant, but he hadn't done so yet. He chug-lugged the bottle of Merlot instead and he glanced around the room for the waiter to order another.

"I'd like to get away more often, Rachel, but this has been such a critical time for me. And as soon as we get back, I'm moving my office to the plant. I plan to replace Allan after I get the process line up and running. The bugger doesn't know what the bloody hell he is doing! All he does is create friction between staff, goes over-budget, and goes behind my back. Everyone's right, you know, I need to engineer it myself. I'm the only one who knows how to do the job. Do you agree?"

"Well no, I don't. I feel you should find a qualified engineer to replace Allan. If you had done a thorough background search on Allan to begin with, you probably would've found that what he and Vera said about his experience wasn't exactly what you needed. The only thing you knew for a fact about him was he and Vera ran a pub together and had to file bankruptcy. Hardly a proper credential. You didn't check him out, so you more or less asked for what happened."

"I know, I know."

"But you were doing your daughter a favor. I would've done the same thing if it had been my son, I suppose. But, it's not good business to hire family or friends. Respect eventually flies out the window. And believe me you're going to have more trouble with Allan before this is over. He's angry and vindictive, Ethan. Be careful."

"Yes, yes, yes. You must think I don't see anything at all. Well, I do, you know. And I'm going to do the engineering job myself. And that's that!" He gulped another glass of wine.

"But, you're the managing director, Ethan. You can't just drop everything to do a process engineer's job. It seems to me, if you were to climb down a rung, it should be to put on the hat of Sales Director. You could sell hammers to a hammer manufacturer. If you don't get some signed contracts, there won't be a reason to engineer a plant. You're paid to haul organic waste from farmers and food companies and then you've got to sell the product you make from it. Sales at both ends. The investors aren't going to finance you forever, not without some kind of return, right? Didn't Harry say no more money? He won't lend you any more, Ethan, without some sort of return. He isn't rich. You've got to get the sales. I can't believe he mortgaged his holiday home in Spain to give you the money. His wife doesn't know anything about it."

"Bloody hell! I don't want to talk about this, Rachel. I don't want to talk about it!" He signaled for the waiter, "Another bottle of wine, please, the same."

She turned quickly towards the jazz combo to hide the hurt in her eyes, and focused on the singer's rendition of 'When I Fall In Love.'

No matter how hard she tried, she could not get used to Ethan's sharp manner in ending conversations that were not to his liking. If she were to single out one of Ethan's faults that annoyed her the most, it was his seeming disregard for his investors. He treated their investments irreverently. He acted like the money was lent to the company indefinitely, and it seemed as if he didn't care whether it was repaid or not, with no regards for agreements and terms. But then again, if the money wasn't there, it wasn't there, so he couldn't repay them. He wasn't spending it recklessly. Maybe she was being too critical. The lyrics of a song by Joe South popped into her mind, *Walk a mile in my shoes, walk a mile in my shoes. Yeah, before you abuse, criticize and accuse, walk a mile in my shoes.*

A lot had happened since Rachel first arrived from the States. She was glad Ethan welcomed her into his business; although not aware it was because he wanted her near. She thought it was because of her stateside, number–crunching experience that prompted him to ask her to join Verde Victory. She knew her financial reporting methods would be an asset and her people sense was usually spot on. So, she'd temporarily set aside the screenplay she had been writing and had given Ethan's environmental company her complete attention for a few months.

It had been a challenging dual role for Rachel, accounting manager and human resources director, but she thoroughly enjoyed learning the British way of doing business. She had excellent business sense as well as being a creative. Ethan owned a bio-process formula to treat organic waste and convert it into animal feed and fertilizer. It was an innovative process, unlike any other in the world, and he owned the patents for it in over forty countries. The possibilities were endless, but it was still in the costly preliminary testing and trial stage.

In the few months after Rachel's arrival, she accomplished more than her predecessor had since the startup of Verde Victory, Ltd. She had set up appropriate accounting systems, budgets and forecasts, reporting procedures, and an organizational structure. She had assisted Verde Victory, Ltd. in acquiring the first bank loan of £500,000 which it had direly needed in order to increase the capacity of the existing processing plant and to start building portable processing plants. Portable plants could be set up on the property of the food grower or food packing company to recycle its green waste rather than send it to land fill, which had been legislated against by the government.

Verde Victory also added to the employee roster and brought everything up to governmental standards and codes, and was now moving in a positive direction to the next plateau, which would unfortunately require more funding.

But, things began changing rapidly between Rachel and Ethan because of the long hours, the constant togetherness, and the increasing growth of the company. Daily flare-ups and confrontations over expenditures, sales, and finances peppered their lives. Rachel finally asked that she be relieved of her duties and responsibilities earlier than planned. She said she wanted to get back to her writing and wanted to go to Paris to do research, but would be on tap as a consultant to Verde Victory.

When she exited the day-to-day operational aspect of the company, Ethan's family reentered. Namely, his daughter and step daughter, Vera and Adele, and his ex-wife, Nora. Nora had been with him in the original company that was registered under another name.

As a result, Rachel was feeling like odd man out these days. She was well aware of Ethan's fickleness when it came to his allegiance to associates and family. One never knew from one day to the next on which side of his favor one would be. It wasn't a secure feeling.

So in that moment while dining at the Ritz after she questioned Ethan about the business and he'd abruptly cut her off and shut her out, she seriously considered leaving him permanently. She felt he treated her as if she'd never been a part of it at all. And when it came to his loyalty to her, well, she knew, at the moment, it was non-existent.

She looked across the table at him as he continued to gobble up his food. *Of course, not sleeping with him doesn't help the cause, if there is a cause, and if that is what one would call it.* But she couldn't bring herself to make love to him. She just couldn't do it. Sure, it made her feel guilty and sorry for him. But then again, their relationship wasn't founded on sex. It was based on friendship and business. And she didn't feel it was right that she should consent to have sex with him just because they were betrothed, regardless of what her dear stepmother, Lee, had said on one of their long phone conversations.

She'd said, "Just give him what he wants, dear. Close your eyes and think of something else. It'll be over before you know it."

Good advice? Rachel thought not, as she sipped and watched the singer. *This engagement is a joke.* The words flashed through her mind again. *It's a great big joke.*

Besides, no one knew how she really felt about sex. She wasn't entirely sure how she felt about it either, but ever since that damn creep date-raped her in L.A. a few months before her father died, everything had changed. She was a very strong person in one sense, but not in another. It had been difficult blocking the event from her mind, although lately it was fainter than ever before. But she still couldn't even begin to think of having sex.

The recollection of that night leapt to the front of her mind once again. She tried suppressing the memory, but it refused to budge. It was to be conjured up right then and there as she gazed straight through the musicians into the space beyond them.

She had heard of Congressman Rollings and seen him on CNN news even before she met the man at a club in Marina Del Rey, where she was living at the time, while writing her first screenplay. Creep Rollings, as she later referred to him, was a visiting congressman from a Northern California district and was very charming, very intelligent, and very attractive. It didn't bother her that he was married because she had no intentions of ever getting married again anyway. Twice was enough. And it was a safeguard to her that he was married, not to mention it was a known fact that he was a ladies' man. So, she didn't feel guilty about it, for she wouldn't be his first adulterous conquest, if it even went that far.

He'd come on very strong and a bit inebriated that evening. He invited her to accompany him to a private cocktail party at the Marina City Club. He'd told her that a few political friends and constituents were throwing a shindig at the penthouse where he was staying. She went.

Surprise! Surprise! No cocktail party. No political friends or constituents. Just the two of them. Before she had a chance to consider a sexual liaison, he grabbed her roughly, hurt her mouth as he kissed her, then talked dirty. She had struggled and fought against his strength and his disgusting lewdness and crudeness until she became so exhausted she couldn't fight anymore. Hardly a romantic encounter. He had managed to rip off her blouse and, during the scuffle that ensued he tied her hands and then her feet to the bed posts with four of his neck ties that obviously had been thrown on the bed in preparation.

She'd worn a short leather skirt, silk blouse, and a leather blazer that evening. Ever since that night, she had converted her wardrobe into the lengthy multi-layered ensembles she now wore.

He'd been unable to yank the leather skirt from her, so he shoved it above her waist and pulled down her panty hose. Now her lower and upper extremities were exposed and available for whatever he wanted to do with them. He stuffed a washcloth in her mouth to muffle the screams and cries. She heard the city noises coming through the penthouse windows, but no one could hear Rachel. She remembered how she had prayed to every God she could think of to spare her. She promised God that she'd never go out with another married man. She promised she'd never again have sex out of wedlock. She promised and promised and promised, until there was nothing left to promise. Her mind had raced, searching for a way out of the hellish nightmare.

He had said over and over he wasn't going to hurt her; had

said that he liked it when his women were tied up. He'd told her to relax and enjoy it, she didn't have to do anything, he just wanted his way with her in every fashion he'd ever fantasized. He had said he'd always wondered what it would feel like to rape a woman. He said some women submitted to his fantasies, but it was never like this. This was the best ever.

"Does it hurt, Baby?" he said in a disgusting, spittled, gravelly voice as he twisted her nipples so hard she thought she would pass out from the pain.

Her muffled sounds didn't interpret as the words she was actually screaming, "You said you weren't going to hurt me, you asshole! How can you possibly think you aren't hurting me?

Rollings had laughed psychotically at the pain in her eyes. He replaced his fingers with his teeth and began biting her, drawing blood.

She felt she was about to pass out any second and wished the hell she would. But she had to stay awake somehow, had to figure out how to get away from this sick prick.

Then, he unzipped his pants.

She wildly strained and yanked at the ties wrapped around the posts. With every fiber of energy that was left and with tears streaming, she growled at him like a rabid animal. *If I could have gotten to the slimy cocksucker at that very moment, I would've killed him!*

He positioned himself between her legs and began to ferociously violate her body with his hands and penis. It had felt like her insides were being pulled out of her body through her vagina.

Rachel had cried helplessly at the unbearable hurt invading every part of her brain and body. She didn't think she could bear it. She was right. She passed out.

Afterwards, he had obviously untied her and fallen asleep, because that was the scenario when she regained consciousness. After momentarily staring at the blood on the bed, she quickly dressed and ran from the penthouse, afraid to stop and assess her damaged body.

When she entered the lobby from the elevator, she lined up a cab and then discreetly called the perp's room on a house phone and left a message on his voice mail.

She could remember it verbatim:

If you ever come near me again, I'll plaster your face and name all over L.A. on buildings, cars, buses, telephone poles, and every possible surface available. I'll go on television and radio talk shows. I'll send mass emails if you so much as communicate or cross my path in any way, shape, or form. My father is a very powerful man in California real estate and politics, and if he ever finds out what you've done to me, he'll make sure you'll never be reelected, not to mention he'll probably kill you first. I'm going to place a blow by blow description of what you did to me in several safe deposit boxes, and with my attorney, and in the event that anything happens to me, this information will surface immediately. I mean every word of this, you creepy sicko!

Whether Rollings had believed her threats or not, their paths never crossed again. She saw him on the news from time to time and wondered how many other unsuspecting women experienced his psycho attacks. Maybe she was the only one. Maybe it was a fluke.

No, it wasn't. She remembered he had said that he liked to pretend to rape, so he'd done it before and probably had done it many times since. Those crimes usually progressed, becoming more and more intense and violent to satisfy the perpetrator's anger towards women or to satisfy his own morbid needs.

She never did report it to the authorities because she had gone to his room, willfully. She'd flirted with him. There were witnesses. Besides, she knew she didn't have a chance in hell against a congressman. Someday she'd write about it and let people figure it out for themselves. Someday, he'd slip up.

Rachel poured herself another glass of champagne as she shuddered at the memory. *How could he do that to a woman? What makes a man do such a terrible thing? Why would a man want to force a woman into submission?* She remembered how she had begged him to stop, had pleaded with him. She remembered how trapped she'd felt when she was tied to the posts and gagged. That same feeling of being trapped was surfacing more and more, lately. She felt trapped when she felt intimacy nearing.

Her two marriages had been very short-lived, producing the one son who was happily married and living in Denver. She didn't see her son Devin as often as she liked, but they communicated by phone and email quite often. Devin was her first husband's son. So he lived through the abusive second marriage too.

It wasn't only the abusiveness and controlling madness that put her off marriage, however. She couldn't stand the time restrictions marriage put on her and she had little patience with the fragile male ego and dominance. It seemed she was forever walking on thin ice when she was married, at any moment expecting it to crack, experiencing non-existence, losing her real self, becoming a nondescript second citizen rather than a woman of her own substance and choice. She felt that a man was happiest with a submissive wife, one who would support him in his endeavors, one who would be the chief cook and bottle washer, who'd be a "yes man", always eager to listen to what he had to say and to agree with him at all cost, and one who'd spread her legs at a moment's notice. *Hell, no! No! No! That is not me!* The thought made her shudder again.

She steered clear of serious relationships after the second divorce. Yes, the trapped feelings had occurred in her marriages long before the evil attack. But Rollings only confirmed in her mind the extent of the depraved male mind. Not all men were evil, just most. She knew she couldn't lump all men into one category. And she felt that Ethan wasn't to be classed as such. He would never force her to do anything. She knew that. He was a gentle man. Sometimes volatile in business, but basically a gentle person with those he loved.

Even so, her claustrophobic thoughts of dreaded intimacy had magnified since the horrid experience in California and although this marriage-to-be was supposed to be a business arrangement only, she could feel sexual neediness from Ethan and that made her nervous. Very nervous! She definitely wasn't into needy.

9

Ethan leaned back in his chair, dabbed the corners of his mouth with the black linen napkin, lifted his wineglass, and noticed how the light was reflecting on Rachel's face. Her almond shaped eyes, turned up nose, and gorgeous lips excited him.

He noticed that she was lost in her thoughts while sipping her champagne and watching the singer. He methodically compared her to every other woman in the room. She was by far the most interesting, he noted, and positively the most voluptuous. He didn't think she needed a facelift at all. Why would she even consider interrupting the natural flow of aging? He couldn't believe the dress she was wearing. It had been several years since he had seen the skin below her collarbones. She'd changed her style since they'd first met. She usually draped herself in artsy-fartsy attire, layers upon layers, making herself look like a shapeless fabric covered box.

Box as in rectangle, he corrected himself, amused at his own off-color thoughts. She would be appalled if she ever heard

46

him refer to her as the slang female anatomical descriptive "box".

They never spoke in a sexual suggestive manner or even joked about such things. She was as serious and straight-laced as they came, although there was something hidden in the glimmer of her eyes and in her demeanor that said otherwise. He'd always hoped she might be totally uninhibited with him. *Yes, I want her.* The betrothal was more than a business arrangement as far as he was concerned. It was a ploy. And tonight he held high hopes after seeing her bold curvaceousness. Although he'd sensed Rachel's physical inattentiveness to him from the beginning, he had not pressed the point.

When he first met Rachel, he knew they would always be connected. It was something he couldn't explain, but it was a strong feeling. Not just a hope or a wish or anything of that sort. Maybe it would take a lifetime, but he felt that the moment would come when she would realize that he was her true love.

He remembered when he and several of his engineers had been in California on business and had decided to take in one of Bakersfield's famous country western watering holes, The Old Corral, or Ethel's as it was called. He was on the dance floor trying to learn the Texas Two Step when he saw a couple of attractive women walk in and sit at a ringside table. One was Rachel. She was laughing, energetic in her gestures, and had seemed to love the music. He loved to dance and even though he hadn't quite mastered the footwork of this particular dance, he enjoyed country western music immensely. He noticed that she had grinned as she watched him bounce lightly around the floor out of sync with the others.

He wanted the music to stop so he could go over and introduce himself before someone else swept her away. In fact he had contemplated walking off the dance floor whether the music stopped or not. He did just that.

"Hello. May I join you?"

Rachel had motioned to him to sit. Her friend left to talk to someone at the bar. "Please do. Where are you from?"

"England. North of London."

"I thought you might be from England."

"Does it show that much?"

"A little."

"May I buy you another drink?" He had gestured to the waitress and indicated a round of drinks.

"Why, thank you. You don't need to do that. But I'll take it, thank you." Rachel laughed, again grinning broadly.

"Has anyone ever told you, you have a lovely smile?"

"Yes, quite often as a matter of fact. Has anyone ever told you, you are light on your feet?" She had teased with her eyes.

"Yes, quite often as a matter of fact," he answered.

They both laughed. He had been amused at her sense of humor. "Would you care to join me in the next dance?"

"No thanks. I don't dance. I like to watch. Go on if you want, I'll watch you."

"I'd rather dance with you."

"Nice of you to ask, but no." She sipped her wine, still making eye contact. "Have we met before?"

"We may have. Have you been to England?"

"No, never. But I want to go. My father's British, and I've felt a pull towards England for as long as I can remember. I love its history, the kings and queens. Read about it all the time. Read British novels, historical romance and otherwise. Love British movies, but then Britain is in my blood."

"Hmmm . . . that's interesting. I might just have to take you back with me. What would you think about that?" He lifted his glass of beer to his lips while watching her eyes widen to what he'd just said.

"Take me back with you?"

"Yes. Would you like to go with me? To England?"

"I am going."

"But would you like to go with me?"

"No."

Ethan smiled as he recalled Rachel's bluntness. If there was one thing he could always count on, it was her curt truthfulness. She undeniably spoke her mind. *Most of the time.*

He wondered what she was thinking right that moment as as they sat on the Seventh Floor of the Ritz. He wondered if she was thinking of him. He knew her mind wasn't on the music, he could tell by the expression on her face.

"What are you thinking, Rachel?"

She looked at him and grinned. "Let's go to Trafalgar Square, Ethan. Right now. Wouldn't you just love to be there at Midnight?"

10

After pulling up to the entrance of the London Ritz, a chauffeur stepped out of an empty, sleek, Mercedes limo, opened the passenger door, and stood waiting. Very few people were leaving the Ritz at this hour – 11 p.m. Most people were already where they wanted to be to bring in the New Year.

Ethan Philips burst out the entrance of the hotel and impatiently signaled a valet to order a taxi. The doors swung open again; this time it was Rachel, carrying two rain coats. She hurriedly joined Ethan and handed one to him.

"How long will it take us to get there?" she asked as she draped the other coat over her shoulders.

"This is ridiculous, you know," Ethan exclaimed. "The streets are cordoned off because of the riots last year. It'll be impossible to get near the fountain."

"We'll get there. We can drive as far as we can and then hoof it the rest of the way."

Ethan looked at her curiously. "You? Walk in the rain in those shoes? You don't realize how far it is, do you?"

"Come on, Ethan, where's your sense of adventure? Midnight at Trafalgar! It's exciting!"

A cab pulled up in front of the limo and the driver hopped out and signaled to them.

Through the hotel doors rushed Paul Newland, tall and handsome, blond shoulder-length hair flying. He led a group of five Japanese businessmen who were wearing their telltale three piece dark suits, white shirts, pale yellow ties, and dark overcoats. Paul motioned them to the waiting limo, chatting with them in their native tongue, as they entered one by one. The last man to enter, who appeared to be the senior ranking member of the group, shook Paul's hand and thanked him for a wonderful dinner at the Ritz, and then climbed into the limo. But before Paul got in, he glanced towards the cab in front of them at exactly the same moment Rachel glanced towards him. Their gaze collided. The impact held them momentarily until Ethan's abrupt voice urged Rachel to step into the cab. He stepped in her line of view and short-circuited the electrifying connection between Rachel and Paul.

Her coat had fallen off one shoulder, revealing the complete upper half of her breasts above her gown. As she leaned forward to enter the cab, Paul glimpsed more of her than was surely intended and he felt a tingling surge zap his body.

Once in the cab, Rachel discretely looked back at Paul through the rear window. He was still standing there, blue eyes staring in her direction, seeming to wait for something more from her. So she gave him a Mona Lisa smile as the cab sped away.

She sat back continuing to smile and then noticed they were in an Austin FX3 Taxi, which she'd learned to recognize because Ethan was big on the history of everything and always passed that information along to her, whether she wanted it or not, a pastime while he was driving. She found it amazing that to change a tire on this cab, you didn't have to place a jack under it, because it had a built-in hydraulic jacking system that allowed the front and rear axles to be raised simultaneously or individually. Equally amazing, the car could turn around between curbs that were only 25 feet apart. It seemed incredible because the cabs seemed so large.

She gazed out the window, watching the rain begin to fall. She liked the rain and wondered why Ethan had been a bit sarcastic when she remarked that they could walk to Trafalgar Square past the cordoned areas. He'd inferred she wouldn't want to walk in the rain. *Where did he get that? I love to walk in the rain. Oh well, it isn't worth the thought. As usual he doesn't know me, and probably never will.*

So, she began thinking about the fantastic looking man that had been staring at her outside the hotel. *I wonder why isn't he with a woman on New Year's Eve. Could be gay. Or maybe a tour guide, since he's with a group of Japanese tourists. What a way to spend New Year's Eve! Maybe he's going to meet up with his sweetheart before Midnight. Only 45 minutes left*, she noted as she looked at her wrist watch.

"Are we getting close, Ethan?"

"No, this traffic's horrendous. It'll be another quarter hour and then we'll have to walk quite a distance," he said, as he leaned forward toward the driver. "Turn here, please, it should be faster."

"And please, hurry. We've got to get there before Midnight," Rachel added. "We just have to."

"I can't believe after paying for a New Year's party at the Ritz, you want to go somewhere else. We could've driven directly to Trafalgar without making the bloody reservations and then spent the night with my sister."

Rachel shot him a harsh look, "Yes, we could've driven straight to Trafalgar or taken the train, but no, not spend the night with your sister. And yes, we could've found a less expensive place to stay, if you would've asked me in the first place, if that's what's bugging you."

"It isn't the money, Rachel. It's your bossy attitude and having to have it your bloody way all the time."

"This isn't a tug of war, Ethan," she snapped back as she looked him directly in the eyes, "I appreciate the Ritz, I really do. It's beautiful. Thank you. And I loved the music at dinner, but the atmosphere wasn't friendly, and you know I'm not crazy about that food. You know that. So, we did that for you, now we're doing this for me. Do you understand what I'm saying, Ethan?"

"All right, all right," he said as he looked out the window.

"And ever since I was a little girl, I've watched New Year's Eve celebrations from around the world on TV with my father. And being this close to Trafalgar Square, one of the biggies, it would be a crime if we didn't go. It's exciting to me. I plan to celebrate New Year's Eve in all the major cities of the world."

Ethan's eyes widened, as he chuckled, "All of them?"

"Yes, all of them. What's wrong with that?"

"Nothing at all, if that's what you want to do." He continued to chuckle.

"Well, it doesn't hurt to have goals and dreams, does it? Besides, it gives me something to look forward to. Thank you very much!" She turned angrily, watching the passing shops through her window.

The calm cab driver darted in and around vehicles with the smoothness and expertise of a man who enjoyed his craft. He muttered an occasional remark under his breath, Rachel noticed, but still he wasn't as deliberate and demonstrative as the cab drivers in Paris.

She'd spent some time alone in Paris a few weeks before, visiting the museums, the riverboats, and the sidewalk cafes. While she was there she had hoped to extract some creative energy from the city, making notes for a synopsis that she sent to her agent in Los Angeles before coming to London. Her first film script had been optioned and Anita had said the second would most likely be optioned too. But nothing of Rachel's had actually been produced. She felt good about it though, at least the projects were being optioned and she had a wonderful agent. She'd never given up her dream of writing for a living, just like she wasn't going to give up her goal of being at the Trafalgar fountains on New Year's Eve at the stroke of midnight. *Next year I'll spend New Year's Eve in Paris! Yes, the Eiffel Tower on New Year's Eve.*

"I can't wait to start writing my novel, Ethan."

"A romance novel, is it?"

"No, a *romantic* novel," and she once again explained to

Ethan, as she had several times over the past few weeks the difference between the two. She told him that a *romance* novel is a simple story - single man meets single woman, love at first sight, conflict between them, man gets woman, they marry and live happily ever after. On the other hand, a *romantic* novel includes death and sometimes murder, extramarital affairs, divorce, rape, abortion, much more than in the "goody two-shoes," boy–meets–girl boy–gets–girl romance novel. And it doesn't necessarily end "happily ever after."

"I think my first one will be a romantic mystery," she said. She didn't know what the mystery would be, but at least that was her plan. She knew from experience in writing screenplays that most plots write themselves, so it could very well end up being something entirely different from what she'd planned anyway. She was even thinking of a second novel, using the same heroine in Highlands, North Carolina.

Pat Conroy, her favorite American author, had written one of his novels in Highlands. He'd stayed in the small lake-ridden, lush green mountaintop town for several months while writing it, even though he lived in nearby Atlanta.

When Rachel first went to Highlands to visit one of her college roommates, she fell in love with the small, upscale, resort town. Her mate, Lana, was happily married to Monte Miller and they lived in a remote log cabin in the land of the Smokey and Blue Ridge Mountains. Both Lana and Monte were talented artists and reminded her of the "artisans" of the '60s. Bohemian love children they were - bearded Monte with his long dark pony tail, and tall, thin, Lana with her massive curly, blond locks. *They'll play a major part in my next novel. And there's so much Indian lore in that area, I'll work that into the story as well.*

"Here we are," the cab driver said as he pulled to the curb. "Can't get any closer than this."

Ethan turned to Rachel and exclaimed, "You're mad! We're a half mile from the fountain and it's starting to rain again."

"We're not quitting now, Ethan. C'mon, let's hurry!" She opened the door and got out of the cab.

Ethan followed, reached into his pocket, and handed the

fare through the window to the driver. Rachel was already on the sidewalk, champing at the bit, umbrella raised over her head.

"Which way?" she pleaded.

"All right, all right," he replied with an impatient frown and pointed. "Come on."

Off they went up the sidewalk, Rachel almost running to keep up with Ethan's fast strides. Although he was heavy and average height, his legs were long and he moved quicker than the normal man of his stature. So when he walked, Rachel jogged. She was always lagging behind, always trying to keep up. But this time, she wasn't complaining. There were droves of people, all going in the same direction, all with the same intent.

"Twenty minutes to midnight," Rachel called out as she glanced at her watch during the breathless run. Finally, as they rounded a corner, she saw the 17-foot Lord Nelson statue perched atop a column looming 170 feet in the air over the heads of the masses congregating in the famous square.

"We made it! We made it! See, I told you we would," she called out to Ethan who was several yards ahead of her.

He paused and waited, "It's impossible! There're hundreds of people here. You won't be able to see anything."

"You just stick with me, Ethan Philips. C'mon," she said with determination as she grabbed his hand and pulled him towards the crowd of people forming a human wall, a hundred deep around the circumference of the monument. More people were rapidly arriving, crowding behind them. The noise level was astronomical - lots of shouting, laughter, music somewhere in the distance. People didn't care about the misty rain and luckily, they didn't bother to use their umbrellas. In those close quarters, a poke in the eye with an umbrella could be disastrous. So, Rachel quickly shut her umbrella and began working her way through the crowds, ever so gently and apologetically, towards the front lines, pulling Ethan behind her.

Daddy, I'm here! I'm at Trafalgar Square in London on New Year's Eve!

11

Around and above Trafalgar Square, television crews and cameras were positioned strategically. One camera was high atop a perimeter building, while roving reporters and other cameramen were standing at the edge of the crowds, interviewing the arriving celebrants. During the minutes leading up to midnight, the media networks would pan the major cities around the world, showing the multi-geographical celebrations to the viewers glued to their television sets. Rachel had programmed the VCR to record it all, in anticipation of possibly seeing herself at the fountains surrounding the base of Lord Nelson's statue. She'd telephoned her son, her agent, her mother and stepmother back in the U.S., telling them to watch ABC's broadcast, which would be an eight-hour difference, and possibly they'd catch a glimpse of her near the fountains. So, here she was, at Trafalgar Square, still pushing through the crowds at eight minutes till midnight.

"Excuse me," she said as she continued to politely work her way through. "Oh, I'm sorry, Happy New Year! We're almost there, Ethan," she said as she gripped his hand tighter, pulling him along behind her. She knew if she let go, he'd be lost in the crowd and it would probably take forever to find him again. It did cross her mind to let go, but she resisted the temptation. Just a few more steps and they'd be at the front. Wrong! She couldn't go any farther. She had to be content with second row back. The front line was shoulder to shoulder and she knew no one was going to step aside and let her take their place. They'd probably waited there for hours to be where they were. Besides, this was a darn good position. She could look over the short Asian gentlemen who were in front of her and still see the police-guarded fountain. There were policeman spaced every six feet to keep the people out of the water where the riot had occurred the previous year.

The multitude was made up of people of all color and race, size and age, with the exception of children. No children. Everyone was in a celebratory mood. They had either left a party to spend a few exciting midnight moments at the fountains or had just left dinner parties to join in the joviality, or maybe had come directly from their hotels and homes to cheer in the new year as Lord Nelson loomed high above them.

At the base of the Lord Nelson monument sat four gigantic bronze lions. The Lion sculptures by Edwin Landseer, the famous animal painter, were objected to when they were placed at Lord Nelson's feet, because they were an afterthought and it was felt that it wasn't befitting. The monument itself was built in 1839-42. The Lions were added in 1868 and Rachel remembered the criticism she'd read about them earlier in the day.

"The Trafalgar Square lions must be quietly damned, because, pretending to be done from nature, they absolutely miss the true sculptural quality which distinguishes the leonine pose, and because a lion crouched like that has not a concave back like a greyhound, but a convex back, greatly ennobled in line from the line of a cat's back in the same position."

But, to Rachel they were beautiful. This was exactly how she thought it would be. Her heart pounded, and the adrenaline rushed. *This is for you, Daddy.*

Ethan was stuck two rows behind her and found it

impossible to move in any direction. He talked to the women surrounding him and seemed to enjoy it.

Every few seconds, a wave of entering people on the outer edge of the gathering reverberated through to the front lines in a manner that almost toppled the first few rows of people who were holding on for dear life. Rachel planted her feet a foot apart and slightly bent her knees in order to sustain her balance against the increasing pressure of the crowd behind her. All of a sudden, one very strong wave lifted and shifted her to the right and forward, smashing her into a tall man in the front line. Their bodies adhered, her front to his back.

She quickly apologized, "Sorry, it's the crowd pushing me." However, although embarrassed, she enjoyed being pressed against this hunk of a man. Much to her surprise, she actually found it quite enjoyable. Their eyes met as he looked over his shoulder down at her. It was the man she'd seen at the limo when they left the hotel. Her face reddened.

He reflected the same surprise as Rachel and his smile broadened as he responded, "Oh, hello. You're the one from the Ritz?"

"Yes, and you're the tour guide, right?" she said as she glanced towards the Japanese men, all in a row, to the right of him. Neither Paul nor Rachel could shift their positions. And if he managed to turn around and face her, they'd be in an even more compromising position. She wondered how it would feel, their fronts pressed together. He was so perfect. At least his backside was perfect. *He's got to be gay. He's too pretty.*

One of the Japanese men turned to Paul and said, "Tomorrow, at nine?"

"Yes. We'll have breakfast and then I'll take you on a pub crawl in Soho and Piccadilly and maybe catch a movie. More local color," Paul replied.

The crowd began the countdown to midnight.

TEN . . . NINE . . . EIGHT . . . SEVEN . . .

Rachel glanced back at Ethan, who was in an animated conversation with a young woman who seemed to enjoy the bodily contact between them. Rachel felt relief. She didn't want to give Ethan the traditional kiss at the romantic moment of midnight anyway. She was so very happy just being here and absorbing all the excitement in the air and feeling the mood of all the people around her. This was absolutely breathtaking. The crowds were pushing forward again and she held her ground against the pressure.

FOUR . . . THREE . . . TWO . . . ONE . . . HAPPY NEW YEAR!

Paul turned his torso, raised an eyebrow, and looked down inquisitively at Rachel. She smiled up at him and nodded.

He slipped his hand behind her and held it firmly to her lower back. She felt her own heartbeat pounding against him and felt every inch of his body as she rose to her toes, tilting her face up to his. Their lips lightly touched. He drew back for a moment, recognized another *yes* in her expression, and then gently returned to the soft, then explosive kiss.

She didn't want it to end. It was just like the descriptions in the romance novels and in the movies. She heard bells and saw stars. She felt faint. *This is crazy, a perfect stranger making me feel this way. I'll never see him again. He's too beautiful, too young, and I'm engaged. What a waste! On all counts!*

Paul loosened his hold. He inhaled deeply and whispered into her ear, "You take my breath away."

Rachel turned to see if Ethan had seen them. No, he was busy kissing the women all around him.

Before she could say anything more to this tall, blond, blue-eyed stranger who'd captivated her mind and body, a huge surge of moving people forced them apart. She could still see him above the heads of the people pushing between them and she could see he was motioning her to go to the North side of the square.

Ethan had managed to push through and reached towards Rachel. "Take my hand, Rachel," Ethan bellowed. "This way, it's the quickest and safest."

She glanced quickly towards Paul as he was swept further away, out of sight. She sighed deeply, took Ethan's hand, and they exited south, through the maniacal throngs.

Belinda peered over a giant bronze lion at the scattering

celebrants scampering across the square. She'd made the last minute decision to come down to the square, even though she hadn't planned on doing so. She'd done it every year she'd been in London and as usual, she felt drawn to the square once again. It was an intriguing place, regardless of the countless others who generally annoyed her. Normally, she would go to Trafalgar Square for a few hours on the weekend and would sit on one of the lions while daydreaming or reading. She felt inspiration in the square until someone would inevitably appear and disturb her thoughts.

She called out and waved to Paul as he passed near her, but he didn't notice or hear her above the noise of the crowd. Obviously he was busy ushering his wards to the next point of interest, wherever that was. She had seen him kiss that woman and enviously wondered who she was. They weren't together. The woman went off in another direction. *A kiss with a total stranger! How romantic!*

12

As they made their way towards a main boulevard to hail a cab, passing through what seemed like an alley to Rachel, she called out to Ethan who was ten steps ahead of her, "I'm hungry, Ethan, let's get something to eat before we go back to the hotel."

He stopped, turned, and glared at her, disbelieving, "Bloody hell! After the meal at the Ritz, you want another one?"

"But, I didn't eat any of it. Remember? Can't we just stop and have something light? Chinese food, maybe? You like Chinese food. And since when does one meal satisfy you for the entire night?"

He laughed and took her arm as they proceeded farther up the narrow alley-like street. They both laughed and chatted about Trafalgar Square, Rachel's unrelenting persistence in getting there, and the outrageous number of people that had surrounded them as they waited for the countdown. Ethan told Rachel about the women who had come on to him and how he'd obliged them with New Year's Eve kisses, but how he would have rather kissed her at the stroke of midnight. However, he seemed delighted and cheerful at the fresh memory of the strangers' kisses.

Rachel complimented him on being such a charming and willing participant in making the other women happy, but neglected to mention the thrilling kiss she'd experienced. All of a sudden they came to a busier, wider street, and rounded the corner.

"Here we are. The restaurant is up this street. It's Mandarin. Is that alright?" Ethan opened his umbrella, put his arm around her shoulder and drew her near him.

"Yes, of course. I love Mandarin," she replied while trying to stay under the umbrella as they hurried over the cobblestones in the rain.

This part of London was one of Rachel's favorites. She loved Piccadilly and Soho and both areas were within walking distance from Trafalgar. Of course, a good pair of walking shoes was in order, not the new, black lizard spikes she wore. But at this moment she was utterly floating and didn't feel the blisters that were beginning to form on the backs of her heels.

The sidewalks and streets were packed with people and it was impossible for vehicular traffic to move. The revelers were in wild gay moods, singing, laughing, and filling each pub and café to the brim then spilled over into the streets. Tonight, people were celebrating everywhere, even hanging out of the windows above the shops that lined the narrow streets. Rachel was caught up in all the merriment, inebriated by it, though the earlier effects of the champagne she'd consumed at the Ritz had worn off.

A drunken passerby stopped and asked her if she would run away with him. She laughed, patted him on the arm saying, "Not tonight, honey, maybe some other time." He went on with his partying buddies who pulled him into a music-emanating avant-garde club full of strange looking characters with rainbow-colored hair and layers of leather and steel. Intimidating guards with shaved heads, dressed in black, were frisking everyone who entered the doors of all the clubs.

"Jeez! This is eerie." she exclaimed.

"You want to go in one of the clubs?"

"Gawd, no!" She replied as they hurried on. "The ones in Newcastle were enough for me. Thank you very much. I'll take a good ol'-fashioned pub or piano bar any ol' day." She remembered their experience in the Northern city of Newcastle, checking out the wild nightlife. It had made her feel very old and out of touch with the new generation. It wasn't something she cared to repeat this very special night in London.

They continued to hurry past dozens of clubs and pubs filled with a bottomless pit of strangers that seemed to appear from nowhere. In spite of the throngs of bizarre personalities and the obvious gap in generations, Rachel found it exciting to be part of the ever-growing crowd on the street. She drew creative energy from the city and liked to come here as often as she could, sometimes the more raunchy the surroundings, the better. It was a mega dose of multiple vitamins to her, a healthy shot in the arm.

Back in California, she had loved L.A. and lived in an apartment near her father in Brentwood. Now, of course, his home was hers. But she had also spent some time with her stepmother, Lee, in Cambria and with her mother, Lily, high in the Montana mountains after Neal had died. She'd also spent a few months in Highlands, North Carolina, before coming to England. It just so happened that all three areas were similar ... were surrounded by bodies of water and forests ... the type of environment that made her feel good.

Rachel thought of Cambria where the tree-covered coastal mountain range met the sea on the central coast of California. Cambria was on the portion of the famous scenic Highway One that stretched from Morro Bay to Carmel. San Simeon, Hearst Castle, Big Sur, Monterrey Cypress, towering cliffs that dropped sharply to the ocean, art galleries, hidden trails, restaurants and self-awareness clinics, majestic homes that blend into the terrain, waterfalls, streams, communes, monasteries, humble huts of struggling craftsmen, a truly eclectic group of ranchers, artisans, writers and professionals - all on a four-hour stretch of highway hugging the coast along the Pacific Ocean shoreline. Although it was one of the most charming, peaceful places in the U.S., Rachel still regularly gravitated towards and needed the hubbub of a city.

She loved the crowded streets of a city, the congested freeways, the overcrowded malls and shops, the thousands of restaurants with every kind of food known to man, the multiplex cinemas, performing arts centers, the jazz clubs, the dives, strip joints, mass transit, the crowded beaches, the street people and street musicians – all of it. She loved it all. It gave her energy of a different sort. It made her feel alive. She always seemed to write with renewed verve and spirit after spending time in a city. And now, London was giving her a tremendous surge of energy. She needed both worlds. She was part her father, her mother, and her stepmother. She was all three and then some.

"How much farther is this place?" she cried in an agitated tone as Ethan pulled her along behind him. "I've got to stop for a minute, my feet are hurting." She leaned against a building.

He stopped and held the umbrella over her head as she held on to his shoulder and removed one shoe and then the other. The skin had been rubbed off her heels, and the raw flesh was oozing through her silk stockings.

"It's just a little farther," he replied. "It's the one up there with the red awning."

She took a deep breath and put her shoes back on. They slowly made their way to the restaurant, as she limped and held onto Ethan for support. Up until now the madness of the night had given her such a high, she had felt no pain. But reality was setting in and her pain sensors were now sending out the message in full from her blistered heels to her brain.

Ethan immediately spoke with the host after they entered. Rachel didn't see any empty seats and she was certain the place was holding more tables and more people than legally allowed. She immediately excused herself and disappeared to find the ladies room. She sat on the marble countertop and soaked her feet in a basin of cool water. Not caring that the stockings were still covering her feet, not caring what anyone would think if they came in. She only cared about soothing the bleeding abrasions.

There were couples still waiting outside when she returned to the dining room. Patrons who had been there before she and

Ethan had arrived. But, as usual, Ethan somehow had managed to ingratiate himself to the restaurant host and was sitting at a table nearby. Although Rachel felt he lacked panache, her fiancé always did have a commanding presence and people of all ranks had always seemed to gravitate towards him and willingly give him what he wanted.

She picked up the menu after she seated herself and asked, "So, what are you going to order?"

"Would you like to share the number four?" he said as he smiled at her. "Are you all right?"

"No, I'm not. I don't know how I'm going to walk out of here. My heels are raw and bleeding."

"Shall I get something to put on them? I'll get some bandages for you." He scooted his chair back and stood up.

"No, no. That's okay. Sit down, Ethan. Order first and then while we're waiting maybe you can find something. Okay?"

He sat down and stretched his hand across the table to hers. "I just want you to be happy."

The waiter arrived and took their orders – two number fours and a bottle of champagne. Then Ethan excused himself from the table to inquire at the host's desk if there were any bandages in the house. Luckily, they had a package of a Band-Aid equivalent. Mission accomplished. When the host brought them to Rachel, she hastily went to the ladies room and removed her panty hose, and then applied the bandages along with the antiseptic that he had handed her. The meal was on the table by the time she returned.

She sat down and looked lovingly at Ethan, "Thank you, Ethan, I feel much better now."

He nodded, not saying anything because his mouth was full of food. She dove into the meal herself, suddenly feeling famished beyond belief. She hadn't eaten anything since the toast she'd eaten in the car that morning and she loved Chinese food, the perfect meal. Italian and Chinese foods were unquestionably her favorites, other than simple American food.

"This has been the perfect night, Ethan," she said as she placed her napkin on her plate and leaned back sipping the champagne. "It really has been. Thank you."

Sometimes, she loved him. Especially times like this, when he was gentle and seemed concerned about her, when he'd go along with her no matter how much he'd rather be doing something else. Sometimes, he could be so easy-going. She wondered if maybe he was right when he said she had to have everything her way to be happy. Maybe that's why she was happiest alone when there was no one else to consider.

Ethan raised his glass to her and then guzzled the remainder of the champagne. He motioned for the bill from the waiter.

They left the restaurant, a little weary from the evening's festivities and noticeably wound down in comparison to how they'd been an hour before. The streets were still full of celebrants. How they kept up the pace was a mystery.

Although the Band-Aids had helped somewhat, Rachel still couldn't walk without pain. So she stood under the crimson canopy while Ethan moved down the sidewalk searching for a cab.

Rachel leaned against the building, suddenly feeling even more exhausted and sleepy. It'd been a long day and after the extreme highs, she was hitting bottom now. All her energy was oozing out through the wounds on her feet. There wasn't a bit of energy left. She wasn't even sure she could walk from where she was standing to a cab even if Ethan found one. She looked up the sidewalk where he was hailing cab after cab in vain. They were either off duty or busy. The thought occurred to her, *what if we're stuck here all night?*

At last, Ethan motioned to her to hurry. He was holding open the door to a private car. In London, on especially busy holiday nights or extraordinary events which fill the town with tourists, private citizens could apply for a permit and were allowed to use their own cars to transport people. This was one of those nights.

13

The driver of the hired Jaguar sedan rounded the corner and they headed down Piccadilly Boulevard. Rachel leaned her head against the headliner of the car near the window and closed her eyes. Even at three in the morning, traffic was as congested as it was before midnight. Rachel opened her eyes and looked into the shop windows on the left side of the street. Then she glanced up ahead and saw a sidewalk café filled with patrons. She wondered how long the people would party - all night probably.

The Jag moved slowly as it neared the sidewalk café. She saw him immediately. *This is crazy.* What were the chances of running into the same stranger three times in one night in a large city? *I can't believe it!* But there he was, lifting a champagne glass to clink with another held by a beautiful, young woman. *At least he's straight.* The traffic halted right in front of the café.

Paul sipped champagne and looked over the glass towards the street when he saw Rachel peering out of the window of the Jag. His reflex was instantaneous, but by the time he reached the street, all he could do was watch her disappear among all the other automobiles jamming down the boulevard. She was looking through the rear window as she had earlier, this time giving him a slight wave and a sad smile.

"We've a bottle of champagne in the cooler in the room. As a matter of fact, I think there are two of them. How do you feel about toasting the coming year before we go to bed?" Ethan asked, as he wondered what she was watching out the back window.

"That would be nice. I'd like that," she replied a little too quickly, turning to avoid eye contact. "But, I'd like to take an oil bath first, if you don't mind. You know, get comfortable. I feel so muggy after this evening."

"Yes, yes, of course." His hopes were instantly ignited at the thought of her taking a bath. He wondered what she'd brought along to wear to bed. Several times, in her absence, he'd looked through her wardrobe in the country house they shared and had carefully opened her bureau drawers, lifting the silk and satin lingerie, feeling the richness and softness of each article. He'd imagined her wearing them under all the layers of black clothing she usually wore. Could it be that on this momentous occasion, the celebration of the Millennium, he would have something even more momentous to celebrate?

As Rachel stared out the windshield and recognized the Ritz up ahead. She breathed in deeply and thought about the ensuing hours. Would she be able to make love to Ethan? She knew what his expectations were, and his need, and she knew she'd stalled about as long as was humane. *It has to be hard on him. But I shouldn't have to make love if I don't want to, and so what if I do take it beyond the limits. It's my body.* She knew that he knew what he was doing, talking about offering her champagne. But, on the other hand, maybe if she drank enough of it, she'd lose some of her inhibitions. It would be easier to relax and possibly get past her fear and could do this "kindness" for him as her stepmother Lee had suggested.

Alcohol used to work when she was younger and when she didn't give a damn. Of course, she didn't give a damn because she partied most of the time. *Maybe if I concentrate on his good qualities, I would appreciate him more, and then I can reward him. What am I thinking? He's not a puppy to be rewarded when he behaves well. And I'm damn sure not a dog biscuit!* Maybe her problem was compounded by the inheritance of Lee's attitude towards sex. In fact, she didn't recall ever seeing anything of a sexual nature between Lee and her father as she grew up. *You'd think they would've at least touched, hugged, or kissed each other in front of me, or I would have heard something going on in their bedroom, or seen one of them naked. But, no, nothing.*

They had managed to smother her with affection, however, but not with touching. It was more like over protective suffocation. She felt she was never allowed to express a thought of her own. She remembered her father saying over and over that he knew what she was thinking and that it was wrong. Didn't matter what it was. He'd continually tell her what she was thinking, which was always a far-cry from her thoughts. He'd make it a point to drill his own interpretive thoughts into her mind, telling her what was appropriate to think and what was not. He never once was curious as to what was going on in her mind, which might explain her rebuff of male authority. Although she could accept authority in the workplace, she didn't handle it well in her personal life from the men she knew. *Maybe that's why it was so difficult for me with my ex-husbands and now with Ethan. Maybe my resentment of being controlled by Daddy is manifesting itself. Maybe it isn't the fear of sex itself. Hell, I don't know.*

But she did know that as one gets older, the early pain and resentment surfaces in unexpected ways. She'd seen how the elderly, those who were out of their minds in institutions waiting to die, would unconsciously act out the hurt and pain they had endured in childhood. They would, unknowingly, dump it doubly on their caregivers in cruel ways; spewing vile and atrocious words, hitting and lashing out at all those around them. She wondered if she would be that way when she was old. *God, I hope not! I don't want to suppress anything that would surface in my old age and embarrass me. I think I have an authority issue to work on, and a sexual one. A double whammy!* But it wasn't only sex Ethan was craving. She knew that. He just wanted to be loved, to be held and touched. *I don't know if I can give him what he wants.*

She wondered if maybe Ethan's mother hadn't given him enough attention when he was growing up. His father hadn't. Although his grandmother was the family matriarch, she was very overbearing, but had loved Ethan. She just hadn't been a touchy-feely kind of person. Rachel doubted that Ethan had received much physical love. *Funny how most men are so close and protective of their mothers, no matter how they're treated. Ethan most certainly is. Maybe the reason men are sometimes overly obsessed with breasts is because it represents closeness, their mothers feeding them, the suckling. Nice, warm, fuzzy feelings. Maybe that's what Ethan misses. And maybe that's why he craves food and physical touching so much. The way to a man's heart is through food and sex, stemming from the babe and mother relationship most likely. But, the more they get, the more they want. So what is that all about?*

She recalled her past marriages. *I'm definitely not needy. Maybe it's because I wasn't breast-fed. But maybe it isn't the same with a daughter and mother. Then again, why wouldn't I be the one most likely to be needy, since I don't recall a whole lot of physical contact during my childhood either?*

Although Lee and Neal had smothered her all through her growing up years, she just couldn't remember being hugged and kissed. She remembered mostly being mentally and emotionally manipulated by her father, then by his third wife, Mary. Sometimes it's the sub-conscious memory of not being caressed and cuddled that makes an adult crave it, but then that wouldn't explain Rachel. She didn't want to be cuddled. *Let's cuddle. I hate that expression. What it really means is - let's fuck! Oh! How I hate that word too!*

Her apprehension continued to build as she stepped out of the cab at the Ritz.

14

When they arrived back in the suite, Ethan pulled out a bottle of champagne from the mini-bar and placed it in an ice bucket filled with ice that had just been delivered along with two crystal flutes by a Ritz valet. He could hear Rachel singing in the bath and heaved a sigh that at least she sounded happy. *Yes, yes, maybe it's going to work out after all. Everything must be perfect.*

He rested a long-stemmed pink rose across the tops of the two champagne glasses on the cocktail table. Then he reached into his pocket and withdrew a small silver rectangular box that was tied with pink ribbon. He placed it in front of Rachel's glass. He'd been carrying the shiny little box with him all evening, waiting for the right moment, but she'd seemed so unreceptive most of the night. He envisioned the scene. *She'll come out of the dressing room in a black negligee, I've never seen her lounge in anything except black satin pajamas and velvet robes. I'll hand her the rose and while she inhales its perfume, I'll pour the champagne. I'll toast her stunning beauty.*

71

Then, after sipping the bubbly, I'll give her the gift. I can see her ecstatic face now. She'll throw herself in my arms and we'll make love all night.

"Ethan, could you please pour me a glass of champagne and hand it through the door. I'd like some while I'm in the bath," she called out through the bedroom interrupting his fantasy. He stood silent, glancing at the well-laid cocktail table before him. His face fell for a moment before thoughts of a wet, naked Rachel replaced his other daydream.

"Ethan?"

"Yes, yes, yes. I'm coming," he said as he quickly popped the cork and poured a glass. "I'm coming." He carried it carefully so as not to spill as he hurried towards the dressing room door and handed it to her. "Here it is." She held a towel in front of her, not realizing her backside was reflected in the mirrored walls behind her. She was holding the door open, just enough to reach for the champagne flute. Ethan rose on his toes slightly, straining to catch a better glimpse of a rearview of her lovely body over her shoulder as he handed the glass to her.

"I could join you, you know. It's a Jacuzzi, big enough for both of us."

"Uh, well, no. I'd just like to relax a little by myself, if you don't mind. And you know how I am, Ethan. I couldn't do that, I just couldn't," she said as she began closing the door. "But, thank you for the champagne, and I'll be out in a minute, okay?"

He silently stood facing the closed door for a moment, then sighed heavily as he returned to the salon and went straight for the chocolates on the buffet. He sat on the sofa, poured himself champagne, and gobbled up three of the chocolate truffles.

Rachel lay back in the marble tub, surrounded by billowing suds and perfumed, steamy water, and sipped her champagne. *How can I possibly have sex with him? But I must. I know I must. It isn't fair to him. I know that. But, how can I? I haven't been able to get close to a man in over two years, except for the handsome hunk in the square tonight. But then, that doesn't count.*

No one had a clue what had happened to her in L.A. It wasn't easy to put it out of her mind, either. She had nightmares

72

of the congressman coming at her with that horrible look on his face, drooling and slobbering, licking his lips. *Ohhhh! I have to stop thinking about it. Maybe if I drink enough champagne, I can get past it and feel lovey-dovey like I used to be able to do, which was why I drank then, and don't now.* She had been quite the sexual adventuress before the congressman got hold of her, but not since. Her promiscuous days had come to a sudden halt.

Damn! I've got to make love to him tonight, it's the least I can do. She gulped the rest of the champagne and grabbed a towel. *I can do this.*

Ethan poured himself another glass and stepped out onto the balcony, breathing in the early morning air, sipping as he thought of the events that had led up to where he was today. He'd been through some rather horrendous times in the past ten years. He'd divorced his second wife, Nora, or rather she'd divorced him. He felt that she had every right to do so; he hadn't been a good husband, and she had let him know he was inadequate in no uncertain terms – demeaned his sexuality and criticized his business acumen. But he hadn't harbored any resentments or animosity towards her. As a matter of fact, she was still a huge part of his life and business. Probably always would be. He still remembered the good times they had early in their marriage. And their union had given them a daughter whom he adored; he grew to love the stepchild from Nora's previous marriage. But Nora was a hard, domineering woman, the kind which Ethan abhorred.

They divorced after Nora met another man during one of Ethan's business trips to the Orient. And, although he came home and found her in bed with the guy, she blamed Ethan and filed for divorce. He wasn't entirely exempt from blame, for he had his share of women in the Orient, although nothing serious. So he'd been unfaithful, too. And since the divorce, he hadn't a regular lover, hadn't remarried. He hadn't the time, but on occasion he would find the time to have his sexual needs satisfied on a weekend jaunt to Amsterdam.

He wondered if maybe he'd been attracted to Nora because she reminded him of his grandmother - the matriarch of his family - who had as much to do with his upbringing as his mother. His father hadn't been much of an influence and had catered more to his sister Elaine. It was a miracle he wasn't a serial killer since he'd spent his whole life dominated and ruled by women. Instead, he continued to be surrounded by them in the workplace, including his daughters who each had an office next to his.

In Rachel, however, he felt he'd found a refreshing element. She was a more sensitive, creative person. In addition to her business acumen, she was a writer, a painter, and a musician. She was gentler than most women he'd known. She didn't nag or castrate, although tonight, he didn't feel much like a man. But, he didn't know how to handle Rachel. *Should I force her to have sex with me? No, how could I do that? No, no, no. I couldn't and I wouldn't. Whatever will be, will be. Que Sera.* He downed the last of the champagne from his glass. *Maybe it was a mistake asking her to marry me.*

Nora had said it was a mistake. In fact, he and Nora had been talking about getting back together before Rachel arrived six months ago. Their daughters were angry, disappointed and dismayed that Rachel had managed to wangle a marriage proposal from their father, not knowing it was his idea. They didn't trust her and neither did his sister. They all felt she was after his money and told him so on a daily basis. He spoke to them every day, living up to his reputation of having a phone receiver attached to his ear. He wore a headset in his office, so he wouldn't have to continually pick up the phone. He wore one in his car, too. He was always on the go, on the phone, and loving the attention from the women in his life, as negative as it was, even from Rachel.

"Okay, I'm ready for another glass, so do we have some more?" Rachel smiled broadly at Ethan as she came through the doorway. Her voice startled him.

He turned, dashed back inside from the balcony, and then stopped. He stood transfixed. *What is this vision standing before me? Maybe I've had too much champagne. Maybe the combination of the chocolate and bubbly has affected my brain. Am I hallucinating? Who is this woman standing in front of me smiling so lovingly?* He was paralyzed.

"Ethan? Do we have more champagne?"

"Oh, yes, yes." He rushed inside. "I'll open another bottle. You look absolutely ravishing, Rachel."

Rachel twirled around, giving him the full front and back view of her curvaceous body under the extraordinary, strapless, thin, long, black nightgown she had purchased that afternoon in the hotel lingerie shop. She'd seen it when she'd arrived and although she wasn't sure what she'd do with it, she just had to have it. It was one of those rare moments when you know an article of clothing was made for you and if you didn't buy it right then, you might never find one as beautiful. Of course, she hadn't felt that she needed it. She hadn't any sexual desires or flings in such a long time, but she was compelled to buy it. Now she was glad she had. Maybe, just maybe, she could go through with it tonight. She certainly felt feminine and sensual.

"You like?"

Ethan laughed, "Do I like? I love! I have dreamed of you like this. I can't believe we're still standing here discussing it." He stepped towards her, removing his glasses.

"No, no, no. Not yet. More champagne, please. Oh, what is this?" She reached for the small silver box on the cocktail table and picked up the rose with her other hand, smelling it as she sat on the brocade sofa. "This is beautiful, Ethan. When did you do all this?"

"While you were in the bath. Go on, open the box." He poured her another glass of champagne as she carefully opened the gift.

"Ohhhhh, my God! They're beautiful! Pearls are my favorite, Ethan. Are these real diamonds?" She lifted the earrings from the box. Each earring had a two carat solitaire diamond set in gold. A pearl the size of a marble dangled beneath. She fastened one to her ear lobe. *Very exquisite, very expensive, very smart.* "I can't believe you bought these for me. Why?" She attached the other earring.

"Why not? I owe you a great deal. And of course they're genuine, and so are the pearls. A good way to begin a new year, don't you think so?" He edged nearer to her on the sofa, placing his arm around her, beaming to the brim. She looked up into his

75

eyes, put her arms around his neck, and kissed him gently.

"Thank you, Ethan. I'm so . . . so . . . flabbergasted. I just don't know what to say. Except, maybe Happy New Year, and I hope we have many more."

Then she pulled away and lifted her glass, "Let's make a toast, shall we? "

15

Across the river, Paul carried a tray of bread, cheese, and fruit into his bedroom. He wore a white terrycloth robe with a gold monogrammed "P" on each pocket.

"There we go. A little sustenance to carry us through. Would you like something to drink, Phyllis?" he said politely, as he placed the tray on the bedside table, and reached for the Jack Daniels. He took a swig right from the bottle.

"Not right now, I'm fine," Phyllis said as she lazily fluffed the pillows between her and the white brick wall which served as a head board for Paul's king-size bed. She pulled the satin sheets over her naked lap and leaned back, ready to snack.

"I'm so relieved you were home when I called. I needed you tonight."

"Yes, me too," she reached for the bread and a slice of cheese. "I like what you've done to the condo, Paul. The lighting is amazing and your paintings are just fabulous."

Two gigantic, abstract, acrylic and oil paintings covered two walls of Paul's bedroom. His style was colorful – glazes of blues, purples, and greens with splashes of yellow and hints of red. His technique was unique; translucent colors layered over dozens of small pen and ink rectangles with nude drawings inside the perimeters - mini-paintings within a painting - very tedious and time-consuming works of art. Throughout the immense loft, he'd sectioned off the various living spaces that included a large screening room with all the most recent hi-tech electronic equipment; there was an entertainment center with surround sound; a plush seating arrangement; a spectacular lighting fixture with waterfalls and oil dripping down metal tubing; and a hi-tech kitchen and bath.

The contemporary bedroom was separated from the rest of the loft by ten-foot high wooden framed partitions of slanted, double-sided, three-inch wide mirrors that served as hanging screens. These provided a sense of privacy from the rest of the loft, while still maintaining an open-airy feeling. The two walls making up the perimeter of the expansive corner condo on the top floor of the newly renovated warehouse were of two-foot by two-foot wood-framed glass window panes. The other two walls of the rectangle were white painted brick. In the ceiling above the bedroom and kitchen were electronic controlled skylights made up of narrow strips of glass that rolled back at the touch of a button.

"Well, I'm glad to be in my own place again. I'd love to have my own gallery, but the bloody ad agency takes all my time, and I can't seem to put away enough money to do it."

He went into the bathroom, and returned with a hand mirror and a rectangular ebony box. He sat on the bed and opened the box and removed a plastic bag of rock cocaine. Then he placed a few pieces on the mirror, and reached into the box again, this time to pull out a small box of razor blades.

"Well, for starters, you could save money by cutting out the damn drugs," Phyllis said as she pulled the sheet up under her neck. "You know, Paul, I really don't like being here when you're doing that stuff. You don't realize how awful it is after you've been doing it for hours."

"Join me and then maybe it won't be so *awful* for you."

"Never! I mean, it's just that . . . well, you seem to totally detach from me and get off in your own head . . . not even needing me here. I should take a video of you in that state, so you can see exactly how repulsive you are."

"You're kidding, of course," he said, as he continued to prepare the coke.

"No, I'm not. Where's your video camera? I think you should see yourself."

"It's over there near the VCR. I'll take some footage of you, shall I?"

"Oh no, you won't. I'm not going to have any nude video floating around of me."

"You know me better than that. Don't you? For God's sakes, don't you trust me?"

"Well, yes, I trust you, Paul. But I don't trust any of your other playmates. I've seen the photos you have in the metal box over there, filed alphabetically, by first names."

"Those are research for my paintings."

"Whatever. I just want you to see how you are with all that coke and Jack Daniels in your system. Your nose runs horribly and you don't even know it. Can you imagine how that turns me off, snot running down over your lips and chin, stringing down to your chest and stomach? And you sit there and masturbate for hours, eyes half closed, Vaseline running all over everything . . . it's just horrible, Paul. When you reach that point, you don't even know I'm here."

"Oh? Then why are you here if I'm so horrible?

"I care for you, Paul. I really do. And I worry about you. You're going to kill yourself one of these nights. That stuff will kill you. If you're lucky it'll only damage your health in general. You're crazy for doing it, you really are." She reached for a robe at the foot of the bed and put it on as she headed for the entertainment center to get the digital camera.

Paul watched her slim curvaceous body brushing against the satin robe and noticed the well-toned muscles in her legs and arms. "You're looking absolutely buff, Phyllis, darling. You turn me on just watching you move."

"Then do without the coke and booze tonight, Paul. Try it. See if you enjoy our lovemaking without the stimulants. Okay?

Have some champagne with me, if you have to have something."
She stood with her hand on the camera, waiting for a response
from him.

He moved slowly towards her, eyes connecting with hers,
smiling sexily, showing his perfect teeth, "Now, Phyllis, dearest,
let's not spoil a perfectly good night by being a bit stuffy. I'll
just do a little. I won't do it all night. I have to take some clients
to Soho today, remember? And I'll know you're here, how could
I not? Deal? Phyllis, darling?" He kissed her warmly, running
his hands down her back and kneading her buttocks softly.

She groaned and said "Oh, you do know what I like. That
feels so good."

He picked her up, took her back to the bed and gently laid
her against the pillows, then filled her champagne glass.

"Now take a few sips and feel the effects of the bubbles. I'll
be right with you to give you more of *everything* you like."

16

"You're so lovely, Rachel, let's have a kiss, shall we? Yes?" He moved towards her when she returned from a brief visit to the boudoir. "You are absolutely delicious."

She took a deep breath and sighed. He crushed her to his chest, then surprisingly kissed her very gently. Taken aback by the softness of his kiss, she pulled away slightly and looked into his eyes. "My goodness, Ethan! Where did that come from? That sent a thrill to my toes and back."

He boldly attempted kissing her again, but this time he was a bit over-eager. He wanted her badly and it was difficult keeping himself at bay. He'd never felt this way about anyone and he wished like hell he didn't about Rachel. She was such a cool cube. But nevertheless, he blurted, "May I make love to you tonight, Rachel?"

Again she lightly pulled back, but continued looking into his eyes.

He held her fast, "I want to feel your body next to me, your lovely soft skin against mine. I know you care for me a little, even though you don't like to show it. I see it in your eyes at times, when you're not thinking about it."

She laughed as she relaxed in his arms, "What does that mean, when I'm not thinking about it?" She stood on her toes and kissed his nose. "Explain that to me, please."

He couldn't contain himself any longer. He almost squashed the life from her as he gave her a bear-hug and laughed while he spun her around, lifting her off the floor, and then explained, "When you let down your defenses, when you stop trying to be the person you think you are and become the person you really are."

"Oh, is that so. And since when do you know me so well? Huh? Tell me that." They both laughed and began slow dancing in place to the music that filtered in through the windows from the garden below. They continued slow dancing all the way to the bedroom and out onto the balcony, grinning at each other, both afraid to admit or question their destination.

As they continued to dance and giggle, thoughts frantically flew through Rachel's mind. *Should I stop him now, before it's too late? Or should I go along with it, just let him make love to me? What if he doesn't like my body? He says he likes what he sees, but that's through this gossamer fabric. What if I'm not good enough in bed? What if I can't do what he wants? What will he want? Will he want oral sex? Will he want me on top? I hate that. Makes me feel so vulnerable. I hope he's not kinky. I wonder how many women he's made love to. What about protection?*

All Ethan could think of was his performance. *Can I get it up? Oh God! What if I can't? Why didn't I get some Viagra? Will she laugh at me? Will my penis be big enough? Will she want oral sex? Will she do what I want? What will she want? What if she is a total prude?*

They reached the bed and Rachel closed her eyes as Ethan tenderly began kissing her lips, her neck. He brushed his lips across the rise of her breasts. He moved his hand to one of her breasts and affectionately caressed it as he felt the hardened nipple through the filmy garment she was wearing. Rachel gasped. She lifted Ethan's eager lips back to hers and held them there for what seemed like forever. Their combined heat and passion fused to obliterate all the needless questions and anxiety that had consumed their minds just moments before.

Rachel forgot about Ethan being overweight, about his poor eyesight, about his clumsiness. She forgot about the night of terror that had reigned in her mind for so very long. She forgot about feeling too old and too fat.

Ethan forgot about Rachel's bitchiness, her aloofness, her recent irritability. He forgot all about Viagra and whether or not he would be good enough for her.

All they felt was the extraordinary pleasure that increasingly mounted as Ethan gently touched and explored Rachel's body as she did his.

17

Rachel awoke to the sounds of the street and distant music. Ethan slept with his back towards her on the window side of the beds. There were two king-sized beds, one for him, one for her, butted up against each other, making an exceedingly large sleeping arena. *This is a wonderful idea*, she thought as she sat on the edge of the bed, stretching. *It makes sleeping with someone much easier. No tossing and turning to disturb the other during the night.* In fact, she hadn't tossed and turned at all, first time in years. The bedcovers were almost as they were when she got into bed. *Fancy that.*

They'd made love on Ethan's bed. The cherry wood four-poster with a brocade canopy had obviously been specially made for these combined mattresses. She had been amazed at how huge it was, which she hadn't actually noticed until they were under the canopy. But her attention had been diverted, as she remembered, when Ethan had begun kissing her and had slowly and carefully removed the fragile diaphanous nightgown from her submissive body. It was hard to explain how she had felt.

She couldn't understand it. *How could I have been so tense one minute, and not the next? It couldn't have been the champagne because I didn't feel inebriated. Maybe a little lightheaded and sensual, but not at all soused like I had to be before having sex before.*

She thought about it as she went into the dressing room, splashed water on her face, and drank a glass of water. "I actually enjoyed it," she said aloud as she looked at herself in the mirror. "Ha! Imagine that. I must be healed!" She slapped the heel of her hand against her forehead on the word *healed*, mimicking TV evangelists. She put her hand over her mouth and snickered to herself, surprised at her happy, high-spirited mood.

"Are you all right?" Ethan called from the bed as he rolled over and saw that she was gone.

She responded "Yes! I feel great! I'm having a glass of water. Would you like one?"

"Yes, please," he said.

She'd always been amused at Ethan's two-word automatic response to almost anything that was offered him. It was as if he wasn't listening, just answering a voice inflection. He always replied the same, in the same tone. Would you like a cup of coffee? *Yes*, please. Would you like a blanket? *Yes*, please. Would you like a pint of beer? *Yes*, please. Would you like a new car? *Yes*, please. Would you like to fuck an orangutan? *Yes*, please.

When he said those words with half-closed eyes, he reminded her of a little boy. She could visualize his ruling grandmother, if not his mother, teaching him to say it when he was a tot. *It's endearing.* She carried a glass of water to him.

"Did you sleep well, Rachel?"

"Better than I have in a long time. I didn't even hear you snore."

"I don't think I did. At least, I didn't hear it."

"You wouldn't hear it, silly. I'll make some coffee. Are you getting up?" she said as she headed for the living room.

"I think I'll lie here awhile and relive last night, if you don't mind."

She hesitated for a moment, thinking the appropriate thing

to do would be to jump back into bed with him and both of them relive the two hours they had spent together just a few hours ago. But she noticed it was noon by the clock on the mantle and she shook her head as she kept walking towards the coffee maker on the buffet table.

While she made the coffee she questioned her feelings about Ethan. *There must be some love there. How could I make love to him if there isn't?* Then her past sexual escapades came to mind, when love wasn't an issue. *But why do I continue to come back into his life? This had been going on for several years now. How and why do I have moments when I really feel like I love him, if I don't? What is that all about? Why can't I totally commit to him? He has good qualities. Why am I drawn to him but yet I hesitate? I don't understand it.*

Ethan decided he needed to get out of bed after all if they were to do all he and Rachel had talked about doing on this wonderful first day of the millennium. It didn't seem possible that the year 2000 had arrived. He remembered when he was a little boy and how his thoughts of the year 2000 seemed so very far away, possibly unattainable in his lifetime. He'd considered 2000 A.D. as only part of the science fiction world he loved so much. He loved reading Isaac Azimov and all the other writers that had influenced him to carry his avid interest into his young adult years. He studied bio-chemistry at Oxford because of it and that had led him to the environmental bio-degradable field which he so dearly loved. He thought of Harry Harrison's story "Make Room! Make Room!" quite often. He'd seen the movie version "Soylent Green" starring Charlton Heston many times over the years. It was remarkable he was nearly doing the same thing the author described in his book and what the movie portrayed. The only exception was he converted organic waste to animal feed and fertilizer instead of recycling warm cadavers into food pellets for the human race. He wondered about that process, what it would take and if it were feasible. He knew it wasn't ethical, but then if scientists are about to clone a human being, why *not* figure a way to recycle human beings, since cloning would upset the balance of nature. As it was, it was an act of pollution throwing ashes and bone fragments into the environment or supplying diseased, decaying bodies to the underground water tables. *Hmmmm. Yes, I might give that some thought.*

"What's the matter with me!?" he said aloud, appalled at his own thoughts, going from a memory of an exotic sexual nature to a spine-shivering view into what the recycling future might hold. He shuddered as he turned on the shower and the cold water hit his body.

18

Paul woke up nude and very cold in his overstuffed leather chair near the bed that Phyllis had vacated earlier that morning. A note rested on the pillow next to the video camera. He rubbed his eyes and ran his hands through his hair as he surveyed the situation. The Jack Daniels bottle laid empty on the floor to the side of his chair, a small table with minute particles of cocaine dust still sat in front of the chair facing the bed, scattered with the other paraphernalia. The last thing he remembered was Phyllis putting on the white lacy, satin panties he'd given her. He had asked her to masturbate while wearing them while he watched. Whatever it was that made him so damned excited when his "girls" did this, he wasn't sure. But he loved it. And he'd rather see that than fuck. Although he hardly ever had an orgasm during this sexual play, he held an unbelievable pre-orgasm high for hours, thus the reason for the huge amounts of Vaseline stocked in his cabinets. Then when his body couldn't take any more whisky, coke, and erotica, he'd pass out. This was his sexual ritual. Normally he didn't deviate from it. Although when he'd meet a new conquest, he'd go through the undesirable "normal sex" the first couple sessions, and then when he'd won her, he'd switch his preferred sexual activity and she would usually go along with it, for a while at least. Some would think he was a total pervert and would drop him right away or shortly thereafter, others hung in a bit longer, like Phyllis, thinking they could change him.

He'd wondered at times if his sexual preferences of not wanting to touch, only wanting to look, stemmed from his pre-teen boyhood experience with his nymphet aunt, who continually, but discretely, exposed herself to him. She'd flash him when she'd be sitting in the parlor across from him at family gatherings - sometimes incredibly revealing flashes, always showing glimpses of white panties as she sat with her legs apart, and stared straight at him. At times he was so turned on, he'd have to rush upstairs to the bathroom and jerk off as quickly as he could before anyone was the wiser. She had known what she was doing to him, of course, and even took it a step further once. On that occasion, his aunt coaxed him out into the back garden, into the gazebo. She'd positioned him right in front of a wicker chair in which she sat with one leg lifted up over the arm of the chair. Slowly she slid her hand from her cheek down her body until she reached her panties. Paul had almost fainted from the blood rushing to his head, both of them. She'd slipped her fingers inside the panties, while Paul had watched, and had brought herself to a quiet, subdued climax. When she'd finished, she'd returned to the house, leaving Paul almost collapsed in a state of exasperation.

Soon after that, she had moved to Canada. Then he heard that she'd run off to Africa with a political dissenter and she forever disappeared from Paul's life. He'd never lost the image, however, and he wondered if she had any idea of the possible influence she'd had on his sexual life.

Yes, of course, Aunt Veronica has to be the impetus.

He picked up Phyllis's note. He knew what was coming even before he read it. She told him to watch the video of himself and then go to hell. He crumpled the note and tossed it aside, then quickly reached for his watch and reacted to the time.

"Damn! I'm late!"

Paul rushed into the shower, scrubbed furiously and shampooed his golden locks, thinking how much simpler it would be to have short hair rather than shoulder length. Something he must consider. In fact a simpler life would be perfect all the way around. Something else he must consider. He thought about the note Phyllis had written and thought about how his sexual life had progressed to the point it had. It seemed as if thoughts of sexual pleasures had taken over the majority of his daily life. It interfered with his creativity at work. Maybe he needed to go to an addiction clinic or at least go to a few therapy sessions.

Maybe that will be one of my New Year's resolutions. Maybe cutting down on my coke habit would be a smart move too. Repulsive? God, that sounds awful! Snot? Nah! No way!

Although he knew she was right. The clean-up after every incident was evidence enough.

He stepped out of the shower, quickly shaved and brushed his teeth; blow-dried his hair and opened a huge wardrobe to select something casual to wear to his afternoon of entertaining the Japanese consortium. Light blue cashmere pull-over, tan corduroy pants, and tan suede loafers would do the trick. He donned a tan leather jacket and was out the door in seconds, still feeling the effects of his debilitating habits.

19

"Ethan, what do you think about this? My usual black, with a bit of color around my neck."

Ethan set his china cup on the saucer, surprised that she'd asked his opinion. He gave Rachel an approving look. "Yes, the color is good. But I do wish you would wear more colorful and form–fitting clothing. Why is it you don't do that? You did when I first met you."

"I don't like the way I look in color and tight clothing anymore."

"I don't necessarily mean tight, just more tailored rather than layered. But the green scarf is quite a departure for you. It looks stunning. Would you like a cup of coffee, my dear?"

"*Yes*, please. Oh! I can't believe I said that!"

" Said what?"

"*Yes*, please. The way you say it."

As Ethan poured the coffee, he laughed, "So, you can borrow my phrases, I don't mind." He handed the cup and saucer to Rachel and then walked to the window overlooking Green

Park. "I figure we can have breakfast downstairs and then go to Piccadilly and Soho."

"That sounds nice. And maybe go to a movie?" Rachel carried her coffee back into the dressing room to do some last minute touchups on her hair while she eagerly anticipated a positive reply about the movie. No reply came forth. She quickly arranged a few out of place curls, thinking about the possibility of seeing the handsome stranger again in Soho or Piccadilly. She had overheard his conversation saying that's where he'd be today. She immediately chided herself for even thinking of him after the lovely experience she and Ethan had earlier that morning. She did a last minute inspection and returned to the parlor with her purse over her shoulder, sipping her coffee.

"I'm ready when you are."

"Good, I'll take the morning paper, then. Off we go."

They headed for the lift as Rachel commented again on the paintings that lined the corridor walls and how much Lee would love to see them. She'd been thinking about her stepmother and mother as she dressed, thinking she should plan a visit to America very soon. Lily hadn't sounded well the last time they'd spoken on the phone.

They arrived at the lift and, as usual, Ethan stepped on first, holding the door open from the inside for Rachel.

She smiled and noted, once again, how he did that rather than holding the door open from the outside and letting her step on first. *Oh well, it's trivial, doesn't matter. I need to be less critical of him.*

It was a silent ride to the main floor and a short walk to the coffee shop—not really a coffee shop in the usual sense of the word, more of an elegant, morning tea room of course.

Ethan ate his huge English breakfast - sausages, bacon, eggs, baked tomatoes, mushrooms, beans, toast with marmalade, as he read the newspaper.

Rachel had toast and coffee while she watched the people pass by. She loved people-watching. She thought again of Trafalgar Square and the memorable kiss at midnight. She wondered about the stranger and what his life might be like. *Is he single? Is he really a tour guide? Why did it seem so natural to kiss him? There was an unexplained familiarity there.* She had a dream about him after she'd finally dropped off to sleep earlier that morning.

The dream was of Cornwall though, not Trafalgar Square. She was standing on a hill overlooking Mount's Bay, looking across the bay towards St. Michael's Mount. She recognized the region from when she and Ethan had been there a few years before. Strange that she would have the dream after their lovemaking. Although, she'd had several dreams of Cornwall over the past year.

But in this dream there were several people standing on the hill behind her, for she was further out on the point and away from the rest. Rachel remembered how wonderful she felt in the dream, how free. Love and connection emanated from the small group of people behind her. She turned to look upon their faces. The dreamboat at Trafalgar was among them, but she didn't recognize the others. Ethan stood a distance away from the rest and beckoned her to follow him. She didn't want to go. And then she woke up.

She gave herself a mental shake. *Maybe I'll take a tour when I come back to London by myself.* She'd looked up all the tour companies one previous trip to London. *I wouldn't mind bumping into that handsome stranger again. Whatever or whoever he is, I am not ashamed that I enjoyed the kiss. That's all it was. Just a kiss. I wonder if he's thinking about me. Probably not. Why would he? Strange how life takes a turn. I never thought I'd ever make love to Ethan. Maybe, I'll be able to put those horrible memories behind me now. Damn that creep! I should've reported him. He might be out there hurting other women. Might? He most certainly is, what would change him?*

"Rachel? Rachel!" Ethan reached across the table and touched her arm.

"Oh! I'm sorry, Ethan. I was thinking of something. Sorry. What did you say?"

"Shall we go?"

"Yes, let's go," she said as she folded her napkin and placed it on her plate. She swallowed the remaining coffee. "There, I'm ready."

They left the restaurant and exited to the valet port to hail a cab. In the cab Rachel thought again of her mothers. "Ethan, I think I might want to go home to see my family, do you mind?"

"No, of course not. I'm going to be rather busy, as you know, with all the changes at the plant, and I dare say, it would be good for you."

"Yes, I think so, too. But, actually, I'm torn. I also want to go to Cornwall. I guess I could do that when I come back. But then, I don't know. Maybe I should go there first. What do you think?"

"Either one, although I think it's rather boring in Cornwall. Why would you want to go there?"

"I loved it when we went. Why didn't you like it?"

"Oh, I suppose it was the timing . . . Christmas . . . I missed my family."

"That was my fault. I didn't realize how traditional you are. I've never been one to want to be with family on holidays because I never had much of a family. But now I'm feeling a bit different about it. That was four years ago, wasn't it? On one of my visits? Anyway, I'd like to go check out some things in Cornwall. I'm feeling drawn to the area. And you know how I am about that. That's how I found my mother."

"Then by all means, go. You know my schedule is full in January, so go as soon as we get back. Who knows what you might find this time?" He was amused and captivated by her child-like imagination, curiosity, and sincerity.

"Yes, I think I will. Then after that I'll go to the U.S." She dissolved back into her own thoughts as they traveled up Piccadilly from the Ritz towards Soho.

20

"Stop! Let's get out here! This is it, please stop," Rachel exclaimed loudly and the cabby immediately swerved to the curb.

"You want to walk from here to Leicester Square? The Odeon and the cineplexes are in Leicester, you know. And I thought we might have tea at Brown's afterward."

"Yes, yes, I know. But we can walk. It isn't very far. Look, here it is on the map."

Extracting a small pocket–sized book of maps from her purse, she opened it to a page where she'd drawn red circles in four areas: Trafalgar Square, Leicester Square, Piccadilly Circus, and Soho.

"Take a look," Rachel said as she thrust the pocket maps at Ethan and quickly opened the door. Not waiting for Ethan, she jumped out and stood on the stone walk and breathed in the cold, exciting air in the hub of London. *I am standing in Piccadilly Circus, the famous London landmark, Daddy.*

At night, the massive, spectacular, neon and digital screen

displays served as advertisements for major international corporations, similar to Times Square in New York. By day, still as energized, the square buzzed with swarms of people traipsing in and out of the surrounding souvenir shops, pubs and other eateries.

After paying the cabby, Ethan joined Rachel. He glanced at the book of maps she gave him.

"Did you know Piccadilly takes it name from a 17th century frilly collar called a picadil?" he asked. "In fact, a dressmaker grew very rich making them and built a house right in the vicinity," Ethan proudly divulged and then put the maps in his pocket.

"Oh, really? Like the collar I painted on the fox in my *Snooty Fox* painting?"

"Yes, like the one on the fox." He laughed as he grabbed her arm and headed towards the square, taking his usual long strides. "When are you going to finish that painting?"

"Ethan, you're dragging me again. Slow down. I plan to finish it now that I've sent that damn script and synopsis off to Anita. Maybe I'll take it to Cornwall with me, finish it there. "

They slowed to a normal pace and strolled past shop windows, stopping occasionally to comment on the displays. Rachel broke loose and headed towards a bronze fountain topped by a figure of a winged archer. Ethan quickly followed and pointed out that the archer was the pagan god of love, popularly called Eros.

"Originally, it was designed in the 19th century as a symbol of Christian charity, a monument to the philanthropist, Lord Shaftesbury, who was a crusader. He had spent his life attempting to improve the lives of the poorest and most oppressed people in Britain, especially the children who were sent down into the mines and collieries to work."

Ethan took great interest in the history of his country. In fact, he loved to delve into world history, his favorite subject. Even owned a series of books called *Early Southwestern History of North America – Cowboys and Indians*.

"The fountain is made of bronze, but Eros is made of aluminum, which was a rare metal in the 19th century," he commented.

"Really?" She walked around it, giving it a thorough once over. "Okay, I've seen enough, let's go to Leicester Square," she said as she pulled the mini-book of maps from Ethan's pocket.

He quickly intervened, "I know the way. We'll take that street over there, past the Pavilion; it takes us right where we're going. Come along."

They continued to gaze into windows and view sidewalk café sippers and diners as they both lazily made their way up Coventry Lane to Leicester Square, occasionally stopping to wait for the other.

"There, that's what I want to see, Ethan. *The World Is Not Enough* – the new James Bond movie. Okay with you?" she exclaimed as Leicester Square came into view and the Odeon Cineplex loomed predominately across its expanse.

"You surprise me, but yes, yes, let's check on the start time, shall we?"

He was halfway to the Odeon before she even stepped from the raised-stone walk to the flat surface that stretched across the square to the theatre and the other cineplexes that bordered the pedestrian area.

Rachel followed Ethan slowly, noticing all the tourists hanging around, some shopping, some chatting in tight little groups, others eating vendor food. On one of the plaques in the square, she read that twenty-two million people visit Leicester Square every year. She moved closer to the center of the square to get a better look at the statue of Shakespeare and then the smaller one of Charlie Chaplin.

The square had so many historical implications, as did most squares in London. She knew that Leicester was originally called Leicester Fields, the site of a house by that name, founded by one of the Sydneys - the Earl of Leicester, who in the mid 1600s had been removed from Sydney House which was to become the Old Bailey, England's criminal court.

It was in Leicester Fields that Elizabeth, Queen of Bohemia, daughter of James the First, ended her unfortunate life. Rachel glanced up a side street and visualized the "Winter Queen", the Queen of Bohemia's nickname because her husband

Frederick died after only one season as King. She was also called the "Queen of Hearts" because she was so very popular, just like Princess Diana. Rachel imagined Elizabeth regally strolling towards her, in white furs, through the imaginary cheering throngs on the sidelines in the square. Rachel imagined her as resembling Sonia Henie, for some unknown reason, sans the ice skates of course. She had no clue why Sonia Henie came to mind except that, like Elizabeth, Sonia Henie was dearly loved by her fans. Elizabeth had died right here in Leicester Fields on one of her stays.

Rachel sat down on a nearby bench and let her thoughts continue to sweep her away, deeper into Elizabeth's world.

Elizabeth's father, James the First, was the only son of Mary, Queen of Scots. James was the result of a miserable and tragic marriage. He was taken away from Mary at a very early age and raised in the remote priories of Scotland. Rachel had thoroughly researched and enjoyed reading about the life of Mary, Queen of Scots and of Elizabeth the First, Queen of England. In fact, Elizabeth the First and Rachel shared the same birthday - September Seventh.

Mary had been given a bum rap by Queen Elizabeth, who was convinced her cousin was trying to steal her "crown." *They just got off on the wrong foot and weren't able to get on track. They could have been friends, could have been neighboring queens, if it weren't for the pack of back-stabbers and ill advisors surrounding them both.* All Mary wanted was to be able to practice her beloved Catholicism and to rule Scotland with the love of her life, the Earl of Bothwell. But when she fled from the Protestant murderers in Scotland to seek safe asylum in England under the protection of her cousin Elizabeth, she was in for a surprise. Queen Elizabeth imprisoned her, sequestered her for nearly 20 years, and eventually had her beheaded, never once having met her cousin Mary, never once having heard Mary's own defense and intentions or her own true story. Queen Elizabeth had been told that Mary was going to make a bid for England's throne.

Mary's son, James the First, son of her murdered husband Henry–Lord Darnley, became quite the literary figure in

England, writing both poetry and prose, having learned from great scholars and from his mother's vast library. Not only did he inherit his mother's love for literature, he also acquired his mother's religious sense and convictions. He was responsible for the translation of the Bible.

Rachel remembered that it was James who also introduced the Masque form of entertainment to the British court.

Ethan had told Rachel that Leicester Fields also served as a "pouting place" for George the Second - Prince of Wales, after the notorious quarrels with his father George the First whose statue originally had been in Leicester Square and who had been a miserable man. He'd been more into sexual activities than kingly duties. George the First had imprisoned his wife and took on two huge, German mistresses known to Londoners as the Elephant and the Castle. His son had fled to Leicester Fields a multitude of times to escape his father's sexual escapades and illogical wrath.

Then came Frederick, George the Second's son. Frederick died in Leicester Fields, same as Elizabeth the "Winter Queen", and it's his bogus epitaph that became quite famous:

Here lies Fred,
Who was alive and is dead,
There's no more to be said.

England was exotic to Rachel. She loved the history and all the stories. She loved the landscape, the villages, and the cities. She loved the people, past and present. As she sat transfixed in the imagination of the surroundings as they must have been, she felt absolutely sure that she had lived here before. She felt such a strong kinship to these characters who were so easy for her to imagine. *Maybe I'm crazy, possibly losing my mind. Maybe I've lived once too often in my dreams and imaginations. I've heard of people who have opted to remain in their dream worlds never to emerge into the real world ever again. Could this be happening to me? It's because of my dreams that I feel I have to go to Cornwall. Even though the dreams are mysterious and a bit illusory. I recognize the terrain in them – Marazion,*

Mousehole and Penzance especially. No, I'm not losing my mind. I'm going to Cornwall where I hope to find some clues of having lived there before. Or maybe to find some long lost relative, maybe an ancestor.

Whatever it was, it coerced and consumed her thoughts and she was determined to find out why she was so strongly summoned to the Southwest region of England. An all too familiar sound penetrated her semi-conscious state.

"Rachel! Rachel, here I am. Rachel!" Ethan waved at her from a pub lined alleyway next to the Odeon. She snapped out of her imaginary world, waved and hurried to join him.

𝟚𝟙

Belinda Bluhm laid her romance novel face down on the overstuffed arm of her chair, picked up an empty can of Diet Pepsi, and went into the kitchen where her mother entertained a neighbor.

"Belinda, would you like to go to the Odeon with us to see the new James Bond film?" her mother, Beatrice, asked.

"Yes, come along with us," the neighbor said as she picked up another biscuit from the china plate Beatrice had so generously filled with sweets.

"Oh, I don't know. I'm really into this good book, and I'd like to finish it today. When are you going?" She reached into the fridge for another drink.

Beatrice lifted the teapot from the tray and poured another cup for her guest, "In an hour or so. If you change your mind, please do come with us. We'll have tea somewhere in the square afterward. Alice is treating us, a New Year's gift."

"How very nice of you, Alice, I'll have to think about that." Belinda left the kitchen and returned to her book in the parlor.

She sat for a moment, tried to get back into the novel, then lifted her gaze to the street outside the window. She watched the children from the building next door playing with their new Christmas toys. She wondered if she'd ever have any children of her own. Unless she found a sperm donor rather quickly, it didn't seem very likely.

"There's a thought," she chuckled aloud to herself as she let her thoughts wander even further along that vein. She thought about Paul Newland. *Yes, there's always the stud of Triple R. I wonder if he would be willing to donate a sperm or two, in the conventional way of course, if I decide to go that route. Just a one-shot event, maybe. It doesn't look like I'll ever get married. No sign of a prince charming or even a frog on the horizon. Actually, I'd settle for just a child to care for and raise, one of my very own.*

"Well, that's something to think about," she said aloud as she picked up the book again and went into her room to get dressed. She decided to go to the movie and tea with her mother and Alice, the spinster from next door, after all.

Beatrice loved her daughter, and was so proud of her. Belinda had been the first in their family to go to University. Then when Belinda was hired by Triple R right out of school, Beatrice was even more ecstatic - her only child working for an international advertising firm in London. She'd worked two jobs to help Belinda get through school. One thing Belinda inherited from her mother was her own willingness to do whatever it took to make a living. Nothing was beneath the two of them. So, when Belinda entered the Ruskin School of Drawing and Fine Art at Oxford, Beatrice went to work as a bar maid at The Lord Nelson in Hastings, in addition to running a bed and breakfast near the pier on the seafront. She didn't mind it at all. It was for her daughter's future and Belinda had helped her keep the B & B afloat all those years; cleaning the rooms, attending to the guests, cooking breakfasts. It had been a team effort, so the least she could do was to help finance her daughter's schooling.

Beatrice knew everyone in Hastings. She was born there, which meant more coins than usual being added to her tip jar at The Lord Nelson when familiar patrons would come to have a pint or two. She was a tough ol' broad, as she referred to herself on many occasions, and was sorry to leave the place when Belinda convinced her to sell the B & B and come to London to live with her after she went to work at Triple R. Belinda knew her mother had always wanted to live in London. Eventually, they found a small, quaint, four-story hotel right smack dab in the middle of Bloomsbury, which was similar to the B & B in Hastings. Beatrice wasted no time in buying it. It was heaven to her, living in lovely London town. If only her Teddy could see her now.

Theodore Bluhm had died in a mining accident in Sussex when Belinda was four years old, leaving his wife Beatrice penniless and alone to be the breadwinner. Teddy was a cheerful sort, easy going, but not very ambitious. As long as he could put the food on the table, pay for the electricity and water, make love to his Beatrice, spend time with his adorable little daughter, and pet his dog each evening, he was happy. He needed nothing more, except maybe having a pint or two at The Lord Nelson on occasion. Their house didn't have a mortgage; it was Beatrice's house, left to her by her mother and father.

After Teddy died, Beatrice sold the family house in which she'd been born and purchased a terrace house on the seafront, where she rented out rooms for an income. It later became one of the popular inns that line the seafronts of the towns and villages along England's southern coastline.

Belinda opened her wardrobe, sat back on her bed and stared at the contents hanging in front of her, all bright colors of the rainbow. She didn't wear white and she didn't wear black, only variations of yellow, red, blue, and green, which of course included all the hues in between.

She lay back on her bed for a moment, closed her eyes, and began daydreaming of a life with a daughter or a son or both. She daydreamed of moving to the country, to a cottage surrounded by a beautiful garden, with a lovely vine-covered stone wall bordering the property and artistic metal gates that she would design and construct herself. She loved working with metal and shared a small studio across the river with a fellow graphic designer, not far from the offices of Triple R.

Every week night, she hurried from work to don her visor

and protective clothing and would create to her heart's content for a couple of hours, while most of her cohorts were out partying at happy-hour pubs. Some of her exotic metal sculptures were showing in galleries in Soho and Brighton. Her work was getting more notice than it ever had before. Every week a few more pieces sold. She stashed her art proceeds towards the day when she would purchase her dream cottage.

Belinda was very excited about a new idea that she planned to experiment with after the holidays. She'd sent off to Canada for several of the most beautiful stones she'd ever seen, Ammolite. Ammolite was the fossilized remains of the ammonite shell. In fact, some shells had been found in Kent and were on display there. She'd traveled to see them, but was disappointed that they were still in their original form, not the mineralized version, in which iridescent colors glowed with the beauty of the rainbow. But she did find a few in a rock shop in Mousehole, on the west coast near Penzance when she was on holiday there the summer before.

She picked up the specimen that she had purchased in Mousehole from the bedside table and turned it over between her fingers. Bright blues, greens, reds, yellows. It was so beautiful! Her "rainbow rock", she called it. Rainbows were among her favorite things. So, of course, she loved Ammolite. It was like the most colorful Opal, only brighter. She'd made it into a good–sized pendant on a chain. Pendants were all the rage. In fact, it measured three inches in length by one inch wide. She slipped the chain over her head. *Yes, this just might make the difference in my sculptures*. Her vision was to incorporate these gorgeous gems into her work; working metal around them and into small to medium sized sculptures. Not jewelry. She hadn't decided on a theme or a subject as of yet, but it could be the start of a new career for her.

Belinda learned from the rock hound in Mousehole that Ammolite was first discovered and used by the Blackfoot Indians in North America and Canada, who called it buffalo stone. They would wrap the shell fossil with buffalo hide and use it for good medicine when hunting bison. The story goes that one winter when the Blackfoot were starving, the "spirit of the rock" came to a woman. It seemed the buffalo had disappeared and the deep snow had prevented anyone from searching for them. The young Indian women were the gatherers of firewood for the evening's cooking. One young woman had been out looking for firewood and she heard a beautiful voice singing. She followed the singing and saw an Ammonite fossil in the crook of a tree branch, on a tuft of buffalo hide. Then the lovely voice spoke. It'd sounded as if its sound came from the fossil and said "Take me, for I am powerful medicine. I am the greatest medicine of the buffalo." So she picked it up, took it back to her people, and told them what had happened. They held a ceremony and the buffalo reappeared the next morning.

Belinda loved folklore and was genuinely impressed by the mineralized fossil. She had purchased it at a rather steep price. She decided to pair the gem with the dazzling multi-colored jacket she'd discovered while searching the back of the store racks in a Soho used clothing shop the previous weekend. It was of crinkled taffeta stripes in bright blue, yellow, orange, & green, lined with pale yellow satin, very different to anything she'd ever owned. She'd wear it with a pale yellow tee shirt and blue jeans. *Perfect,* she thought as she dressed. *Perfect for a new day in a new year.* She brushed back her short blond hair and then shook her head so it would fall into place naturally. She quickly added a touch of mascara to her long lashes and spread some lip gloss on her lips. She didn't like makeup, but today she'd make an exception. She pulled on her camel-colored leather boots and grabbed a matching three-quarter length leather coat as she left the bedroom.

"I'm ready, let's go," she called out.

22

Rachel and Ethan sat at a sidewalk table in front of a pub just a few steps away from the Odeon, sipping drinks and watching people queue for tickets. Out of nowhere, in the last twenty minutes, hordes of people were arriving to catch the new James Bond movie.

In the States, Rachel would be watching reruns of the Annual Rose Parade in Pasadena this time of day, because she usually missed the parade as it was being televised live early morning. She'd make a point to watch one of the reruns that went on all day and night on New Year's Day. *In fact, the actual parade is ready to begin in California right now*, she thought to herself as she glanced at her watch.

"We're missing the Rose Parade, you know," she said as she smiled at Ethan and reached across the table to touch his arm. "Remember that time we were going to the Rose Parade and ended up at Disneyland instead?" she laughed.

"Yes, we were driving the company RV. We changed our minds on I-5, and instead of turning left to go to Pasadena, we went straight to Disneyland. Whose idea was it to do that?" He grinned as he stood and picked up his glass for a refill.

"I'm not sure. It could have been Reg's. He'd never seen Disneyland or maybe it was Carl's. Neither one of them was too keen on a parade, having just come all the way from the UK. And I had to agree, going to Disneyland was a much more attractive proposition. Four adults going to Disneyland on New Year's Day. That's funny," she laughed again as she handed her glass to Ethan. "I'll have a refill, too, do you mind?"

She watched Ethan as he went after the refills and remembered the first time she'd met him seven years ago.

Rachel had been away from Southern California for almost a year. She had spent the time in the Northwest, where she had found her mother, before she returned to the Southland with a much renewed spirit and vigor. She had felt infallible and very happy at the end of the first week back in L.A. as she drove north to the San Joaquin Valley to visit her father and tell him all about finding her mother Lily. His horrid third wife, Mary, had already divorced him, so Rachel had been thrilled to have the time alone with her father. He had begged her to forgive him and had attempted to make amends with Lily, Rachel's long-lost mother, through several phone conversations during that week.

Later that week, while still in Bakersfield, Rachel had been invited by an old high school chum, Carey Rose, to go to Ethel's to hear some country western music. Rachel loved music of all kinds and had jumped at the chance to do something a bit different. Ethel's was unique in that it was advertised as being "half way between the dump and Oildale". Actually, the full name was Ethel's Corral, and it looked like a shed surrounded by a corral. Horses were actually stabled there.

On the dance floor that Sunday at Ethel's had been Ethan trying to Texas Two Step with the best of them. He hadn't seemed to mind that he was not doing it like the rest, and he had been enjoying himself so much that it just didn't matter to him or anyone else that he hadn't mastered it.

Rachel had been amused and amazed that someone could be so uninhibited. She couldn't take her eyes off him. She had been captivated by his foreign flair and joviality. She would never be

107

able to get out there and be as loose, without a care in the world, like he was demonstrating. In a way, he had reminded her of her father when he had been younger.

He must have noticed Rachel while he danced, for he had joined her table before the music had ended, and had ordered drinks for both women. Then he had motioned for his buddies to join them – two other UK engineers – and they all had a wonderful afternoon. That had led to dinner at one of the famous Basque houses in Bakersfield: *The Woolgrowers.*

It was at dinner that night when Ethan had revealed what he was all about. He told Rachel about his UK environmental company and how they had traveled to the U.S. to seek partners for a joint venture, targeting the farmers in the San Joaquin Valley near Bakersfield. Rachel had learned he was looking for someone to work for him in the area to set up accounts and to take care of follow–through and communications between the UK and the States. Since she had plans to reenter the work force after being away from California for a year, she offered her services.

Rachel sighed. So much had happened in the seven years since then. One happenstance was that she severed her relationship with Ethan's company in California only a couple months later, and in spite of her sudden resignation, their friendship had endured through the years.

She remembered one of her trips to England when Ethan had met her at the airport in London. It was on August 29, 1997. She'd needed a respite from L.A. after quitting another job she hadn't liked. She would never forget the next morning and the week that followed.

They had driven to Elaine's home in Kent to spend the night when Rachel had arrived at Heathrow, since it was too late to drive north to Stamford. Elaine was away on a holiday in Florida. They decided to spend the night, then continue on to Ethan's home in Stamford the next morning.

Rachel couldn't sleep. She had taken her pillow and had gone downstairs to watch television in the living room. Ethan was upstairs asleep in his sister's room. Once or twice, Rachel dozed on the sofa, but she awakened with a start when the increasing din of the television had become more convoluted.

It was 4:30 a.m. and the words "breaking news" had appeared on the screen in large block letters. She watched as the newsroom seemed to be in chaos. Captions appeared on the screen, "Di is Dead!"

"Ethan! Ethan!" she called out. "Ethan, wake up!"

Rachel heard Ethan's feet hit the floor above her and heard him bumping and scrambling down the stairs.

"What is it? What's wrong? Are you all right?"

"Princess Di is dead! She's been killed in a car crash! So has Dodi. I can't believe it!"

He plopped down on the sofa next to Rachel and wrapped his arm around her. They both sat and watched in utter disbelief as the tragic story had unfolded. They had huddled together long into the morning when at last Ethan went into the kitchen to make coffee and breakfast. Rachel had wept as the news media revealed the disheartening drama that had surrounded Princess Diana's death.

Over the next two days, even after they had returned to Stamford, Rachel had been glued to the television. She read and saved all the newspaper coverage of Lady Di, her family, and the questionable mourning house of Royals. The reaction of the public had been astronomically sympathetic. Mountains of flowers and gifts had been placed at Kensington Palace and television coverage had been rampant throughout the world. They had never seen anything like it; nothing of that magnitude had been expressed for anyone ever before, not even for heads of State, historical and literary figures, super stars or entertainers.

Ethan had taken off work to join Rachel in front of the TV the day of the funeral.

"I just can't believe it," Rachel had voiced through her tears. "Why her?"

"Yes, seems unfair, doesn't it?" Ethan's words had been noticeably shaky.

"They said they're driving to Althorpe straight away after the funeral to bury her. Where is that?"

"It's only an hour's drive from here. Maybe an hour and a half."

She sat up quickly with excitement in her swollen red-rimmed eyes, "Let's go there. Can we? Maybe we can get there before they do. They're moving at a snail's pace. What do you think? We'll take flowers. I want to give her something."

"All right. Let's go."

"I'll cut some flowers from the garden and make a card; it'll only take a minute."

They drove to Althorpe in under ninety minutes, but couldn't get near the Spencer property. All the roads had been blocked in a six–mile radius. So they had to park the car alongside a country road north of Althorpe and walked at a very fast pace, almost a jog. Multitudes of people had done the same - all hurrying to reach the Spencer family estate before Princess Diana arrived, to see her enter the gates to where she would be laid to rest.

As Rachel hastened along the narrow road, urging Ethan on, she noticed a car coming up from behind them - a black London cab. She had thought it was odd to see the cab so far out in the country and stopped to watch it work its way through the people on the road coming towards her. As it neared she recognized Prince Charles and his two sons seated somberly inside. They'd arrived by Royal train in the nearby village and had been driven to Althorpe.

"It's them!" She whispered to Ethan as he reached where she stood. They both had reverently nodded in respect as the vehicle passed by; hoping they'd expressed their sadness in an acceptable manner. Rachel had touched the car as if she wanted the boys to feel her deep affection and understanding of the heartbreak they were going through.

Wiping tears from her eyes, she tugged at Ethan's arm. "Come on, let's hurry." She walked fast, unable to jog any longer because she had a side ache and had been out of breath.

They saw the gates of the estate up ahead as they rounded a bend in the road. The cab had already driven through. The news media had set up at every angle, focusing on the gate. Diana hadn't arrived yet. They had made it in time.

"Here we are," Ethan interrupted her reminiscences of the events surrounding Di's death, cheerfully handing her a glass of champagne.

"Oh my, champagne? So early?"

"It isn't early. It's nearly half past six. The movie begins in fifteen minutes. Are you hungry?" He sipped his brew, leaving froth on his upper lip.

"Yes, I'm famished, actually, but I can wait till after the movie. I bet you're starving, you haven't had anything since breakfast."

"Well, you must remember we had breakfast in the early afternoon."

"Oh, right. I forgot. You know I was just thinking about when Princess Di died and we went to Althorpe."

"Yes, that was quite an extraordinary day, wasn't it?"

"Remember waiting at the gate with all the news media crowding around? We were standing right in front below one of the network's tripods. And some of the newsmen were up in the trees."

"I wouldn't have believed we could have done that, you know. You were rather insistent, as I recall. I couldn't believe we were right across the road, right in front of the gate."

Rachel sipped as she remembered. "I still get all teary-eyed when I think of Di in the casket with the flowers all over the hearse, people still throwing them as it came down the lane towards us, and the boys' small white rosebud arrangement sitting on the front of the roof of the car. People were actually sobbing and wailing. I caught myself doing it a time or two. It was impossible not to. And it was absolutely moving to place our flowers and the card against the fence. I just had to do that, Ethan. I'd never felt that way about someone I didn't know. It was incredible."

"Yes, I believe it was a matter of being caught up in the moment with a nation mourning for the princess and possibly the end of an age."

"I think you're right. You're absolutely right." She continued to sip the champagne and glanced at the crowd that was forming in double lines at each of the five doors to the theatre. The doors finally opened. Her eyes seemed to automatically zoom in on the back of a tall blond man, just entering at the far line.

"Oh, my God!" she blurted out.

"What is it, Rachel? Something wrong?"

"No, no. I'm sorry. Uh, the . . . the drink just hit a cavity in my tooth. The coldness, you know. Nothing to worry about. It's okay." She breathed in deeply as she quickly glanced back where the blond vision of *Trafalgar Square* had disappeared into the theatre.

Ethan accepted what she said, but began wondering where they could get her tooth fixed on a holiday, if need be.

"Drink up, shall we? We should go so we won't have to sit on the top row in the upper balcony. It's frightening up there."

23

All the ground floor seats in the theatre were taken. *No chance of sitting here*, Belinda thought as she led her mother and Alice towards one of the stairways that led to the First Floor Balcony. It's a good thing they got there when they did, because she absolutely didn't want to sit in the Second Floor Balcony, and even worse way up in the Third Floor Balcony. She always got dizzy looking down from there.

With the crowd, they slowly made their way up the stairs leading from one balcony to the next. Beatrice ate popcorn as she walked and Alice dug into a box of chocolate-covered raisins. Both women chatted and laughed, oblivious to the crowds surrounding and bumping up against them. It didn't bother them in the least. They were having a good time. Belinda seemed more stressed about it than they.

"Okay, let's stop here and take a look," Belinda said as she scanned the balcony in the center section. "I see the perfect spot, come along."

They began to climb the second of four aisles of stairs to the seats Belinda had pegged for them.

"Isn't that a lovely striped blazer, Rachel," Ethan said as he motioned to the young woman who carried a leather jacket and climbed the stairs towards them. She had stopped to hurry the two elderly women who were right behind her. "Now, why can't you wear something colorful like that? It's absolutely marvelous!"

Rachel couldn't believe her ears and eyes. *It's colorful alright. Blindingly colorful! How many colors are in that jacket? Maybe as a throw pillow it would be fun, in a Bedouin tent in the Sahara. How could he even consider that I might look good in something like that? It's way too bright for me!*

As Belinda continued to climb the stairs, she glanced to her right, instinctively. "Ohmigod! Mother, it's Paul Newland. He's here. In this theater."

"Where, dear?"

"Up there, don't look. Blimey, he's seen us! Hello, Paul," she called out and waved. Not waiting to see if he responded, she hurried to her left to the seats she'd selected. She just wanted to sit down and disappear.

Paul Newland actually waved back. He had seen the bright jacket coming up the stairs, but hadn't realized that it was Belinda until she waved. He admired the colors and the fit of the jacket. *That must have set her back a few. She seems to be more radiant today. Must be the jacket. And one of those two women with her must be her mother. I wonder which one it might be?* He couldn't see the faces now because they were sitting with their backs to him. He felt most women resembled their mothers.

As his eyes wandered further down the section from where he sat, a portly gray-haired man stood up, then leaned down to say something to the woman beside him. Paul's gaze went to the woman. He saw her profile as she whispered into the man's ear. *Wait a minute! It's the redhead from Trafalgar. Damn, she's sitting in this very section!* He sat up straight and leaned forward, scanning the seats right behind her. He noticed that the one on the aisle was empty, possibly vacated by someone who must have gone to the snack bar or wash room. Paul excused himself from his row of clients and moved quickly to the aisle on his right and stood there until her companion had left. Then he made his way down through the people that came up the aisle and sat to the right, behind Rachel. He tapped her shoulder. Startled, she turned around and came face to face with the grinning Prince of Trafalgar.

"Hello," he said with a sparkling smile.

"Oh, for goodness sakes! I can't believe this."

"I've thought of nothing else since Trafalgar, believe me. You are absolutely gorgeous. Quickly, I want to give you my card." He reached into his pocket. "Do you have a pen?"

"Yes, I do," she breathlessly replied as she unzipped her purse and pulled one out. "Here. You know I overheard you say you were taking those people to see a movie in this area today. So, I thought it might be this one, typically a man's movie. I guess I was right, wasn't I?"

"You're very perceptive." After Paul wrote his private phone number on the back of a business card, he handed it to her.

She was stunned. *Is this really happening? He's actually giving me his phone number?*

Belinda watched the exchange between Paul and the woman.

She is without a doubt older than him, Belinda noted. *Damn! She's the one he kissed last night at Trafalgar. They do know each other.*

At that very moment, Belinda decided to quit Randolph, Ross & Remington. *I'm fed up with it and with men! I don't want to see that fickle friggin' lover boy Newland ever again.* Even though he wasn't and never would be interested in her, she felt he was cheating on her fantasies at that very moment with an older woman. It was just too much to see him flirting right there in front of her. *To hell with his damn sperm! And to hell with Triple R! I'll quit the agency and become a famous metal sculptress in spite of him. I'll get a boob job, get a personal trainer, and then the men will grovel at my feet, since it seems they're only interested in how a woman's body looks anyway. Paul will be sorry. And I'll have tons of babies without him. So to double hell with him! Although, our children would have been beautiful*. She sighed in disappointment.

"Do call me as soon as you can. Where do you live?" Paul asked as he touched Rachel's shoulder again.

When she felt the warmth and grip of his fingers, she almost lost her train of thought, but managed a weak answer, "Stamford, north of Cambridge."

"Only an hour by train. Please, call me. Let's do lunch, either here or there. I must see you again. This is more than coincidental - running into each other this often." He saw Ethan come 'round the corner heading towards the aisle and stood up to leave. "Are you married?"

She shook her head as she read the card.

"Then, please, call me." Paul hesitated and thought twice about leaning down to kiss her as she looked up and nodded. He turned away just in time, before Ethan began his ascent up the stairs to his seat.

24

It was late when Paul pulled into his parking space on the eighth floor garage, adjacent to his apartment. He was happy to be rid of the Japanese faction and was looking forward to his evening with Sheri. He'd telephoned her from the car and asked if she'd be willing to come over tonight rather than tomorrow. He knew she wouldn't give him any lip service like Phyllis had. Sheri was young and a bit on the naïve side, which is how he preferred his women. He'd remembered what his father had told him, "Pick a young one, Paul, that way you can mold and shape her like you want." *Good advice, Dad.*

Paul's mother and father had divorced when he was 13. He had lived with his father after that. His mother hadn't believed she could handle a teen-aged boy and didn't want the responsibility. Besides, Paul and his father had always been very close and she hadn't wanted to interfere in that sacred man's world that they both seemed to covet. So Paul's teen-age education of women came from his father's view and values. After Paul left for college, his father, who was a womanizer of

117

the first degree, had moved to Toronto where he continued his life of eternal skirt-chasing. Paul hadn't visited his father in a couple of years, but had managed to spend time with his mother in Los Angeles when he went there on business. Their relationship was strained and far from perfect. She'd become a successful restaurateur in West L.A. and was a very busy woman, no time for family.

He unlocked the apartment and immediately began setting the scene to match his vision of a night of his brand of sexual adventure. He didn't have to woo or do anything special to put Sheri in the mood because they'd reached that point in their relationship where Sheri knew just what he liked and made no bones about doing it. She was there to please her man, thinking she was the only one of course. Very naïve! He thought of Phyllis and felt sad at losing her from his bevy of babes because he undoubtedly loved to look at her body. It was a knockout. But then he didn't need the continual aggravation from her. *I'll have to find a replacement for Phyllis right away.*

He brought the ebony box of cocaine into the bedroom area, dimmed the lights, selected soft music, poured himself a tumbler of Jack Daniels, then sat, drank, and waited.

Fifteen minutes later the doorbell rang.

Sheri entered, wearing a white see-through top, a short, flimsy, pink skirt, and pink spike heels. She was a curvy young woman, had youthful breasts that were firm and a bit on the large side. Her hips were very narrow and her legs were perfect. There was only one flaw on this pretty blond if one had to find a flaw. Her eyes were slightly crossed. So when she looked directly at him, it appeared she was looking elsewhere. But Paul didn't mind in the least. He wasn't interested in her eyes.

He took her coat and told her to have a seat on the bed. She did. He returned with a glass of red wine, her drink of choice. She sipped as he sat across from her in the chair he'd placed facing the bed. He began masturbating as he watched her drink the wine and fondle herself without taking off her clothing. No words were spoken. *This is perfect. This is exactly what I want,* he thought to himself in excitement.

After a few minutes of watching her perform, he closed his

eyes; usually he didn't need continued inducement from his women. He only needed a visual to jump-start his fantasies. After the initial moments, he would be off on his own, high as a kite in his mind, and would only glimpse at his subject if the images started to wane.

"That's it, that's it, keep doing that. Yes, yes, oh yes."

Sheri rolled her eyes as she listened to him repeat the same words over and over. She couldn't believe a man like this reverted to masturbation when he could have any woman he wanted. *What is wrong with him?* He was sitting there totally out of it, eyes half closed, acting like he was watching her, talking like he was looking at her, but he wasn't. *He's definitely got a problem.*

All of a sudden, he stopped, his eyes opened wide, he gasped like he couldn't breathe. She wasn't sure if he was having an orgasm or what. He normally didn't. *No, something is wrong.* He was very flushed.

"Are you alright, Paul? Paul?"

He gasped and started breathing again.

"What is it, Paul?" she said as she quickly moved to him.

"I'm fine, just fine. No, don't touch me. Please go back. Please. Start in again. I'll be fine. Just had a sharp pain. Indigestion. I'm alright."

She reluctantly returned to the bed, positioned herself, and continued with the established ritual.

He globed more Vaseline on his hand. Four hours later, after several more lumps of cocaine, a giant jar of Vaseline, and another fifth of Jack Daniels, Paul clutched his chest, dropped the full bottle of whiskey he had just opened, and gasped in pain again. This time it didn't stop.

Sheri immediately leapt from the bed, clad only in her blouse and white panties. She was frightened and scattered and didn't know what to do.

"Call . . . ambulance," he whispered. "Hurry."

She raced to the phone, dialed the emergency number, and relayed the situation. The ambulance arrived six minutes later and Paul was pale, bluish, and unconscious. Sheri was still screaming, "He's dead, *he's dead!*"

25

For two weeks the doctors had been telling Paul the extent of the damage caused by his drug and alcohol abuse and had been showing him the results of various tests they'd run on his body tissue and internal organs. They managed to scare him half out of his wits with their doomsday prognoses. If he continued to drink the excessive amount of Jack Daniels he'd come to habitually consume, his liver would be nothing but diseased scar tissue in just a matter of months and he would die. His system was so screwed up as a result of using cocaine, it was going to take weeks to rid himself of just the substance lingering in his cells and organs. His body had become dependent upon the abuse. He couldn't believe it. He'd never considered himself an addict. He only dabbled on weekends. Now they were saying he was a junkie, and that his habit would undoubtedly increase, and not only his liver, but his damaged heart would not take the strain. The next heart attack would be his last. He was told he could not drink or use again, if he wanted to live.

Damn! How did this happen to me? His thoughts took him

back to his youth, as he lay in his hospital bed hooked up to all the monitors. He thought back to when he was a teenager. He had begun experimenting with drugs and alcohol after his parents divorced. Living with his dad had given him much more freedom than he'd ever had when his mother was there. His dad had been cavorting every night, so Paul had hung out at the Santa Monica Pier where he'd meet up with the other rich kids, all of them using or imbibing on the beach. That was also when he had begun acting out his sexual fantasies.

The psychologist in the hospital suggested he examine his sexual addiction and warped sense of sexual activity, which turned out to be the result of his aunt's persistent wickedness, just as he had suspected.

Evidently, from those early days of pubescence, he had continued to search for that same initial thrill of his aunt's perversion, but had to revert to the use of cocaine and booze to sustain the thoughts that perpetuated the imagery. He was addicted to imagery instead of touching.

He experienced a tremendous change in his thought processes as a result of the discussions he had with the psyche doc. He agreed to continue the sessions after he left the hospital, as well as attend A.A. and N.A. meetings. It didn't take him long to make up his mind and commit after he heard all the damage he'd done to his body and what might happen if he continued. He didn't need another nudge from his higher power. This painful one was more than enough.

Belinda peeked through the doorway and hesitated for a moment before she timidly asked, "May I come in, Paul?"

"Of course, you may come in. What brings you to the hospital, Belinda? Are you visiting someone?" He wondered who it might be. At any rate, it was a surprise seeing her. He hadn't had any visitors - a few phone calls, but no visitors in the two weeks he'd been there.

She entered the room and stood wide-eyed for a moment, staring at the monitors that surrounded Paul. "Are you okay?

"Yes, they say I am if I change my entire living-breathing lifestyle, so I guess you might say I'm okay. All I have to do now is do what they tell me and I'll be up and at 'em in no time at all. So, you didn't say who you've come to see."

"I've come to see you, Paul."

"Me? You're kidding."

"I've been here several times, but you weren't allowed any visitors yet. The food in the cafeteria is rather good as a matter of fact and the gift shop has some lovely novels. Would you like me to bring you a book to read?"

He looked at her as if he'd never seen her before. "You have been coming here to see me? Why?"

"You know, you really gave us all quite a scare. And you seemed so alone. No visitors, no family. I'll not come anymore if that's what you want." She began backing up towards the door. "Oh, I forgot. I brought this." She reached into her bag and handed him an envelope. "It's a card from everyone at work. I'm the designated delivery service, you see. I've been carrying it with me for a few days. Waiting for you to— well, I'll go now that you're going to be all right."

"No, wait! Stay, talk to me. The only people I see in here are the doctors and a couple of aging ex-Army nurses. It's nice to see a pretty face for a change. So, please, please stay."

"Okay, I will."

He caught the bright sparkle that suddenly appeared in her eyes. "Pull up a chair, tell me something. Anything. Have you always lived in London?"

PART TWO

Cornwall

26

Rachel decided to travel to Cornwall by train from Stamford. She charted her leisurely trip through London in order to have a meeting with a producer, which her agent Anita had set up, to discuss Rachel's recent screenplay synopsis. They had met and he told her he was eager to read the completed screenplay, which hadn't been written, of course. Rachel wasn't planning to write it until after she spent some time in Cornwall, but she promised him she'd get to it very soon, and as soon as she finished it, she'd send it to Anita and then he could deal with her. It wouldn't take long to put it on paper once she got started, she told him, because the story was already written in her mind.

Her mind worked constantly on all her projects, it never rested. When it wasn't working on storyline and characters of one screenplay, it was outlining the next one. It also continuously speculated about the new series of novels she wanted to write, how the characters were to unfold, who would be in each book, the plot lines, the drama, the point of it all, same as in real life. Rachel's mind wrote without her complete

125

attention, even wrote without her fingers striking the keyboard. It wrote while she slept, while she was awake, while she was busy doing other things, as if the story had a mind of its own.

Maybe I have two minds, she thought as she looked out the window at the rolling green hills moving past the train. *Maybe I'm Siamese twins without the extra body.*

She leaned her head against the curvature of the seat and continued to gaze out the window while one of her minds thought only of Paul Newland. After the meeting in London with the producer, she'd telephoned Paul from a payphone at the train station and when he answered, she quickly hung up the receiver.

Why can't I talk to him? What would it hurt to meet with him?

She'd dialed his number at least ten times over the past month, sometimes waiting for him to answer, then she'd hang up. If his machine answered, she'd listen to his voice before hanging up. Sometimes she'd hang up after only a couple of rings. She just couldn't talk to him.

What am I afraid of? Is it because of Ethan? Or am I afraid of the possibility of sex?

With Ethan, their relationship was easy these days. He didn't bug her. He just seemed to be thankful she was there with him, whether they did anything together or not. He hadn't even hinted or suggested they have a repeat performance of their New Year's Eve session. Anyway, she didn't want to start up another relationship with anyone else, especially a physical one, and she suspected that's exactly what it would be with Paul.

Oh yes! Absolutely! And he's way too young for me. So, what the hell? Why am I thinking about him? It can't be the real me feeling this. It has to be the animal me.

She smiled at her thoughts and straightened up to check the map to see where she was.

The next stop was Exeter in Devon, then only three and a half more hours to Penzance in Cornwall, where she'd take a taxi to Newlyn. She'd rented a cottage over the internet in Newlyn, which was two miles west from Penzance. She was eager to get there and do her research without interruptions. She'd usually managed to isolate herself rather well, even while living in cities, but it couldn't compare with being far and away from the hustle and bustle of city life and people. Plus, she loved the adventure of traveling alone and did it quite often these days. She wasn't a complete loner, though. She needed to be with people on occasion. She just preferred to be the one to select the occasion - the why, when, and where.

This is a lovely part of the country.

The train approached Exeter and she began making notes about the things she was finding rather quaint. One was wash hanging out on circular clotheslines, which she hadn't seen in years. Circular clotheslines were extinct in most California areas. Most people used clothes dryers, at least in the cities. Of course, it was nice to let your linens flap in the summer breeze, it made them smell so good, but she doubted that these were hanging out for that reason. She couldn't remember when she'd last seen or even had a clothesline in her own backyard, or garden, as she remembered what it's called in England. Then she couldn't remember if they had a clothesline in Bakersfield when she was growing up. They must have because that was before dryers. Then in her mind's eye she saw Lee hanging out the clothes on a circular one that moved around and around, just like the ones she saw now as the train rushed past the suburbs of Exeter. She remembered how she used to get it going really fast and Lee would come out to stop her.

That had to be a good 40 years ago. And here the things are still being used in England.

She had the strongest urge to get off the train and go twirl one of them, for old time's sake.

Everything seemed so familiar as she looked out the windows at the far rolling hills and at the swans floating on the stream that ran alongside the railway amidst the thick foliage and trees that flanked the rail bed.

I know I was here in a past life.

Somewhere deep in her memory, she remembered a dream of swans on a small lake or pond in an exquisite garden. Swans were symbolic to Rachel. They represented splendor, serenity, and security - security as in safeness, a safe haven, and protection. She'd gone to the Los Angeles Zoo many times to watch the swans and flamingoes as they raised their young–teaching them, protecting them. They were in abundance in this southern British landscape, as common as the blue jay and sparrow in California. She wondered why there weren't as many swans in the lakes and rivers of America. She made a note to find out. *There must be a reason.*

Oh, there are the towers of St. Peter's Cathedral.

The train slowed down as it ran through the outskirts of Exeter and neared its scheduled stop. Rachel peered to see the remains of Rougemont Castle.

A lovely town.

She craned to see more and wrote the following: *I'd like to come back here sometime and roam the streets, maybe stay a couple days. It looks like a very interesting town. Exeter University is here, too.*

She always carried a small notepad in her purse, to record what she saw and heard during her daily comings and goings. She'd been doing it for years and had a huge drawer full of writings in pocket pads back in California, and the collection in the UK was increasing ever so quickly.

A group of teenagers boarded the train at the stop in Exeter and sat at three tables surrounding Rachel. Twelve kids in all. Noisy kids. She felt like moving into another car to maintain the quiet and solace she'd been experiencing thus far, but she stayed put, thinking maybe they'd be getting off soon. If she moved, it meant she'd have to pack up everything that she'd taken out to make herself comfortable over the lengthy trip. Three and half more hours to Penzance and she knew she couldn't bear traveling with these wild, pubescent beings.

Please get off at the next station, was the message she sent via mental telepathy to the teenager who seemed to be the leader of the pack.

It worked.

27

"I don't care to speak to him!" Ethan yelled into the phone receiver before he slammed it back into its cradle. His secretary, Pamela, had entered just as he finished the conversation.

"I'm sorry. I should have asked if you would take the call. So sorry. Shall I take a message when she calls back?" she said as she nervously laid papers for him to sign on his desk.

"I do not want to talk with either of my daughters or my ex-wife when they call. Do you understand? I've told them to get on with their own lives and I'll handle my business myself, without any interference from them. And please have my personal phone number changed and unlisted, right away." He signed the papers and handed them back to her.

Pamela quickly left his office and closed the door without any intention of changing his phone number. She'd learned from past experience that this was only a temporary spat, that when he got over it he'd give the new number to them anyway. She'd just screen the calls till then.

Ethan had made a few decisions in this first month of the

new millennium. The repercussions from firing his son-in-law were extremely exaggerated. His daughters and ex-wife were volatile and on his back daily, which had impeded any progress he tried to make in the business. So he ordered them all out and now the sparks flew more than they ever had before.

He felt Rachel had left at such an inopportune time; she could be helping him get through this critical mess, although he understood her wanting to go to work on her own projects. *Yes indeed, I understand, I just wish she were here.* He thought about how much he missed her and needed her soothing presence. So many times he'd wanted to take her in his arms and experience again that wonderful New Year's Eve. He dreamt of their love-making every day and every night, but he didn't want to chance scaring her off by being aggressive. *I'll wait for a sign that she wants me again too.* A sign that hadn't been forthcoming. Now she was gone and for how long, he didn't know. He was so lonely without her. With her, the increasing chaos at the plant was bearable. He could come home and dump all his worries and woe on her, and she'd always managed to help him clear his mind and make him feel better so he could tackle the next day with a semblance of success.

However, a heavier storm was unquestionably brewing over the firing of Allan Brigstock, his daughter Vera's husband. He couldn't believe both his daughters had ganged up on him, bringing his business to a halt. Vera and Adele were heads of departments and they'd been sabotaging his edicts and orders, usurping his authority with staff members, and spreading ill-will. Although his stepdaughter Adele had recently shown feelings of remorse for causing the latest debacle when several key people had resigned.

Thank God, Elton didn't quit! He thought of his chief shop steward as he put away the file he'd been working on. Elton Whitehall was a middle-aged man with loads of grit, who had been with him since he first began his business and was his most loyal employee. He could always count on Elton.

But Ethan's ex-wife, Nora, continued to bash him daily with angry phone calls, only to make matters worse.

It all had centered on Allan's dismissal. It had finally come to Ethan's attention that great amounts of money had been spent on items not requisitioned and approved, and that some items were missing - motors, generators, etc. - and that Allan might be responsible. He addressed him about it. Allan denied purchasing any items without approval and since there wasn't a paper trail pointing to him, Ethan hadn't a leg to stand on. Allan also denied removing any equipment from the property. In every case, Allan's backside was covered. There was a good possibility that he wasn't the culprit.

But when Allan began to shirk his duties, taking off in the middle of the day, taking off a few days each month, coming in late, it became evident that the engineering department was dangerously behind in expenditure and production reporting and it was affecting the overall performance of the company, its staff, and its income.

The straw that broke the camel's back was when Ethan saw his personal assistant and Allan in a rather sensual embrace after returning from a "liquid" lunch. Allan didn't know Ethan had seen them, and Ethan had never revealed the incident to his daughter, nor to anyone else for that matter, but at the very moment he saw them together, Ethan could have killed Allan for the snake that he was.

He replaced his assistant shortly after and now was suffering the backlash of firing Allan. He could put a stop to their criticism if he'd just tell his family about what he had seen, but he couldn't hurt his daughter Vera, and he couldn't bear the assured wrath of his ex-wife Nora. She already thought every man was a cheat and a liar and reminded Ethan of that every time she talked to him. She'd never forgiven his transgressions, although she had been as guilty as he.

Women! I'll never understand them.

Ethan opened his briefcase and inserted a few files he'd planned to work on at home. He still wondered which of the four had punctured his tires yesterday. The girls had denied doing it, but he felt they knew who did and he was suspecting Allan. Although back in the old days, Nora would be the prime suspect. Before they divorced, she did worse than that to him. He had witnessed her deliberately crashing into his car once and he

131

suspected she had set fire to his house once and he knew she had been the one who demolished his kitchen while he was out of town, breaking everything in sight. She was a very vicious woman when she wanted to be and so were her daughters.

Seeds from a flower produce more of the same. Yes, this situation is getting out of hand.

He closed his briefcase and stood still for a moment, seeming to be unsure of what to do next. He paged Elton Whitehall, but didn't receive an answer.

Elton was more than a shop steward. He knew all there was to know about Verde Victory. He had worked with Ethan from the beginning - which was coming up on 15 years now - and his duties had stretched over into the engineer's functions. He'd been taught by Ethan and was able to do the work of any process engineer, without the formal degree. He knew the processes, knew the proper settings to treat green waste and convert it to a usable product, knew the mechanics of the machinery, and actually knew the business inside and out. He'd accompanied Ethan into the field to give presentations at food-packing corporations and farms telling the advantage in hiring Verde Victory to haul their green waste to their processing plant and to explain the mechanics of the bio-chemical conversion of that waste into animal feed and fertilizer.

Elton had often wondered why Ethan didn't promote him from the floor of the plant into the office. He took pride in his abilities and was furious at Allan for all the pain he caused Ethan and Verde Victory.

Elton and Allan had clashed on many occasions. Elton was the one who had informed Ethan about the problems Allan was causing within the company.

"Something has to be done," Elton commented to his shop staff as they were having their afternoon tea break, "Allan stuck the tires, you can be assured he did."

"We should do the same to his car," one of the workers replied.

"No, that won't do it. He needs to be taught a lesson he won't take so lightly," Elton stood as he washed his cup and put it away. "Something that will surely stop his insults and cruelty once and for all."

He referred to the rumor Allan had been telling their chief suppliers that week. Allan had telephoned some of the suppliers and told them that Ethan had spent time in prison 20 years ago for absconding with funds from one of his business ventures.

It hadn't happened exactly that way and Allan made it sound worse than it was, however Ethan did spend seven months in jail because he innocently moved funds from one of his companies into a new venture. Before his environmental segment, he had opened a string of boutique salons–beauty and fashion–for Nora and his two daughters. They had managed the chain and he was the director of sales and marketing and in charge of increasing the number of locations throughout England. During that time, however, he began a new venture, a construction company. One of his many dreams was to remodel older buildings, vacant farm houses, and water mills and turn them into suitable residences. It was a definite high point in his career until he made a huge blunder. He took money from the salons to finance his building company, creating a major deficit in the salon business, and creating a tax fiasco.

Pretty soon it all caught up with him. He was overextended, couldn't pay his taxes, and ended up in court. He lost everything. Then on top of it all, he had to face the embarrassment of jail for seven months for not declaring true income and for trying to short change the government. Nora and the girls had never forgiven him for losing their business and their home.

So, Elton was more than aware of the long-standing animosity Ethan's family felt towards him, and he figured the anger had passed from them to Allan when Allan married Vera. He felt they were being unnecessarily cruel and knew Ethan couldn't take much more.

Elton was surprised when Adele had telephoned him just that morning to ask him to keep an eye on her father. She said she was going out of town for a few days and was worried about him. She said Allan had made some very heated remarks about getting even and she was afraid he was actually going to physically harm her father. She told Elton she didn't agree with the family and said that Vera was blinded by her feelings for

Allan, unable to see Allan for the fool he was. Adele told Elton she was sorry for making things worse and that she was not going to be a part of it anymore.

It was at that point in the conversation that Elton told Adele about the rumors Allan was spreading about her father, how the suppliers had been calling him every day that week, asking if what Allan was saying was true. Elton said that he'd had to admit it was mostly true, but that Ethan had paid his debt twenty years ago. He assured them that Ethan could be trusted implicitly. He told Adele that he didn't think Ethan knew what was going on and he was reluctant to tell him this latest ploy of Allan's devious vengeance.

Adele was shocked. She became enormously livid that Allan had misused the confidentiality her mother and sister shared with him. She screamed over the phone about Allan being "the slime-bucket of all times!" Then before hanging up, she announced that she was going to stop the bloody bugger from ruining her father's life. She'd had it with him. He had to be stopped.

Elton agreed.

28

It was dark in London and cold for February. Belinda parked her car in the underground garage of the warehouse in which she'd rented a new space for a studio all to herself. She'd given her notice to Triple R a week after New Year's Day and even though she felt she was taking a big chance, banking everything on the acceptance of her new sculptures, she was happier than she'd ever been and her countenance bore her feelings. She'd been working out in the gym every morning to tone her problem thighs and buttocks, and had scheduled breast implants, but at the last minute cancelled. She figured if she couldn't fix her body the natural way, then it didn't need to be fixed and to hell with it. But she was doing everything else she said she would do in her New Year's declarations. Her dream was unfolding and if her works of art were successful like she hoped, she would buy a cottage somewhere in the country and live happily ever after. Only one chink in her plans - still no man in her life to make her babies.

I can adopt, she thought as she sat in the parked car for a moment, thinking of her future. *No, I want my own blood child.*

Paul wasn't a contender, she knew that. Although he had been nice to her while she visited him in the hospital, she'd only seen him once since he was released. She'd hoped he would call her, she even gave him her phone number, and he seemed to have shown an interest, but he hadn't called.

When she got out of the car, a chill came over her. Not the kind of chill that comes from the weather. This was an eerie chill with goose bumps, hair rising on her arms.

Someone's here.

She scanned the empty floor of underground parking spaces to see who it might be. No one. Still feeling a bit uneasy, she made a quick bee-line for the elevator. She repeatedly pushed the button.

Damn! Must be jammed or something.

Her hands shook as she peered about and considered her options.

I can get back in my car and get the hell out of here and park on the street, or take the stairs.

She took several deep breaths to calm herself. She elected to take the stairs.

I'm just imagining things. No one is here.

Several times she'd felt as if someone had been watching her when she had arrived at her studio in the evening, but of course no one ever was. Although she had felt it probably wasn't wise to come back at this hour when the building was deserted, she did some of her best work at night and wasn't going to let some ridiculous uncomfortable feeling keep her from it, despite the fact that the docklands weren't a safe place for a woman at night.

Damn! The door to the stairway was locked. *This is not good.*

And then it began. First, she heard one person laughing, then another, and another - forced laughter resounding from all parts of the garage. A man stepped out from behind one of the supporting columns and stood between her and her car.

She literally stopped breathing.

"What do you want?" she asked, barely able to get the

words out.

The man stopped laughing as four other leather clad figures stepped out into view from various sections of the garage. Their faces were covered, two with ski masks, two with masquerade masks. The leader wore a Halloween devil's mask. She found that amusing in the midst of her fear. Then he motioned for the others to stop where they were.

"I been watchin' ya come 'ere every day, and then ya come Hammer and Tack at night chicken pen the bloomin' buildin' is empty. That Kathy Burke for us, don't it china plates?"

One guy responded loudly, "Yea, yea!"

Another repeated, "Kathy Burke for us!"

Another laughed, "I got summit special for ya wite 'ere, Basin Of Gravy!"

"Yea!" the rest of them agreed.

Belinda's adrenaline reached record heights as her mind raced frantically. The Cockney rhyming slang wasn't all that familiar to her, but she got the gist of the moment. She backed up and quickly turned to run farther up into the parking structure. She called for help, over and over, as loudly as she could, hoping someone would hear her.

The man in the Devil's mask signaled the others to go after her. They did, caught her and wrestled her to the floor. She screamed and thrashed until they gagged her with a neckerchief. They bound her hands behind her with masking tape. Her kicks and struggling made it difficult to hold her, but between the four of them they managed to press her down onto the oily cement as they began to cut away her clothing with knives, not caring about the nicks and cuts they made in her skin.

The leader stood above her, watching with excitement. When his eyes weren't skimming her body, they fed on the terror in her eyes.

She focused on his bright red hair that hung out of the back of the mask. It was an unusual red, more of an orange, but not dyed. For a moment, she thought she saw some pity in his eyes, almost as if he might change his mind, might call the whole thing off. She pleaded with him, hoping he could read her eyes.

But she misread him.

Then the unmerciful rape began. One by one they assaulted every orifice of her body in every unimaginable way, sometimes together, sometimes separately while the others watched and cheered. There was nothing she could do, they outnumbered and overpowered her.

After struggling in vain to exhaustion, she began drifting to another plane - not conscious, not totally unconscious – hovering just outside of her body. She almost reached a painless level. Something she'd learned the one year she practiced Zen.

The invasion was brutal. She urinated and it had mixed with the blood that was coming from the abrasions in her anus, and now she was lying in a warm pool of both. Her elbows were nothing but raw flesh and the front of her shoulders and knees were scraped skinless from the attack upon her while she was face down. They'd flipped her from one side to the other as if she were a rag doll.

Her mother's distressed and tearful face flashed into her mind. She squeezed her eyes tighter as she felt a sharp pain low in her abdomen. She drifted further to a place where she thought she saw her father, dressed as an 18th century gentleman. *Papa, is that you?*

Hold on to me, Luv, the man in her apparition replied as he reached for her. She placed her hand in his and they floated through a field of flowers towards a quaint cottage on a hill where an adorable, cheerful, little, orange-haired boy hugged a black dog while holding a furry white kitten. A woman stood at the door of the cottage and blew a kiss to her. Then everything went black.

29

I can't believe it! One of the graphic artists had just come into Paul's office and told him what had happened to Belinda. He opened his rolodex, found Belinda's home telephone number, and dialed it.

"Mrs. Bluhm? . . . Hello. This is Paul Newland at Triple R. I'm calling about Belinda. How is she?"

He listened while Beatrice went on to tell him of Belinda's condition. "Oh, my God!" he exclaimed as he leaned his head back on the chair and stared out the window. "Will they let me visit her? . . . I'd truly like to see her, if I may . . . Right . . . Okay, I'll wait here for your call. I'm at 206-105 . . . 206-105. Yes. I'm so very sorry. Thank you, Mrs. Bluhm. Bye."

He sighed heavily as he hung up the phone. *No, no!* He ran his hands through his hair as he thought about how exuberant Belinda had been after she handed in her resignation at Triple R, setting out to make her fortune as a sculptress. She came to the hospital right afterwards and told him all about it. She'd even brought a sample of her work, one of the most extraordinary works of art he'd ever seen. It was a combination of steel, copper, and tin, twisted and cut into shapes that were welded together to form a group of buffalo about 36 inches long and 12 inches wide at the base and 24 inches high at the tallest buffalo. The group of five tapered back, gradually decreasing in size. Each animal had oversized eyes of the most marvelously brilliant stones. Her "rainbow rocks," she had called them. "That piece is not for sale," she'd said. "It's to remain in my private collection."

Damn, damn, damn! Please, God! Not Belinda.

Her mother said she was not only bludgeoned and raped repeatedly, but stabbed in the abdomen and left for dead.

I have to do something. The phone rang and he quickly answered. "This is Paul . . . Thank you. King's College . . . Yes, I know where it is. Will it be alright if I go this afternoon? . . . Thank you, thank you so much. And please, if there's anything I can do for you, call me. My home phone is 205-145, and you've got my number here . . . Yes, 205-145 . . . Anything, anything at all, you just call . . . Yes, I'll keep in touch . . . Thank you again, Mrs. Bluhm . . . Okay, Beatrice it is. Thank you, Beatrice. Bye now."

He buzzed his secretary; he told her he'd be out for the afternoon and to put his messages on voice mail so he could check them later. He wouldn't be back to the office until the next day. He grabbed his jacket and rushed from the building.

As he sped to the hospital, he recalled how Belinda had looked on New Year's Day at the Odeon. He remembered the rainbow-colored blazer she'd been wearing and how she seemed to glow. He'd never noticed that about her before. He thought about how she looked when he'd seen her just a week ago. They'd bumped into each other at Palm Court and had actually had a drink and a delightful conversation together. He'd noticed that she had lost weight and was looking rather trim and had planned to give her a call to ask her to dinner. But he was so caught up in the finalization of the new client contracts that time got away from him. Now he regretted having been such a neglectful ass.

If only I had called her, it might have been the night she was attacked. I could have prevented it from happening. She might have been with me at some intriguing café and we could have been discussing art. Damn, damn, damn!

He saw King's College Hospital up ahead. It wasn't very far from his office on the south side of the River Thames. It was the closest hospital to Belinda's studio, which was very lucky for her. A homeless man who slept in the parking garage regularly had discovered Belinda soon after the tragedy occurred and had called an ambulance. She was taken to King's, which was a major London teaching hospital in Denmark Hill that utilized all the newest techniques. It was ranked as one of the best in the country.

Paul pulled into the parking area near the main entrance. *Flowers, damn it! I should have brought flowers.* He rushed through the doors and quickly searched for a flower shop. He found one in the Cheyne Building which was next to the Intensive Care Unit where Belinda was. After selecting a bouquet of flowers to match Belinda's precious rainbow stones, he asked at the information desk for her room number. The attendant gave him directions and he thanked her.

He was rooted to the spot in the doorway to her room. He couldn't move, he couldn't blink, and he couldn't believe what he saw. The nurse said he could stay for just a few minutes as it was almost time for her meds again. He wondered what other meds Belinda might be taking. It appeared she had every conceivable type of drug running into her body from an outrageous number of tubes as it was.

Oh, Belinda! What have they done to you? Tears filled his eyes and overflowed so fast, he wasn't aware it was happening until they spilled onto his whitened knuckles that gripped the bouquet of flowers.

She slowly opened her reddened, swollen eyes, blinked a few times to clear her watery vision, and thought she saw Paul Newland standing there holding a bunch of beautiful flowers. *Where am I?* She looked to the left and saw a nurse nearby, then saw tubes coming from all over, leading into her. *Oh yes! I remember.*

"Belinda, can you hear me? Can you see me?" Paul asked as

he leaned in closer.

"Dream . . . ing . . . right? Night . . . mare's . . . gone."

"If only I had—" He couldn't speak another word. His voice wavered and faded as he tried to choke back the sobs that were building up in his throat.

"Those . . . for . . . me?"

He gently placed the flowers on her and, at the same time, bent down to kiss her bandaged forehead.

She looked into his eyes as he raised his head and said "Thank . . . you." When she raised her bandaged arms to lift the flowers for a whiff of the scent, she groaned in pain.

"Here, let me help you." He gently held them closer to her nose. He could see the extent of the abrasions, bruises, and scratches that caused the terrific swelling and made her face seem like that of a horrid mutant instead of the pretty, blemish-free, oval, pointy–featured face that once belonged to her. Her lips were swollen all out of proportion, split, and bruised. All he recognized was the bright green of her eyes, her voice, and the pale blond hair that curled from beneath the bandages. He didn't even want to begin to imagine what must have happened to her body. The tears welled up again in his eyes.

She closed her eyes and slept.

30

"Oh what a beautiful morning, oh what a beautiful day," Rachel sang as she got out of bed and pulled back the curtains to open the second story bedroom window. "I've got a wonderful feeling, everything's goin' my way." She saw the tips of the masts on the boats in the Newlyn fishing harbor just over the rooftops, and she heard the ever present cries of the sea gulls and assorted dock noises. The Pilchard Works, the one and only of its kind, was a thriving factory on the Newlyn docks and she heard the men and the equipment working from her bedroom window.

"Cornish salt pilchards are pressed wi' traditional screw presses over at the factory and then packed in wooden barrels that 'uv been go'n to Italy since 1905," her new friend Pete Bell had divulged to her. "The Italians call them Salacche Inglesi. Same as salted anchovies, they also come in fillets, dry, or in oil. But their traditional form is as oole fish packed in wooden boxes or barrels."

"What does oole mean?"

143

"Oh, I'm sorry 'bout that, it means "whole".

When she first arrived in Newlyn, she saw Pete standing in front of the Swordfish pub across the street from the Pilchard Works. He was leaning against the wall smoking a cigarette. She asked him what was happening over by the docks. He was happy to explain the pilchard factory to her.

"What is your accent, I can't quite pinpoint it?"

"I'm a Scouse, from Liverpool."

"Scouse?"

"Yes, sea-pie, or Scouse, a mixture, like an Irish stew, it's the scran o' liverpuelians."

"What is scran?"

"Means food."

Every morning, she walked to the wharf to talk to the fishermen and packers and then, would double back for her morning coffee at the Swordfish, where owner Pete Bell would have a pot brewing. She'd been doing this for nearly two weeks and this morning would be no exception.

She donned her jeans, slipped on some walking shoes and a black turtle neck sweater, washed her face, brushed her teeth and quickly combed her hair back to tuck it up under a knit cap. She wasn't too fussy these days about her looks. She never was when she was away from home. After grabbing her favorite coat and gloves that she'd purchased at a Navy surplus store in the States, she went off to her usual morning ritual. It was truly a beautiful morning, and she wanted to sing it out for the entire world to hear, but thought it might be best not to.

I don't think the Cornish are quite ready for my singing. But then again, some people might like it. Those who can't hear well.

But she confined herself to humming. Her singing-in-public days were over, short-lived as they were.

She recalled the one and only paid gig she'd landed. She was hired by the owner of a club in Bakersfield and fired by his girlfriend three nights later. The reason given was the guy hadn't cleared it with his gal who was the manager and did all the hiring and firing. Rachel felt the truth of it was that she just didn't like her singing, which had been quite an ego blow. That was the end of her mini-career, although she would sing in piano bars when the occasion or mood struck. No stress involved and no work schedules. She had a problem with work schedules.

As she continued on to the wharf, humming along the narrow cobblestone pathway winding in an alley-like space between and around the cottages and buildings, Rachel made a mental note to stop by the Co-op and pick up a few groceries on her way home. She was already familiar with the Co-op or as it was technically called, The Co-operative Group. It was a very large company that offered a multitude of discount services, one of which was a grocery chain that catered mostly to towns and small villages. According to Ethan, they were all over England, at least 1600 stores at last count. Ethan filled her in on the Co-op and its history when she first arrived in the U.K. Even Newlyn and Penzance had Co-op stores. She was thankful for that, because it was the only source for groceries in Newlyn, except for a fruit and vegetable stand just around the corner from it. Otherwise, she'd have to walk to Penzance to purchase food, which would be okay once in a while, but not on a regular basis. She didn't rent a car so that she was forced to walk everywhere and thereby, made sure she exercised.

There were tourists at the Pilchard Works this morning, which also housed a museum. On weekends, it was a very busy place. She decided to skip her visit this time and go straight on to the Swordfish instead.

"Hello, anybody home?" she called out as she went through the side door that led into the "grown-up" section of the Pub. She called it that because the area in back was a very lovely room, with warm décor in emerald greens and ruby reds, upholstered chairs, and carpet. The grown-ups congregated and drank there. The "wild" young beer-drinking adults frequented the pub up front, which was filled with wooden benches, tables, and floor, and the music was as loud as the patrons. Pete and Sarah ran the place. When one tended bar in the back, the other was in the front. They'd switch off periodically, but as a rule, Sarah was in the front.

Pete and Sarah. Rachel hadn't quite figured out what their relationship entailed. She wasn't sure if they were a "pair," although they both lived upstairs and were partners in the business. They weren't married. That's all she had gleaned so far, without asking the out and out question - *Are you sleeping with each other?* Anyway, she liked to figure things out through observance and listening.

"I'll be rite down, Rachel. 'Elp yourself to the Everton Toffee," Pete's deep voice echoed down the stairs.

She smiled as she took off her gloves, amused at his dialect. She laid her jacket on one of the green and red plaid, upholstered chairs that lined the room. Then she grabbed a glass mug and poured herself a cup of coffee. She noticed that coffee always tasted better when someone else made it.

"E'yer ay come, ready or not," Pete joyously called out as he bounded down the stairs and entered the pub. "And y'alright this custy sunshiny morn, Miss O'Neill?"

"Yes, wonderful! Thank you." She watched him pour his coffee as he ducked to keep his head from hitting the hanging glasses. He had to be at least 6 feet 5 inches in height. His hands completely covered his china mug as he used it as a hand warmer while he sipped. He had very large hands, well-formed muscular arms, and a darn good body to go with them. There were a few tattoos on his arms. From his Navy days? She didn't find the tattoos offensive as some might. In fact, she found him very attractive in a rugged sort of way - a cross between film star, James Coburn, and mostly, musical star Howard Keel. She was quite fond of having her morning coffee at the Swordfish with the handsome proprietor, Pete Bell.

He'd invited her for morning coffee on the second night she'd patronized the pub, after he learned she was staying in a cottage just up the hill. She'd asked him about a few of the locals and the history of the harbor, and had mentioned that she loved to walk around the docks early in the morning, so he suggested she stop by the next morning and have a cup with him. He wasn't open for business that early, but told her that the side door was always open to the locals who liked to come in for a cup and shoot the breeze. So, she did just that.

There usually would appear three or four other people as well to share the hot steamy brew filled with milk. White coffee they called it, but she drank hers black. She was getting to know the locals and in the process spent more time with Pete, which didn't bother her in the least. He was fascinating. Something about him intrigued her.

"So, what ay your plans today, luv," he asked as he set his cup on the bar and lit a cigarette. She even liked the way he smoked cigarettes, although she wasn't a smoker.

"Oh, I thought I'd do a little grocery shopping before heading back to do some writing. Then I think I'll take the camera out for a photo shoot. Maybe walk to Penzance, go to the library."

"Custy day for it." He squinted as he blew smoke.

"What are your plans today?" Rachel asked.

"It's me day off. I'm pick'n up me daughter and tak'n 'er to the Eden Project."

"Oh yes, that's something I've wanted to see. So, where is your daughter?"

"She lives wi' 'er ma', and this is me weekend to 'uv 'er. Once a month. She's 13. Mingin age."

"Mingin?"

"Horrible."

Rachel laughed as she nodded in agreement and stood to go for a refill. Pete stopped her, took her cup and poured it for her.

"You juss relax. You've gotta long corky and chalk ahead o' you today, must welt all you tinnie when you tinnie." He smiled broadly and teased her with his dark eyes that matched his curly dark hair.

"I must rest all I can when I can? Are you saying I should rest because of my age? I think I'm beginning to understand you more and more, Pete Bell," she teased back. Her eyes twinkled at his endearing uniqueness.

He laughed and sat on the bar stool beside her. "Would you like me to take you to the Eden Project next week on me day off?" He looked at his mug, not at her as he asked the question, almost as if he was afraid to face the answer.

It took her totally by surprise and she didn't know what to say even if she could speak. She sat and stared into her cup for what seemed like eons. A million things zoomed through her mind. *What would Sarah say? But then it wouldn't be a date, surely not. I think I'd be too nervous to be alone with him.*

"You don't 'uv ter give an answer now, luv. Juss think about it," he said as he squeezed her arm and stood to go behind the bar. "E'yer comes Dudley. 'E spent most o' the day in e'yer yesterday. Ay don't see 'ow 'e tinnie stay in business be'n closed all the time. 'Ey, Dudley!"

Dudley was a nice looking man. He was a bit shy and had difficulty looking at people when he talked to them. He always seemed to be searching for something, either in his pockets, out the door, out the window, or around the room. He was terribly fidgety. He'd done the traveling rock show circuit for years and finally had decided to settle in one place and open a rock shop. He figured that instead of going to the masses, the masses could come to him. At least, that was his theory. Unfortunately, he selected Mousehole, which was a tiny fishing harbor, off the beaten track, just up the road from Newlyn. The town was busy in the summer, but dead in the winter.

Rachel certainly enjoyed Mousehole. She thought it was a quaint little village that was full of interesting history, touristy shops, and a few pubs and cafes. A delightful place to have lunch and spend an afternoon. She'd first explored it with Ethan on one of their trips to Cornwall.

"Mornin', Pete. Hello, Rachel." Dudley reached for the cup of coffee Pete handed him. "You still here, Pete? Thought you'd be off to fetch your daughter."

"I'm go'n after ay 'uv me Everton Toffee and visit wi' de two o' you for a few more minutes, after Sarah comes down. So, ay you open'n yer shop today, or ay you closed again?"

"You make it sound like I'm never in my shop." he replied, flashing a mischievous grin. "I'm there most of the time."

"'Ow tinnie you be there when you're e'yer most o' the time. Ay don't know, but it appears to me you close more than you open. Ay you independently wealthy, mate?" Pete teased him.

"Well now, it appears to me if you tossed as much coin in my shop as I do in yours, I would be independently wealthy."

Pete laughed as he poured more coffee into Rachel's cup.

"So, av you been to Dudley's shop, Rachel?"
    "Twice. It was closed." They all burst into laughter.

31

Such a lovely day for a stroll.

Rachel headed for the path along the shore. She loved walking on seashores, any seashore, anywhere. She felt her best in villages near oceans. But it didn't have to be an ocean, just near a body of water, in general. It could be a lake, a river, a stream, or a pond. There was something about water. It calmed her, created a mood of reflection, and allowed her to think clearly about past, present, and future. The path from Newlyn to Penzance fit the bill exactly. As she sauntered along, she gazed up onto the hillsides, noticing the many different styles and colors of the dwellings. It was the same here as most parts of the world, always an interesting assortment.

Well, maybe not most. Maybe not Greece or the Middle East. Here they're brick and stone houses, houses covered with plaster, some painted, and some left in their natural state.

She loved the pink and yellow houses the most. Many of them were overgrown with climbing vines, some flowering, some not. Roses were in abundance.

150

It seems rather early for roses.

She glanced back to the shore where there were rocks and stones of all sizes, huge boulders, and flat slanted sheets of granite. A huge spur of granite ran from the north across the bay to the south, which had always been an undersea hazard. Sand alone was not the norm on a lot of the British beaches, pebbles combined with sand was the norm. But on this stretch it was predominately rocks, with little sand. She spied a flat boulder, headed for it, and sat down to ponder the dream she had the night before.

She dreamed she was in a small boat, crossing over to St. Michael's Mount, a tidal island of earth and granite on which a castle stood across the bay from where she sat. The view she saw at the moment was the same as in her dream. She could have boarded the boat in her dream from this very spot on the beach. There had been people waiting for her at the wooden jetty below the castle. The more the boatmen rowed, the more they drifted backward, like one row forward, two rows back. It had seemed so futile. They couldn't reach the dock where the people were making beckoning gestures to them.

Rachel believed dreams had important meanings and interpreted hers to mean she or her ancestors lived here at one time. Maybe the dreams were meant to guide her. Maybe it meant she was having difficulty getting to where she should be in this life. The dreams had been recurring over the past year and they centered on this particular area – Marazion, St. Michael's Mount, Penzance, Newlyn, and Mousehole.

Since 1660, the St. Aubyn family owned the castle on St. Michael's Mount and she wondered if she had a connection to that family in some way. Or maybe she had lived in Newlyn in a past life and had been a school teacher to the St. Aubyn children. She had an open mind about the possibilities. She'd always felt that she would be a good teacher, even though she hadn't gone in that direction like her mother. Maybe Rachel hadn't because she'd already done it in an earlier life. She was under the impression that your vocation as well as your gender might change from lifetime to lifetime.

Which made her wonder why there was such a hullabaloo

against a person wanting to change their gender in their present life.

The spirit and soul are a constant no matter what and if genders change from lifetime to lifetime, why not do it in the present if you want?

She'd seen a BBC television program the previous night about a man going through surgery to become a woman. They'd said that Thailand was the country of choice for transgender surgeries and that the majority frowns against the procedure. It made sense to her, though.

After all, the person inside remains the same, so what's a body got to do with it? She laughed. *That would be a good movie title about transsexuals 'What's A Body Got To Do With It?' Hey, if it makes a person happy to have a body to match his or her emotions and mentality, then why not? Thank God, I'm satisfied with who I am!*

She wouldn't go under the knife for any reason. Not even for plastic surgery, even though she'd threatened to do so, many times in the past year.

As she sat there gazing across the bay at St Michael's Mount, her mind drifted from transgendering back to wondering how it would have been to live in the 17th and 18th centuries. Tomorrow, she planned to take a bus to Marazion from Penzance to visit the castle. Maybe she could find something linking her to a past life, or maybe an ancestor, or a living relative. Something was pulling her there, she was certain of it, and she knew to follow her acute intuitions.

She stood up and made her way over the jagged rocks back to the concrete walk leading to Penzance. She ambled past the lawn bowlers who were adorned in white. They were all older men with hair same color as their uniforms. Usually, she stopped to pick out the best players and cheer them on, but today she was on a quest. She was out of lipstick, the only makeup she used while traveling, and had been digging into the tube with her little finger to smear it on. She was tired of a color-stained pinky. So to Boots she must go. Boots was England's equivalent to California's Walgreen's, Thrifty, Longs, Rite Aid, and Sav-On drug stores. Although Boot's didn't handle as much merchandise as its American counterparts, it stocked an assortment of cosmetics and toiletries, which was all she needed anyway. She wondered why it was called Boots. She'd have to look that up on the Internet. *How did I ever live without the Internet?*

Her thoughts shifted to Ethan as she rounded the corner to go up Chapel Street, her favorite walking route into Penzance. She had called him last night and he was feeling blue. He said he missed her, asked how the research was coming along, and asked when she was going to return to Stamford. She didn't tell him she might not return, that she might go to the States directly from Cornwall. She didn't want to hurt his feelings. But then, she wasn't exactly sure what she was going to do, nor exactly what her feelings were towards him. He was a nice person. A very nice person, basically. She knew she was too hard on him in the sense that he didn't quite fit the picture of her perfect man. *But then, who does?*

She doubted very much that there was a man out there who would ever fit that picture.

32

Allan slammed down the receiver, swearing to himself. He'd just been on the phone with another supplier of Verde Victory to spill his guts about Ethan's imprisonment and to warn the guy about Ethan's "unusual" practices in handling other people's money. He had come up against a brick wall with this one, however. The supplier had told him that he ought not to spread such vile gossip about Ethan Philips. He said that he admired Philips and would not repeat anything Allan told him. He also told Allan to go to hell. He said that Elton had already informed him of the slanderous rumors Allan Brigstock was proclaiming against his past employer and father-in-law, and he'd hear no more of it.

Allan dialed his wife Vera to tell her that he was leaving his office - a small cubicle on a piece of property he had leased in Stamford, where he turned his lifelong hobby of buying and selling used sports cars into a living. He told Vera he would be home in an hour, or so, after he met up with Adele at the George Inn for a pint. He said Adele had telephoned him and wanted to

154

tell him some good news. Vera questioned what her sister's good news might be. She'd run into her earlier that day in Oakham where Adele said she'd bought a gift for a friend's daughter, but she hadn't mentioned anything about any news. She wondered what it could be. Allan told her he'd find out and tell her when he got home. He hung up the phone, gathered his belongings, and left his office.

It was half past five. He'd been waiting at the George Inn for an hour. Adele told him she would meet him at half past four. He'd already had three pints and was drinking a fourth. For the past hour the pub patrons half-listened to him rake Ethan over the coals. In an inebriated state he usually became obnoxious, and this was no exception. Finally, the barkeep cut him off after drink number five, so Allan belligerently paid the tab and stormed out the door.

He sped west from Stamford towards Oakham, wondering what the hell happened to Adele. She normally wouldn't stand him up. They'd had many of these clandestine meetings over the past two years and this one wasn't even secretive, since he'd told Vera he was going to meet with her. *What is Adele up to?*

The two of them had been having an affair since the company Christmas party, two Christmases before. Adele came on to him, he'd swear it to anyone, although it was a mutual combustion, coupled with an overabundance of spirits. Vera had a headache that night and left early, leaving the two of them to cavort. Both Allan and Adele didn't hold liquor very well, which was well known. Shortly after midnight they had disappeared, unnoticed by the rest of the partying staff at the holiday soirée. That was the beginning of a very hot and wild affair. This past week he had told her it would have to end, because it was starting to interfere with his marriage. He didn't want to lose Vera. He loved her. Adele had been furious. He had tried to calm her, while at the same time telling her he would never divorce Vera.

Bloody hell, what's that? Something instantly appeared out of nowhere in the road up ahead of him, almost as if it jumped down from the trees that canopied the road.

My God! It's a girl! He violently braked, but nothing

155

happened. *No brakes!* He screamed as he struck the child and saw her flip up over the hood. The car fishtailed, skimmed a tree, flipped and rolled over and over until it slammed broadside into another tree further up on the opposite side of the road.

33

Ethan was horrified. He ran from the building to the parking lot towards his car while the Verde Victory staff stood by in absolute shock. The call had just come. Allan was dead!

Vera had cried uncontrollably when she called her father from a Peterborough hospital. Allan had smashed his car into a tree on the road between Stamford and Oakham. In between sobs, Vera said that his car had struck a little girl, but they couldn't find her. She said that Allan had been screaming when the paramedics got there, "Help the girl, please, help the girl." But there was no sign of anyone else at the scene, only Allan bleeding profusely from head and bodily injuries. He slipped into shock very quickly. Others had arrived at the crash site and immediately assisted by looking into the nearby fields on both sides of the hedgerows and in and around the shrubs. They even had searched the trees whose branches spanned the road from one side to the other, hoping to find a live little girl who Allan said had appeared out of nowhere. They found nothing. Now Allan was dead.

As much as Ethan disliked Allan, he would never have wished this upon him. However, the thought did cross his mind that the thorn in his side was now removed. He instantly shook his head to rid himself of the evil thought and concentrated on getting to the hospital as fast as he could. He thought about Allan driving the road between Stamford and Oakham, had traveled the route many times himself. It was a narrow, curvy road with many blind spots. Allan was a speedster and always took chances. Ethan was a fast driver too, but it made him nervous to be a passenger with Allan, who had two accidents the past year and had wound up in ditches both times. Both times, Ethan had gone to retrieve him. In fact, Allan's accidents were a joke in the factory lunchroom. Everyone knew how wild he was behind the wheel. He loved fast cars, sports cars. This time, he had been driving a BMW Roadster. This time, Ethan wouldn't be retrieving him.

Ethan shut the engine off in the car park and literally ran into the hospital. Vera was waiting for him with Nora.

"Popsie, he's gone! I can't believe he's gone," she cried as she buried her face into his shoulder. "What am I going to do? I don't have any money."

"Come along, let's go in here for a moment," he said as he directed her into an empty waiting room off the corridor.

Nora followed and put her arm around Vera's waist, trying to calm her as they huddled closely, "Popsie will work things out for you, Luv. Won't you, Popsie? You mustn't worry. Come now, don't cry. Everything's going to be alright." She looked at Ethan and frowned, "You must do something quickly. She'll need some money."

Ethan felt helpless. He didn't need another financial burden. He didn't need an ex-wife telling him what to do either. Unable to bear seeing his daughter cry, he excused himself and stepped into the corridor and blew his nose and wiped his eyes. He felt like running away from it all. He wished he could.

Further down the hallway, he saw several policemen and a few paramedics standing near a doorway. He walked towards them, thinking maybe they were the ones who had attended Allan.

"Excuse me, but are you the medics who brought Allan Brigstock in?" he questioned one of the uniformed attendants.

"Yes sir, we are. Are you a relative?"

"I'm his father-in-law. Ethan Philips. Can you tell me, please, how the accident occurred?"

One of the policemen turned and introduced himself to Ethan. He told him the accident was under investigation and as soon as they could determine the cause of it, they would certainly make it known to him. He asked for his card.

As Ethan handed it to the officer, he asked about the little girl that Allan said he saw.

The officer told him he would contact him when the facts were clearer. At this time no one had any information about the girl. He said they would be getting in touch with him to ask some questions as soon as they determined whether or not it was an accident.

Ethan thanked him and slowly walked back to his grieving daughter.

Whether or not it was an accident?

34

Paul rushed into the flower shop, picked up his daily order, and made his way to Belinda's hospital room. He had visited her every day since the first day he came to see her. She was out of ICU and in private accommodations now, and was mending extraordinarily well. The abrasions and cuts were disappearing. The stab wounds had just missed her bladder. There was a question, however, about whether or not she would ever be able to conceive and it was doubtful that she could carry a child to full term even if she were to become pregnant.

She still wouldn't talk about the gruesome details to anyone, not even to the detective or psychiatrist that'd been assigned to the case. She couldn't bear to remember.

On his daily visits, they discussed each other's artwork. He'd told her he was completely fed up with Triple R himself and had admired her decision to strike out on her own. He told her if she could do it, so could he. They'd struck up a rather amicable relationship, friendly and easy, a huge departure for both of them. Belinda had never had a friendship with a man.

Paul had never experienced friendship with a woman – his quirky kind of sex had always been his priority.

"Ah, my little Chickadee!" he exclaimed as he stood in the doorway, making her laugh at his poor imitation of W.C. Fields.

"Paul, come in, what took you so long? Oh, more beautiful flowers. You're spoiling me you know, flowers every day. We're filling up the children's ward with them."

"At least they're not going to waste. So, how are you this fine, lovely day?" he asked as he bent over to kiss her forehead before sitting near her.

"I'm feeling so much better. The doctor said I could go home sometime this week." *I can't believe this gorgeous man has been visiting me every day. I wish I could stay in the hospital so it could go on and on.*

"That's great! I'll take you home when it's time, just tell me when."

She'd thought about going home, thought about going back to her studio to work. She wanted to get back to her sculptures, but being in the studio in that building didn't feel like the right thing to do. It frightened her. Her anxiety rose just thinking about it. "Paul, I'm thinking about going to Cornwall to set up a studio. Thought I might be able to work there without the fears and dread I'm feeling about the studio here. What do you think?"

Oh no. I was just getting to know her, and now she's going away. He understood her reasoning, though. The time wasn't right for her to face her fears. They hadn't caught the bloody buggers yet. That alone was scary.

"I think it's a good idea, Belinda. In fact, I can help you move all your things from the studio to Cornwall, if you like. I'd love to do that for you, would you mind?"

Mind! I'm ecstatic! Calm down. Mustn't read anything into this, than what actually is. He's just being sympathetic. Feels sorry for me and is returning the favor for when I visited him in the hospital. Yes, that's all it is. But, I don't care what it is. I'll take whatever he offers. "That would be wonderful, Paul. I'd feel much safer with you helping me gather my things from the studio. Thank you so much! I owe you."

"No, I owe you," he gently answered as he ruffled her short blond hair.

She loved it when he did that. He did it quite often. It was such an endearing action and reminded her of her papa who used to always greet her with a grand hair-ruffling. *Papa loved me more than life itself. Maybe Paul thinks of me like a sister and he feels protective. Yes, that's what it is.* "I was thinking about finding a studio in Mousehole, you know, where I first found my rainbow rocks?"

"Yes, I figured that's why you've decided to go there. In fact, it's a marvelous spot. We can drive down and locate a suitable rental, then come back and move your things. It'd be a holiday for me, for both of us. I have an old school chum who has a holiday house near Mousehole. It's huge, as a matter of fact, on the side of a hill facing the sea between Newlyn and Penzance. Five bedrooms. Beautiful place. I'll call him tonight and set it up. I mean, well, I don't want to presume too much, it'd be on the up and up, of course. That is, unless you'd planned to make the trip with your mother?"

She couldn't believe her ears. She just stared into his face and his clear blue eyes. She was stymied and confused. *Who is this guy?* It wasn't too long ago that he wouldn't give her the time of day, now he'd become a major part of her life. *My whole life, as a matter of fact.* If it hadn't been such a horrific, traumatic, life-threatening and painful event, she would have arranged to have been raped much sooner. *No no, mustn't think that way.* She smiled as she realized she was definitely on the road to recovery, being able to joke about it to herself.

"Actually, my mother can't leave the B & B right now. So, as soon as I find out when I'm getting out of here, let's do it!"

35

Rachel stepped off the Marazion bus into one of the most charming villages in Cornwall. She didn't know what to do first, roam around the village, have lunch, or go directly to the castle on the Mount. She opted to roam first and have lunch before trekking to the castle, although it was important to catch the tide just right, since the age-old stone pathway to the island across the tidelands was only accessible when the tide was out. She asked a shopkeeper if there would be a problem getting to the castle if she had lunch before she went out. He said "no" and commenced to give her a little history of the castle.

He told her Marazion was an ancient medieval town, first chartered by Henry the Third in 1257, then reaffirmed by Queen Elizabeth in 1595. The town used to be a major commercial port. But then Penzance later took over the area's commercial importance and became the chief draw in that part of Cornwall.

"The castle on the Mount originally was a Benedictine Monastery," he told her.

"Really?" she interrupted. "Does the St. Aubyn family still

live there?"

"I believe they do maintain private quarters, but the castle is part of the National Trust now. If you come by before you leave town, I'll try to have some information on the family for you."

"Oh, that would be great! Thank you very much!" She shook his hand and then went to find a place for lunch.

As she strolled down the street, peeking into the shops and taking in the quaintness of the town, she spied the Godolphin Inn. It looked like an interesting place to have lunch and it had a view of the Mount across the bay. As she walked through the door, she hesitated for a moment. *Déjà vu.* She passed on through the entry and was surprised at the immensity of the dining area. She glanced at the menu lying on a table in the foyer and then went to a dining table by one of the windows. It had an excellent view of the castle and the causeway leading to it.

People hiked the causeway in both directions. *Quite a distance to walk*, she noted as she sat near the window. She was glad she'd changed her boots to walking shoes. The walk up to the castle looked quite intimidating, a very steep incline of steps and winding stone walkways. At the foot of the Mount were structures that bore a close resemblance to the village near the dock in her dreams. The realization startled her.

As she gazed across the causeway, she visualized life in the days of old, a busy village that housed the workers of the castle and supplied them with the provisions their families needed. In her imagination, she saw the children playing near the edge of the rocky shore, saw the women hanging wash and preparing food on huge timber tables near the outdoor granite ovens, saw the men and women busy at their crafts and tending the gardens leading up the hill to the castle. She wondered why in her dream, she had been in the boat that went to Mount St. Michaels.

"Are you having lunch?" an attractive middle-aged woman asked as she handed Rachel a menu.

"Oh yes. Thank you. May I have a cup of coffee, please, to start?"

"Yes, of course. Do you want to know about our lunch specials?"

"No, thank you. I know pretty much what I'm going to

have. Thank you."

Rachel watched the waitress go to a service area and make coffee in a small French press coffee maker. After a few moments, the vibrant, cheerful server placed the press on a tray along with a flowery china mug and carried them to Rachel's table. Rachel thanked her and ordered a cheese and fruit plate.

While she sipped her coffee, Pete Bell came to mind as did Ethan. She mentally drew a comparison between them. Pete seemed to be a very perceptive man and able to read Rachel pretty well, whereas Ethan was just the opposite. *Pete's of the earth. Ethan's a bit loftier. But they are both gentle souls.*

She hoped that Pete hadn't picked up on the slight attraction she felt towards him or on the fact that she couldn't wait to get to the Swordfish every morning to have coffee with him. Funny how thoughts of her New Year's Eve encounter with Paul Newland had almost disappeared since she'd been in Cornwall. She wondered how she could be so caught up with one man and then shift to another so quickly. Of course, both were strictly affairs of the mind, harmless and imaginary. No intimacy involved. Living in her mind wasn't such a bad way to go, it certainly was a much safer way to experience infatuations. She could take the storyline in any direction she wished. She was in control.

I wonder if I'll ever give myself totally to a man again. Of course, why should I? I have everything I want. She had more than enough money to live on and she was on the verge of supplementing her income with her writing. She had a home in California and loving relationships with her mother, step mother, and son. She could come and go as she pleased, whenever and wherever she wished. She'd reached a point in life where she loved the freedom to travel and the freedom to be herself. And she didn't have to deal with sex. *Why am I even considering marriage with Ethan and having to rearrange my life and schedule to include him?*

She noticed a very nice-looking, middle-aged man enter the restaurant. He was dressed in casual clothing, a bulky wool sweater over his shoulders, sleeves looped on his chest. His camel-colored shoes were expensive and were the same color as his corduroy trousers. He carried himself as only the affluent would. He looked in the adjoining dining rooms, methodically working his way towards the area where Rachel sat, obviously searching for someone. Other tourists had arrived since Rachel had been seated and now there were two other waitresses working the room. Rachel's waitress entered, carrying a fruit and cheese plate.

"Margaret!" The man opened his arms towards her.

Margaret quickly set the plate in front of Rachel, and ran to him. They embraced tightly and kissed right there in the middle of the room, oblivious to the patrons and the growing applause. It was reminiscent of one of those scenes in movies where the lovers fly into each other's arms right before the happy ending.

Rachel was thrilled to witness such a public display of affection. She was very curious about this reunion. Obviously it was more than just a welcoming embrace between friends.

The happy couple reluctantly separated after a few moments and moved to a small table tucked away in a corner, upon which already sat a silver ice bucket and a bottle of champagne. The man poured two glasses and they toasted each other, then the waitress hurried back to Rachel's table.

"I'm so sorry," she said to Rachel. "I knew he was coming, but I haven't seen him in a year and I was a bit overwhelmed."

"Hey, that's alright. Really. I'm fine."

"Is the food all right?"

"Yes, of course. It's perfect. But may I ask you a personal question?"

"Yes, you may."

"Well, I can tell he's someone special to you."

"Yes, he is. We've been lovers for six years. He holidays here once a year and this time he plans to stay."

"So, are you going to be together?"

"That's the plan," she said through the most magnificent grin Rachel had ever seen. After she was sure Rachel had all she needed, she took off her apron and joined her handsome admirer at his table.

This is a first! Rachel had never seen a waitress join a patron at a table in the middle of her shift. Another waitress came by with more coffee.

"Excuse me," Rachel said as she nodded towards the couple in the corner, "is that gal off work now? I want to make sure she gets the tip."

"Oh, she's the manager, Ma'am, and that's her fiancé from Spain. They're getting married up at the castle next month. She's a St. Aubyn, you know, her relatives own the castle. And he's related to the Royal family in Spain. It's a lovely story, theirs is. They've had such a hard time, so many obstacles to clear. And now they're getting married. Aren't they beautiful?"

"Yes, they are very beautiful." Rachel was thinking how that was the way she should feel about getting married.

36

Paul and Belinda arrived in Brighton at noon. Even though it was out of the way, they'd both agreed to make a holiday of the trip to Cornwall, take a couple days to see the countryside along the sea.

Belinda had been released from the hospital two days before, and Paul had worked non-stop moving everything from her studio into a storage area in his building while she was still in the hospital. He'd convinced her that was the best thing to do, and when she was ready, he told her he'd move it all to her studio in Cornwall, where ever that was going to be.

"Doing it this way," he told her, "you won't have to go back to your old studio."

Although she'd recovered remarkably, there was still an abundance of healing to do, so there was no point in going back to the scene of the crime just yet. Paul wanted to help her and she was willing to let him. She still couldn't believe he was her new best friend. She didn't even have an *old* best friend. He was her *only* friend. It was extraordinary.

"Shall we drive down to the beach and have a hot dog in one of those beach cafes?" she asked gleefully.

"A hot dog? You really want a hot dog?"

"What else would you have at the beach? Please, please, please, let's have a hot dog."

Paul laughed as he turned towards the boardwalk. He drove slowly and looked for a parking place.

"There's one," she said. "Perfect."

He pulled into the space, grabbed their sweaters, and crossed over to open the door for Belinda. As he helped her with her sweater, he noticed how much weight she had lost while in the hospital, which only reminded him of the unforgettable horror she had gone through. He wasn't feeling pity for her. It was something else, but he wasn't quite sure what. He knew he liked her company more than anyone else he'd ever known. He liked to do things for her and to see her smile, especially when her eyes would light up. He felt protective, like a brother would protect a sister.

She wore a light yellow, loose fitting, cotton shirt dress and light brown leather sandals. Simple, but classic. Paul admired her short sun-bleached hair and the way she dressed. He was so surprised when she told him she'd found the dress in one of the charity shops, where she bought most of her clothing. Charities in almost every town sold used clothing and home furnishings to increase their funds. She'd told Paul that there was a fantastic one in Brighton she wanted to go to, but when they drove by it on the way into town, it had a "closed" sign in the window.

"I can't get over the fact that you buy clothing from charity shops. It totally blows my mind," he said as they walked towards the stairs that led down to the beach and the beachside cafes.

"Why does that surprise you?"

"I just assumed you were one of those clothes-horsy women, who filled her charge cards to the hilt and was up to her ying-yang in uncontrollable debt."

"Ha! That'll teach you to assume the worst. I would never do that. I'm saving for my thatched cottage," she said, smiling up at him. "My life-long dream is to have a thatched cottage, and a fam—" Her voice faltered and she staggered.

169

Paul reacted quickly and put his arm around her as she turned and buried her head into his chest, muffling the soft sobs that suddenly overcame her. He'd been through this once before with her since she was released from the hospital. The doctors had come to the conclusion that due to the nature of her internal injuries and the repair, it would not be possible for her to have children. Even though they had given her encouragement earlier on, they felt that even if she could conceive, it would be dangerous for her and the child. They wanted to tie her tubes, or better yet, give her a hysterectomy right away, but she had refused. She couldn't bear that happening to her, too.

Paul held and consoled her as they stood near the railing. After a few minutes, she gained her composure and pulled away, still a bit shaky, but able to talk once again.

"I'm so sorry. Sorry." She took the handkerchief he handed her to blot her tears. "I feel so terrible for putting you through this."

"It's okay, I don't mind. You need to just let it go, Belinda. Crying is healing. Remember what the doctors said? Let it surface. You can say or feel whatever you want with me, because I want to help you. I do. Just call me Brother Paul."

"As in priest or relative?"

"Either. Whatever works for you," he said as he lovingly ruffled her hair.

Belinda sighed, unsure of what to think about him just being a brother to her.

"Then, Brother Paul, let's get a hot dog." They both laughed as they skipped down the steps to the beach on the most beautiful, sun-shiniest day of the year.

37

"Bloody Hell, the man is insane!" Ethan screamed as he slammed down the receiver. He rushed from his Corby office to the shop and directly to Elton's office.

Elton was searching through some files when Ethan burst through the door. He was taken aback at the intensity of Ethan's expression.

"They want me at the constable's office to question me on the murder of Allan Brigstock. Can you believe that? It's absolutely ludicrous! How dare they infer I might have something to do with it. It was an accident, that's what it was. Everyone knows he drives like a bat out of hell, don't you agree?" He furiously paced Elton's office.

"They say he's been murdered, do they? What proof do they have? Did they say?" Elton calmly reached for a cigarette. "Why do they suspect you? Or maybe they just want you to shed some light. It might just be a routine questioning. Not that they suspect you. Would you like a drink, Ethan? Let's go down to the pub, I've just finished up here." He stood, put on his jacket, and gathered work to take home.

Thirty minutes later, they sat at the Black Horse Pub in Elton, a small village east of Corby, west of Peterborough, which was Elton Whitehall's namesake. He was born in Elton and had lived there all his life. The place filled up with the usual patrons, mostly workers in the area, bankers, lawyers, carpenters, salesmen, but very few women at this hour. It was only 5:45 p.m. and the women usually arrived around 6:30 p.m., nearer to dinnertime.

The Black Horse boasted of the best pub food around. It truly was right up there with the best of them. Ethan had eaten many meals at the Black Horse, and although he was very upset at the moment, he was also very hungry. He ordered a hearty meal of duck and vegetables, boiled potatoes and sausage, although food wasn't served till much later,

He gulped his lager as he sat on the barstool near the rock fireplace and thought of Rachel. *How I wish she were here. I must call her tonight and tell her about this new development, and that I will be going in tomorrow for questioning. At least they didn't arrest me. That's a good sign.*

When he'd first called Rachel and told her of the accident, he'd told her how Vera had fallen apart. But since then he'd sent Vera to Tuscany with her mother to holiday. It was the least he could do and he couldn't bear to have the two of them hanging around depressed and crying all the time.

Ethan hadn't seen Adele lately. She hadn't telephoned every day as she usually managed to do. He wondered about that.

"Have you heard from Adele, Elton?"

"No, I haven't. Saw her at the service, but the last time I talked to her was the day Allen died. She called that morning to ask that I keep an eye on you, she was worried."

"Worried about me?" Ethan laughed, took another swig.

"Yes, she said she was concerned about what Allen was saying and doing to you. In fact, we all were talking about it in the shop that week. We thought someone ought to teach him a lesson. You don't think one of our blokes could have done something so dreadful, do you?"

"I wouldn't worry about it, Elton. It wasn't murder. It was

an accident. How could it be anything else? I don't know where they're getting their information, but I'll find out tomorrow."

38

What should I wear? My usual jeans and black sweater?
Walking shoes, without a doubt.

Rachel was getting ready to go to the Eden Project with
Pete. They were to meet at the Swordfish pub in thirty minutes.
It'd been a week since he first asked her and when she stopped
by the pub the night before, he asked her again. This time she
said "yes." He seemed happy she'd accepted, but she wasn't sure
if it was because he loved the Eden Project and jumped at every
opportunity to visit it or because he actually wanted to spend
time with her.

At the Swordfish Pete was sitting on one of his sofas in the
"grownup" bar, smoking a cigarette and sipping a cup of strong
coffee. "It's juss a friendly geste, that's all."

"Does Sarah know you're taking her?" Dudley asked as he
held a cup of coffee tightly, trying to control the morning shakes.

"O' cose, she does. And what difference does it make
anyroad, whether she knows er not. Yew know us relationship is
ed de outs and we're not married. It's beun more platonic than

not, de past few munths. We're juss business partners," replied Pete drawing in a deep breath of smoke as he spoke. "I'm rather attracted to our interestin' visitor from the states. A writer, nah less."

"She might put you in her book, better watch out. It might be one of those tell-all women's books. You might even make it to the big screen."

"'A! That doesn't scare me, yew trouble maker. But then again, I'd be an interestin' subject, don't you think?" He stood up, stretched and went for more coffee. "She's due any tick now."

"I'll be right back," Dudley said as he set his coffee on the lamp table and headed for the men's room.

Pete leaned against the bar and took a gulp of coffee. *I wonder what her story is. She hasn't really said much about herself. Only that she's here to write a book.* He walked over to the open door, gazed in the direction from which she'd be coming, and replayed the night before in his mind. *She must have come to the Swordfish last night just to tell me she'd go to the Eden Project with me.*

She'd actually stayed till closing, which was a departure from her usual routine. So he'd decided to ask her again. Her answer had totally surprised, yet pleased him. Of course, he knew there'd be no future with a woman like her. They were from far different worlds and generations. He figured she was probably ten years older than him, not that it mattered. She didn't look it.

Then Rachel had told him about her adventure in Marazion, how she'd found valuable information about the castle, and how she'd actually stumbled across a relative of the St. Aubyns, plus some other names of family members living in the area. That piqued his interest.

He wondered where he'd take her to dinner after visiting Eden. Of course, it all might take a different course depending upon how the day went, so he pushed the thought from his mind.

Last night he thought he'd seen more than a flicker of interest in her eyes. She seemed to be watching him all the time. It warmed him all over to think that she just might be feeling like he did. *But, didn't she say she's engaged to be married?*

Here she comes.

He turned quickly, looked into the mirror behind the bar, gave his hair one last combing, and then popped a breath mint.

Dudley reentered at the same time Rachel appeared at the doorway. "Good morning, Rachel," he greeted, "I understand you're putting your life into the hands of our mutual friend, Pete Bell, today."

She laughed and greeted them both, taking the cup of coffee Pete handed her. *Pete is such a gentleman. Charming. Handsome to boot. How am I going to be able to contain myself today? Then again, maybe I'm being premature. Maybe he'll do something to totally annoy me and the relationship.*

"Bright, Milady, ay we ready? We'll take ar' Everton Toffee wi' us," Pete said as he reached for his jacket that hung in the alcove beyond the bar area.

Sarah bounded down the stairs, fluffing her bangs, or fringe as the British say. "Good morning, all." She was a tall, attractive, curvy woman, long hair in a pony tail. A bit brash around the personality edges, but pleasing to the ears and eyes nevertheless.

They all responded awkwardly.

"So, you're off to see the wizard, Rachel?" Sarah asked as she went for the coffee.

"Yes, I'm so grateful that Pete has offered to take me. I hope you don't mind."

"Why should I mind? It'll be nice to get rid of the bloody fool for the day. I'll get some work done around here, for a change."

"'A! Now that'll be somethin' to celebrate, won't it? Juss what is it you're plann'n ter do, doll?" Pete asked.

"Now, wouldn't you like to know. So, off with you! What are you waiting for? Go to your lovely Eden Project. Maybe you should open a pub in St. Austell? Eh? Then you could be there all the time, couldn't you? He can't get enough of the place, Rachel. Takes his daughter, takes his friends, takes anyone who wants to go. So, you're his latest victim."

Pete laughed good-naturedly as he zipped up his jacket and

reached for Rachel.

Dudley raised his eyebrows before saying, "So, have you been to the Eden Project, Sarah?"

"No, I have no interest whatsoever in seeing a bunch of plants in a giant terrarium."

"But, it's a 'istoric undertak'n, Sarah," Pete said, "it's one o' the gaffer wonders o' the world now."

"I haven't seen any of the other *gaffer* wonders of the world, now have I? So why should I see this one?"

"Come along, Rachel. We should get started." He nodded to them both, "See you, Dudley. Sarah." Then as they left the pub, he turned to Rachel, smiled and said, "Me car's around the corner, this way."

39

"Ay thought we might take the A394 through Marazion to 'Elston, then a quick jaunt over to Falmouth, if you 'aven't seen it, then the A39 to Truro and cut over to St. Austell from there. What do you think?" Pete said through the whitest of perfect teeth.

"I couldn't repeat what you just said to me, but it sounds fine, whatever you want." She wondered how his teeth were so white in spite of the abundance of coffee and nicotine he consumed. She'd used whitening toothpaste to keep the coffee stains to a minimum, but then was told by a dentist that it might be too abrasive, since her teeth had become so sensitive to hot and cold. So now she used *Sensodyne*.

"How do you keep your teeth so white?" she blurted out, wishing she hadn't the very moment after.

"Ay brush after every meal and 'uv them cleaned every six months. Isn't that the Yank way to do it?" he grinned as he glanced over at her.

"Well, yes. I just wondered, I mean . . . well, you've such

178

perfect teeth and a beautiful smile." *Shut up, Rachel. What's the matter with you?* She quickly turned, clenched her own white teeth, and looked out the window.

"Ta, Rachel, that's a laughin' compliment." *She's a lovely woman.*

They drove along in silence through Penzance, both seeming a bit uneasy.

"I told you last night about the manager at Godolphin's in Marazion, didn't I? That she's a St. Aubyn?" Rachel questioned.

"Aye, you did. Ay know exactly who you saddy. Margaret Trimble, she is. Ay know 'er. Let's stop thuz fe a moment, 'uv a cup o' Everton Toffee and see if she's in, shall we?"

"Oh, that would be fabulous, thank you! I'd love to ask her a few questions, although she might be off with her handsome man planning the wedding or something like that."

She instantly thought of Ethan. She wished she could be as enthusiastic about an upcoming marriage as Margaret and her Spanish prince. It just wasn't the same. She wasn't excited about it, nor the thought of it. She needed to listen to her inner voice. "The answer lies within," her mother, Lily, would say.

Rachel wouldn't be attracted to Pete as much as she was, and she wouldn't have had such sensual thoughts of Paul like she did, and she wouldn't be off gallivanting in Cornwall if she were madly in love with Ethan and wanted to be married. She knew she had to face it and come to terms with the fact that marriage was not for her. Not for business reasons, nor for personal reasons. There was no reason she could think of to be married.

"You're in such deep thought, Rachel. Wanna share?" Pete pulled to a stop sign. He reached across the seat and squeezed her knee. "Wanna tell me?"

"Oh, it's nothing, really. Just thinking about something I have to do tomorrow. It's . . . well, it's just something I've been putting off, and now I'm going to have to face it."

He grinned, "That sounds rather ominous, and intrigu'n. Ay you sure you don't wanna rabbit about it? Sometimes a lend'n flapper is 'elpful. I'll lend you mine. As a matter o' fact, you tinnie 'uv both o' them." They both laughed.

Rachel relaxed. "Okay. You asked for it." She hesitated. "I'm engaged to be married, and I don't want to be. It's as simple as that, and I've got to break the engagement, it's dragging me down."

"Now there's a subject ay tinnie without a doubt relate to." He pulled into the left lane and turned left off the round-about heading for Marazion.

Rachel found it interesting that most intersections were round-abouts, not the usual American four-way intersection.

"Sarah and ay were at that point in our relationship," he continued, "When ay felt marriage wuz not for me. Not that she's in any way a bad git, she isn't. She's a 'ard worker, and sensitive, lov'n. But there's firkin miss'n there for me." He reached for the pack of cigarettes. "You don't mind if ay smoke, do you?"

"Of course not, it's your car. And cigarette smoke has never bothered me. Go on."

He held the steering wheel with his elbows as he lit the cigarette, then said, "I'll try to explain this to you, so's you can understand me language better. It's jess like the Eden Project. Ay love go'n there. It's a paradise, a storehouse for our future. Outside and under the domes are all the plants o' the world, flowers, trees, and scran. All o' it, be'n grown and perpetuated there, never to be extinct. But, it's more than a collection o' plants. It's about the environments they come from, and a study o' those environments. It's about cultures and scientists com'n together, under one rewf, to learn about each other's environments. It's about teaching. It's about communication and giv'n each other a voice. Oh, I'm sorry. Ay tend to get carried away about it. Yew'll experience it when we get there. Sorry 'bout that."

"No, go on, I want to hear what you have to say."

"Bright, it's juss that Sarah and ay aren't on the same wave length. And it isn't a criticism o' 'er. It's juss that ay 'uv so much more I wanna see and learn in this world. And ay can't do it with a git in tow."

"That sounds familiar," Rachel interjected with a laugh.

"I'm afraid I'm not marriage material. Ay joined the

merchant marines to see the world, met me ex-wife and married 'er onna shore-leave, should 'uv settled down, but kept go'n back out to sea. One day, ay came round to a dead starved and angry relationship, and decided it wasn't worth it to 'er or to me. So, ay moved on, but always lived near the sea. 'Uv to 'uv me sea, you know. After ay left ships, ay met Sarah in one o' de pubs ay worked, we both decided to bowl into de bewzer business together and e'yer we are. And ay 'uv de one daughter as evidence o' me ex-marriage."

Rachel felt so comfortable with Pete. She found him honest and very compelling, difficult to decipher at times, but charming. She told him of her own life, briefly; about finding her mother, about her first and second marriages, about her son and step mother.

Then in exchange, Pete told her of growing up as an only child, of spending his youth in Liverpool. His father had been a sailor. They'd moved to London when he was a teenager where his mother had died unexpectedly when he was 15. He had adored his mother and had always blamed his father for not getting the proper medical treatment for her. He believed she would be alive today, if he had. His father had died the same year as Rachel's.

Pete drove straight to the Godolphin in Marazion and stopped near its stone walkway. He kept the car running as he jumped out his door and went to Rachel's, opened it and said, "I'll meet you inside, afti ay find a jam jar park."

Rachel figured he meant a car park, which he did. It was another beautiful day in Cornwall, no mist or fog. Here it was 10 a.m. and one needed only a light sweater or jacket. Rachel breathed deeply, taking in the fresh sea air as she walked up the stone path to the Godolphin. She felt a strong sense of belonging this morning, more than she had since she'd been in Cornwall. She knew this part of the world could become her home very easily. She was considering looking for property to buy in Cornwall so she could split her time between the States and England.

As she neared the entrance of the restaurant, her breath was taken away by a quick, sharp breeze that whipped by in a flash.

Where did that come from? There wasn't a wind blowing, not a cloud in the sky. And she suddenly felt Déjà vu again, same as the last time she neared this spot. *I've been here, in another life, I know I have.*

There was a bench outside the entrance. She sat and closed her eyes and listened. She heard the ocean waves gently lapping against the rocks and sand and visualized the boat from her dreams. It came closer and closer to the beach on the other side of the Godolphin. *Yes, I see the Godolphin up on the bluff. And it definitely is me in the boat.* She felt the sea spray and the rocking of the boat. In her vision she looked down at her hands, on one she wore a beautiful blue sapphire surrounded by tiny pearls, where a wedding ring would be worn. A large silver medallion ring was on the middle finger of the other hand and a silver bracelet of hearts on that wrist. She smelled the salty breeze, felt it on her hands and upon her face. She looked down at her feet and saw pale brown leather boots laced to just above her ankles. She wore a long cream colored dress, a simple dress with layers of soft linen underneath and stockings. Someone helped her from the boat that had landed and been pulled up onto the wet sand.

"All rite, me luv. Come along, the jam jar is parked and I'm ready for a wee bit o' Everton Toffee. 'Ow about yew?"

She opened her eyes. The man in her visionary thoughts melded with the grinning, handsome vision who stood before her with his hand reaching out to her.

Ethan left the Constable's office, not knowing what to think.

Are they actually accusing me of cutting the brake lines of Allan's car? Bloody Hell!

He was also thinking of what the constable said about some fibers caught in the grille and on the hood ornament of the car.

"Similar to that of an acrylic wig," the constable said.

That's rather puzzling. It couldn't have anything to do with the accident. Allan's blood alcohol content was indeed high enough to cause him to imagine a girl wearing a wig, standing in the middle of the road, but it certainly is far-fetched. He was hallucinating. I'm not going back to the office.

It was a beautiful day and Ethan thought about driving home, packing a bag, and driving to London to see his sister, then driving on to Cornwall to be with Rachel. He needed to get away from Verde Victory and all the crap. *A week away will do the trick. Yes, that's what I'll do.*

As he drove towards Stamford from Peterborough, he wondered where Adele might be. He tried to call her from his cell phone. He'd been dialing her number for several days with no answer. She was old enough to take care of herself, he knew that, but he'd always been more protective of her than he was with Vera. Adele was older than Vera, being from Nora's previous marriage. But he felt as if she were his own. She certainly needed more attention. She was much more insecure and withdrawn than Vera, but had the innate ability to jump into battle with all fours blazing, just like her mother. And like her mother her mood swings were extreme at times. Several times Ethan had suggested that she see a doctor, but Nora wouldn't have it, she would always come to Adele's defense, saying that there was nothing wrong with her, that she was going through a phase, and that she would be all right. *Right, a lifelong phase.* He thought the effect of Adele not knowing her biological father might very well be part of the problem. He'd died of stomach cancer soon after Nora and Ethan were married, before Adele was old enough to know him.

Since she'd become a young woman, Adele would disappear for days at a time, with no mention of where she was going. At first, it worried Ethan, not knowing where she was, but over the years it had become an expected way of life for her. She was different and that was all there was to it.

So, Ethan wasn't really worried when he couldn't reach her. He just wanted to let her know where her mother and sister had gone, which she probably knew already, but he wanted to let her know that he would be away for a week himself.

He called Elton at the plant to tell him what the constable had said. He told him that he'd be in London overnight, then he'd be going on to Cornwall and would call him from Penzance.

Next, he called his sister and said he was on his way to spend the night, if she didn't mind, which she didn't.

He turned onto the road leading into Stamford.

He dialed Rachel's cell number. No answer. It irritated him that she refused to carry her cell phone. She said she wasn't a phone person and if anyone needed to reach her, they could always leave a message and she'd return the call. *Nothing seems to be urgent in her life.* He decided not to leave a message because he wanted to speak with her directly to let her know that he was on his way to Cornwall.

As he gazed across the fields, he marveled at the beauty of the landscape. The hedgerows in this part of England were lush and green. From one newly–plowed field, a massive flock of birds lifted off, after eating seeds, bugs, and worms. They flew in synchronization to the next field. He pulled over to the side of the road to watch in total wonderment the mysterious way they remained in tight formation. He thought of his family. In times of sadness, they seemed to be close and synchronized, but any other time, they were scattered and distant.

He knew his daughters were more their mother's offspring, and he'd felt the estrangement that occurs when little girls became big girls. They were both pushing forty now and wanted to lead their own lives and start their own families. But regardless of their ventures they always landed right back in his lap and pocketbook.

Before leaving for Tuscany, Nora had told him that Vera was pregnant. At first, he was flabbergasted and sad for Vera, but then he thought maybe it would be good for her

Maybe she'll have a son. I've always wanted a son. But all I got were conniving, vindictive females.

All except his sister, that is. She seemed to be the most sane and genuinely loved him. She was always happy to see her younger brother and coddled him when he was at her home in Kent, just outside of London. Elaine's affection for Ethan hadn't wavered when he was in prison those many years ago. She stood by his side, was very supportive, and never treated him like a criminal. In fact, Elaine didn't like Nora, didn't think she was good enough for her brother. She'd given Ethan her opinion before he married her and continued to give it to him every chance she got thereafter until they divorced. She was worse than a disgruntled mother-in-law to Nora.

Ethan smiled with thoughts of endearment towards Elaine. She was such a loving person and he couldn't understand why she'd never married.

He pulled onto the road that headed home, where he packed a bag and lost no time in getting back on the road to Kent.

As they entered the Godolphin, Rachel was acutely aware of Pete's hand against the small of her back. She was sure that he wasn't conscious of it, but she was super-sensitive to a man's touch. Even when he touched her knee in the car, it momentarily stunned her, in this case, thrilled her. She didn't know why her system reacted so incredibly much when a man touched her. *It was just a natural gesture to him. He probably thinks nothing of it. He's just a personable and warm person, that's all.*

Margaret was standing, talking to a young couple at a table.

"Ah, she's e'yer. That's 'er, rite?" Pete quietly asked Rachel.

"Yes, it is. So you do know her?"

"Ay do. Let's sit at the table by the window," he said as he directed Rachel to the exact same table she'd chosen when she was there before.

"This is where I sat when I was here before. You've chosen the same table." She was amused at the coincidence.

Margaret turned in their direction. "Pete Bell, you ol' fool,

186

how the hell have you been?" She quickly reached for him and gave him a friendly hug. "What brings you to Marazion?"

He leaned back as he held onto her arms, "Ay brought someone to meet yew." He stepped aside. "This is Rachel O'Neill, from America, a writer, and she's do'n some research on St. Michael's. Thought maybe yew could give 'er some information."

"Hello, Rachel," she said as she extended her hand and Rachel gladly shook it. "I'd be more than happy to help you." She looked questioningly at Rachel, "Have we met before?"

"Well, I was in here last week, when your fiancé arrived from Spain."

"Oh yes, the cheese and fruit plate. It's good to see you again." She smiled. "Would you like some coffee or tea?"

Pete answered before Rachel had a chance to say anything, "Everton Toffee would be the bee's knees. White for me, black for Rachel. We're on our way to the Eden Project and ay juss wanted to stop and introduce yew two, so yew tinnie set up a time for 'er to come back and rabbit to yew about things. Is that all rite?"

"Of course, it is. In fact, I'd love to invite you both to a little party we're having next week to celebrate the upcoming marriage. Will you come?"

In unison, they both replied, "I'd love to."

"Then that's settled, I'll be right back with the coffee and the invitations." She left them alone as they sat and stared at each other with wide eyes and bright smiles.

Rachel was flabbergasted. Not only was she going to be interviewing a member of the St. Aubyn family, she was going to a celebration of a St. Aubyn marriage. It was astounding! And Pete would be going too.

"Do you think Sarah will want to come to the party?"

"Nah, ay don't think so. She'll 'uv to weerk most likey. Someone 'as to, you know." He laughed as he winked.

"The party sounds like it might be fun."

"Thank you for com'n wi' me today, Rachel." He reached across the table and squeezed her hand.

"I'm the one who should be thankful. You're not only

showing me the countryside and the Eden Project, but you've given me the opportunity to step right inside the St. Aubyn family. You don't know what this means to me. It isn't just a piece I'm doing about the castle. There's more to it than that. And, I'll go out on a limb here and hope you won't think I'm nuts, but I get the feeling I've been here before. I mean long before last week. Uh, do you believe in reincarnation?"

Pete sat back with raised eyebrows, looking at Rachel quizzically.

Before he could say anything, Margaret returned grinning with the coffee and two envelopes. She had a glow about her. She was one of those people who always stood out in a crowd because of her effervescence. This morning, she was especially vibrant and there was something about her that truly fascinated Rachel.

"Here we are." Margaret cheerfully placed the mugs of coffee on the table. "And here are the invites. Next Sunday evening it is and it'll be up at the Mount. There'll be boats to transport all the guests. The information is there for you. I do hope you'll both come."

Rachel was already opening her envelope, "Thank you so much for including me, you don't know how much I appreciate this. I really was in complete awe of the obvious love the two of you have. It warmed my heart. One doesn't experience that very often."

Pete quickly retorted, "'aving the love or witnessin' it?"

"Both," she laughed as she tapped Pete's arm lightly.

Margaret pulled out a chair and sat, sipping a third cup of coffee that she'd brought on the tray. "So, what have you been doing with yourself, Pete? Have you seen Andrew lately?"

"Nah, ay 'aven't seen 'im inna month or two. Last ay 'eard 'e'd gone off to the Big Smoke to weerk onna project, some apartment build'n er firkin. It's 'ard to keep up wi' 'im."

"Well, if you see or hear from him, invite him to the party, will you?"

"O' cose ay will," he answered as he sipped.

"So, how's Sarah?" she asked.

"She's the same ol' Sarah. A total workhorse, she is. When

she takes a day off, she usually goes into de Big Smoke to see 'er ma', but that's the extent o' 'er interests and travels. Ay think she'd like to return to the Big Smoke. Talks about it a lot. We're not gett'n on, Margaret, so it's juss a matter o' time." He glanced at Rachel, hesitating as she returned the glance.

Rachel suddenly felt uncomfortable, not with Pete, but with herself. She would rather that Pete would not be available. She preferred affairs in the mind, not in reality. *But then what's reality? Reality is what one imagines and imagination creates one's reality. How many times have I imagined a reverie and then that reverie became real? Dangerous stuff, imagination. Be careful what you imagine, Girl.* "I'm assuming that Big Smoke means London?" Rachel asked.

"Yes, Dearie. Sometimes he goes a bit over the top with his Beatles dialect." Margaret was amused at the glances Pete shared with Rachel. *I wonder if something is developing between these two. That would be nice,* she thought to herself as she sipped.

Her friend Andrew had told Margaret most of Pete's story one night when they were partying offshore on Andrew's boat. Pete had been there with Sarah, one of the rare appearances Sarah made in Pete's world. Margaret liked her, but hadn't thought she was right for him. Sarah had a strong character and had been a bit reluctant to join in the merriment. She stood back and watched, more of a serious sort. Pete was a social butterfly, moving from person to person, joining in conversation and laughter. Margaret had been instantly drawn to him and if she hadn't already fallen in love with her Spanish "Prince," she'd said many times she would have gone after Pete. He was such an easy, likable guy.

"So, what were you asking Pete, just as I got here a moment ago? I heard a familiar word." Margaret looked directly at Rachel, waiting for an answer.

"Oh, you heard me, did you? I was asking Pete if he believed in reincarnation, because I've felt such strong connections with places and people since I've been here. I've felt like I may have lived a previous life in Cornwall maybe. So I'm doing some research in that direction. Do you believe in it,

Margaret?"

"As a matter of fact, I do. And so does Pete, don't you, dearie?" She smiled as she watched the grin spread across Pete's face.

"Ay wuz wait'n till we got e'yer to tell 'ye. Margaret and ay are part o' a group in Cornwall oo do believe in reincarnation, Rachel. There's a couple 'undred o' us oo meet from time to time, not all at de same time, juss small groups. Once a year we 'uv a grand meet'n. Andrew's one o' us, in fact ay met Margaret on Andrew's boat at one o' the meetings, isn't that rite, luv?" He patted Margaret's left hand resting on the table, and scraped his fingers on her gigantic, diamond engagement ring. "My God, that's a huge diamond, Margaret! It must have set the bloke back a quid or two!" he remarked loudly.

"It's an heirloom, actually," she said as Rachel leaned closer to take a gander.

The three of them behaved and talked together as if they'd known each other forever. If one were observing, one would have thought they were old friends.

And it felt exactly that way to Rachel.

They were back on the road leading to the Garden of Eden, as Pete referred to it. After a few miles, he pulled into a petrol station for a fill-up and went inside for a pack of cigarettes.

As Rachel sat and watched him walk towards the convenience store, she questioned herself. *Okay, so what's most important to me? A relationship, writing, or travel? And what about my legacy?*

Lily had popped that unexpected question on Rachel's last visit to Montana. Her mother was much more spiritual than Rachel. Not spiritual in the religious sense, but 'on the path to enlightenment' spiritual.

Rachel had asked herself over and over what Lily had meant. It had stymied her at the time and still did. *What legacy will I leave behind? How do I want to be remembered? I don't know.* She did know that she wanted to be remembered as someone who never said "I wish I would have." That was a given. She grew up hearing her father say those words over and over and she'd vowed never to repeat his regrets. It was probably the reason that he'd not only made her promise to see the world for him, but for herself as well. *Yes, that's what I want more than anything else. To see the world and write about it. But that isn't a legacy. Did my mother mean a legacy that is tangible?*

Inheritance was tangible, but she didn't think she meant that. No, Lily had to be referring to something more indefinable like one's values, love-giving abilities, and honest character, giving something of oneself to mankind. *Well, I've basically an honest character. That's one. Mostly honest.*

She was still asking and answering her own questions when Pete returned to the car.

"Here you go, luv. Brought you a biscuit and a drink." He handed them to her and turned on the ignition. "Did you miss me?" he asked, grinning from ear to ear.

Rachel was captivated by his boyishness, "If you'd been gone any longer, I might have," she teased.

"Off we go then, only an hour more to Paradise."

They rode along in silence as they ate their cookies and washed them down with cola. Out of the corner of her eye, Rachel watched Pete chew his food. She was delighted that he ate with his mouth closed, didn't smack, and didn't attack the cookie as if it were the last snack he'd ever swallow. *He has manners. By God, there is hope for the male species!*

"So tell me, Rachel. When are yew gett'n married?" Pete kept looking forward while munching his biscuit waiting for a reply.

Rachel choked unnoticeably, swallowed a gulp of cola, and cleared her throat. "Well, I—I'm going to cancel, like I said."

"Why is that?"

"I just don't think I'm ready to be married again."

"But what about the sorry bloke who's in love with yew? 'Ow's 'e go'n to take your rejection?"

"Pete, it would be worse if I married him, not knowing if I love him enough or not, wouldn't it?" She was irritated.

"Bright, yes, ay suppose that's gallant o' yew. But why did yew consent ter marry, if yew aern't sure?"

"Oh, I don't know. I just don't know. It was all such a good

192

idea at the time. We were both thinking of business, mainly his controlling shares. That's how it all began. We were joking that with my 5 percent and his 47, he'd control the company votes if we were married. So, one day on the train leaving a board meeting in London, we decided that's what we'd do. Hence the engagement. And things just went from there. I care for him, I do. He's been very kind to me and I believe he does love me. I'm the one with the problem, as usual. And I don't want to be unfair to him."

Pete set his cup in the holder and began to light up a cigarette. "Ay tinnie cotton why yew'd wanna be sure, but ay don't think anyone is ever a 'undred percent sure, do yew?"

"Probably not," she said as she looked out the window at the countryside nearing Eden.

Ethan pulled onto the gravelly lane that led to his sister's cottage. He'd always loved visiting her because she made him feel so welcome and loved. Since their mother's death there was a terrible void and only Elaine seemed to be able to ease that loss for him. Now she was his sister, mother, grandmother, and father, all rolled into one.

He honked his horn as his excitement grew. Out the front door bounced an eager Elaine. She waved cheerfully, so jubilant to see Ethan. In looks, Elaine was a reflection of Ethan. They could have been twins. It was uncanny.

They'd always been close, even when they were growing up, except Elaine was daddy's little girl and Ethan was a mama's boy. A natural phenomenon when one parent favors one child was that the other would take up the slack with the disfavored one. The Philips "twins" were a classic example.

Ethan barely had time to open his car door before Elaine descended upon him with her doting ways and hugs, as if she hadn't just seen him two weeks prior for lunch at The Ritz.

"You look marvelous, Ethan! You sounded as if you were at the end of your tether when you called." She held him at arm's length to look him over.

He giggled like a little boy. She always made him feel like the little brother that he was. It was as if whenever he was around her, he reverted back to his childhood. He knew he did it and couldn't help it.

"Of course I look marvelous, why shouldn't I?" He giggled as they traipsed arm in arm into the cottage.

They went directly into the kitchen where Ethan usually headed to forage for food. Elaine took his jacket and hung it on a hook near the door.

"I've made some pork pies, your favorite. Shall we have them now or later?"

"I'll just have some tea right now, thank you. I ate on the M1 when I stopped to make a phone call. I've been trying to reach Rachel since yesterday. She doesn't have her cell phone turned on. She's rather independent that way." He retrieved the cell from his shoulder bag and dialed her number once again. "She doesn't know I'm coming to Cornwall. Must let her know, you see."

"Oh. Well, why not let it be a surprise then? It might be an interesting moment for the both of you."

"Now just what do you mean by that, you trouble-maker. What is going on in that deranged little head of yours? Eh?" He laid the phone on the table and put some sugar in the cup of tea Elaine handed him.

She laughed and sat in the chair across from him, and took a sip of tea. "Well, it's just that if I were engaged to be married, I'd want to plan the wedding and be with my love, not take off to other parts of the country for an undetermined length of time. Does that sound right to you, Ethan? My only concern is for you."

"Elaine, I know you like the back of my hand, although for the life of me I don't know what that really means." They both laughed. "And I know you don't approve of Rachel, but that doesn't matter now, does it? We're going to be married and that's the end of it. And I don't think it's proper to surprise her in Cornwall. I want to let her know I'm coming. Is that alright with you?"

"Of course, whatever you wish, dear. It's your life. I wouldn't want to interfere. And I do like Rachel, so you mustn't think I don't." She plugged in the electric kettle to warm up the water and then reached for some jelly biscuits. She placed two on a china plate and handed it with a smile. "Your favorite."

"Ah, yes." He took a bite from one, "This is superb! Absolutely superb!"

"Thank you, Ethan. By the by, what is happening in the investigation of Allan's death? Have you any news?"

"Oh dear, they questioned me this morning to great lengths. I felt like they were accusing me of his death. Why would I want to kill him? Although the thought had crossed my mind, I must admit. But I would never do anything like that, you know that, don't you, Elaine?"

"Of course I do. So why do they presume his death was not an accident? I don't understand. He was driving too fast as usual and he crashed his car." She reached for a jelly biscuit and dipped it in her tea before munching.

"The brake lines had been snipped, not all the way through, just enough to prevent him from stopping at a high speed. And there was something else. Some sort of material was snagged on the grill, which might corroborate the story of the girl he claimed he hit. It's all so very confusing. I can't imagine who could have cut the brake lines and I don't understand what happened to the girl if he hit her. Surely she could not have gotten up and ran away." He picked up the cell phone again and dialed Rachel's number. No answer.

"How is Vera taking it?"

"Well, just as you would expect, very hard. She's with her mother in Tuscany at the moment. I sent them off to get them out of my hair. They were bloody nuisances, driving me crazy with their brooding telephone calls. I don't know where Adele is, haven't been able to find her since the funeral. I suppose she's off on one of her mysterious holidays again. Very mysterious, I might add. Leaving right after the funeral, not saying a word to anybody."

"You don't have to worry about Adele. She's self–sufficient and strong. I would imagine she's just as you say, off on a holiday. I need one myself. I'm thinking of going to Florida this week, would you like to join me?"

"Is this an effort to divert me from Cornwall, my darling sister? He rose from the table to get more tea.

"Wouldn't you rather go to Florida than to Cornwall? You despise Cornwall. You should go with me to Florida, Ethan."

"I should go to Cornwall."

Rachel gazed out the window at the lights that twinkled on the masts of the ships moored in the tiny harbour village of Charlestown. She listened as Pete gave her a brief history of its port. She was delighted that he wanted to treat her to dinner in the historic Rashleigh Arms. It had that endearing familiar "old world" lure that she loved and a raw elegance which warmed the depths of her soul. She could very easily spend hours, maybe days here. Maybe she had.

Her mind drifted back to the Eden Project and how it had been as spectacular as Pete had said it would be. She'd told him that she'd have to see it a couple more times, it was just too much to absorb in one afternoon. Pete still radiated at showing her one of his favorite places and her reaction to it.

She couldn't think of anyone, ever, with whom she felt so at ease. He was witty as well as sincere in just the right combination. He was quiet mannered and gentle with no roughness in his demeanor and actions. He had a wonderful accent, even though she couldn't understand him half the time, and he was always smiling. He was smart and well-informed without a display of haughtiness or self-proclaiming intellect. He ate normal foods, simple foods. He was polite and friendly to everyone. He was perfect.

She watched the excitement in his face as he continued to tell her of the tall ships that were docked near the Arms.

"They're famous owd ships which are used in film projects all over the world and they provide a liv'n to the people o' the quays."

"They're beautiful. Do they give tours on the ships?"

"Yes, on occasion, but not this late in the even'n. This bewzer wuz named after Charles Rashleigh, by the way, oo founded the china clay industry e'yer in the 18th century. 'E built Charlestown 'arbo to accommodate shipp'n o' tin that wuz be'n mined in Cornwall, and the china clay. Tinnie you believe the village population wuz only nine persons before 'e built the 'arbo?"

"Only nine people before he built the harbor?" She laughed. "That's incredible. I wonder who they were."

"If we would 'uv been e'yer earlier, we could 'uv gone to the shipwreck and 'eritage museum which tells the 'istory. It might 'uv a registry o' the names. Charlestown is an intrigu'n place." He reached for the bottle of Merlot and poured more into their glasses. "I love comin' here."

"Yes, it's restful and peaceful. You just don't know how much I love this, Pete. Thank you very much." She lifted her pewter goblet to him. They clanked them together and continued to sip while gazing into each other's eyes. Rachel felt a sudden heat creep up her neck into her face and quickly shifted her gaze to the goblet.

Pete felt the warmth of their gaze, too. He reached for her hand as it rested on the table, "Rachel—"

"Please, let's just enjoy the moment, shall we? No intimate words, no regrets. Is that all right with you? For now?"

He raised his chalice in the air, toasted in agreement, then gulped the contents down. "Bright, this is a custy plonky, shall we 'uv anuvver bottle?"

199

Paul covered Belinda more than himself with the umbrella as they strolled back to the Channel View Bed & Breakfast on Brunswick Terrace. They'd just finished a delightful late dinner and chat at a wonderful Chinese restaurant on the Weymouth sea front. The restaurant was on the upper level and gave them a complete panoramic view of Weymouth Bay. The skies had been filled with stars just an hour ago while they sat watching the last of the sailboats returning to the harbor. A storm was blowing in from the southwest, prefaced by a light rain.

They'd taken their time driving the coastline from Brighton, stopping first in Bognor Regis for tea and a stroll along the beach. Then they drove to Chichester and along Langstone and Portsmouth Harbours, pausing just long enough to see the huge shipping vessels and pleasure boats traversing the channel. They almost called it a day in Southampton, but decided to continue on through Bournemouth to Weymouth. Although Bournemouth was the most popular of the two sea towns and more upscale, Belinda preferred Weymouth. She'd spent time there before and knew just where they could stay. She called ahead on her cell phone for reservations. Besides, that would put them in Penzance the next day easily. However she wanted to visit the Abbottsbury Swannery, which was just a short distance from Weymouth, before they left for Penzance. She'd told Paul about the swannery, and he was just as eager to see it, for he had never been to one.

They arrived in Weymouth at the Channel View around eight o'clock in the evening and their accommodations were ready for them. The proprietors, Ali and Martin Weller, a vibrant couple in their 40s, weren't at all cross for having been disturbed during their dinner, and were happy to greet Belinda once again. She'd been staying with them for several years as she traveled the southern coast of England on holidays and weekend getaways. The last two available rooms were lovely, cozy, comfy cocoons on the second floor on the sea side of the quaint 19th century building.

The Channel View was one of a dozen clean and pristine bed and breakfast guest houses lined up side by side along the Weymouth promenade. Much like the one Belinda's mother had owned and operated in Hastings. Each was painted a different color, each with a different façade and personality. But Belinda preferred the Channel View because of Ali and Martin Weller and because of all their personal touches and service, the flowers in the window boxes and front patio, but mostly, because of the view. The Wellers were such a pleasure to be around, full of energy and laughs, and they made all their patrons feel special. It was Ali who initially told Belinda about the quaint village of Abbottbury with all the thatched roofed cottages, and the swannery that she'd grown to love so much.

Belinda and Paul were served tea upon their arrival at the Channel View, and a brief chat in the parlor with their hosts. Martin suggested they should hurry over to the Chinese restaurant across the street for dinner before it stopped serving. As they headed for the door, Ali asked Belinda if she wanted her to unpack the bags while they were at dinner or if there was anything else she could do for them. Before Belinda or Paul could respond, Ali headed up the stairs as she continued on to say she would place fresh towels on the beds for them and would bring up some of Belinda's favorite chocolate.

During her previous stays, Ali would give Belinda extra coffee packets and biscuits, and every evening, she'd place a bar of Cadbury milk chocolate on her pillow, a bar that got bigger with each visit. The last one was a giant bar for her to take home. She had even laundered Belinda's clothing, which was not one of the usual services offered. On her first visit, Belinda had asked Ali where the nearest Laundromat was. Ali wouldn't hear of it. She insisted on laundering Belinda's clothing, even though it wasn't a service she usually offered, and after that, it had become a ritual. Ali was one of the most giving and sincere people whom Belinda had ever met. She had such energy, lots of nervous energy - a blond, trim, dynamo that ran at full speed all day and night.

Martin was the perfect mate for Ali. He was a trim, muscular sportsman, who gave of himself as much as Ali, but was more of a laid back kind of guy. He knew how to relax, whereas Ali didn't. He loved to read and he'd had many discussions with Belinda about their favorite novels and authors.

Belinda called up the stairs to Ali that she needn't unpack anything because they would be leaving early in the morning and they wouldn't need anything else that evening. Martin handed them their keys and sent them off across the street to the restaurant. Told them he'd take the bags up for them and not to worry.

Such a wonderful, friendly couple, Belinda reflected as she and Paul returned to the Channel View after a very satisfying Chinese meal.

"So shall we call it a night or would you like to have a cup of tea in the parlor before retiring?" Paul asked as he closed the umbrella and locked the entrance door behind them.

"I think we should get some rest, that's what I think. You've been driving all day and I'm not so sure you should be doing all that just yet. Maybe it would have been easier on you if we would have taken the train. Don't you think so?"

"Hell, no! It's more like a holiday this way. Are you sorry I came with you?"

"Of course not, silly." Belinda patted his arm. "That's not what I'm saying. I worry about you. You must have rest, the doctor said so."

"The doctor said no more drink, drugs and sex. That's what the doctor said. He didn't say anything about driving. And what about you? You're the one who was in a hospital last. Not me."

Belinda laughed and turned to go into the parlor. "A fine pair we are. All right. One cup of tea and off to bed we go. Did you bring a book to read?" She went to the familiar book-laden shelving opposite the fireplace and browsed through the assortment. "Here's a good one. I gave these to Martin last time I was here. Jack Whyte. Have you read him?"

"No, I don't believe I have. One lump or two?" he asked as he prepared the tea.

"None, thank you. He's a fantastic writer. Usually, I read only romantic novels, but this particular series of Jack Whyte's is absolutely profound, called the Cumulod Chronicles. There are seven books in the series and I've read them all. This is the first one. Want to try it?" She held the book towards him.

"Sure, why not? I haven't read a book in years. Guess it wouldn't hurt to make another drastic change." He took the book and then poured two cups of tea. They sat on the sofa together, both perusing their books in silence. She'd selected *Mary, Queen of Scots*.

Paul read the prologue and commented immediately after, "This looks interesting. I've always been intrigued with the mystery surrounding King Arthur."

"I'm sure Martin wouldn't mind if you borrowed it."

"You are good for me. You know that? I've never had a female friend. I really haven't. A real friend. I feel I could talk to you about anything, tell you anything, and you wouldn't pass judgment."

She stared at him for a moment, letting what he said sink in before she replied. "Of course I wouldn't pass judgment. Do friends do that to each other? If they do, they're not true friends."

Paul reached over and touched her knee. "I honestly haven't had any friends since college. And those were just guys I grew up with. It's the women in my life who have been rather judgmental. But then I suppose they had a right to be. I've been a real prick. Sorry. A jerk."

"You needn't clean up your vocabulary for me, Paul. I can pitch the words with the best of them. So, please, be yourself with me. So you're referring to the women you've dated?"

Paul leaned and switched on the radio which was sitting on the sofa side-table. He selected soft music which felt very soothing. "Yes, the women I've dated. And the women at work. And of course, my mother. I just have a problem relating to women. All women, as a matter of fact."

"Hey, I'm a woman. You're relating to me. Although, I recall when you didn't. You wouldn't give me the time of day when I worked at Triple R."

"Oh, so sorry about that, I am, I mean it. I'm really sorry, Belinda. And that's what I'm talking about. I've lived my whole life treating women badly. I want to change that." He looked directly in her eyes. "I hope you believe me."

"I believe you."

He leaned and kissed her lips softly, lingering longer than he'd intended.

She quickly backed away and stood up, then picked up her cup and saucer and blurted out, "Uh, I think I'll go— I'll go up to my room now. And I'll— I'll see you in the morning, Paul."

He watched her as she left the room as if in a daze. She bumped into the door jamb then into the table in the corridor.

"Are you all right?" he called out as he rushed to the corridor, but she had already disappeared up the stairs. *Damn, damn, damn. I shouldn't have done that. I frightened her. What's the matter with me?*

46

Another glorious day!

Rachel woke up hearing the cries of the sea gulls as they searched for food for themselves and their young ones. She looked out the back window of the rental cottage at the three baby gulls who were marooned on the roof of the shed in her back garden. Mama Gull had deposited her eggs in a nest which was positioned up under the eaves of the neighboring cottage that abutted the shed. Minnie, Mack, and Moe, the names Rachel had given the babies, were huddled together, bleating. Their open beaks were raised skyward towards the direction in which their mama usually arrived with delicious crab and other fish meat. Any minute now, she would arrive.

Rachel had spent hours on her walks witnessing the gulls, as they hunted for little crabs in the beds of the moss infested streams that led to the ocean. She'd stood on the stone bridges to take photos of the hunt and attack. It was incredible how the tiny crabs would scurry and hide under the moss, but the wise gull was never fooled. He would peck at the crab until it lost consciousness and became precious gull food. The sea gulls also found plentiful bits of fish on the docks, since Newlyn was still one of the few remaining fishing villages.

She quickly brushed her teeth, splashed cold water on her face, donned her usual jeans, boots and sweater, brushed her hair, and headed out the door for a walk along the beach. She'd decided to skip coffee at the Swordfish this morning. She felt the need to regroup and distance herself from Pete for a day or two. It was getting too close for comfort.

Last night in Charlestown, the situation could have become one she regretted today. After they had a second bottle of wine, Pete suggested they spend the night at the Rashleigh Arms, separate rooms of course. But she asked that they return to Newlyn. She offered to drive so he could sleep, since he'd drunk most of the wine and was concerned about driving under the influence.

It would have been so easy to spend the night in his strong arms.

It appeared her fear-of-sex days might be a thing of the past, thanks to New Year's Eve and Ethan, and meeting Pete.

As she drove the night before from Charlestown to Newlyn, occasionally glancing at Pete's handsome face while he slept, she resisted the urge to pull over and smother him with kisses.

She had tossed and turned most of the night in her own bed, fantasizing about the two of them making love. But she knew she couldn't even begin to think about that reality, if it was a reality, until she sorted things out with Ethan. She planned to call him today.

The morning was clear and crisp. Never had she felt such sparkling fresh air. How can it be any fresher anywhere else in the world? What constitutes fresh air? Absence of pollution? Sea air is the most innocent air. It was as if the sea filtered the air somehow. She thought it must be, by far, the best air to breathe.

She strolled along the promenade leading from Newlyn to Penzance, pausing only a moment to watch the smooth, frothy waves rolling over the rocks and pebbles. She gazed up at the pastel-colored houses on the hillside as she passed. She walked past the early lawn bowlers, past the Penzance sea-water swimming pool on the beach, and up Chapel Street into the heart of town, and then to the Blue Snappa, a coffee shop that she liked. She'd decided to have breakfast this morning. A vegetarian breakfast – vegetarian sausage, egg, beans, toast, and a huge cup of coffee.

After eating, she sat, sipped the coffee, and watched the people parade by while artisans were setting up for what looked like a sidewalk bazaar.

Thoughts of Ethan crept into her mind. She decided to call him on her cell phone when she finished her coffee. The phone was in her pocket. She had turned it on before she left, but hadn't checked the messages yet. Her dislike of phones stemmed from the days in corporate America. Since then, phones annoyed her, she didn't like to hear it ring, she didn't like to feel she had to answer it, and she didn't like having to talk to someone at their convenience. To her that's what a phone constituted – being at the caller's mercy, on his time schedule. If she answered, she had to talk to whomever, whether she wanted to or not, whether briefly or not. So, she just didn't turn on her phone. She listened to messages once every couple days and then decided who and when she'd answer. Made her life very simple. Nothing was ever so urgent that it couldn't wait. At least, that was so in her life. If someone wanted to email her, that was different. She would return the emails immediately and checked them several times a day. Just a matter of communication preference.

She thought about how she was going to tell Ethan that she didn't want to marry him.

How can I not hurt his feelings? Maybe I shouldn't do it over the phone, definitely not in an email. I should wait until we're face to face. That means I'll have to go back to Stamford before I go to California.

She didn't want to do that. She wanted to fly from Southampton to L.A., via Paris, stay in Paris a couple days, then go on to L.A. She was considering buying a house in Cornwall when she returned and planned to leave most of her things, especially items she'd accumulated since she'd been there, in storage in Penzance. She knew this was where she belonged. It felt right.

Her cell phone rang. She hesitated. Two more rings. *Dammit!*

"Hello? Oh, Ethan! How are you? . . . It's good to hear your voice too . . . Yes . . . No, I'm in Penzance, having breakfast . . . I'm alone . . . Oh? . . . When? . . . Great. Call me when you get here and I'll direct you to the cottage . . . Yes . . . I'll have the phone with me . . . Yes, I promise, I'll answer it . . . Okay, see you tonight. . . . Bye."

Problem solved. Oh dear, I'm not ready for this.

Rachel ordered another cup of coffee and began making notes in her pocket notebook. She flipped back through the pages to glance at a previous entry: *St. Aubyn family, Marazion.*

The Penzance Library was just off Chapel Street. She'd planned to spend some time there today doing more research on the St. Aubyn family and St. Michael's Mount. She also wanted to find out about the nine people in Charlestown who lived there before Charles Rashleigh built the harbour. She felt there was a connection between Marazion and Charlestown. Both places had been in her dreams before she'd seen either of them. She hadn't mentioned it to Pete Bell.

But when Pete took her to Charlestown the previous night it was uncanny how familiar it had all seemed. This morning, she remembered why. She had seen Charlestown in one of her dreams. So she had to have been there in a past life. She'd never been there in this life and she hadn't seen any travel shows or write ups of either place. Pete might have been there in a past life too because he had said that he also felt a kinship to Charlestown. Here they were, both thrown together by chance.

Or is it? Souls travel in groups from lifetime to lifetime.

She had begun to believe it. The fact that Pete knew Margaret and believed in reincarnation was a convincing factor. Pete had said he felt like he was home in Cornwall. So did she. She felt she had been led there.

But, why?

"This is perfect, Paul. I'm so glad you thought of it," Belinda gleefully remarked about their temporary quarters in the pink house on the hill that overlooked the promenade to Penzance and the tranquil sea. "Look at this view, will you? I could live here forever."

Paul was thrilled that she liked it. "But what happened to your thatched cottage? I thought you said that's what you wanted."

"Of course, silly. I just meant that this is what the doctor ordered for now. Are you sure your friend doesn't mind us being here? It's so elegantly furnished." She marveled at the velvet upholstered chairs and sofa. "This is not what I expected at all. I was thinking beach house, not a formal residence."

"It belonged to his mother. She was extremely wealthy and used this as her summer home when she was alive. He also has homes in Scotland and France. A nice guy to know." Paul grinned at Belinda, "Do you want to choose a bedroom? There are five to choose from. Come on, pick one."

They both went through the house laughing, giggling, and admiring. Belinda chose a bedroom on the second floor facing the sea and Newlyn. It was a floral feminine suite and had an adjoining sitting room and roman bath. Paul selected a bedroom on the first floor with a view of the sea and Penzance. It was a wood-paneled room, much like his office in London. It was also reminiscent of the staterooms on the Queen Mary, docked in Long Beach, California. He'd spent many intimate evenings on the Queen Mary. The thought reminded him that he mustn't forget to book a flight to Los Angeles to attend the major week-long meeting in Triple R's Brentwood office next month. He'd become so involved with Belinda's move that he wasn't thinking of anything else these days.

Paul was relieved that Belinda wasn't angry at him that morning when they met for breakfast in the parlor of the Channel View. He had worried all night about startling her with that kiss. But she hadn't mentioned it at all and acted as if it hadn't happened, so he hadn't mentioned it either. From now on, he vowed that he would be careful not to let his feelings make him do stupid things. He found himself more and more attracted to Belinda, and not in the usual perverted sense. *Thank God!* It was much more than that. She had a way about her that was utterly captivating. From that first moment when she had come to see him in the hospital he had felt a difference. Her vulnerability and timidity that day had captured his heart. He still beat himself up for not calling her after he left the hospital. He would always regret that. But now, here they were, in Penzance in a house together, planning Belinda's artistic future. It flabbergasted him to think of where they were just two months before compared to where they were now. Being with her felt right, but he knew she wasn't ready for a commitment. There was far too much pain in her eyes.

As a matter of fact, since he was not doing cocaine and alcohol these days, he could feel and think about other things, even his own future. It was strange how he hadn't the desire to have a drink or a snort at all, and sex was totally out of the question. He was seeing a therapist twice a week and was working through his distorted sense of juvenile desire.

They unpacked the car and made their individual spaces theirs. Then they decided to take a walk down the promenade to check out Penzance. It was a short jaunt down to the sea after crossing the main road between Newlyn and Penzance. They stopped to watch the lawn bowlers for a moment.

"Have you ever done this, Paul? Lawn bowl?" she asked looking up into his bright blues.

He returned the gaze and was momentarily shaken by the beauty of her emerald eyes, brighter and clearer than they'd ever been before. "Yes. I mean—no, I haven't. Sorry, I—I was—I'm sorry. What were you saying?"

"I've always wanted to try lawn bowling. Maybe we can do it while we're here." She wondered what he could be thinking that had totally distracted him. She'd tried not to show how shaken she'd been since he kissed her last night. She'd wanted to throw her arms around his neck and be forever held by him. She felt safe with him. But she knew he had many other women, and she didn't want to be lumped into their category - falling all over him. Besides, he had so much to deal with at the moment that she didn't want to stress him out any more than he was. Although, it didn't prevent her from thinking about him all night long.

"I'll see about setting it up in the morning while you're still getting your beauty sleep. How's that?"

"I'd love that. Thanks."

They continued on towards Penzance.

Up ahead, Rachel sat on a bench, resting on her return to Newlyn from Penzance. She noticed a couple coming down the promenade towards her and wondered about them as they walked along the sea front. She wondered who they were and where they were going. She loved to watch people and guess their story. As they got closer, she couldn't believe her eyes. *What's he doing here?* She even thought the woman looked familiar. *Omigosh! She's the rainbow coat in the movie theatre! They know each other? This is too weird.*

Paul and Belinda stopped to admire the granite boulders on the beach. He noticed in his peripheral vision someone sitting on the bench ahead of them and he nonchalantly turned to look at

211

the person.

"What the hell—" he said, as he began to walk towards Rachel.

"What's the matter? Belinda called after him. "What is it, Paul?"

"I think I know this person." He reached out his hand to Rachel, "It is you, isn't it?" She looked very different he noticed, quite plain, but glowing. No make up, very casually dressed. He'd wondered what had become of her, she'd never called.

"Yes, Rachel." She shook his hand. "How are you, Paul?" *He is absolutely stunning!* She was feeling terminally dowdy. "What are you doing in Cornwall?" she asked, trying to conceal her fluster.

"I was just going to ask you the same question?" He was still holding onto her hand.

Belinda stepped forward, introducing herself. "Hello, I'm Belinda Bluhm."

Paul dropped Rachel's hand. Rachel reached for Belinda's. "Rachel O'Neill. Nice to meet you. You were at the James Bond movie on New Year's Day. You . . . you were wearing a very colorful, striped blazer."

Belinda laughed, "You remember my blazer? I love that ol' thing. Found it in a charity shop. So you know Paul, I gather?"

Paul cleared his throat, stepped back, and rested his hand on Belinda's shoulder. "Well, not quite. We met New Year's Eve at Trafalgar Square and then we ran into each other the next day at the theatre. That's been the extent of our friendship. Seems like we keep bumping into each other."

Belinda remembered now. He had been talking to Rachel at the theatre. She remembered thinking to herself at the time how Paul had reverted to seeing older women. He had even given her his card. *She looks rather young and appealing up close, not an older woman at all.*

"Are you staying in Cornwall?" Rachel asked.

"Yes, we're staying at a house up there on the hill. The pink one, that one up there," he pointed to the huge three-story house that Rachel had admired since she'd arrived in Newlyn.

"That one? Omigod! I love that house. I look at it every

time I go on this walk. It must be a marvelous place."

"Maybe she would like to come see it, Paul?" Belinda questioned. *May as well get them together if it's meant to be. Who am I to stand in the way. So what if it breaks my heart to bits.*

Rachel was excited about the possibility of seeing the house. "I'd love to see it."

So Paul invited her to meet them there around seven that night for starters and cocktails, then they'd give her a tour.

Then Rachel suggested that they all go to the Swordfish afterwards and she'd introduce them to some local color. She figured that would be about the time Ethan would call, so he could join them at the Swordfish because the pub would be much easier to find at night than her Jasmine Cottage. *Strange how I don't feel the same attraction to Paul as I did New Year's Eve. He's good looking, yes. But he isn't affecting me now as he did then. Maybe it's because of Belinda. Or Pete.* She didn't know. But once again, she couldn't understand how she could feel so strongly about a person one minute and then relatively nothing the next. She felt friendly towards him and drawn to him, but in a different sense. Now, it was like running into an old friend. It was very confusing. *Such a crazy coincidence to run into him here! Mind-boggling!*

As Paul and Belinda continued on their way to Penzance, he was deep in thought.

Belinda felt alone, and remained silent.

He couldn't understand the feelings he was having towards Rachel. He hadn't felt aroused like when he first saw her. But he was still drawn to her. He wanted to know more about her and was compelled and genuinely interested in becoming better acquainted with her. *Oh dear, I'm ignoring Belinda.*

"Thank you for inviting Rachel to see the house, Belinda. You're very perceptive. She genuinely seemed interested." He glanced sideways at her, sensing something was askew and asked, "Are you all right?"

"Of course I am. It's quite a surprise meeting someone like that out in the middle of nowhere, isn't it? She appears to be a nice person. And I may as well start making friends if I'm going to be living here. Now is as good a time as any, isn't it?" She looked away tearfully, out over the waves rolling in with the tide. *He likes her, I know he does. Oh, God. Help me not to make a fool of myself.*

Belinda was in love with Paul. That morning at the Abbotsbury Swannery, Cupid's arrow struck her heart. She knew she could never be with another man. Her heart had been so full, it felt as if it would burst. It actually hurt and pushed against the inside of her chest and lungs. In fact, she'd lost her breath and had to breathe deeply until the dizziness had left her.

At the swannery they had been walking through the overgrown garden where hundreds of swans congregated and were waiting to be fed. They'd stopped to watch a mother swan and her four small babies swimming in an emerald pool that branched off from a stream that led to the sea. She had been transfixed by Paul's face. His features had transformed into angelic softness. An aura surrounded his body. He had tears in his eyes when he turned to her and said he was moved by all the beauty surrounding him. He told her how wonderful it would be if she could have a cottage right in the middle of the swannery. He told her he loved being with her and loved sharing her favorite spot with her.

She was smitten.

The Swordfish was more crowded than usual for a Wednesday night. Hump day, as Rachel recalled the reference to partying on Wednesdays back in her early days of clubbing in Los Angeles. Middle of the week, like a hump on the middle of a camel's back. The weekends were the head and the tail. Sounded logical to her, although she never knew if that was the true meaning of hump day and never really cared anyway.

The pink house on the hill was incredible. Paul had been a perfect host, as was Belinda. Rachel wondered about them. There seemed to be a fondness, but they didn't display any of the usual physical niceties, such as holding hands, putting their arms around each other. No kisses, no caresses. But they were unusually kind and polite to each other, the look in their eyes revealed mutual affection.

She had introduced them to Pete who was bartending when they arrived at the Swordfish earlier, and they all three settled on the bar stools after ordering drinks – a bottle of wine for Rachel and Belinda to share, a bottle of mineral water for Paul.

Rachel was impressed with Paul's will power. He told her about his heart attack, which he said was the reason he wasn't drinking, then excused himself and went to the men's room.

"Tell me, Belinda, is he alright, honestly?"

"Yes, he's doing exactly what the doctors tell him. Doesn't veer off the plan at all. He's wonderful, isn't he?" The question not only expressed how Belinda felt, but gave her the opportunity to see just how much Rachel knew and felt about Paul.

"Yes, he must be. I can't imagine him being up and around so soon after experiencing something as serious as a heart attack. It's amazing."

"I know. And when he came to the hospital to visit me, I was overwhelmed. He was barely out of the woods, himself."

Rachel sat up straight, took a closer look at Belinda and inquired, "Why were you in the hospital?"

Belinda breathed deeply and closed her eyes for a moment. *Didn't mean to get into this.* She hesitated a bit longer before she looked Rachel straight in the eyes and said quietly, "I was attacked and raped by five men."

Rachel was stunned and flabbergasted. "What happened?" she whispered as she held her hand over her mouth, while old memories she'd thought she'd forgotten about her own horrid experience flooded her mind.

"I'm all right, really. But— but you wouldn't have recognized me then. I still have some discoloration on my body, some bruises, cuts healing. But, I'm fine. Truly." In spite of the strong professions, her hands shook as she took a couple quick gulps of wine. "Thanks to Paul. I don't—"

Rachel touched Belinda's arm, "You don't have to say any more, really. If you don't want to."

"No, it's all right. I'm supposed to let it out. It helps. And for some reason I don't mind telling you. Is it okay?"

"Yes, of course. Please, go on."

"I was just going to say, I don't know what I would have done if Paul hadn't been there for me." She took a deep breath before another gulp of wine. "The doctors wanted to give me a hysterectomy. Said if I ever got pregnant there would be serious complications. They stabbed me, you see. In my abdomen."

Rachel flinched and covered her face with both hands.

"They did a lot of damage. Not to mention the damage by repeated raping and—" She took another deep breath and winced in memory as she reached for the wine bottle. "And—and sodomy." She noticed Rachel had turned away. "Are you alright?"

Rachel couldn't trust her voice to be steady, so she remained silent, trying to hold back the sobs that were rising in her throat. Pete saw the change in Rachel's demeanor and immediately reached across the bar for her, questioning with his eyes.

She whispered, "I'm okay."

"I shouldn't have been so blunt, Rachel. That wasn't the right way to tell it. I'm sorry."

In a quavering, tearful voice, Rachel managed to say, "For heaven's sake, Belinda, there's no right way. I'm just feeling miserable it had to happen to you. You're so beautiful and young." She wiped her nose and eyes with a napkin and attempted to finish, "You know what? We always think our own tragedies are the worst ever, until we hear someone else's. Yours just made mine seem like a romantic comedy. I was date-raped a couple years ago and I'm just now coming to terms with it. And you seem so normal so soon after something so horrible. I can't even imagine what you must be going through. I'm so sorry." She hugged Belinda while she whispered, "You are so strong. Do you mind if I absorb some of your strength?"

"Take all you want," Belinda offered and smiled, at the same time found herself moved and mysteriously drawn to this American woman whom she'd just met that afternoon.

Paul returned from the men's room and sat at the bar next to Belinda, wondering about the embrace between the two women.

At that moment, Dudley entered the pub. Rachel immediately saw him, stepped back from Belinda, and motioned him over. "Dudley, I want to introduce you to some friends that just arrived today. They're staying at the big pink house on the hill. The one I talk about all the time. This is Belinda Bluhm—"

Belinda gasped, "Oh my goodness. The rock shop in

Mousehole?"

"Well, yes, actually, I own the rock shop. Yes. Do I know you?" he asked as he shook her hand.

"Paul, he has the rock shop I was telling you about in Mousehole. Dudley, you are totally responsible for my new career." She turned excitedly to Rachel. "I bought my first rainbow rock from him."

Her eyes are as brilliant as her rainbow stones, Paul thought as he admired Belinda. "So, this is the man that caused you to quit your job. Thank you, Dudley. Good show." He and Dudley shook hands. "Paul Newland here."

Pete joined them on his side of the bar and handed Dudley a drink. "Bright, ay 'ope yew did de rite th'n, Belinda. Quitt'n yer job because o' a alley apple ter become a beach bum." He laid on the accent a bit more than usual for the new guests.

They all laughed. Pete liked this group of people–Rachel, Dudley, Belinda and Paul. He felt good with them. They liked to laugh and were all artistic souls. Even though he had just met the two newcomers, he already felt a warm kinship and was looking forward to getting better acquainted.

Belinda and Dudley discussed a studio that might be available right next door to his rock shop and Paul suggested that they go look at it the next day.

As the night wore on, the pub thinned out considerably, and after meeting and talking with a few more locals, Paul announced that Belinda and he should be calling it a night. They were saying their goodbyes when Rachel's cell phone rang.

"That's Ethan. Don't go yet, Paul. I'm sure he's close by." She answered the phone. "Hello? . . . okay . . . come into the middle of Newlyn near the docks and you'll see the Swordfish Pub. Yes, that's where I am and I want you to meet some friends . . . Okay? . . . Great. Five minutes . . . Bye." She put the phone back in her bag. "He's on his way."

Ethan made his grand entrance, bounding through the doorway as if he'd frequented the pub many times before. That had always amazed Rachel. He had such presence. He entered a room as if he knew everyone in it. As it turned out, he usually did before the evening was over. He was the epitome of a super sales person, which was why she'd always thought he should be out in the field more, with Verde Victory. He could sell any idea he chose to sell. She admired him for that. She was just the opposite, not into sales at all, and didn't want to be.

Rachel introduced everyone and Ethan ordered a lager and drinks for all.

Rachel's phone rang again. "What? Who would be calling me here? At this hour. I'm not going to answer it." She lifted her glass of wine and sipped. It kept ringing.

"Answer it, Rachel, bloody hell!" Ethan commanded. "It might be for me. I left your number with my sister if she couldn't get me on mine."

"Dammit! I don't like to answer my phone," she said as she lifted it out of her bag and answered harshly. "Hello! . . . Yes, this is she . . . What? I'm sorry could you speak up a little louder." She got off the stool and walked towards the doorway, then motioned to the rest that she was going outside for the call.

Ethan laughed and told the others that he found it rather annoying that she wouldn't answer her phone most of the time. He'd lost several important calls that were meant for him because of it.

Pete stood back and observed. Wondered what in the hell drew Rachel to this man in the first place. He seemed to be an insensitive bloke, insisting she answer her phone when she didn't want to.

Sarah appeared from the front bar and asked Pete how he was doing. They moved off into the corridor and were still having a conversation when Rachel reentered. She was pale and appeared to be faint. Pete pushed past Sarah and caught Rachel as her eyes rolled back and her body went limp. Sarah ran for the smelling salts. The others crowded around, fearful for what might have happened. She gained consciousness when Pete put the salts under her nose, then she wept in his arms.

Ethan knelt and removed Rachel's hand from Pete's shoulder, "What is it, Rachel? What's happened? . . . Rachel? Can I do something?" He felt her forehead.

She looked up at Ethan and through her sobs she said, "Lily is dead." Then she said to Pete, "My mother . . . dead . . . . I have to go . . ." She tried to get up.

Pete gently lifted her to her feet, feeling such empathy for her. "Get back. Make room." He guided her to one of the plaid sofas that she loved. Sarah arrived with a cool, damp towel to put on her forehead. Dudley had poured a shot of Irish whiskey for her, his remedy for everything. She took it and grimaced as she swallowed it in one gulp.

"Thank you. It was Lee. Said Lily had a massive stroke." She continued in what seemed like a confused, rambling, broken dialogue, "She didn't know . . . what hit her. Gardening. She loves to garden . . . you know . . . lives in Montana . . . I mean, lived . . . I have to go there, now . . . I mean, tomorrow . . . tomorrow. I was going to go visit her, remember I said that, Ethan? But now I'm too late . . . *too late!*" She covered her face and began sobbing.

Ethan grabbed his jacket off the hook by the door and returned with keys in hand. "I'll take her. Thank you, you've all been very kind. Come along, Rachel."

He helped her to her feet and as they left, she glanced back over her shoulder at Pete, who was suddenly feeling helpless and lonely.

Paul had his arms around Belinda, holding her tight against him.

Sarah's arm rested across Dudley's shoulders, the two of them holding shots of whiskey.

All had sad eyes turned towards Rachel and Ethan as they went out the door.

Adele lifted another vodka bottle to her lips and took a swallow. She'd been in the hotel room for how long, she didn't know, but it had to have been for days, maybe weeks. She didn't know and didn't know if she cared. *I'm sick, I don't feel good.* All she could remember was leaving Allan's funeral, driving to the train station, and buying a ticket to Boston and then to Skegness. She knew no one would think to look for her in Skegness. It was Britain's east coast's answer to the west coast's Blackpool, only on a much smaller scale. A carnival atmosphere, not as in Rio de Janeiro, but carnival as in pin-ball and other arcade games, vending machines, cotton candy, ice cream, plentiful pubs and fish and chips, all smashed together in a small area near the Eastern U.K. sea wall. She'd always looked down her nose at places like this, where all the common people took their grubby little brats on holiday, and here she was wallowing in remorse and pity in this godforsaken ugly sea town, wishing to die.

She wanted her father. Where was he? Why hadn't he called? He always called her.

"Oh, wait a minute. He doesn't know where I am. And I'm not going to tell him. He'll get mad at me. But, I didn't mean to do it, Popsy. I just wanted to scare him, just a little bit. You should hear what he said to me. He said he didn't want me anymore. And I wanted to get even for what he did to you, Popsy. Popsy, where are you? I need you. Come help me, please! Where's my baby?"

She reached across the bed for the life–size life–like doll that she'd bought in the toy store in Oakham. It looked so much like a five-year old girl it was scary.

"Vera almost saw you, sweetie. But nobody saw you except Allan. Right? Right?" She laughed hysterically. "Scared him out of his bloody wits, didn't we?" The chilling laughter stopped as suddenly as it began. "Ohhhh, he almost hurt you, little one. If I hadn't pulled you back up into the tree in time you would be all gone. Poof! In a million pieces. Yes. I saved you. I did. That's okay, I know you love me."

Adele picked up a comb that lay on the lamp table next to the bed and combed the doll's mangled hair. "Look at what the mean old man's car did to you. Pulled out some of your hair. But, it'll be okay. Mama's going to fix it for you."

PART THREE

England and USA

50

It was a beautiful memorial service for Lily O'Neill. It was as if the entire Blackfoot Indian Nation were in attendance - Siksika, Peigan, Kainai, Blackfeet - all 16,000 of them.

The gathering stretched as far as Rachel could see across the snow-covered meadow near Browning, Montana, and the Blackfoot Indian Agency. Everyone wore heavy parkas or furry animal coats, shawls, and hats. Ceremonial dancing and music combined with bonfires and feasting made it an astounding celebratory event. Lily had been a prominent member of the tribal council and it was obvious she was well-loved by her people and other community members. She'd taught the Blackfoot reservation children for years. All the years that Rachel thought she was dead.

Rachel felt as if she was watching a panoramic movie stretched across the big Montana sky, rather than a festival of her own mother's life. It didn't feel real at all. It was surreal. A huge party for a superstar celebrity, not her own mother. This was a part of Lily she never knew. She regretted not being a part of Lily's very special world. Many times after she'd found her mother she had felt resentment towards her father because he had robbed her of 35 years of life with her mother.

Now for another brief moment, as she stood and gazed out at the faces in the crowd that had shared her mother's magnificent life, that old resentment crept into her heart as she witnessed immense love and respect for Lily's memory. But in the very next moment she quickly rejected the stabbing hurt because she'd forgiven her father. She knew she mustn't feel animosity or be judgmental, not only for her own well-being, but out of respect for Lily and her brilliant teachings.

As she gently touched her mother's face, she wondered in what direction her own life would have gone if she had been raised by Lily.

Would it have made a difference to have had this remarkable spiritual woman by my side as I grew from a child to a teen to a young woman? Would it have made a difference to have had her as my mentor, guide, and confidant? Just knowing her the past eight years has made a difference. But it wasn't fair, it wasn't enough.

"I need more, Mother. I need more." Rachel stroked Lily's cheek. She felt guilty that she hadn't visited her more often.

Why didn't I take the time to come here, to make sure she knew I loved her? Why didn't I come here to learn more about her while she was alive? But then how could I know our time together would be cut short?

As she gazed upon her dearly beloved mother lying on the deerskin pallet on a heavy oak table in the cocoon of a shelter, a cry escaped her lips. "Mama! I'll never see you again." She dropped her face into her hands and wept.

Although anguished beyond any level she'd ever known, Rachel was at the same time grateful she'd arrived in time to view her mother. The cremation was scheduled for later that afternoon.

She held Lily's cold lifeless hand while she scrutinized her smooth olive skin. Suddenly she felt an unmistakable electric current shoot from Lily's fingertips into hers. At first, she thought she imagined it, but then it jolted her. It felt like a warm illuminating transference. Again she just let it happen as she closed her eyes and remembered the day she had found her mother, here on the reservation. She remembered Lily's loving words in those first few hours they spent together and later that evening at her mountain cabin. It was as if Lily was repeating it all to her once again.

Rachel tried but couldn't stop the heartbreak that was overtaking her. It developed into a deep-throated wail, a wail that released all the pain of the years of isolation and loneliness she'd felt as a child and teenager without her mother - never feeling she belonged anywhere or to anyone. The tormented sounds tugged at the heartstrings of those within hearing distance, reminding them of their own sadness. But finally, all the weeping ended and there was no more.

She reached for her bag and grabbed another handful of tissues. She breathed deeply in exhaustion as she glanced around the room at the tokens of Lily's life, lovingly placed by friends and members of the tribe.

Against all odds, Lily had put herself through college while Rachel was a baby. After she'd been frightened off by Rachel's father, she had returned to the Blackfoot reservation where she spent the rest of her life serving her own people and fighting for their rights all the way to top government levels.

Flowers, plaques of honor and awards, along with framed photos were positioned on all the flat surfaces in the huge outdoor shelter. They were of Lily with presidents, governors, entertainers, writers, the less fortunate, and the sick. Crafts, art work and paintings by the children of the tribe were in abundance. The books of poetry Lily had written that were filled with her own drawings were standing in a display case. Rachel wondered how she could not have heard of Lily during any of those 35 years. True love was felt in this room. Rachel felt it. *This is legacy.* This is what her mother had meant when she'd asked Rachel if she had considered what her legacy would be.

Rachel squeezed her mother's hand and she placed her other hand on Lily's forehead. She closed her eyes prayerfully for a moment. Then she took a final look at her mother's glorious face and leaned to kiss her beautiful, frozen lips.

"I'll always love you, Mama."

227

51

After the funeral, Rachel spent several soul-searching days at Lily's cabin, tucked away high in the Montana mountains. She forced herself to go through her mother's belongings, to box the things that needed protection from the elements, and to place clothing in plastic bags to preserve them. She gave the potted plants and trees to the children on the reservation as remembrances of her mother.

Then she drove straight to Cambria, California, stopping only for food and short rest breaks. She needed to be with her stepmother, Lee Dearmore.

When she got there, she told Lee about Lily's memorial service, about the kudos and affection that had been displayed so flamboyantly and sincerely. She told her about how difficult it was at first to sift through her mother's things at the cabin. She explained how it had evolved to a sacred and enlightening experience, and how being there had given her added strength and peace.

They discussed and questioned what legacy she herself

could possibly leave behind, that could even begin to compare with her mother's. Lee told her it would make itself known to her. She just needed to remain open and receptive.

"I'm going to miss mother's conversations over the phone, her letters, and her emails, all her wonderful words of wisdom." Her eyes began watering up again.

"Oh honey, I'm so sorry." Lee leaned over and hugged her. "First your daddy, now your mama. It's heartbreakin', it is. But you still have both of them. When you want to feel near your daddy you can find him in his house in Brentwood. When you want to be near your mother, you can always go on up to the cabin. It must be pretty up there in Montana, is it? And you still have me, if that's any consolation." She patted Rachel on the shoulder and returned to the coffee pot.

"Oh, I know. I guess I'm just a bit depressed right now. I could go back to Montana this summer or in the fall, I guess. Sometime before the heavy snow. Maybe I'll go there to write a book. I don't know."

"Well, I'm just so happy you've come to visit me, honey, before you go back to England. I've missed you more than a bad shot misses a target."

Rachel laughed.

Lee kissed her on the top of her head and then poured a cup of coffee. "You know, I think of you all the time. I've even painted some pictures for you. They're at the gallery."

"For me? What are they? I can't wait to see them, Lee. In fact I want to see everything you've painted. But, please, sit back down with me. Tell me all about your life here in Cambria. It's your turn. Tell me all about you. Are you meeting people and selling lots of paintings?"

"Well, you know me, honey. I'm not really all that good at gettin' out there meetin' with people. If they come to see me in the gallery, that's okay. I can deal with that."

They continued to catch up on each other's lives for the rest of the morning, and then Lee took Rachel to her gallery in the West End of Cambria. She pointed out the Pewter Plough Playhouse, a community theatre where she told her she volunteered for box office duties occasionally.

"I'm so happy to hear you're doing that, Lee. Why don't you audition for a part? You'd be good onstage."

"Oh, honey. I could never do that. No, I could never do that, I'd get as tongue-tied as a mute. Believe me. I'm doing all I can do just sellin' the tickets and takin' the money."

"Well, I'm so happy you're involved in the community. It's such a lovely little town. I've always liked Cambria. I'll have to roam around while I'm here and see what's new." She stretched and said, "You know, I think I'm going to need to go back to the house pretty soon and get some sleep, if you don't mind. It's hard to keep my eyes open. It was a long trip."

"That's alright by me. Your room is all fixed up for you. I'll just lock up. It'll only take a minute. Wait, I almost forgot why we came down here. I want you to see the pictures I did for you. They're right here in the closet."

She opened a closet door and pulled out three canvases wrapped in cloth. "Now, you go sit over there so you can get the full effect."

The first one she unwrapped was of Rachel sitting beside her son Devin when he was three years old, as he rolled in the grass playing with a white furry kitten.

"Oh, that is so precious, Lee! I remember that photograph. You took it. It was at Shamel Park that time we stayed two weeks with you after I filed for divorce. We were hiding out, remember?"

"How could I forget? That man was plumb crazy, Rachel. I knew it from the get-go, when you brought him up here to meet me before you married him. I was glad you left him. He would have killed you eventually, I know he would. Abusers don't get better, honey, they get worser."

Rachel was always amused at Lee's unpretentious Midwestern drawl and her own brand of English grammar.

"Well, we don't have to worry about that anymore, do we? You know, Devin always loved to come here. Maybe he and Kellie could meet me here some holiday."

"Oh, honey. I'd love that. I haven't seen him in a coon's age. Yes, I'd sure love that."

"And I have to have that painting. I'll buy it from you."

"You can't buy somethin' that's already yours, Rachel. Now let's look at the next one." She removed the wrapping slowly.

Rachel's eyes opened wide in disbelief. It was a painting of a British sea port with tall ships docked near a group of white stone buildings. It was Charlestown. "How did you know about Charlestown? It is Charlestown, isn't it?"

"I don't know where in tarnation it is, honey. I only know how much you like the ocean and the old English villages, so I thought I'd paint one for you. I took it from a postcard I found in one of our antique stores. Do you like it?"

"Of course I like it. I love it! I can't believe it! I just visited Charlestown a few weeks ago. It's amazing, Lee. It really is." She stood and hugged her step-mother. "Oh, thank you so much. Now all I need is a house in Cornwall in which to hang these beautiful works of art."

"Wait now, sit back down, there's one more of 'em. Then we'll go back home."

She carefully removed the wrapping from the third and largest of the three paintings.

It was a remarkable painting of a family of swans on a pond in a lush garden. Rachel gasped and covered her face with her hands. She began crying and couldn't stop. Lee quickly leaned the painting against the wall and went to her.

"Oh, my lord! Now what have I gone and done. I'm so sorry, honey. Here, let me get you something." She hurried to the small restroom at the rear of her shop, not sure of what she was going after. Maybe a glass of water. Maybe a wet cloth. She was frantic.

Still sitting, Rachel looked up at the painting again and dabbed her eyes with the sleeve of her sweater when she saw Lee's confusion. She gave a happy laugh. "Lee, I'm all right. Really, I am. Come back. It was the shock, the surprise. It's just that my emotions are hovering just a micro-second above me."

Lee returned and squeezed Rachel's arms and kissed the top of her head.

"You couldn't have painted anything more touching, Lee. Lily gave me a book the last time I saw her. She'd done pen and

231

ink drawings of swans and their babies - hatching, feeding, and learning to fly. She had written poetry to go with the pictures. You just don't know what this means to me. Swans are special to me. Lily was a swan, you know."

52

He hoped like hell she was answering the phone. *Please, please, be there.* Ethan was frantic as he waited for Rachel to answer. She'd left all the numbers where she'd be staying in the States. The cabin in Montana, Lee's in Cambria, her place in Brentwood, and her son's in Denver. If she was on schedule, she'd be at Lee's home right now, probably still sleeping since it was only one in the afternoon in England. *Come on, come on, answer the phone!*

"Hello?"

"Hello, Lee. This is Ethan. Sorry to bother you. May I speak to Rachel, please? It's rather urgent . . . yes, please." He picked up his cup of tea as he stood near his desk, sighing and heaving his chest, shifting from one foot to the other, as if he needed to make a quick trip to the men's room.

"Ethan, do you know what time it is?"

"I'm sorry, Rachel, but I had to talk to you. I don't know what to do. It's all such a grand mess, it is. Adele has been arrested and they're holding her for observation in a psychiatric hospital."

"Why? What happened?" Rachel nodded *yes* to Lee who was standing by asking her if she wanted coffee.

"They found her wandering the streets in Skegness, of all places. She'd been there for days, evidently, in some filthy hotel. She was dirty and covered with sores and drunk out of her bloody mind. They say she was carrying a doll the size of a little girl and wouldn't let anyone near her. Kept screaming she didn't mean to kill him, she loved him, it wasn't her fault. Oh, what am I going to do, Rachel? She's been arrested for killing Allan!" He began to weep quietly with his hand over the receiver, not wanting Rachel to hear him. But she did.

"Ethan, listen to me. Do you hear me? Ethan?"

"Yes . . . I'm . . . listening."

"Okay, find the best attorney you can. Call Ian. He'll put you on to someone. Get the best. If she's truly out of her mind, there might be a chance. Do you believe she did it?"

"Yes. She says she did. Why would she do that, Rachel? I just don't understand it. Her own sister's husband. It just doesn't make any sense at all!"

"Did she say she cut the brake lines?" Rachel sat down at the kitchen table and took a swallow of coffee.

"I don't know what she's admitted to specifically. But the constable said the hair of the doll matches the fibers they found on the grill of his car. That would explain him thinking he hit a little girl. It's all so very horrible! I just can't believe she would go to such lengths, Rachel. Why would she do that? They found fibers on a tree branch over the road, proof she was up in the tree with the doll."

"Okay, but do they have proof she cut the brake lines? He wasn't the best liked person in the world, Ethan. Find out about that. Promise me you will?"

"Yes, yes, I will. It is possible someone else could have cut the brake lines. That would make that person the murderer, wouldn't it?" He perked up, feeling rejuvenated.

"Well, it's worth a try. As soon as you find out something more, call me back, okay?"

"I will, I will, Rachel. I always feel so much better after I talk to you. When are you coming home?"

She took a deep breath, hesitated, then answered, "Well, you know I have to meet with my agent in L.A first, and I also want to visit my son in Denver. You know that."

"Yes, I'm aware of that, but when will you be returning? You are, aren't you?"

She looked up at Lee for a moment, Lee nodded in understanding of what was being said. "I'll come back to England after I visit Devin, but I'll let you know before I do. In the meantime, keep me posted and stay calm. At least they're not on your case anymore. You have to look on the bright side. Right?"

He laughed, "Well, I guess you have a valid point. You always find something positive in everything. You know that, don't you? I think that's one of the reasons I love you so much." There was silence. "I do, you know." More silence. "Rachel, did you hear me? I said I love you."

Rachel's eyes were closed as she rested her forehead in her hand, "And I'm fond of you, too, Ethan. Hey, just keep hanging in there, okay? Everything's going to be all right."

"Yes, I feel like it is now. Bye." He hung up the phone abruptly as he had the habit of doing. He leaned against his desk and smiled. *She loves me.*

53

Rachel opened her eyes after a long nap to see moonbeams streaming through the window of her loft in Lee's lovely A-frame home in the pines. She had always loved coming here. She was thankful Lee wasn't the kind of person that had to have Rachel's company every waking moment. Lee would always go about her business leaving Rachel to make her own plans on how to fill her day.

After freshening up in the charming wall-papered, flower-filled bathroom, Rachel reached for her laptop to check her email messages. There were several - one from her agent, one from Devin, two from Pete, and one from Belinda. What a surprise, an email from Belinda? She opened it first.

It read – *Hello Rachel. I've waited a couple weeks before emailing you, didn't want to intrude upon your sorrow. I hope all is well with you and the pain has lessened. I empathize with you. When I lost my father, I thought I would never be happy again. But soon my mother more than filled his void and we are so very close today. I just don't know what I'll do when my mother goes. It's unfathomable. But it happens to all of us at one point or another. It's supposed to happen, I figure. Then we become that adored mother to someone. I guess I better get busy if I'm ever going to be a mother. Ha ha.*

Rachel laughed out loud. She was amazed at this woman. After all that had happened to her, she could still talk about having children.

She stood up and quickly ran downstairs to get a cup of coffee before reading the rest of Belinda's message. It looked like a lengthy one. This was quite surprising, considering they'd only just met the day before she left England for Montana. At any rate, Rachel's cup was empty and it was a habit to have a full cup of hot coffee nearby when she worked at the computer. *A bad habit.* She knew it contributed to the storage of cellulite on her body.

"Oh Rachel, honey. I didn't see you. Did you have a nice nap? " Lee rose from the chair where she'd been reading.

"Yes I did. It was the best sleep I've had in days. I just want to grab a cup of coffee, Lee, I'm checking my email. Seems I can't do it without a cup in my hand."

Lee laughed as she sat again. "Well, let me know when you're ready and I'll cook us some dinner."

"I'm taking you out to dinner, and don't try to talk me out of it. I'll be finished in a few minutes and then we'll go to the Brambles." She hurried back up the stairs to the loft.

Lee picked up the phone and called the Brambles to see if Dennis Dillow was bartending in the Pub. He was. She made reservations for dinner in the bar so he could be their waiter as well as bartender. She knew Rachel loved to talk to him about art and writing. He did pen and ink portraits and wrote short stories. Every time Rachel visited, she would always encourage him to put together a collection of his cleverly written short stories and publish them.

Rachel settled in front of the computer with her mug in hand and read more of Belinda's message.

"Since you've been away, Rachel, I've settled in quite well. We found a studio in Mousehole next door to Dudley's rock shop, with living quarters above it. It's perfect. So Paul returned

to London and arranged to have my belongings sent to me. My
mother and her friend drove my car down last weekend and took
the train back to London. We had a wonderful visit. My flat is
just about in order, and then I need to focus on the studio. It'll
be open to the public. They'll be able to watch me work, and I'll
have pieces for sale, of course. It's all so exciting. Dudley's
never around. I don't see how he can make a living. He's always
closed."*

Rachel chuckled as she read, thinking about Dudley. She
wondered if he had an email address. She'd ask Pete.

*"I hope you don't feel I'm out of line emailing you out-of-
the-blue like this. Pete gave me your email address. I found out
after you left that your mother was Blackfoot Indian. I couldn't
believe it. My rainbow stones were discovered by the Blackfoot.
Did you know that? It was a lucky charm to help them find
buffalo. It's Ammolite, a fossilized shellfish. Are you familiar
with it? I buy a lot of it from Canada near where your mother
lived in Montana, and Dudley says he thinks he can get it at a
better price for me. That would be nice of him. I'm working on a
very special piece right now, amidst all the chaos, believe it or
not.*

*"Well, I just wanted to touch base with you. I feel so
connected to you, Rachel. Maybe it's the Blackfoot Indian
connection, and then again maybe it's because of the horrid
experience we both had, I don't know. But I prefer to think it's
because we were destined to meet. Both such free spirits and
artistic souls. Have you had time to work on your book? Luv,
Belinda. P.S. Pete said to tell you hello, he misses you".*

Rachel sat staring at the screen. *I like that girl.*

True, they barely had time to get to know each other, but
when Belinda blurted out her brush with death as they drank
together at the Swordfish, Rachel was reeled in. Rachel was
drawn to people who had a story to tell, especially if they were
willing to tell it. She sensed a vulnerable side of Belinda, in spite
of the strong image she portrayed. Although, she had to be
strong to have survived such a horrendous attack, mentally,
emotionally, as well as physically. She suspected they were both
of the same ilk. She could very easily be friends with Belinda.

Such coincidences, Belinda's stone being connected with the Blackfoot nation, both of them being sexually assaulted, both acquainted with Paul Newland, and all three of them connected to Cornwall. It seemed destiny or whatever was in the mix, once again.

Cambria was beautiful at this time of year. Winter was just ending. Buds and bulbs were sprouting early. Rachel carried her digital camera over her shoulder on a hike to Moonstone Beach, which took about thirty minutes. Lee lived at the top of Huntington Drive on Park Hill overlooking the East-West Ranch down past a shore-lined row of upscale houses onto a magnificent panoramic view of the Pacific Ocean. Lee had been very fortunate when she bought her house those many years ago as it resulted in owning one of the best views in Cambria.

Again Rachel thought of how wonderful it was to breathe pure sea air. The only other smells were those of flora, fauna, and occasional chimney smoke. *Invigorating*. She walked slowly along the boardwalk on Moonstone Drive. It was a lovely walk and she greeted the cheerful people as they passed by, some with dogs, some with children.

At the northern end of the walk was Leffingwell Landing where she climbed over the faded redwood railings and crouched down to shoot views of the sandy cove below through a clump of winter flowers. *I could create a Cambria photo calendar. This could be February's photo. I can't believe tomorrow is the first of March already. It would be fun going to villages and towns, creating calendars for locals and tourists. A damn good idea! I could do that in England and sell them in Belinda's shop.* The day before she had purchased a small book written by Gayle Baker about Cambria's history. Evidently, Ms. Baker had written several town histories while traveling the California coastline. The booklet was more defined and more interesting than the usual tourist brochure of a town. The writer had told the story of the early settlers and carried it right up to the present, including photos of the historic families that were still in residence. *That's what Marazion and Charlestown need.* Rachel had been successful at finding the names of the people in early Charlestown, but hadn't had a chance to research them on the Internet since her trip to the Penzance Library.

She smiled as she thought of the past two weeks in Cambria. Lee spent every day at the gallery, deliberately giving Rachel all the privacy and quiet time that she needed to write. Lee ran the television at such a high volume when she was home, she knew it would break Rachel's train of thought. Lee's hearing aids weren't all that effective with the TV, it seemed. But Rachel had seen a hearing device advertised on the Internet that enabled a person to hear a TV without turning the sound up. So, she found a source locally and planned to surprise Lee with it as a parting gift.

Rachel cherished her visit with Lee because she'd come to realize that she'd been so caught up with her own life the past few years, had let relationships with her loved ones pass by unnoticed, just as the one with her mother had. How she'd wished she would have spent more time with Lily, which was one of the reasons she was determined to go to Denver and be with her son before returning to Britain. She also had some personal items of his grandmother's to give him. *One never knows when this life is finished. A scary thought.* Again she wondered what her legacy would be.

She shook the thoughts from her mind as she walked over to the grassy slope on the bluff above the tide pools, and stood where she could see the coastline of Moonstone Beach to the south. While thinking about Devin and Lee, she snapped the charming seaside motels and homes that were nestled in the trees at the top of the hills or on the slope down to the beach. It could almost be a British landscape if the motels were terraced four-story B&B's, and if the homes on the hill were of stone, brick and masonry. In Cambria, most dwellings were made of wood and stucco. But she noticed how slate roofs had become popular in the States now, more than in the past. Slate was a given in Britain. If it wasn't slate, it was tile or thatched.

Her mind wandered to wherever it wanted as she sat at one of the picnic tables near the artful Monterey Cypress trees. She closed her eyes and lifted her face towards the sun.

Ethan. She thought of what he'd said to her over the phone. That he loved her. She thought of how it would be if they were married. He was a kind man. *Too kind, maybe. No, there isn't such a thing as too kind.* But he was too permissible, especially with his family. He wouldn't give them an argument even if he disapproved of their activities and actions. Sure, he'd shut them out temporarily, but he'd always open the door again after a while. He was too easy. Rachel wondered how he continued to love them sometimes, considering all they had done and said about him, especially lately. But then, even though she and her son were at odds for years, Rachel still loved him dearly and would do anything in the world for him. So that must be how Ethan felt about his family.

He was even friendly with his ex-wife Nora and they'd been divorced several years. Nora had been married before, had left her first husband before she knew she was pregnant with Adele. She married Ethan when Adele was a year old. They were happy those first few years. But Ethan was a complete work-a-holic, which didn't set well with Nora at all. She wanted him to spend more time with the family, but he'd traveled continually in those days. And when he was at home, their personalities clashed terrifically. *Sounds a bit like Pete and his first wife. Maybe traveling husbands and stay at home wives don't mix.*

She thought how even today Ethan sped through life working-working-working and very rarely slowed down for personal time. That might be okay for Rachel because she too had a full schedule and many interests and usually didn't need constant attention and togetherness.

So there were things about Ethan that worked for Rachel, in spite of her impatience with some of his habits and mannerisms. *But everyone has offensive habits and mannerisms to someone.* She and Ethan hardly ever exchanged harsh words. But then again, she refused to be part of any heated conversations, so maybe that was why they didn't clash. She'd usually leave the room. It was her answer to any sign of confrontation. Just walk out.

Aside from that, if we were married would he be able to accept my free-spiritedness and encourage me in my own endeavors? Not that she needed encouragement. She'd given up all hope for that years ago. She'd learned to depend on herself for encouragement. *But it might be nice to have a nod of approval from time to time, from someone, other than my agent.*

So will Ethan be demanding and disgruntled when I announce I'm going off to Africa or to Russia or to China or to wherever? Could he endure my long absences? Could he accept my independence? How will he feel when I want to be alone at my mother's cabin in Montana or my father's Brentwood home or Lee's home? And how will he feel about my plans to live in Cornwall? What will he think about that?

No, it's not fair to expect him to give his blessings on my lifestyle. How could I dare ask him to understand, anyway? Then again, how much would I travel if I were married? The Internet supplies a tremendous amount of information, and although I prefer seeing first hand, most information can be gleaned from cyberspace. Two trips a year wouldn't be too much to ask, would it? One month every six months? That shouldn't be too much.

But what about the sex? He'll want it. Why shouldn't he? Why wouldn't any husband? That still was a problem for her, she had to admit. She knew that sex was a major contributor to a healthy marital climate.

Damn it! Why am I even thinking about marriage? I don't want to be married! Didn't I tell Pete I'm not going to marry Ethan?

Pete. Oh boy. How do I feel about Pete? She stood up and began walking back to the boardwalk.

Men! I was doing so well without them. She shook her head like a wet dog slinging water drops from his fur.

I've got to stay focused!

55

Rachel checked her email when she got back to the house. There was one from Pete, another from Belinda, one from her agent Anita, and one from Ethan.

Pete's said, *"Hello, Rachel. I think of you every day, and am looking forward to your return. Attached is a photo of a house in Newlyn, near where you specified, which appears to be what you are looking for. It's reasonably priced and has a view of the sea and sea port."*

Rachel was astounded at his writing. It didn't reflect his Liverpudlian accent at all. An Instant Messenger pop-up appeared on her screen. It was Pete. She answered.

"Hello, Pete. I'm just reading your email."

"It's good to see you, Rachel. Well, I mean, see your writing, in real time. How are you?"

"Wonderful. I just returned from a lovely walk and now I'm going to settle in and get some more writing done today."

"Then I won't keep you from it. I miss you, Rachel. Get on with the book. Ta ta."

"No, wait. I'm not in that big of a hurry. Tell me what you've been doing. Or is it in the email?"

"Yes, it's all in the email. You can read it there. When are you coming back to England?"

"After I visit my son in Denver. Then I'll come directly to Cornwall. Maybe five weeks from now? Something like that. Maybe sooner."

"Okay, I'll take you to dinner wherever you want. Oh, I forgot to mention in the email about the party on the Mount. Remember, we were going to go to it together?"

"Oh my God! I forgot all about that. Too much happening, you know."

"Yes, I know. And Margaret said to tell you hello and she hopes to see you when you return."

"Tell her, yes, I'm looking forward to that."

"I will. I really do miss you, Rachel. You've become a major part of my thoughts."

Rachel hesitated, reading his words over and over. "And I miss you, Pete. Every morning when I have my coffee I think of you at the Swordfish having coffee with Dudley and the rest. Tell them all hello for me, will you? I keep thinking of our trip to Eden and Marazion and Charlestown. Lovely memories. And funny thing, I feel like I've known you forever, Pete. Got to go now. I'll write more in an email, okay?"

"Yes, that'll be fine. Bye."

"Bye."

Rachel went for a cup of fresh coffee, figuring it would be ready by now. She'd made it when she returned from her walk. She hesitated a moment and gazed across the open fields to the sea, through the bay window, thinking about how previous lives were said to be connected with the present one. She knew from her studies and the conversations she'd had with the experts on the subject that the more she could remember from a past life and those around her then, the easier it would be to understand and live this life. She wasn't sure if she totally understood and believed in it, but she felt that because the relationship with Pete was so familiar and easy, it might mean they were very close in a past life and were possibly "twin" soulmates. There were two other kinds of soulmates as well - "companion" soulmates and "twin flame" soulmates.

She thought about how *companion* soulmates are people who you feel good to be around, they are helpful, encouraging, very positive, but are usually only in your life for a brief period. But if a bond is formed with a *companion* soulmate, they sometimes become a *twin* soulmate in a future life.

A *twin* soulmate is someone you've been close to in other lifetimes. When you meet this time around, you immediately feel comfortable and feel like you've known the person your entire lifetime. Actually, you're continuing the relationship from where you left off in the previous life. You already have a strong bond with this person, which lasts for years, if not the rest of your life. You're in tune with each other, and together you help each other grow and your friendship becomes stronger. If you have disagreements, you are able to understand each other's view and can get on with the friendship without it coming between you.

I think Ethan is a twin soulmate, too.

As she watched a sailboat make its way south out of sight, she thought about the *twin flame* soulmate, someone who is your one and only true soulmate. You've been special, loving and caring soulmates in many of your past lives together and there is a deep spiritual bond between you this time. Supposedly, your *twin flame* soulmate is always of the opposite sex. The others could be any sex.

So is Pete or Ethan my twin flame soulmate? And where does Paul fit into the equation? Or does he? She sighed deeply and went after her coffee, shaking her head in utter confusion.

56

On the last night of her stay in Cambria, it was Lee's turn to take Rachel to the Brambles for dinner before she was to leave. Dennis was working, which had to be a prerequisite of going there, of course. It was a bittersweet day for Rachel. She had come to love Cambria even more because of its quiet ambiance. Her relationship with Lee had grown more loving and stronger. If she hadn't believed that her providence was in England, she would have considered making a home among the pine-covered hills on the central California coastline.

Dennis had iced a bottle of champagne and it was waiting for them at their table as they entered the Brambles pub.

"Good evening, ladies. I'm ready for you, as you can see." He motioned to the corner table in front of the window seat.

"Oh, look what he's done, Lee. Dennis, you are the best. You really are. I'm going to miss you and our wonderful discussions."

He uncorked the champagne as he added, "Yes, I agree, it has been wonderful. I would only hope you'll be back very

248

soon."

"Or you could come to Cornwall for a visit. Why don't you do that? You and Christina come over for a holiday? I found a cottage in Newlyn. In fact, Pete found it for me. I've told you about Pete."

"Yes. You'll have to email me a photo of you and your cottage."

"I will. And I hope you'll send me a copy of your book of short stories when it's published. Or better yet, I'll buy it on the Internet." She lifted the glass of champagne he poured, waiting for Lee to lift hers. "Join us, Dennis, for a glass. A toast. Can you?"

"Yes, Dennis, that would be nice." Lee interjected.

"Of course I can."

He went behind the bar and got another champagne flute and poured himself a glass from a bottle that was already open behind the bar. They toasted the future success of Rachel's new life in Cornwall and the publishing of Dennis's new volume of short stories.

"And let's not forget to toast your new novel, Rachel," Lee added.

The night was a pleasant event. A few acquaintances of Lee's wandered in and joined the conversation. Lee was proud of Rachel and told everyone about her being an author and that she was on her way to live in England. Told them she had raised Rachel and that Rachel also was a talented painter, as well as a singer.

Rachel hadn't thought about singing or painting lately, but the comments reminded her that she wanted to start painting again as soon as she got settled into her new home.

She thought of the photo of the cottage that Pete had attached to his email. It had won her over. The three-bedroom, refurbished 19th century dwelling had a slate roof, instead of the thatched roof she'd dreamed of, but was nevertheless a most charming cottage with a beautiful garden, climbing rose vines and ivy front and back. It sat on top of a rise and from its windows, one could see the fishing docks as well as the expanse of the sea outside the Newlyn port. It was perfect. It had a view of the promenade, of Penzance, and of St. Michael's Mount. Pete knew just what she liked in spite of the short time they'd known each other, more proof to her that they might be twin soulmates.

She immediately made an offer on the property and it was accepted. The arrangements were made through her bank. It was in escrow and would be hers by the time she returned to England. She made the final decision to return directly to Newlyn and had not included Ethan in her plans thus far. She hadn't yet informed him about the house that she'd just purchased.

It was late and all the dinner patrons had left the dining room at the Brambles. Only two other people were in the bar area, across the room from Lee and Rachel.

"Well, Dennis, this is it. I'll be leaving early in the morning. Join us for one more drink?"

Dennis poured three more glasses of champagne from the second bottle that Rachel had ordered, that unbeknownst to her, was on the house. "It's been wonderful seeing you again, Rachel. And I think you're making the right decision. Your eyes light up when you talk about Cornwall. And it really isn't that far away in cyberspace."

She put her arm around Lee and held her glass high, "To the three of us. May all our dreams come true and may we know our hearts and listen to our souls."

"That's lovely, my dear." Lee gave Rachel a kiss on the cheek and her eyes glistened as she lifted her glass to her lips and drank the toast with Rachel and Dennis.

"It's getting a bit too emotional around here," Dennis said as he grinned in an effort to conceal that he was moved by the moment.

"Let's keep in touch, Dennis. You're very special to me, you know," Rachel responded.

"To Cornwall," he toasted.

57

That night when she returned to the loft to check her email before trying to sleep, Rachel found three emails waiting.

She opened the one from Pete first, which was her order of preference these days, and he said,

"Hello, my dearest Rachel. I am so happy you purchased the cottage. I'm happy for several reasons. One - it fulfills your dream of living in Cornwall. Two - now I know you'll be here for a long time. Three – we can have coffee together every morning and that's the best news for me.

Sarah is in London making arrangements to live with her mother while she finds a place to live. She's going back to university, which is something she's longed to do. Everyone should do and be who they are.

That is one of the most admirable features I've recognized in you. And I want you to know I'm here for you, Rachel, just as I know you would be for me.

Isn't it amazing how one can feel in such a short time? But I think we both know it's been more than a short time.

251

Email me when you reach your next destination. Have a safe trip as you travel from Cambria to Los Angeles, and know that my spirit is with your spirit.

Much love and affection . . . Pete B

Rachel smiled as she read his message again and again. There was so much to read in his words. Here was a recognition she'd never had or felt before. Yes, he was truly a twin soulmate.

She read Belinda's email next. *"Rachel, I have so much to tell you, but first . . . I am happy to hear you are coming back to Cornwall to live, and that you bought the house Pete told you about. I've seen it and it is absolutely gorgeous! I'm so excited. Now you can visit me in the studio every day.*

And I've another reason to be happy, Rachel. I'm going to have a baby! I'm pregnant! There's a sad part, however. It happened when I was raped. I haven't told Paul yet, but I will the next time he visits. I might have to have hospital care if it becomes dangerous, they say. But, I don't care. I know this baby is meant to be and I know he will survive. He's mine, all mine! Yes, he's a boy. I'm so so so so happy!!! Words do not describe how much. When are you coming home? Many Hugs from Belinda and Baby Jake. (I've already named him.)"

Rachel was spellbound. *Baby Jake. Belinda's having a baby.* She was overjoyed, but at the same time worried about her going the term without mishap.

She didn't feel like reading Ethan's email, so she signed off and decided to read it the next morning before she left for Los Angeles. She would answer Pete and Belinda at that time, too. She got ready for bed and fell asleep the minute her head hit the pillow and for once, she didn't dream.

58

Anita Schwaber was waiting for Rachel in her seventh floor office on Bundy and Wilshire in West L.A. She knew the drive from Rachel's Brentwood home was just ten minutes away, taking traffic into consideration, so she made lunch reservations for one o'clock. She figured that would be about right since signing the papers wouldn't take long. There'd been an option extension request on Rachel's first film script. Anita was so sure it would make it to the big screen, if not, then maybe a television movie. Either way, it would give Rachel a produced property and would give her more clout on subsequent projects. She'd been on Rachel's case to write the film script she'd promised the producer in London, but Rachel told her she wouldn't be writing it until she wrote a novel. The novel was more important to her at the moment, she said. She said it was a love story set in England and France.

Although it sounded interesting to Anita, she still hadn't seen an outline or even one page of the manuscript. Hopefully, Rachel would have something to show her today because Anita wanted to have something to pitch to a publisher.

Anita was one of the west coast's top agents. She even rivaled the larger entertainment companies that specialized in film and fiction. She'd begun her one-agent company six years before and had built up quite a reputation for selling her client's projects. A. J. Schwaber was known throughout the industry and throughout the world as A. J. – a first-class wheeler dealer.

Rachel had been one of her very first clients when A. J. was taking whoever she could get. They had to show promise, however. She wouldn't take an obviously bad writer, but all were first-time authors and screenwriters. At first, it was very difficult to get into the agent race, but Anita soon figured out the system and the timing and was galloping to the finish line as fast and professional as any of the thoroughbreds on the literary agent track.

"Hello? A. J.? Where are you?" Rachel stuck her head through the inner office doorway that led to A. J.'s private office.

"Come on in, Rachel. I'm on the phone." She was always glad to see her most promising client. She believed Rachel would be taking the industry by storm one of these days and she would be riding the current right along with her.

"There you are. How are you, Anita? I mean A. J. I just can't get used to calling you that."

"I don't mind. It's my name, isn't it? I use A. J. to throw the chauvinists off track. They don't know if I'm a man or a woman. It gets my foot in doors I wouldn't get in otherwise. I'm still Anita to you." She hung up the phone after no answer and stood up to hug Rachel. "How are you, girl? All rested and ready to get back to work?"

Rachel set her briefcase beside an arm chair, sighed deeply, and sat down. "Yes, I'm really into my book now. Have finished the first few scenes, oh I mean chapters. It's tough getting out of the screenwriting mode. I keep writing in the present, use all the "ing" words instead of the "ed" words. It's amusing at times. One paragraph will be in the present tense, another will be in past tense. But I'll get used to it. It's a whole new experience for me. And I love it. I actually enjoy it more than screenwriting."

"You're kidding? I wouldn't have thought that. I would have thought it'd be much more difficult and time-consuming."

"Well, it is. Maybe that's why I like it. It's more challenging. Anyway, don't ask me about the new screenplay, I haven't written it yet, and I'm not going to until I finish the book. Okay?" She got up to pour herself a cup of coffee that was warming on the credenza in front of the window.

Anita swiveled her chair to get up, "Would you rather have a glass of champagne? I have some on ice."

"No, no, no. This is fine. Too early for champagne. So, what's up with the extension? What's the delay?" she asked as she gazed out the 15th Floor window and took in the distant view of Santa Monica Bay. Sailboats were in abundance, their owners taking advantage of the sunshine and the cool offshore breeze.

"John says he's having trouble finding the Dorothy character. Every time he thinks he has someone, she gets a better offer and off she goes. And he's working on a tight budget, so that limits the choices. Independent filmmakers, you know how they are. But he wants to do the picture. He believes it's another *Thelma and Louise* with a good ending, one that the audience will love. Actually, I think it's a two-hour M.O.W. kicking off a weekly series."

"I agree. That's how I see it. I've even written the outline for ten one-hour episodes. Maybe he'd be interested. Ask him." She returned to the chair and pulled it up to Anita's desk. "Okay, where do I sign? And is he paying more for the extension? I'm buying a house, I could use the extra money."

"Of course he is. That's good business. Here's the check, take a look." She handed it to Rachel and grinned.

"Wow! I thought you said he was on a tight budget?"

They both laughed as Rachel signed where Anita indicated. Anita made copies, gave Rachel a set, and the two of them left the office to have lunch at the Pacific Dining Car in Santa Monica, one of Rachel's favorite haunts.

As they headed down the corridor towards the elevator, Paul Newland came through the doors of the offices of Triple R at the end of the hall. Rachel couldn't believe her eyes.

"Paul?" she said as she continued walking towards him.

"What are you doing here, Rachel?" He grinned from ear to ear as he gave her a big bear hug.

"It seems we keep asking each other that, don't we? What about you? Why are you in this building? I didn't know you were in L.A." She leaned back while perusing his handsome face and flowing blond hair.

"That's Triple R at the end of the hall. Our west coast office." He noticed Anita staring at him. "Oh, I'm sorry, Rachel and I are old friends from England. Sort of." He grinned at Rachel.

Rachel introduced them to each other and they chatted back and forth for a few minutes about why he was in L.A. and what she was doing there. He invited her to dinner later in the evening and she accepted.

59

At lunch, Anita grilled Rachel about the absolutely gorgeous man they had just encountered in the corridor near her office. "How did you meet Paul? Did you date him in England? Why hadn't you mentioned him in your emails? What are you going to wear to dinner tonight?" She fired a stream of questions at Rachel.

So Rachel told her all about their chance meeting on New Year's Eve, told her about seeing him outside the Ritz, about the thrilling kiss at Trafalgar, and how they saw each other again a few hours later and even ended up at the same movie the next day. She told her about struggling against contacting him because she was afraid of a relationship. She described the startling moment she met him again in Cornwall. "But by then, it was different," she said. "And now we're just friends."

Anita asked her about the decision she had made to live in Cornwall, about the house she'd purchased, and about her plans of settling there. "What about Ethan?"

"I'm not going to marry Ethan. He doesn't know it yet. I

257

want to tell him in person."

Then Rachel told her about Pete. About the feelings she was having and how she thought they might be soulmates of the highest order.

Anita said that she understood all about soulmates, believed in the premise, and had once been married to her soulmate. Or at least she thought he was until he slept with her best friend.

"Speaking of non-soulmates," Anita said as she looked over her glass at Rachel, "did you hear about your Senator creep?"

"My Senator creep?"

"That guy you told me about, Rachel. Oh, I'm sorry, he's Senator Rollings now. You probably didn't know that. He was just arraigned on rape charges and is going to be appearing in court a week from Monday."

Rachel sputtered her coffee and wiped her chin with her napkin. "Rape charges?

"Evidently there were several women who were going to testify. They had him cold. I'm surprised you haven't seen it on the news?"

"I haven't watched or read any news lately. So tell me, what's happening?"

"Well, now the victims aren't talking, the media says. And his people are saying it's nothing but a smear campaign against him to keep him out of the presidential race. He really hurt the last girl, they say. He cut her up pretty bad. I cringe when I think about it, but they say one of her nipples was sliced off. *Oh!* That just gives me the heebie jeebies! Can you imagine?"

"Yes, I can! And I hope they hang the bastard!" She took a deep breath and sat up straight in her chair, shifting uncomfortably. "So, what do they do now that the so-called victims aren't going to testify?"

"Well, they're saying on television that the D.A. is trying to build a case without them, but it doesn't look promising. The guy has surrounded himself with an army of people who all substantiate his alibis and cover for him. And his family is standing by him, of course. They had him though, until someone got to the victims. Now their lips are sealed. They haven't found one girl yet. She just totally disappeared. How's that for convenience?"

"Bullshit! That's what it is."

"I know. Even a friend of his last victim told the media that someone came to see her last week and scared her half out of her wits. Her friend's the one he mutilated. Of course, she immediately withdrew her statement. The guy has government covert operations experience, for God's sakes. He's dangerous!"

Rachel stared at the food on her plate. She'd lost her appetite. Suddenly, she called the waiter over and ordered a glass of champagne, then changed the order to a bottle.

"Rachel? What are you doing? A whole bottle? We'll have to cab it home for sure." Anita laughed as she excused herself and went to the ladies room.

That damn friggin' creep is going to get away with it again, and now he's worse. Rachel looked over at the bartender and the early afternoon alcoholics sitting on the stools. The place was filled with men, mostly middle-aged. She wondered as she looked them over what it was that made some men so cruel and evil. *What motivates a man to rape and mutilate and sometimes kill a woman? What snaps in his mind? Is he born that way? What kind of a person was he in a past life? If each life is to be a better one, a chance to learn and improve oneself, what must that horrible savage have done in his past life? Or would this be his first life? Some say you keep coming back until you get it right.*

She wondered if serial killers passed from one life to another as serial killers. *What if they never got it right? Maybe Jack the Ripper became the Boston Strangler in another life.* She took a healthy swig of the champagne that the waiter poured for her.

Well, this bastard's life is certainly going to fast-forward and he's moving out of this one into the next one if I have anything to do with it!

60

As Rachel drove Anita back to her office, she told her about Belinda. About what had happened to her in London and how Belinda had been afraid she'd never be able to have a baby which was what she wanted more than anything in the world. She told Anita specifics about the brutal attack and what the five men had done to her. She told her that Belinda was pregnant by one of the assailants. She relayed how she was thrilled she was going to have a son, but was afraid to tell Paul whom she loved very much.

Rachel told Anita that she was going to put away the friggin' bastard senator for all the Belindas and the Rachels and the whomevers of the world who are victims of such vile crimes against women. If it was the last thing she ever did, she was going to make it her own personal vendetta to put Rollings away.

"Rachel, I've never heard you talk like this. Are you alright?"

"You're damn right I am! I should have reported Rollings

when it happened to me. Maybe someone else would have stepped up then, since I'm sure I wasn't the only one. He might be living his life in jail right now. If by chance he killed or had that other girl killed, it wouldn't have happened if I had pressed charges over two years ago."

"You can't blame yourself for what he's done, Rachel. You did what you thought was right at the time. Never fear, he'll get his, you just wait and see." Anita gathered up her purse and jacket as they neared the building. "I'll get out on the corner. You don't have to pull into the parking structure."

"Okay."

"So, what are you going to do, Rachel?"

"I'm going home to call the D.A.'s office to tell them my story and offer myself as a witness - for Belinda, for me, and for all the rest of them."

Anita saw a wild and determined look in Rachel's eyes that she had never seen in the five years they'd known each other. It worried her. "Honey, take it easy, will you? And you have a good time tonight with Paul, okay? Call me tomorrow."

"I will, and please don't worry, Anita. I'm okay. I'm just pissed. Don't worry." She stopped the car and Anita blew her a kiss as she hurried up the sidewalk.

Rachel pulled away from the curb and headed towards Brentwood to her father's mansion. Her mansion. It was an English Tudor style house of course, her father having been British. It had an expansive front garden through which a cobbled-stone driveway wound through the trees and shrubs to the ivy-covered, stone entrance to the house, then wound back out to the street - a circular drive-way of sorts, an *irregular* circular driveway. Rachel pulled just past the entryway, and parked. She hadn't used her father's car while she was there. She preferred to drive the rental that she'd driven from Montana to Cambria and now to L.A. She would turn it in at the airport when she left for Denver to see her son. But now, she wasn't certain when that would be. Things had suddenly changed.

61

The early evening weather was beautiful in Marina del Rey. The marina was one of the largest pleasure boat harbors in the U.S. Paul and Rachel were seated on the heated patio of the Cheesecake Factory where the sun cast an orange glow above them on its way to the other side of the world. A waiter lit oil lamps and chatted with strollers passing by along the walkway on the beachfront.

"I love this place, Paul. Brings back mostly good memories," she remarked as she leaned back in her chair and looked out across the docks and boat slips. She listened to the lines slap against the masts, making harmonious soothing sounds. When she lived in the marina, she'd go for coffee at the Washington Street coffee shops near the pier and would walk out on the pier and breathe in the fresh salty air.

"It reminds me of Cornwall . . . the smell, the boats, the gulls." Paul lifted a glass of mineral water to his lips and glanced at Rachel. *She seems to be on edge tonight.* He hoped it wasn't because of him. He didn't want to make her feel uncomfortable.

"Is something bothering you, Rachel?"

She turned towards him and thought a moment before answering. "No, not really. I've just got a lot on my mind. Sorry. So, did you see Belinda before coming to the U.S.?"

His eyes brightened. "No, I wasn't able to get away, but I try to visit her every other weekend. She's doing such wonderful pieces, you know. I believe she's going to be a huge success in Mousehole. She makes friends easily and people are finding her studio and actually buying. It makes me want to chuck it all and open my own studio."

"You do sculptures?"

"No, I paint. That is, I used to paint. Haven't done anything the past couple years. Triple R takes all my time." He poured himself another glass of water.

"Isn't it strange how we've come from a most tantalizing kiss on New Year's Eve to this?" She smiled at him, noticing a flush in his cheeks.

"I—well, I—I don't know what to say, Rachel. At the time—the way you looked, the mood. Well, what I mean is—"

"No need for explanation, Paul. Really. I understand, I do. It was the moment. I felt something when I saw you at the Ritz, I was drawn to you too. I didn't know what it was at the time. Of course, you're only the handsomest man I've ever seen in my life."

They both laughed. Paul blushed even brighter.

"And you know it doesn't matter, because I believe we were destined to meet again and again until we struck up this friendship. There's a reason for it, I'm sure. And now you have Belinda and I have Pete. Although I still feel very much connected to you."

"That's the word. You're right. Connected. I mean why else do we continue to bump into each other, if it's not meant to be?"

"I know. But can it be possible we can be close friends after the way we began? I mean—"

"Of course we can. Of course. For me, it was more of a physical attraction at first, but now it's— well, it's more like a close friend attraction, if there is such a thing."

"Evidently, there is." She laughed. "And it's just as well

because Belinda really does need you. Besides, I'm more of a loner. I don't need anybody. Do you love her?"

Paul sat up straight, blinked his eyes at Rachel's bluntness, then he nodded his head slowly, as the realization set in. "Yes, I think I do love Belinda. As a matter of fact, I know I do." He leaned forward, set his glass on the table, and ran his hands through his hair, "Rachel, I believe I do. You know I hadn't admitted it to myself until this very instant. Why haven't I realized that 'till now? I adore her. She is all I think of. She makes me want to quit Triple R and create right along beside her. Damn! I don't know what to do. She's so fragile, still."

"She's stronger than you think she is, Paul. You haven't told her you love her?"

"Of course not, I just realized it myself. And no, I couldn't. It might frighten her. I mean . . . because I'm a man. But don't take me wrong, I would never impose myself on her. I still have some issues of my own that I'm working on anyway."

"Issues?"

"Someday I'll tell you about the skeletons in my closet. In any event, considering what has happened to Belinda, I think it's too soon to even ask for a relationship."

"It isn't too soon to hear that someone loves and cares enough for you to want to spend the rest of his life with you. Especially when she loves you just as much." She waited for him to grasp what she had just said.

"What are you saying, Rachel? What has she told you? I know she emails you every day. Tell me." He was like a little boy waiting to hear that he could go to the candy store and have all the candy he wanted.

"She loves you to death, pardon the expression. She adores you and has been afraid to tell you. Afraid it would frighten you away. You're both having the same thoughts about each other. And there's something else, Paul. And you've got to promise me that you'll not let on you know. I feel it's in her best interest that I tell you. You're going to know very soon anyway." She leaned and placed her hand on his forearm.

Amidst his glee, he looked quizzically at Rachel. "What is it? You're scaring me."

"She's pregnant, Paul. By one of the rapists."

His facial expression morphed into a deep frown. He closed his eyes tightly, clenched his lips. It remained that way for a few moments before he covered his face with his hands and rested his elbows on the table.

At first, Rachel thought she heard someone crying elsewhere on the patio. Then it became obvious it was Paul.

He was trying to muffle his sobs, embarrassed that he was crying, couldn't control his emotions. His tear-drenched eyes peered over his hands at Rachel in desperation.

She slipped a napkin to him, gripping his shoulder at the same time.

He took the napkin, but turned away to hide his pain.

Rachel felt helpless, not knowing what to do. So she just sat and waited, sipping her drink, feeling so sad for him.

Finally he hoarsely whispered, "Why? Why didn't she tell me? I don't understand. The doctors said she couldn't do this. That it would be dangerous for her to have a baby."

"Yes, she told me. And she also told me this baby is going to live because he might be the only child she'll ever have. She's not going to let anyone take him away from her, Paul. She's already named him Jake."

His eyes widened and brightened a little. "Jake? That was my twin brother's name. I told Belinda the story. He died at birth. She named him Jake? I've got to call her." He excitedly began to get up to go to a phone.

Rachel grabbed his arm, "Paul, no. Wait a minute. Wait until you can talk to her without giving away how much you know. It must come from her, do you understand? She must be the one to tell you everything I've told you. Let her do that. Please." She held on to his arm a moment longer, and then let go.

"You're right. But all I want to do right now is hold her and tell her how much I love her and that I want to be the father of her child. Our little Jake."

62

Rachel spent the next few days tying up loose ends on the option deal and in the D.A.'s office. She'd given a deposition and had been put on the witness list for the prosecution. The trial was to begin the middle of April, so she decided she would go to Denver and spend some time with her son in the meantime. She planned to leave on Thursday.

Tuesday morning, she called Paul at his hotel and told him she'd be leaving for Denver in two days. He asked that she join him that evening for dinner and maybe a movie. He was missing Belinda and England and felt closer to both of them when he was with Rachel. She understood exactly because she felt the same way. He was to pick her up at 6:30. They'd go to an early movie, then have dinner in Malibu at the Moonraker.

At dinner, Rachel told Paul of her plans to testify against Senator Rollings. The news media had accelerated their reporting on the upcoming case and the missing girl who was now thought to be dead. Investigative reporters for the tabloid magazines were actually linking the missing girl to Rollings and

266

some rather incriminating tidbits had been surfacing. The major newspapers had mentioned that a previous victim was coming forward to testify. They hadn't used her name, but Rachel knew it was available to anyone who wanted to know, including Creep Rollings. That bothered her.

"I think it's a good idea that you're going to Denver until the trial begins. I understand the guy's a real prick. Goes to any lengths to cover his tracks."

"Yes, and believe me I'm eager to get out of town for a while. I've had the most uneasy feeling the past two days, like I'm being watched. It's probably just the D.A.'s office. I shouldn't be paranoid." She looked around the restaurant and noticed only two other couples in the room. Out the window the night waves were lapping at the spotlighted beach. "He's not going to frighten me into not talking, though. No way. But I'm not foolish. I know firsthand the guy is dangerous."

Paul glanced around the room and felt an unnerving panic. "Has he tried to get in touch with you, Rachel?"

"No, it isn't that. I don't believe he'd do that. He'd send a henchman. That's more his style. I feel an evil presence, though, lately."

After dinner they strolled on the moonlit beach while talking about England and life in Cornwall.

Paul told her that he was going to quit Triple R and move to Cornwall and open a studio. He was planning to tell Belinda in his next email. He said Belinda hadn't mentioned the baby yet.

Rachel reassured him that she would because it was impossible to keep a pregnancy secret for very long.

They talked about Rachel's book, about her new house in Newlyn, about Pete and Ethan. Then he took her home to Brentwood.

63

Rachel handed Paul a pint of her favorite chocolate chip ice cream which she bought by the case. Both of them ate right out of the individual containers. When he had finished, he gave her a hug and a kiss and went on his way.

What a lovely way to end an evening! I really do like Paul. She washed the spoons and made a cup of tea to take into the bath with her. One of the mainstay luxuries in her life was a frothy, oil bath. To her, if she had only a computer, a large bath tub, plenty of chocolate chip ice cream and marshmallow crème, she'd be happy. But she needed to cut down on the ice cream and marshmallow crème because she knew they were culprits to her recent weight gain. She decided when she returned to Cornwall, she was going to get back on her *Fit For Life* regimen. And if she had to have a man to round out her new life, well, Pete would do nicely. She giggled at her simple list of happiness needs.

She ran the water into the sunken marble, oversized tub and squirted baby oil under the stream of water spraying from the gold faucet.

Her father had spared no expense remodeling this house. He used marble in the bathrooms, granite countertops in the kitchen, and other stone materials throughout. He loved stonework. The immense fireplace in the family room was made of white rock with huge semi-precious stones worked into a design. Polished Malachite, Amethyst, Onyx, Aquamarine, Peridot, Tourmaline and a host of others created a beautiful work of art in the rock wall. A bit over the top, but nevertheless extraordinary. Rachel wished Belinda could see it. She'd love it. She must take a picture of it and email it to her, although a photograph wouldn't do it justice.

She reflected on the evening while undressing. Paul had been charming as usual. *What a sweet man he is, and a perfect match for Belinda.* It made her happy to witness real love between two people. *Yes, they are definitely soulmates. Twin flame soulmates.*

She dangled her hand in the water. *Whoops, too hot!* She opened up the cold water tap a bit more and sloshed the water with her hand, cooling it off.

"Okay, a couple sprays of perfume and that ought to do it!"

She climbed in and as she laid her head back on the inflated pillow that was suctioned against the tub, she heard a noise coming from the bedroom. *What is that?*

Before she could react or think about it any further, a black-clad, masked figure appeared in the doorway holding a bungee cord.

She grabbed her towel to her chest as half of it sank in the water. "What do you want? Get out of here!"

The man moved closer. She began throwing perfume bottles and whatever else she could grab while she tried to scramble out of the tub. There wasn't a phone in the bathroom, so she couldn't call for help even if she could. Her only option was to stun him with something and escape.

He dodged the barrage of plants, glass, and porcelain that was coming at him and grabbed her arm, quickly wrapping the cord around one wrist and then capturing the other, pulling it behind her back and binding her wrists together. She screamed, kicked, and squirmed with all her might. But he had accomplished what he came to do. She was disarmed and naked.

Holding her tightly with his arms while she spat at him and continued to kick, bite, and butt him with her head, he took her into the bedroom and tied her to a heavy wooden desk chair. It was solid and she wouldn't be able to move it. He gagged her with one of her own scarves. Then he stood over her and watched her angry, frightened eyes, as he slowly removed his mask.

She was instantly terrified beyond anything she could have ever imagined.

"Hello, Rachel. Isn't this nice? Here we are again. Did you think I would let you testify against me? Huh? Are you that stupid?"

Rachel couldn't move. She couldn't think. She was frozen and scared out of her wits. This man was crazy. His countenance and the look in his eyes were of the devil. *He is the devil!* She was sure of it.

"So, my little friend. What little pleasures shall we have tonight? I've learned some new tricks since our last encounter. Oh yes." He punched her in the face with his gloved fist.

"How's that? You like that? Huh?" He did it again. "No, you're not going to talk to anyone about me ever again."

Blood was spurting from her nose and busted lips. She felt like all her teeth were knocked loose, but couldn't tell if any had been knocked out because of the gag. The pain from the two punches was beyond belief.

He reached down and grabbed her breasts with such force she screamed into her gag.

"Oh yes, I remember these babies. This time I'm going to add a little bit of you to my collection of souvenirs. You should see my collection, Rachel. Lots of little nipples. In assorted colors. Did you know they come in all colors? For instance, yours are beige. A nice pale pink beige." He drooled as he hysterically laughed. A psychotic laugh. He pulled a knife from his pocket and opened it.

"This is a very special knife. I always carry it with me because I never know when I might want to use it, you see." He swiped it across her breast. "It's cool and smooth like silk, do you agree?"

Rachel flinched when the cold steel touched her. "You asshole!" She screamed at him, but of course he heard only a muffled screeching noise.

"No, no, no. No more talking for you my little peach tree." He flicked her nipples with the dull edge of the knife. "After I take my keepsakes, I'm going to fuck you to death, my angel. Then I have a very loyal, hand-picked crew just a phone call away, who will come in here, dispose of your body, and remove any trace of my DNA. No one will ever know what became of you."

64

Paul pulled up in front of the hotel and waited for the valet. He'd stopped at a drug store for some toiletries before returning to his hotel and had also bought more chocolate chip ice cream. The pint he had at Rachel's had only teased his palate, so he decided to pick up another pint for a midnight snack. Since he stopped drinking and using he found he craved sweets more than usual.

The parking valet reached for a ladies purse from the floor of the passenger side. "Sir, do you want to take this with you?"

"Oh damn." It was Rachel's. He took back the key from the valet and drove back to Rachel's house. His hotel was in Westwood, so it was just a few minutes to her Brentwood home.

When he parked in front of Rachel's rental car, he noticed a car further up in the shadows on the exit half of the circular driveway. *That's strange. That car wasn't here before. And it's parked near the street, not where a visitor would park.*

"No!" he screamed as he bolted from the car and ran to the front door. The door was locked. He rang the doorbell, but remembered it hadn't been working when he had picked up

Rachel earlier. He pounded on the door. No response. Then he ran around to the French doors that led from the side garden patio into the den. Locked. *The solarium.* Good choice, it was unlocked. He slipped into the house through the solarium and listened.

A chilling inhuman cackle echoed down the dark stairs. He quickly climbed the first flight and hurried down the carpeted corridor carefully looking through doorways. Another pair of French doors opened into what was most likely the master bedroom at the end of the corridor. Candles flickered and shadows were reflected on a section of the wall he could see from his vantage point. He stopped and listened. If she has someone in her bedroom, a lover maybe, he wouldn't want to barge in like a fool. But he couldn't imagine her being with someone who sounded like that.

"Yes, my dear Rachel. I know you want to talk to all those stupid little people about me. You want to tell them what I did to you, don't you? Baby, nobody rats on Miles Rollings. Nobody! You understand me?"

Rollings! Paul was frantic. The strange sounds he heard had to be coming from Rachel. She must be gagged. *God, no!* His glances searched the hall quickly for a weapon. He didn't know if Rollings had a gun or a knife or what, but he knew he had to act now.

His mind raced. He was in good physical shape, worked out with weights at the gym every day, but since his heart attack he wasn't as agile as he had once been. Although he had an age advantage over the senator, he didn't know what to expect in a scuffle. He knew karate.

Rachel screamed.

Too late to strategize, and he didn't care what the odds were. He stepped into the room and stood staring at a horrific scene. Rachel was naked and tied to a chair. Her nose and mouth bled profusely and her face was swollen. Rollings had pulled and stretched one of her nipples out from her body and appeared be about to cut it off.

"You bastard!" he yelled as he flew through the air and tackled Rollings like the USC football star he once had been. In lightening moves, he grabbed and twisted the creep's wrist, causing the knife to drop. Then he threw him to the floor. Before Rollings had a chance to react, Paul pinned him with his knees, and furiously punched and beat the holy shit out of him. He wasn't sure how long he had been in that violent mode, but at one point he realized Rollings was unconscious, his face bloodied beyond recognition.

Paul's face was blood red too, not only from the specks of blood that had flown from Rollings, but from a deep flush that had begun to spread from his neck up over his face. He sat back on his heels, breathed heavily, felt a sharp pain in his chest and felt dizzy. Rachel got his attention and he managed to cut her bindings just before he fainted.

65

Paul woke up in intensive care with Rachel at his side.

"Welcome back," she said lovingly when he opened his eyes and smiled at her. "You almost left me, but I couldn't have anything happen to my hero, now could I?"

"Are you all right?" he whispered.

"Of course I am, just a few cuts and bruises, a bit sore, a disfigured face, but nothing to worry about. You're the man of the hour, you know. You rescued the damsel in distress. It's all over the news."

"I'm in the news?"

"Yes, and I've talked to Belinda, she's on her way. Left Southampton this morning. She'll be here tonight. She'll be staying with me in Brentwood."

"Will you be safe?"

"Oh, yes. Cops are all over the place."

Paul beamed. "Well, then it was all worth it. I mean, I don't mean—"

"I know what you mean. You don't have to explain."

"I'm going to ask Belinda to marry me as soon as she gets here."

"Oh Paul, I'm so happy. I feel like you're the brother and she's the sister I never had."

"But that would be incest. How about I'm your brother, she's your best friend?"

They both giggled and squeezed each other's hands like siblings.

"What about Rollings?"

"It's over. He is never going to plant his feet on free soil again. I hope he gets the gas chamber. Does California have the death penalty?"

"I don't know."

"Well, when he goes to court, which will most likely be in a year or so they tell me, I'll be there, you can bet your life on it. That snake is dead in the water. I'm going to make sure of it."

"Have you heard from Pete?"

"Yes, he called this morning. He saw it on CNN and Belinda called him before she left. He wanted to come, but I told him to stay put. I'm going to visit my son in Denver for a couple days after the law finishes with me, and then I'm cutting the trip short and going home to Cornwall. Can you believe we both have such wonderful people who love us? He told me this morning, Paul, that he loves me. "

"What did you say?" Paul winced as he tried to sit up.

"He stopped me before I could say anything. Said he just wanted to tell me how he was feeling and that we have plenty of time to explore our feelings when I come home. I'm glad because I didn't know what to say. I think I love him, but I'm not sure. I adore him to bits, but I don't know if that's what love is. Is it?" She frowned as she looked Paul straight in the eyes waiting for an experienced answer.

"Rachel, all I know is that I can't fathom living without Belinda. Honest, I'm totally lost without her. Can't focus, can't think. I never thought I would ever feel this way about a woman and we've never had sex. That's the strangest part. If you only knew. It's been awful, Rachel, being away from her. If you hadn't been here, I would have wrapped it up and gone back before now. But I'm glad I didn't, as it turned out."

Rachel's eyes shimmered. "It was supposed to happen this way." She patted his arm as he continued.

"Anyway, I just want to make her happy by giving her everything in my power to give and to raise our little Jake to be like his mother, a gentle, caring, loving human being. I think that's how you feel when you're in love." He reached for Rachel's hand. "You'll know when it hits you."

"Hey, no more hitting," she said as she rubbed her jaw. They both laughed.

66

Belinda's eyes expressed the high regard she had for Rachel as they parted in the corridor outside Paul's hospital room.

"I'll be waiting in the lobby," Rachel promised, "take your time."

"Thank you," Belinda whispered as she opened the door slowly, not knowing what to expect, and fearful of what she was about to see. Rachel told her that he was out of danger and that she shouldn't be discouraged or put off by all the tubes and equipment surrounding Paul.

But that hadn't been warning enough, she began crying the moment she saw him. She couldn't prevent it any more than she could ever stop caring for the man lying before her. She moved slowly, her hands cupped over her mouth, not wanting to wake him as she choked back the tears. *Oh, my precious Paul.*

She stood near the bed looking at all the lines running in and out of his body, one from his side it appeared, one into his nose, one from somewhere else which she couldn't determine, one into his arm, too many to count. There was a heart monitor, a blood pressure monitor, and countless other monitors. It was a huge reminder of when they'd both been in hospitals not so long ago, only this time he looked worse. He'd told her then that the doctors said he wouldn't survive another one. But he did. She touched his hand. *Please, don't die. I need you.*

At her touch, Paul opened his eyes ready to be defensive, thinking it was the nurse who would wake him from his dreams of Belinda only to force him to move his arms and legs again.

"Belinda?"

"Yes, I just got here. How do you feel?"

"Now that you're here, I feel like a million bucks. Come closer." He lifted his hands to pull her closer and said, "The doc said that kisses mend the heart quickly. Shall we go for the second one of many to follow?"

Her lips pressed gently against his, tasting and savoring the love. They both felt warmness flow from her body to his, and back to hers again.

If nothing more ever happens between us, physically, this will be enough for me, Paul honestly felt. "Will you marry me, Belinda?"

Belinda stiffened and pulled back.

"What's the matter?" He held on to her tightly.

She turned her head away for a moment and took a deep breath. With tears filling her eyes, she grasped his arms. Their eyes locked. "Paul, there's something I must tell you."

"Then, tell me."

"I'm, I'm—oh, this is so hard for me. I'm afraid you'll hate me, that you won't want me anymore."

"Nothing could ever make that happen, Belinda. There is nothing that could ever change how I feel about you. You understand that, don't you?"

"It's so difficult—"

"Well, I'm going to break a promise and give you a bit of help here. Okay? Other than the fact that I love you with all my heart and can't live without you, we need to get married so our baby Jake will be legal and will have a mother and father who will love and adore him forever and raise him to be an artistic warm human being like his mother."

Belinda was paralyzed with mixed emotions. *Rachel must have told him. How could she? But he loves me. He loves me! He knew about Jake before he asked me to marry him.* Coming to her senses, she excitedly, but carefully, kissed Paul all over his face as they both giggled and caressed each other, until calmness overcame them.

"You know, I've never told you my big dark secret, from before you, other than the drug and alcohol addictions. I need to do that."

"There is nothing more you need to tell me, Paul. I love you with all my heart and I know you love me, and that's enough for me. Whatever was before me, can remain there." She kissed him once more on the lips and managed to find enough room to climb up and lie next to him. With her arm across his chest, she snuggled as close as she could.

Paul clung to her as if his life depended on it. His quivering chin nuzzled her golden hair, his eyes were moist with happiness, and his heart felt like it was exploding with gratefulness for this beloved blessing from God.

I promise I will never harm this angel.

67

The flight to Denver was practically empty, which made it easy to spread her things out on the seat next to her and do some writing. Rachel thought mostly of the moment when she would be settled into the cottage in Cornwall. Then she could seriously concentrate on finishing her book.

My God, she wrote in her pocket notebook. *What an eventful year so far! Ha! That's an understatement if ever there was one.*

She decided to read the rather lengthy email from Ethan she'd printed out that morning and stuck in her purse. She hadn't the time to read it before she left.

"*My dearest Rachel,*

I've just read about the terrible thing that has happened to you. I've called your cell phone and your home phone. No answer. I don't know how to reach you otherwise, although I know you are not harmed, according to the media. Please advise."

Rachel smiled at the phrase, "*please advise.*" *True to form.*

"*I am worried about you, however, when I should be giving*

all my attention to Adele. She's been sent to a facility in Wales, a mental institution, and I feel I need to go there for a few days to give her support. It doesn't look good, Rachel. She has lost touch with the outside world.

As it turns out, the brake lines were cut by one of our shop mechanics, thinking he was doing the right thing by stopping Allan from sabotaging the company. He's been charged with manslaughter as has Adele although neither knew the other had such plans. It's all so very upsetting. I need you here to help me get through this. Can you understand?"

Can I understand? She shook her head as if to wipe out the words she just read. It was interesting that he was more concerned about himself and Adele than what she'd just gone through. *Sure, Ethan is a kind and caring man. I know that. Of course he's worried about his daughter. And he knows I'm unharmed. At least physically. So, what's the matter with me? So what's so wrong with him saying he needs me? He probably does.* She didn't know why she was suddenly a bit perturbed at him.

She continued to read, *"If you will please cut your trip short, I'll meet you in London and you can go with me to Wales."*

She stopped reading. He's so different than Pete. Night and day. She couldn't read any more. She leaned her head back against the seat, and shut her eyes.

As the plane landed, she freshened up her makeup, wanting to look her best for her son. A few slight bruises remained under her eyes, but she'd managed to hide them with foundation. It gave the impression she'd had a sleepless night.

In the terminal, Devin and Kellie were first in line, waving and grinning, calling out to her.

Seeing her son triggered the most unexpected deluge of emotion she'd ever experienced. It seemed as if every emotion she'd ever had in her entire life, good and bad, began to pour from her soul. She couldn't stop crying. Devin held her tight.

"Mom, it's okay. It's okay." He'd been so worried about his mother and had been terribly upset that he couldn't go to her in L.A. because of the constraints of his job. But now, she was here and he could see she was okay. That's all he needed. He glanced over Rachel's shoulder at Kellie who was wiping her eyes and sharing his love for his mother. He reached for her and drew her into the warm huddle.

Kellie rubbed and patted Rachel's back as she felt the pain and tragedy her mother-in-law must be feeling. First the death of her father, then her mother, and now the assault on her life was too much. She wondered how much more this extraordinary woman could take.

After a few heart wrenching moments, all three took deep breaths, stepped back, and began to laugh at each other.

"We're nothing but a bunch of crybabies. Hey, shit happens!" Devin wiped his eyes as his signature comment broke them up even more and they were soon on an even keel, excitedly chatting as they made their way through the crowded terminal.

They spent two extraordinary days together. Devin had planned every minute of it. Kellie and he had taken off work to be with his mom.

Devin was a superintendent with a major construction firm. He'd worked his way up the ranks in just five short years after coming out of a twenty-year alcoholic stupor. Kellie had been loving and supportive of him, but it hadn't been easy. She had made it perfectly clear from the beginning that she would leave him if he didn't stop drinking. So he stopped. Just like that. Not only for Kellie, but for himself. He realized the time had come and there wouldn't be any more chances for him. He'd been on a spiral that could only end in early death, a death that was one of the worst to experience. When he was told how tragic it was when hopeless alcoholics were found dead in a pool of their own blood, because they bleed from every orifice, the result of organs bursting, that got his attention.

Rachel had tried to help Devin countless times, but her own life was too unstable and chaotic in itself. It made it difficult to lead the way or be a perfect example to her son. Actually, she had always felt she was the perfect example of what not to do. So, he had to learn on his own. Now, she was so proud of him, even boasted about his becoming sober over night, which was the exact truth. It had been touch and go those first couple weeks when he quit. Devin suffered withdrawal and had been deathly sick. But Kellie stuck by him and he made it. A wonderful woman and a wonderful man. Two more soulmates. Rachel was grateful that Kellie had come into her son's life.

"Hey, Mom!" Devin entered the kitchen where Rachel was making another pot of coffee. "Let's take a ride up to Vail this afternoon. We'll go to dinner at that lodge that has a piano bar. Remember? For your last night here, you can sing for your supper." He giggled.

"Oh, Devin, I don't need to sing. We can go someplace closer, we don't have to go that far. I haven't sung in a long time."

"Nope. I'm taking you to Vail. You like it there, and that's where we're going."

She was tickled at Devin's uncanny resemblance to her father Neal, in actions, words, and looks. She noticed that he had become so sure of himself. And decisive. She'd never really thought about the similarities before. But then Devin definitely had been influenced by Neal as he grew up.

"You sound just like Daddy. You know that?"

Kellie came through the doorway. "So, what's the latest plan?"

Devin poured his mother and Kellie a cup of fresh coffee and told Kellie the change in plans. Kellie thought it was a good idea. She loved Vail too. Devin delighted in making his women happy.

Rachel felt a new closeness to her son as he stood there watching her smile. She realized just how much she loved him. It didn't matter what had happened over the years between them. Theirs was a prime example of unconditional love.

Thoughts of Ethan immediately surged through her mind as she sipped her coffee. *I shouldn't be so hard on Ethan. He loves his family too.*

Then she thought of Pete and his daughter. She would wager that Pete felt the same way about his daughter, the same as Ethan felt about his daughters, same as she felt about Devin. She was glad she had come to Denver.

68

Rachel's plane was due to land at Birmingham International any moment now. It had been circling for quite some time. Backed up departures and landings had delayed the landing, but it didn't matter to Rachel. Soon she would be in Cornwall to start a new life.

She'd contacted Ethan and asked him to meet her at the Birmingham airport. She had a three-hour layover there before she was to board another plane for Newquay where Pete would be waiting for her. She wasn't looking forward to this stop, but the next one she was.

She'd chosen Birmingham because it was more convenient for Ethan and would be on his way to Wales if that was still his plan. He said that it was, when they talked on the phone. He was disappointed when she said she wouldn't be traveling with him, but was happy at least he'd be able to see her before she went on to Newlyn. She still hadn't told him about the cottage. She still hadn't told him about not wanting to marry him. This was going to be one of the most difficult conversations she would ever

285

have. She wished it didn't have to take place, but knew it wasn't humane to keep him dangling any longer.

Rachel spied him right off as she came down the corridor into the terminal. He waved, grinning from ear to ear. He reminded her of her son who was in the same position just four days ago. *How can I hurt this man?* But she had to tell him, it wasn't fair to either of them.

They hugged and Ethan kissed her on the cheek as he led her to a fashionable restaurant not far from the gate.

He ordered champagne and a combination starter.

"And for you, madam?" the server asked.

"Nothing, thank you," Rachel replied.

"Did you eat on the plane?"

"Uh, no. I'm just not hungry, have a bit of a tummy upset. Sorry," she lied. She planned to have dinner with Pete in Newquay.

"That'll be it, then," Ethan told the waiter. "So, are you happy to be back in England? I expect you are."

"Oh yes. You can't imagine. But I enjoyed visiting Lee and Devin and Kellie. Highlights of the trip, you know, visits that were long overdue. And of course, Lily's funeral was the most beautiful I've ever seen."

There was a moment of silence as Ethan ate the bread that had just been served and Rachel sipped water. It was as if her brush with death hadn't happened. It wasn't even mentioned.

"Are you going straight on to see Adele tonight?"

"No, I've decided to stay in Birmingham 'til tomorrow. Actually this is working out perfectly. I have an appointment with a client in the morning and then I'll be off to Wales. Are you sure you wouldn't like to join me?"

"I can't, Ethan." *Now's the time, tell him!* "Ethan, there's something I need to tell you. And I don't want you to take it the wrong way. I mean, I don't want to hurt you. It's just that—well, it's just that I can't marry you. Please try to understand. Please."

He leaned back in his chair, more of a collapse, actually. "Go on."

"It isn't you. It's me. It's just that I don't want to be married right now. I don't want to have to consider someone else's feelings, to be accommodating, to have to report to anyone about my comings and goings. There's so much I want to do, Ethan, and so many places I want to see. I need a clear vision. I can't do it and be married. Not to mention that I want to be positive that I truly love the man I marry. I'm not saying it won't be you, I'm not. I'm just saying I don't want you to wait for me. It isn't fair to either of us."

She breathed deeply. *There, I've said it.* She questioned her choice of words, however. She hoped she wasn't still leading him on. It sounded like she might be. But then how could she say anything other than what she said when she wasn't exactly sure how she felt anyway. She was fond of Ethan. There was no question about that. She hadn't forgotten about how they seemed to fit so naturally and sensually New Year's Eve. It was very confusing to her how she could have felt as she did and now not want to be with him. Especially since she felt they might be soulmates. *Maybe I have to go off and deal with other issues before we can ever be together. It's possible. And that's exactly where I'm going to leave it. At least I broke the engagement. Didn't I?*

"Are you breaking our engagement, Rachel?"

"You read my mind, I wasn't sure if I was clear enough on that point. Yes, Ethan, I am. I'm so sorry." She felt the emotion building.

He quickly reacted to her emotion and knelt before her, and put his arms around her.

She leaned into his shoulder and whispered, "Please forgive me. I'm so sorry."

Taking her hand, he replied, "Rachel, it isn't that either of us must forgive the other. I understand your hesitancy. And I'm not certain of it all myself at the moment." He moved back to his chair, still holding her hand.

She gently removed her hand from his and wiped her eyes.

He continued speaking as the waiter brought the starter and opened the champagne. "Now, all of a sudden, I've got a family once again to contend with and believe me, it looks as if it's going to be a very time-consuming possibility. And with the possibility of new contracts, which I hadn't mentioned to you yet, Elton is managing everything for me. And I'm going to be running helter skelter all over the world, selling, it seems. So you have your agenda and I have mine. I do understand. You needn't feel sad. If we're meant to be together, one day it will happen. Do you agree?" He forced a smile as he reached across the table and gently wiped her tears and then his own with the cloth napkin.

She couldn't say a word and didn't try.

There was nothing left to say.

69

Pete had not left her side since he picked Rachel up at the Newquay airport. When he stood at the end of the ramp waiting for her to disembark, he held a bouquet of roses which made Rachel emit a single chuckle. The roses were a stark contrast to his tattooed, rough exterior.

Rachel lost no time when she stepped off the plane. She ran to him and flung herself into his arms. They had their very first heavy-duty all-consuming series of passionate kisses. Applause from the people in the terminal brought them back to earth. They quickly grabbed Rachel's bags and hurried from the terminal, playfully teasing each other on the way to Pete's car. A good thirty minutes of kissing, caressing, and touching ensued in the car. They couldn't get enough of each other and it seemed impossible to drive anywhere because neither of them wanted to stop.

Finally, they laughed at their situation and decided they must pull themselves together and move on. But, it had not been easy for Pete to keep his hands on the steering wheel and it'd been difficult for Rachel to think of anything else.

Through dinner, their continual amorous behavior had prompted a few glances and comments from fellow diners. They tried to tone down their obvious immersion in each other. All in all it had been a fantastic evening and neither of them wanted it to end. They'd spent the entire night talking, first in the restaurant until the place closed, then in the car until they approached Newlyn.

The sun rose and the fresh rays bounced off the cottages on the hill just ahead of them. Rachel knew exactly which one it was the moment she saw it. It was out of a fairytale, a storybook house. The photo Pete had sent her didn't do it justice, didn't even come close to it.

"Oh, Pete! I love it! It's exactly what I wanted. How could you know?" She leaned over and kissed his cheek, careful not to disturb his driving. The cobbled road up the hill was a narrow one, almost an alleyway, and inattention by a driver could possibly cause one to lose a neighbor or two. She appraised her new neighborhood with pleasure. Flowers were in abundance in gardens and window boxes. Vines and climbing roses covered rock fences and walls. Sea gulls squawked and flew overhead. Some perched on buildings and watched over their young. She saw the fishing boats in the harbour. *Yes, this is home.*

"Oh, Pete! It has a gate with a lovely heart on it. Did you do that?"

"Nah, it came wi' the house. Notice the name?"

All the houses and cottages had names, like the Jasmine Cottage, the rental where she had been staying. There was the Bluebird, the Rosebud, the Seagull, and dozens of other meaningful names to the owners. This one was Heart's Nest.

"That is so perfect."

Pete opened the car door for her. He unlatched the gate to Heart's Nest and waited as Rachel walked along the fence touching and smelling the flowers. Finally, glowing with pride and anticipation, she stepped into her very own front garden.

Rose trees lined the stone pathway that wound through the grass around to the front of the cottage. The roses were blooming in all colors. Ivy covered the sides of the cottage and around the diamond-paned windows. Wisteria and jasmine had eagerly climbed the walls and crept above the entrance and along the top of the windows. There were beds of tulips, iris, and daffodils, purple and yellow daisies. A white wrought-iron table and chairs with an intricate heart pattern sat on the grass under a huge flowering tree near the edge of the cliff.

Pete bounded across the lawn and sprawled in one of the chairs, grinning from ear to ear. "This is a gift from me, luv."

"You're going to make me cry." She turned and inserted the key in the lock, opened the door, and instantly stepped back, mouth gaping in awe. There in the entry way, displayed on a pedestal, was Belinda's newest creation in its entire splendor. A luminous family of swans, a life-size white swan spreading her wings over three cygnets and a black swan standing nonchalantly to the side. Rachel was overcome to the point of dizziness. The beauty of the piece and the excitement of the moment were too much for her.

Pete caught her as her legs buckled and she actually fainted. He lifted her in his arms and carried her over the threshold to the bedroom.

When Rachel awoke, she was in Pete's arms. Rays of sunlight and the aroma of fresh flowers drifted through the open windows. Pete's love-laden eyes gazed into hers.

"What happened to me?"

"In Tuscany, dee 'uv a name for it, luv. Dee call it Stendhal's Syndrome because de 19th century French novelist is said ter 'uv been de fairst ta write about de dizzy'n disorientation some tourists experience whun dee encounter masterpieces o' de Italian Renaissance. I would wager Belinda will be cheddered at yer reaction." He touched her nose with the tip of his and she noticed the sparkle of his white teeth as he grinned before following up the nose rubbing with a light peck on her lips.

"Cheddered?"

"Thrilled."

"Oh."

He kissed her again. And again. Not another word was spoken. He kissed her neck, her shoulders, gently opened her sweater and nuzzled the space above and between her breasts. Rachel brought his face back up to hers, kissed his eyes, his eyebrows, his nose, his mouth again. And for the rest of the morning, they pleasured each other and became as one. In spirit and in flesh.

70

Rachel awoke with a start.

"Are yew alright?"

"I just had another dream," she replied and looked out the car window to get her bearings. She didn't know how long she'd been dozing.

"Tell me about it," Pete encouraged, as he signaled for a right turn.

"Well, I was sitting inside a coach. Not a bus, but a horse-drawn fancy coach with a coachman sitting on top."

"Now, that defo piques me interest."

"Defo?"

"Certainly."

"Oh. Well, I looked down and saw that I wore a light green velvet dress with layers of crinolines underneath, and a dark green velvet cloak wrapped around me. I had curly red hair that tumbled to my shoulders in ringlets. I heard a man tell the coachman to take us to Charlestown. Can you believe that? And then he stepped up through the door and sat next to me. He was a

293

stately gentleman. Wore blue wool breeches with black leather patent boots, white linen ruffled shirt, a tailored matching blue jacket with tails, and he laid a navy blue velvet-collared wool cloak across the seat on the opposite side of the coach."

"Yew defo 'uv a way o' remember'n the details, luv. Did yew recognize 'im?

"No, his face was hidden in the night shadows. But he held my hand and then reached into his pocket. He pulled out a ring and placed it on my finger. It was the same as the ring in my other dream, a huge blue sapphire surrounded by pearls. So he must have been the one who gave it to me."

She didn't tell Pete the rest of the dream. She'd dreamt she was excited and thrilled. She had felt a tremendous feeling of love for the man. When she had reached up to draw him to her, the instant before their lips had met, his face came into full view in the moonlight beaming through the coach window. *It was Ethan!*

She craved her notebook, wanting to jot the details down before she forgot them. Margaret had been working with her in interpreting her dreams–specifically, the one reoccurring dream with the rowboat that had left Newlyn, against the tide. They'd also discussed the one where she had seen herself in period clothing with the same Sapphire ring, disembarking at Marazion. Margaret recommended writing the dreams down immediately upon waking. *Oh, why didn't I bring my notebook?*

Pete read her thoughts and reached into the glove compartment and pulled out a small notebook and pen.

She kissed him on the cheek and quickly wrote notes describing everything in detail before she would forget it.

"I think this might have something to do with that collection we're going to see today," she said as she closed the notebook.

"Who is this git we're visit'n?"

"Margaret says he's a lord and an ancestor of a family stemming from one of the nine original inhabitants of Charlestown. Her mother knew the man and wrote about him in one of her journals."

Margaret and Rachel had formed a special bond that summer. They discussed metaphysical and spiritual subjects, just as Rachel had with her mother Lily. It was almost as if Lily was kept alive through their alliance. But that wasn't the only thing that drew Rachel to Margaret; they had become very good friends. Margaret and her prince of a husband, Felipe, were now part of Rachel's close-knit circle of friends which included Pete, Paul, Belinda, and Dudley. They managed to get together several times a month.

Rachel never had a support group like this, never felt she needed friends, hadn't wanted them before now. She hadn't wanted to open herself to anyone, didn't want anyone privy to her thoughts and desires. She'd always been a loner and preferred it that way. Besides, she'd always felt that she couldn't trust anybody. She'd spent a lifetime of being manipulated and fooled by others, or being rejected, or being abused in one way or another.

But now, after reaping the short-lived care and guidance of Lily she had been able to finally break through the self-inflicted subterfuge and had begun to embrace life and the people around her with the trusting innocence of a child. She marveled how just in the past few months she'd made such giant strides and had been able to cultivate genuine friendships in a manner she'd never before experienced.

"E'yer we are." Pete stopped the car and switched off the ignition. "Ay you ready?"

"I'm ready. I've got a good feeling about this, Pete. I really do."

Pete hurried around to the passenger side and opened her door, reaching for her hand at the same time.

"Then let's get on wi' it, luv."

The grey stone manor house loomed before them. They walked up the granite steps to the first landing, then up the next set of steps that lead through an arbor-like entrance. Two huge timber doors immediately opened upon their approach. A butler appeared, standing before them.

"Ms. O'Neill, I presume?"

"Yes, I am."

"Come along, please."

They entered a huge marble foyer with stairways leading

upwards on either side. A magnificent chandelier floated from the center of a fresco dome above them.

"Wow! I didn't expect this." Rachel held on to Pete, tightly squeezing his hand.

"I must say ay didn't expect it ta be this elegant myself."

"Please step into the library. Lord Evans will join you shortly." The butler motioned to a doorway leading off to the left.

They entered and found a warm, inviting room with overstuffed furniture, and bookshelf-lined walls. Rachel walked over to the French doors that opened to a view of the fabulous garden. Rachel was curious and stepped out onto the veranda. A sudden gust of wind surrounded her, giving her a chill, but before she turned to reenter the room, she felt compelled to look to the left and down over the railing. There she saw the most beautiful mossy pond, filled with blooming lily pads and a beautiful white swan.

"I've been here before, Pete!" she exclaimed. "I saw this in a dream. I really did."

Pete hurried to her side to see what she was talking about and noticed she was shivering.

"You've got a chill, luv. Back you go." He drew her away from the veranda back into the library.

As Rachel let herself be led to one of the floral chintz sofas, she ran her hand along the back of it and commented as she sat, "Not what one would expect from a stuffy old lord."

"Why not?" a voice asked from behind them.

Lord Evans stood in the doorway, trim and tan. A handsome grin had spread across his face, looking not at all like he'd lived 92 years on this earth, which he had. He wore gray slacks with a light blue, pullover, V-necked, cashmere sweater covering a navy blue, open collared shirt and a yellow silk cravat.

Rachel stood immediately and faced him. "Oh, I'm so sorry. I didn't mean–I mean I didn't know–"

"Uh, that's quite all right. Quite all right." He reacted with obvious surprise when Rachel faced him. It appeared he was awestruck, unable to find words. Finally, he managed to gain his composure, although a bit shaky. "Uh, come along . . . sit, sit."

He motioned them to sit on the sofa, which faced another sofa with an ornate Louis XIV cocktail table between them. He never once took his eyes off Rachel.

"Uh, Charles will serve tea and coffee. Whichever you prefer. You see I'm not at all the stuffy old lord as some might suppose. I do allow my guests a choice."

Pete immediately took up the conversation, realizing Rachel's embarrassment and the awkwardness that hovered in the air due to Lord Evans's stares and seemingly obsession with Rachel.

"You delightfully sprise us, M'lord. We didn't know what to expect. This is quite an 'oner, be'n in your presence," Pete said.

Rachel chimed in. "Yes, thank you so much for inviting us."

"Quite all right. Yes. Uh, I understand you are interested in viewing my collection because you believe you might have a Charlestown ancestor? Is that correct?"

"Well, yes, I mean– well, to tell you the truth, and I hope I won't offend your graciousness. It's either that or maybe I was one of the original people of Charlestown, or as you might say, connected to one. Not necessarily as an ancestor. And then again maybe so. I mean—I know this is a bit confusing. You see, I'm actually thinking I lived here before, in a previous life."

Lord Evans raised an eyebrow as he stared even closer at Rachel. "Surely not?"

"Yes, yes. I know everyone doesn't believe in reincarnation. I'm not sure I do, really. It's just that I—I just—well—"

Pete jumped into the dialogue, "She 'as dreams, you see. Dreams 'uv things that couldn't be known to 'er unless she wuz there inna past lifetime. This is what she's so curious about, M'lord. The events in 'er dreams, connect'n wi' them. Investigat'n 'er deep feelings about places in Cornwall and the people she's met. She isn't dewlally wack. She's sincere. And she's a writer."

The Lord laughed. "Dewlally wack? I haven't heard those words in years. No, she doesn't appear to be crazy. In fact, I find you rather charming, Ms. O'Neill. A writer, you say?"

Charles entered carrying a tray of tea and coffee, followed

by a young girl carrying a plate of newly baked cinnamon bread.

They continued to have a friendly visit while drinking the hot brew and relishing the delicious cinnamon bread. Lord Evans told them about his family and Charlestown in the old days. He gave the impression of being captivated by Rachel as he hung on her every word.

Pete noticed the Lord's behavior towards Rachel. *If 'ay didn't know any better, 'ay'd suspect he is 'itt'n on me Rachel.*

After they finished their drinks, Lord Evans stood and invited them to follow him. He climbed one of the set of stairs in the foyer and then continued down a long corridor which led to a narrow, steep winding stairwell. At the top, there was another set of rooms. As they entered the first room, a life-size portrait of a young woman faced them on the wall above a carved, marble fireplace mantle.

Pete exclaimed aloud, "Me God, it's yer spittun image, Rachel!"

Rachel didn't move. She couldn't believe her eyes.

"I'm sure you noticed that I was a bit shaken when I first saw you, Ms. O'Neill. I apologize, but this is the reason. Meet Jane Bolton Rashleigh, who married a cousin of Charles Rashleigh who built this seaport, also namesake of Rashleigh Arms. Jane was my father's aunt by marriage, lived in this very house after my father died. I was just a child then, but I remember her very well. She lived until she was 98. Aunt Janie, I used to call her. The similarity to you is astonishing! Extraordinary!"

"Rachel, look on her finger! Pete pulled her towards the painting, pointing to Jane's hand that was resting on her lap.

It was unmistakable! The ring on Jane Rashleigh's finger was the ring in Rachel's dreams, the one she'd sketched for Pete and Margaret.

She gasped and appeared to be ready to faint.

"Oh no, e'yer we bowl again," Pete exclaimed, as he caught her.

"Please, place her on the sofa." Lord Evans motioned to the settee.

But Rachel was conscious, she wouldn't have it. "I'm fine,"

she said as she moved on shaky legs to the portrait.

Pete was doubtful of her stability and held on to her arm.

Rachel reached out to touch the painting, almost as if it were alive. "It's uncanny. Everything is just like my dream, the dress, the hair, the ring."

Lord Evans glanced back and forth between Rachel and the painting, astounded with the similarity. "Uncanny, indeed." He gently shook his head to dispel the trance. "I have Jane's diaries. Shall I fetch them?"

"Ay think dat would be a grand idea," Pete grinned widely, his eyes sparkling, as he answered for Rachel.

Lord Evans left the room. Pete put his arm around Rachel as they both gawked at the face in the painting.

"This proves it, doesn't it? That I lived in Cornwall in a past life? I was Jane Rashleigh."

"Aye!"

Lord Evans returned, carrying two worn slim volumes.

"Here we are. You may have a read with your tea, if you wish. I have a few matters to attend to, so please ring the bell when you're finished. Is that all right?"

Rachel held the precious diaries close to her. "Oh, yes. Thank you. We'll just sit right here and look through them. Thank you so much."

"Then if you'll excuse me, ta ta. Have a good read."

Pete sat with Rachel on the sofa and took one of the diaries from her lap. Rachel curled up into the fluffy, chintz pillows and entered Jane Rashleigh's world.

A few minutes later Pete broke the silence. "She's tellin' about de proposal in de coach, Rachel. Juss as yew dreamt it. It's all e'yer. Rite e'yer. Look."

Rachel took the diary he held and read the passages about the engagement. She read on. "It says here that they spent the first New Year's Eve after they were married in London. Rashleigh owned a house in Leicester Square. That explains why I felt so comfortable there, Pete. I could feel the familiarity."

"You're shiverin', Rachel."

She welcomed his chivalry as he placed his jacket around her shoulders. She hoped it would stop the involuntary shaking.

"Thank you. I shake like this when I'm excited about something. It should stop soon. I hope."

Jane Bolton Rashleigh had written in her diary about being a school teacher before she became a Rashleigh. She had written about living in Newlyn and teaching the children in the village below St. Micheal's Mount. She'd go by row boat several mornings a week to the small village at the base of the Mount where the children would be cheerfully waiting for her. It had been on the village grounds where she had met young Rashleigh. They had fallen in love at first sight and on occasion had met in Marazion for a meal. It had been on a trip to Charlestown with Sir Rashleigh, that she had accepted his proposal.

"I don't know what to do with all of this, Pete. What do I do?" she tearfully reacted.

"Yew live this loife know'n dat yew lived one before and that you'll live anuvver afti this one. You'll discover that what yew once thought wuz important is not. You'll find mean'n ter this loife by learn'n about yer past lives, so don't worry yer pretty little barnet, it'll come ter yew.

71

Paul and Belinda married in June. It was a divine wedding. They made arrangements with the Abbotsbury Swannery in Dorset to hold the ceremony on the property, at the very spot they'd fallen in love with a family of swans.

The cygnets were still hatching in June, so it was an absolute joy to be surrounded by the beauty of the ducklings and their protective mothers.

Pete and Rachel arrived with Margaret and Felipe. Dudley was there, too. Belinda's mother Beatrice and her friends rounded out the wedding party. It was a small gathering, a perfect wedding.

Belinda wore a vintage, fluffy, white chiffon gown trimmed with lace and a head adornment of white feathers that wound around a band of rainbow stones that she'd fashioned. A gossamer veil fell from the band to the hem of her dress. She was spectacular and stunning and appeared to be right out of a ballet production of Swan Lake. Onlookers took a multitude of photos, in fact it was suggested she be on the promotional brochures for the swannery.

Rachel cried all through the ceremony while Pete held her close. Seeing Belinda's beaming face had been enough to make anyone react with gushing emotion. At one point, Dudley had turned away to discreetly dab his nose and eyes and Pete had reached to place a hand on his shoulder. A bright smile had brightened Dudley's moistened face when he had seen the wetness in Pete's eyes, too. Such big sentimental saps! They grinned at each other.

Three months later Belinda gave birth to an orange-haired, beautiful baby boy. Although it was fearful there might be serious complications the last two weeks, Mother and son did splendidly, and so did Paul. He was ecstatic. No one could ever possibly be as happy as those two lovebirds were, although Rachel came close when Belinda and Paul asked her to be Baby Jake's godmother.

The marvelous pink house on the hill, where Paul and Belinda had stayed their first two weeks in Cornwall, now belonged to them. Belinda couldn't believe it! What a palace it was! She'd never lived in anything as large and grand. Paul had worked out a reasonable purchase deal with his friend who had inherited the wondrous house. With their unique individual brands of creativity, they had turned it into an artistic showplace with a spacious nursery for Baby Jake.

They'd also converted the upstairs portion of the studio in Mousehole into a working gallery for Paul. They spent joyous days working in their studios with Baby Jake nearby in a bassinet, where he was constantly being coddled by none other than Dudley Mayfield.

Dudley's behavior was mind-boggling. He brought gifts daily to Baby Jake, toys and books that were obviously too advanced for a newborn. But he explained that Jake would use them very soon because he was such a bright child. So he would sit and read to him, while Belinda was busy with customers and Paul worked in his upstairs studio. They had cut an illegal doorway between Dudley's shop and theirs, which made it much more convenient all the way around. When Dudley was out, they'd watch his shop, when they were out, he'd watch theirs.

The proud parents, too, were inundated with gifts from Dudley. He gave them beautiful geodes, in all sizes, sliced in half, to expose quartz crystals, amethysts, and calcites for exhibit in their lovely home. They had quite a wall display of them, mixed with an assortment of Belinda's prized rainbow rocks.

Everyone was amazed at Dudley's exuberance and newfound interest. It was as if he had never held or seen a child before. He was enthralled with Baby Jake, his only godson. Lately, he was drinking less, spending more time in his own shop selling to the tourists, and visiting with the neighboring Newlands. He was actually enjoying life. His visits during the day to the Swordfish had dwindled down to Mondays only, when he would close the shop. He reserved that day to do his laundry, shopping, errands, and to drop in on Pete at the Swordfish for a cup or two of coffee and maybe a pint to toast his godson Jake.

72

"Move in with me, Pete. I have a lovely home to share. You were the one to find it for me anyway. You like it, don't you?"

"O cose, ay do, luv. But, it's yer space. Yew need yer space, don't yew?" He had just poured a glass of champagne for the two of them at the Swordfish.

It was nearly closing time and Rachel had been talking to the locals for the past couple hours. Some nights, she enjoyed being there with Pete, watching him in his element. She had wanted to ask him to live with her for a couple of weeks now, but had put it off. She wanted to give it some more thought. So she made the on-the-spot decision to ask right at that very moment, while she had the nerve.

"It's not like you'll be crowded, it's bigger than the living space you have upstairs here at the pub. Come live with me. No strings. She reached for the glass he handed her while she watched his grinning eyes. "You want to. I can see it in your eyes."

"Aw, we ay be'n dead perceptive ternight, ay we?" He leaned across the bar and kissed her nose. "Alright. Nah strings."

So he rented out his apartment, and moved in with her. Then he hired a manager for the Swordfish to handle some of the day to day operations of the pub. Since Sarah had left and Rachel had come into his life, his whole world of interests had shifted.

Then on one of his regular visits to The Eden Project, he had approached a worker and asked him about his job and about the project and ended up going into the personnel office to inquire about future employment opportunities. He had gone in on a whim, hadn't thought it would hurt to inquire, but there had happened to be an opening and they had offered him a job which he accepted on the spot.

So every week, he spent three days at the Eden Project, working in the domed gardens as well as the exposed-to-the-elements sections. He had learned about various soils and climates indigenous to the native plants of all regions of the world, which was how Eden was laid out.

Pete was thoroughly consumed by a desire to learn more and had crossed over into the mineral and mining education program as well. Never had anything fascinated him more. This was what he wanted, to be a part of this amazing global center, preferably in the post-mining regeneration department. There he felt at home. There he belonged.

It was inevitable that he would be selected to give tours to the eager visitors who arrived every day to see this eighth wonder of the world. His verbosity and sense of humor, apparent excitement, and earnest interest in what he was doing made him a likely candidate to guide and educate others. So after a full day of working in the gardens, in the early evening he would guide a group through the complex, just one group, before returning to his room to study all night. He had rented a hotel room nearby for two nights each week and would return home to Rachel the remainder of the week. But he felt the time would come when he would be spending more time in Eden.

In the meantime Rachel had made several trips to Charlestown to visit Lord Evans. She'd found peace in reading Jane Rashleigh's diaries.

Lord Evans was a step-son of a Rashleigh, not a Rashleigh

by name or bloodline, but connected through his own mother who'd married into the family after his father died. He hadn't wanted to lend Jane's diaries for Rachel to take off the premises, and whether that was the real reason or that he just wanted her company, she had obliged. He was a charming man, and she grew to be very fond of him. As for him, she felt he was reliving his days with his Aunt Janie through her, which suited her just fine.

She still wondered about Ethan's face being that of Rashleigh in her dream. *Was he Rashleigh? Could he be her flame soulmate after all?* If he was, maybe the reason they'd parted was that she still needed to find her way to a legacy and needed to become that which she was destined to become. Maybe it was because he had to resolve some of his own issues as well, before they were to come together again.

It made it easier for Rachel, thinking this way. The guilt she'd felt was tremendous, she knew she hurt him badly. She hadn't been able to shake the anxiety over it. He had called wanting to visit her in Newlyn, but when she told him about Pete and that he was living with her, he gracefully withdrew his request and quickly hung up the phone. She knew that had hurt him. But, she felt in her heart that since she and her soulmates were traveling together, if not in this life, the issue would resolve itself in the next. If nothing else, she'd learned that the most important thing was to love herself first, the rest would follow, and to live in the moment.

Rachel went to Newland Studios nearly every morning to visit with Paul and Belinda. She laughed at their quirky sense of humor when she first saw the sign over their doorway - "Newland Studios near Newlyn". Of course, Rachel went there to spoil Baby Jake even more than he was already. But the topic of conversation most mornings was of Jane Rashleigh and the possibilities that Rachel had been her. They carried it even further and kidded about who Paul could've been, who Belinda was, and how they were all connected. They had great fun guessing and surmising. It was decided that Dudley was old man Rashleigh himself and he played along with great enthusiasm, keeping them in stitches with his humorous portrayal.

73

It was 11:15 p.m. on New Year's Eve. Rachel asked the cab driver to wait for her as she dropped off her luggage and checked in at the hotel. The flight from LAX to Heathrow had been uneventful and swift, but she was running late due to an unbelievable amount of traffic from Heathrow into London. Originally, the plan was to be at Trafalgar Square by 10:30 p.m.

She'd just returned from a five-day trip to L.A. The screenplay she had carried around in her head for six months finally made it to the printed page. It had sold immediately to the producer she'd met in London on her way to Cornwall in February. So she'd gone to L.A. to sign contracts. The film had been cast and would be shot in late January and February. She was surprised it had sold so fast. Here a screenplay that she hadn't spent much time writing, one that didn't seem to her to be her best had sold immediately. It didn't make sense. The previous two were better, she thought, although one was still being optioned, but neither had been produced yet. Well, maybe after this one was in the theatres and did well, the others would follow suit. *Oh well, it certainly isn't going to take up much of my thought processes.*

Her interest now was the novel she'd just written, which at that very moment, Anita was probably reading. Rachel had handed it to her at LAX right before the return flight to London. She didn't want to be around when she read it. She felt a bit insecure about it, since it was her first novel. The story had taken a complete turn from what she'd originally planned. It ended up being a story about a young Swiss painter in Paris and a struggling middle-aged American jazz singer, both trying to make their mark in Paris, both living in houseboats on the Seine River. Rachel felt it was a good story, but wasn't sure if she'd successfully got the point across. Sometimes her message was too subtle. *Oh well, I'll soon find out. Anita will probably call me tomorrow.*

The driver pulled under the canopy of the hotel and took the two bags from the boot and handed them to the waiting valet. Rachel disappeared into the hotel, while the cabby waited. Fifteen minutes later she appeared in an amazing outfit which made the driver wonder if this was the same woman. He'd never known a female to make such a terrific transition in under fifteen minutes. She looked as if she'd spent hours preparing for New Year's Eve.

As they drove towards Soho, Rachel thought of the main reason she'd gone to L.A. She'd been invited to appear on a national network TV show with the President and CEO of a newly formed foundation – WUTAV – *Women United Together Against Violence.* They'd contacted Rachel several weeks earlier, after reviewing some clips of interviews she'd given about her horrible ordeal with Senator Rollings and had asked her to head up a new branch of the foundation in the U.K. Rachel didn't have to think twice about it, she accepted immediately. It was exactly what she was looking for . . . a cause. Maybe this was to be her legacy – women united together against violence.

So after a bit of coaxing and pleading, she had convinced Belinda to join forces with her. Her argument was, "Who would be more qualified to understand the psyche and recovery of violence victims than the two of us?" So they planned to open a national center in Southampton in the spring, focusing on rehabilitating victims and perpetrators. Belinda was already designing a newsletter and the brochures. They both were working on a fund drive. They'd been communicating via email with the American organization and were well on their way in an endeavor to change and restructure sex and violence crime laws in England. Rachel was excited about the possibilities.

The night she flew to L.A., Rachel telephoned Ethan from the airport to tell him the good news about the screenplay, since he had been in on the early days of formulating the idea. But he seemed distant and detached when she called.

"Congratulations, Rachel. I'm happy for you."

"Thank you, Ethan. I just wanted you to know that it's a done deal. It's being made into a movie, isn't that wonderful?"

"Yes, it is." Silence.

She thought that she heard him say something, but couldn't make it out. "What did you say, Ethan? Are you alright?"

"Of course, I'm alright."

"So then, how are you? I'm so sorry, I should have asked you before. But I was so excited about how things have gone for me."

"And rightfully so." Silence.

"How is Adele?"

"She's well. Is due to return home from Wales next week. She must be on medication, however." Silence.

"Well, I guess I better get off here, my plane's leaving."

"So in which city will you be spending New Year's Eve, Rachel? New York? Rome? Sidney?"

"Trafalgar Square again. With some of my friends. And you?"

"I've been invited to several parties, but haven't decided. Well, I must get on, Happy New Year. Bye."

He hung up the phone abruptly in his usual manner.

* * * * *

"Pull over right here, please."

The cab driver did as he was told. Rachel paid him and took off down the sidewalk to Trafalgar Square. She couldn't believe it had been just a year since she and Ethan had tried to get to the square by midnight, as she was doing right that minute. She tripped and almost fell over someone's discarded trash, but held her balance and kept running. *There he is! Lord Nelson on top of his pole.*

It didn't matter that she wasn't in another major city on New Year's Eve. She had not forgotten the promise to her father. It had been put on hold. She had not forgotten the slight, sarcastic question Ethan had asked her about where she was spending New Year's Eve, either. Right now, all she wanted to do was live her life, today.

She heard her name being called.

"Rachel, over here." It was Paul. He and Belinda were waiting at the edge of the throng to direct her to where they would be standing as the countdown began. They swiftly pushed through the crowd until she saw Pete reaching out over the top of the people for her. He grabbed her hand and pulled her toward him.

Margaret and Felipe were there, too. They greeted her with smiles and hugs of fondness while being crushed by the surrounding celebrants.

Then Pete drew her back to him, held her close, and gave her a great big, mushy kiss. She kissed him back.

"Hey, guys. It isn't midnight yet." Paul offered with a moist sparkle in his eyes as he and Rachel exchanged glances, both remembering their own special New Year's kiss.

"'A! Yew mind your business," Pete said as he kissed Rachel again. "Ay 'aven't seen me angel in a week."

Paul still felt protective and drawn to Rachel, although he was mad about Belinda, but he believed it was just as Pete and Rachel had agreed. They all had to have lived in a past life together in some capacity. *So who's to say who was with who, whenever.* He smiled at the thought. Over the summer, they'd been to some of Margaret and Felipe's parties and had met more people who were into the past life theory. It was a comfort to Paul to know that the people he loved would always be near him in some capacity. He wanted to believe it because he was truly happy for the first time in his life.

Rachel was beaming. *Here I am in London on New Year's Eve with my magnificent adopted brother Paul, who I met on this very spot just a year ago, and now he's with my adorable friend Belinda who loves him, too.*

Rachel adored them all, especially the little orange-haired Baby Jake, her godson, who was at home being tended by Belinda's mother and card-playing friends at that very moment.

The authorities hadn't found Belinda's rapists and had no clues to give them any leads. It was as if they had vanished into the universe. But Rachel had hopes they'd be found and brought to justice before they struck again.

And here were Margaret and Felipe, for whom she felt such affection and envy. Their devotion to each other was of such fairy tale proportions, except that it was real, very real! She hoped and prayed that someday she'd feel that way about someone. She wanted what they had, and in her heart and soul she knew she would have it, if it was meant to be. She just needed to be patient.

As the bells rang in the New Year, Rachel's thoughts drifted back to Ethan and she suddenly felt his presence. Quickly turning her head to search the crowds behind her, she wasn't aware that he watched her from a window high above the square.

Ethan smiled in spite of the dull ache in his heart. *I'm here, my lovely one.* He knew she couldn't see him. And although he knew their time had not yet come, he felt hopeful that she'd come back into his life again someday. And that was all he needed to believe right now. He blew her a soundless kiss.

Pete tipped Rachel's chin gently towards him and when their eyes met, he crooned in a dreamy voice, "Happy New Year, luv." Then he kissed her softly and wondered when he should tell her that he had moved his things out of her house into a rented place in St. Austell to be nearer to the Eden Project. They'd made him an offer that he could not refuse; he needed to be there fulltime. He hadn't noticed how Rachel's eyes had glazed over and hadn't realized how her thoughts had slipped to another space in time.

Rachel smiled as she gazed at the clear, starry sky and saw a brilliant shooting star leaving a phosphorous trail in its wake.

Oh, my dear mama, you left me too soon. But I have a new life now and I'm free. No more fear. You were right, Mama, happiness and freedom come from within; no one can make that happen for me. So I'm okay. I really am. I promise.

She looked up at Lord Nelson's statue atop its towering column while tears of sadness and happiness dampened her cheeks.

And one thing is for sure, Daddy. Next year it's the Eiffel Tower. I promise you that!

Born in Oxnard, California, in 1940, Rebecca Joan McMullen spent the first ten years of her life in Ventura County with her parents and Sister Mary Elizabeth. Then in 1950, after another sister was added to the mix – Martha Katherine – the family relocated to Wasco, California – a small farming community in the San Joaquin Valley. Here she remained till she graduated from high school and married an out-of-towner and moved away.

After several marriages, birthing four children, and presenting a resume that looks like several pages of Craig's List job listings, she decided to focus on her passion and pursue a career in writing.

Living in several States over the years and in England, coupled with extensive world travel add to her ample stockpile of information and research as she continues to accomplish her goal of writing one book a year.

Now as Rebecca Randolph Buckley, she resides in Queen Creek, Arizona, with her adorable pets – Princie, Oreo, and Albee.

www.rebeccabuckley.com

www.ingramcontent.com/pod-product-compliance
Lightning Source LLC
Chambersburg PA
CBHW060424030726
47495CB00003B/728